SOUL
OF
CINDER

By Bree Barton

Heart of Thorns
Tears of Frost

SOUL OF

Stars

BREE BARTON

 KATHERINE TEGEN BOOKS
An Imprint of HarperCollins Publishers

Katherine Tegen Books is an imprint of HarperCollins Publishers.

Soul of Cinder
Copyright © 2021 by Bree Barton and HarperCollins Publishers
All rights reserved. Printed in the United States of America.
No part of this book may be used or reproduced in any manner whatsoever without
written permission except in the case of brief quotations embodied in critical articles and
reviews. For information address HarperCollins Children's Books, a division of
HarperCollins Publishers, 195 Broadway, New York, NY 10007.
www.epicreads.com

Library of Congress Control Number: 2020937813
ISBN 978-0-06-244774-6

Typography by Joel Tippie
20 21 22 23 24   PC/LSCH   10 9 8 7 6 5 4 3 2 1
❖
First Edition

For Anna, aw yea

AUTHOR'S NOTE

Writing the author's note in *Tears of Frost* was a given. I wanted readers to know from the very first page that the book would delve deeply into sexual assault and depression.

This time, I didn't know what to say or where to start. In *Soul of Cinder*, characters are still processing the aftermath of assault and coping with suicidal ideation. Trauma does not vanish after one moment of connection, magic or no.

"How do I write an author's note?" I asked a dear friend. "What should I even say?"

"Bree," she said, "you've been preparing for this author's note your whole life."

She's right, of course. I've spent my whole life seeking out meaningful ways to heal. This final book is really my love letter to healing, a story about finding your way back into the light. But there's still plenty of darkness, messy and painful, the kind that doesn't fit neatly into prescribed boxes. Which sounds suspiciously like real life.

I believe healing is personal, psychological, physical, political—and it *always* starts with doing the work. If we want to shift the shadows around us, we have to first confront the shadows within ourselves. Then we must find ways to heal that feel good and right to us.

Therapy, medication, physical movement, activism, creativity, storytelling, meditation, supportive friendships, safe communities—there are many paths to healing. I've included some resources at the back of this book that I've found helpful. Keep in mind that no two people heal the same way. If others tell you your way is wrong, remember that they're not the ones inside your head and heart.

If it takes a while to find what works, that's okay. Don't give up. And when you're in the darkest places, find people who will fight for you, until you're strong enough to fight again.

Bree Barton

Flesh of my flesh, bone of my bone,
I give you my body, my spirit, my home.
Come illness, suffering, e'en death,
Until my final breath I will be yours.
Till the ice melts on the southern cliffs,
Till the glass cities sink into the western sands,
Till the eastern isles burn to ash,
Till the northern peaks crumble.
Promise me, O promise me,
You will be mine.

—Glasddiran wedding vows

ACT I

Once upon a time, in a castle carved of stone,
a boy plotted murder.

Chapter 1

EVERY SCRAP

QUIN WANTED TO HURT him.

From the moment he saw the man standing precariously on the horse's back—his forehead sheened with sweat, wrists bound, a dirty rope noosed around his neck and tied to the tree branch above—Quin yearned to send the horse bolting. To hear the wet, clean snap of bone.

"Is someone there?" the prisoner asked, his voice a dusty croak. Quin wondered how long he'd been strung up. The mare seemed content to stay in one place, flicking her tail against the white flies.

"Please," the man said. "If you're there, please help me."

Quin stayed silent, hidden behind a copse of swyn trees. His fingers ticked with restless energy. He still marveled at it, the twitchy heat in his hands.

Magic.

He no longer had the two stones: the red fojuen wren and the black wheel with seven spokes Angelyne had wielded beneath the Snow Queen's palace. *Death is the final axis,* she'd said. *It tilts your tidy elements askew.* As the walls crumbled down around him, he'd almost lost far more than that. Somehow he had managed to stagger out of the palace, only to be buried moments later in an avalanche. Face crushed against hard-packed snow, arms pinned to his sides, the surrounding whiteness so complete it turned to black. He couldn't breathe.

Seconds before losing consciousness, he'd felt his hands warming. All around him the ice lit with a smoky red glow. The snow began to shift, softening to slush.

Only when he had stumbled onto his knees, gasping, did he see the scarlet flames flickering between his palms. He had burned his way out.

The prisoner's boot started to slip on the horse's back. He caught himself just before falling.

"I don't know who you are," the man whimpered, "but I'll give you everything I own. I swear by the four gods . . . the Four Great Goddesses . . . whoever you believe in."

Whomever, Quin thought.

The question of belief was really a question of power. And power, it seemed, boiled down to magic. The real question he'd been asking himself since crawling out of the snow was this: Had the two stones given him magic? Or had it been lurking inside him all along? A quiet, growing power, even during his most vulnerable moments?

Perhaps it existed *because* of those moments. Since escaping the snow kingdom, he'd spent long hours recounting his litany of losses—including the first. The memory came in brutal slashes. The shifting shadows of the crypt. The coldness in his father's eyes. His music teacher's screams as Quin stood by, doing nothing.

When he thought of the horrors of that night, his palms ached with hungry heat.

No Dujia had bothered to give him magic lessons. Why would they? They assumed he was powerless. Everyone had assumed that, his whole life: First his father, shaming and abusing him for who he was. Then Mia Rose, dragging him on an adventure he'd never asked to go on. Then Pilar d'Aqila, who had launched the arrow that nearly killed him—and the arrow that *did* kill his sister, Karri.

Of course, Angelyne Rose had rendered him more power-less than anyone. She had controlled him for months, hurt and abused him, burrowing into his head and heart so successfully that even after she'd stopped enthralling him, he did her bidding so mechanically she no longer had to ask.

If magic was born of a power imbalance—one person being stripped of agency in body, mind, and spirit—it was only a matter of time before he bloomed.

As Quin had risen from the avalanche that should have been his grave, he'd seen a boat sailing out of the harbor. He had only been able to make out three shapes, but he'd had no doubt to whom they belonged. *Angelyne. Pilar.*

Mia.

In that moment, he realized the truth. They had never loved him. Not a single one of them. The Twisted Sisters had chosen each other, and always would. Quin's thoughts darkened as he watched them sail toward Pembuk, the glass kingdom to the west. They had betrayed him and left him for dead, thinking him too weak to survive. He wanted to burn them for it. He wanted to burn anyone—*everyone*—who had ever thought him weak.

And now, finally, he could.

"I beg you," pleaded the prisoner, jolting Quin from his thoughts. "I beg you to have mercy."

Mercy. In the old language, the word meant "reward."

Through the prickly swyn branches, Quin scrutinized the man's gaunt, pale face. Brown stubble cut a sharp contrast against his sallow cheeks. Strong chin. Bloodshot blue eyes.

Quin knew the face well. They were, after all, cousins.

He thought of another copse of trees, where he had discovered Tristan on top of Karri, attempting rape. It felt like a dozen years ago, and yesterday. Half feral with rage, Quin had barreled into his cousin to save his sister—perhaps the one true courageous act of his life.

Now he tapped his fingertips together, watching the thin red flame begin to flicker.. His aim had gotten quite good. Since leaving Luumia he had killed three creatures with a spike of fire straight to the throat. With the rabbit he'd felt a pang of guilt. With the ermine the pang had been smaller. Smaller still with the cwningen. Quin had cured the meat himself.

His cousin would be his biggest game yet. Not that Quin had

4

any plans to eat him. Tristan's death was its own reward.

Quin stepped into the clearing.

"Hello, Cousin," he said.

Tristan's face brightened for only a moment before twisting into fear.

"Qu-Quin," he stammered, clearly wishing his would-be rescuer were someone—*anyone*—else.

The mare nickered, whisking the flies with her tail. She was growing restless.

"Please," Tristan whispered. "If she runs, it won't even break my neck. I'll strangle."

Quin had always had a way with animals. He could calm them easily with a gentle touch, a soft word.

He gave neither.

"Say something, won't you?" Tristan begged.

Quin thought of all the things he could say. A passionate monologue regarding the depravity of his cousin's soul, delivered to a captive audience hanging (literally!) on his every word. Quin had a gift for the pretending arts. As a boy he'd written, directed, and performed whole plays. Occasionally one or two of the cooks would make the trek from the castle kitchens to see the production, but more often than not, he was his own audience, alone on the stage.

What good had words done him? They had no power. They reeked of frailty, a lonely player hiding behind a soliloquy. Empty gestures spoken to an empty room.

"Goodbye, Cousin," he said, and lifted his hands.

He could aim for the chest, cut a blade of fire into Tristan's heart and kill him instantly. But Quin didn't want instant. He wanted his cousin's feet to slip. He wanted to watch the life gasp and gurgle out of him, this rapist to whom he was bound by blood.

The flame leapt from Quin's hands. The scarlet arrow singed his palms as it shot toward Tristan's ankles.

But at the last second, the fire arced upward, corkscrewing a ribbon of red sparks—and searing through the taut rope binding his cousin's neck to the tree.

Tristan fell, landing sideways on the horse. He cried out in pain. Quin charged forward, but it was too late: the horse galloped into the forest, Tristan clinging desperately to her flanks.

Quin cursed his feeble hands. He'd been clear in his head what he wanted, focused on bending his magic to his will. Why had it failed him?

Deep inside his chest, a wisp of relief wafted through like morning fog. Despite all he had done, all he had been forced to do, he had yet to take a human life.

He felt a scorching sense of shame. The relief belonged to the boy he once was. The good, gentle prince of the river kingdom who would never wish harm on anyone—and who had paid the price. Quin resolved to find every scrap of weakness within himself, every pathetic speck, and burn it down to ash.

Next time he aimed to kill someone, he wouldn't miss.

Chapter 2

OVERBOARD

MIA COULDN'T GET IT right.

She had struggled, tirelessly, to understand the mechanics. She knew that this type of boat, with its single triangular sail—a lateen sail, Nelladine had told her—could not turn into the wind. She'd scrutinized the delicate maneuver Nell did with the long coconut ropes, loosing the eucalyptus pole, leaping across the hull, and swinging the sail from one side of the mast to the other.

Mia knew all the right words. In theory, she could apply them.

In practice?

"I can't," she said, shoving the rope into Nell's hand. "I'm a lost cause."

Nelladine sat easily in the teakwood hull, face tilted toward the sun, black braids coiled in a regal bun atop her head. The hint of a smile played on her lips.

"It's all right, Mia. It's your first time on a dhou, you're not supposed to know everything."

Mia plunked down sourly beside her. She was gifted at most things, and on the rare occasion she *didn't* understand a concept or idea, she picked it up quickly. If you couldn't do something perfectly, why do it at all?

"It takes a while to get the knack with the ropes, really it does," Nell assured her.

"Maybe she's more useful as boat meat," said a voice behind them. "But high marks for effort, Rose."

Mia glanced over her shoulder. Pilar was tucked into the stern, her favorite spot, hugging her knees to her chest. Grinning as usual.

"I should never have taught you that term, it's not meant to be an insult!" Nell shot Pilar a disapproving look, then turned back to Mia. "Those"—she nodded at the sandbags lining the hull—"are boat meat. *I* am boat meat. Every crew member is ballast when you're on a dhou, the whole thing is about balance. You're always shifting as the wind changes."

"It's called trimming," Pilar said, maddeningly smug.

Mia resented how easy Pilar was on the water, how she seemed to have absorbed Nell's sailing lessons with no difficulty at all.

"You're hardly bigger than a sandbag yourself," Mia sniffed. "I imagine we could trim *you* right off the boat."

"Behave yourselves, you two!" Nell admonished, though she was clearly amused. "I did always want a sister."

"Sisters are overrated," Pilar said. "All they do is try to kill you."

Mia couldn't argue. Considering this whole sorry mess had started with her little sister, Angelyne, sending an assassin to put an arrow in Mia's back . . . an assassin named Pilar d'Aqila, who had turned out to be the secret first daughter of their father, Griffin Rose . . .

"On Refúj I grew up with hundreds of Dujia who were supposed to be my *sisters*," Pilar said. "My mother always said the bond of magic was even stronger than blood." She grunted. "The only thing worse than sisters is mothers."

Mia couldn't argue with that, either. She'd journeyed all the way to Luumia to enlist her mother's help, only to discover she had no interest in helping. Wynna had turned her back on her daughters and started a new life, a new family, with the Snow Queen. And she had paid for it. She, like everyone else in Valavïk, had been buried under the avalanche.

As Mia studied Pilar's face, a gentler emotion stirred in her chest. When it came to rough edges, Pilar was practically a dodecahedron. But why wouldn't she be? The people who should have protected her, including her mother, had done unconscionable things. Zaga made Wynna Rose look like a slice of strawberry cake.

"I do have a brother," Nell said.

"Really?" Pilar unfolded her legs, leaning forward. "We've been on this toothpick for the last month, and *now* you decide to tell us about your family?"

"Not a toothpick, thank you—I'll ask you to show *Maysha* the respect she deserves." Nell stroked the side of her boat, thoughtful. "I haven't seen my brother in four years, not since I left Pembuk. He'd be fifteen now."

9

Mia felt a twinge of guilt. Why had she never thought to ask Nelladine about her family?

"He would like you," Nell said to Pilar. "He's a fighter, too."

Mia felt another twinge. Not guilt. Envy.

Perhaps it was inevitable they were grating on each other. They had, after all, been stuck on a twenty-foot sailboat, on a choppy and capricious sea, subsisting on a diet of fish, fish, and—would nature's bounties ever cease?—fish with a seaweed garnish.

Mia's feelings toward Pilar were complicated. Her half sister was truculent and ill-tempered; she loved picking fights and wore her sarcasm like a second skin. Pilar lorded over Mia her superiority in sailing, magic—just about anything.

Mia had spent a lifetime trying to decipher the world and apply that knowledge logically, like any good scientist. But long before she failed at sailing, she had failed to understand her own sister, which meant she had failed to recognize the plots Angelyne had set in motion. Mia had failed to understand magic, including the magic in her own body. She had failed to save Quin, sweet, innocent Quin, the boy she might have loved.

As they sailed away from Luumia, Mia saw his smoldering green eyes more often than she cared to admit.

Now he and Angie were both dead, crushed beneath the snow palace. Pilar was the only family she had left. Sometimes Mia was struck by a tide of compassion so strong it knocked the breath out of her. She had seen Pilar's past: not just the rape, but the aftermath. She knew that the whole Dujia sisterhood had turned against her. The island of Refúj, whose very name meant "safe haven," had proven to be anything but.

Mia ached to be that safe haven for Pilar. She knew in the marrow of her bones that she could do it: be the kind of sister Pilar needed. Mia had failed to *see* Angelyne, and had thereby failed to save her. She would not make that mistake again.

"Mia, your face!" cried Nelladine. "Great sands, you're reddening up like a roasted beet! What did I tell you? You have to apply the cream every hour—it absorbs fast." She reached for the scooped banana leaf. "Apply evenly or it'll streak."

Grateful, Mia accepted the leaf. After a solid month of unrelenting sunshine, Nell's deep brown skin had grown a few shades darker, as radiant and dewy as ever, while Pilar's olive-gold complexion had tanned nicely. Mia, on the other hand, had sprouted a veritable pox of orange freckles and was burning to a well-seasoned crisp. No matter how many times she or Nelladine healed the sunburn, she'd be just as pink an hour later. The endless cycle of burning and healing, burning and healing had become almost comical.

From their first day on the sea, it had been clear their lives were in Nell's hands. And what capable hands! Watching Nell captain *Maysha* was like watching a weaver weave or a blacksmith smith. She could chart the stars, tie a one-handed knot, balance barefoot on the edge of the dhou without holding on to anything.

Her magic didn't hurt, either. Nell could do things Mia had never imagined: extract salt from seawater to make it drinkable, catch fish by chilling a modicum of ocean until their heartbeats slowed. A few days into their voyage, she had plucked a floating sea urchin from the water, crushed it down to powder, and used her magic to melt a sprig of seaweed into paste. After blending everything into a pale yellow cream, she had handed it to Mia.

"To protect you from the sun," she'd explained. "So we don't exhaust ourselves healing you fourteen times a day."

Now, as Mia smeared the cream onto her cheeks and forehead, she braced herself for the inevitable gibe from Pilar.

"Still smells like fish carcass," Pilar said, right on cue.

Mia turned to Nell. "Could you do my shoulders?"

Their benevolent captain smiled. "Of course."

As Nell's rope-callused fingers massaged cream into her shoulders, Mia closed her eyes. She had tried dozens of times to re-create the night they fled the snow kingdom, when Nelladine had touched the indigo frostflower inked onto Mia's wrist, spilling warmth over her skin. Results should always be reproducible: that was a cornerstone of the scientific process. Over and over, Mia had entreated her friend to touch the moving fyre ink again. When that didn't work, they would try the other wrist. Then hands. Then arms. Then shoulders.

"Magic?" Nell asked, accurately predicting what Mia would ask next. Magic was a critical variable in the equation; they'd tried it both with and without.

"Yes," Mia said. "Thanks for asking."

Nell's hands stilled. Mia knew she was channeling all her magic into her fingers, trying to spark sensation. Hot, cold, tingling, soothing—whatever Mia requested, Nell would attempt to conjure. Once or twice Mia had thought she detected the faintest flicker of feeling. Her heart would soar. Finally, *finally* she had climbed out of the dark box. But the sensation was so ephemeral she suspected her own yearning was yielding a false positive.

"Can we try the enthrall?"

Nell hesitated, the way she always did when Mia asked to be enthralled. And, like always, Mia had her defense at the ready.

"You told me magic is about being attuned to other people. That you must only touch them if it's what they truly want. It's what I truly want."

Nell sighed. She reached for Mia's inked wrist with one hand, her heart with the other.

Nothing. No thrill of sticky heat, no melted chocolate, no warm honeyed hum.

"Look on the bright side, Rose," Pilar said. "You're immune to magic."

"Yes," Mia said, unable to mask her frustration. "But I'm immune to everything else, too."

"Don't give up hope." Nell gave her arm a squeeze. "We're not far from Pembuk now, and there are powerful Pembuka elixirs, all kinds. Like the one your mother gave you that got lost in the avalanche. They could help you, really they could."

Mia had a hard time believing anything could help.

"Want me to massage *your* shoulders, Nell? You've been doing so much for me."

Nell shook her head. "I'm perfectly fine."

Sometimes when Mia looked at Nell—she was afraid to even *think* it—she felt a softening in her belly. As if a tiny knot had been untied somewhere, a satin ribbon unfurling. The thought frightened and confused her, but it calmed her, too.

In those fleeting moments, she wondered if perhaps the enthrallment had worked a little after all.

"She's quiet today," Nell said, assessing the smooth black sea. Mia had marked this many times: to Mia, the ocean was an *it*; to Nell it was always a *she*. So was *Maysha*. Their first day at sea, Nell had told them, "A dhou moves and breathes, same as we do. Why shouldn't she have a name?"

Pilar groaned. "I hate when it's quiet. With no wind it's like we're treading water. At this rate we'll never get to Pembuk."

"We will."

"But I can see land *now*." She waved an impatient hand to the north. If Mia shielded her eyes from the sun, she could see a sandy blur in the distance. That had been true for days.

"Why don't we find a harbor?" Pilar said. "We could eat something that isn't fish."

"We're close, I promise. Don't forget I know the Pembuka coast better than you do. We're looking for Pata Pacha, the cove I sailed out of four years ago. We'll make landfall and take a caravan to the first of the glass cities."

Pilar yawned. "I'm bored."

"How can you ever be bored on the ocean?" Nell said. "Sailing gives me the same feeling as when I throw a fresh slab of clay on my potter's wheel. Anything is possible, and everything can shift. The sea is always changing, always transforming."

"But isn't that what makes it dangerous?" Mia said, loathing the sound of her own voice. Sometimes she felt as if Pilar had stepped into the role of rash, petulant child, whereas she'd assumed the role of cautious, fretting mother.

"I don't think so, no," Nell said, "though I suppose it depends on your definition of dangerous. The sea swings high and low, wild and tranquil, but she is always honest about who she is."

Like you, Mia thought. Nell laughed and cried so freely, her emotions crashing over her like giant waves before dissolving into sea-foam. She spoke the same way, sentences flowing into one another, words rising and falling in a fluid tumble. Mia couldn't imagine being that free with her feelings. She wasn't sure she'd want to be.

"The sea doesn't pretend to be sweet and docile when she doesn't feel like it," Nell said. "I'd choose the ocean any day over Prisma."

Mia cocked her head. "Prisma?"

"I thought I'd told you about the island! Very controversial in the glass kingdom, some think it's an abomination, some think it's a gift. The Isle of Forgetting, they call it. Home of the glass terrors. I told you about those before, didn't I, Mia?"

"You didn't tell *me*," Pilar grumbled.

"It's a natural phenomenon. The wind whips up the sand and the sun melts it into a glittery glass cyclone, and when you look into it you see your life . . . only it isn't really your life. All the grief and sadness are gone, along with the mistakes you made, the people you lost, so you're looking at the life that might have been, the better one, and you don't just see it, you're *inside* it."

Pilar shrugged. "Doesn't sound so bad."

"Sure it doesn't. Until you walk toward the whirling shimmer of glass with your arms wide, heart open, and you don't even feel it when it slices you apart."

Mia shivered. "Why would anyone go to Prisma?"

Nell blinked at her for a moment. Then she turned away, hoisting herself up into the bow.

"Ask the Shadowess," she said.

This had been happening more and more: little moments where Nelladine pulled back and drew into herself when one of them mentioned the Shadowess. Strange, considering it was Nell who insisted on taking them to the Shadowess. "The only person who can help," she'd said as the glacier crumbled around them.

"Things will be different once we get to the glass kingdom," Nell said, her eyes fixed on some distant point Mia couldn't see. "*I'll* be different."

"How do you mean?"

"You'll see. There's a reason I left home."

"But you won't tell us what it is," griped Pilar. "Or why you're dragging us back. All we know is that we're going to Pembuk."

"You really haven't put two and two together?" Nell laughed her husky laugh. "It'll all become clear soon enough. We're going to a sacred place where the greatest minds have gathered since the beginning of time: people who have learned how to heal not just the world around us, but our own hearts and minds."

"Great, more riddles," Pilar groaned. One thing Mia had learned from a month on the sea: her sister was keen on groaning.

Sister. The word still felt strange and out of place, like a blackberry drupelet stuck between her teeth. She still had trouble reconciling the fact that, after seventeen years, she'd lost one sister and inherited another.

"Mia." Nell nodded toward the lateen sail. "The luff—that's the edge closest to the mast—is a little loose. Can you help me reroute the halyard?"

"Yes," Mia said, although "probably not" would have been a more honest answer.

Pilar dropped from the stern, landing evenly on both feet. "Need a hand?"

"I'm fine."

"There's no shame in it."

Mia was caught off guard—in part because Pilar was being kind, in part because she had invoked shame. Shouldn't Mia be the one telling her big sister not to feel ashamed? She'd tried so many times to initiate a conversation about their night under the snow palace; the more Mia replayed her own words, the more tweaks she wanted to make. She should have done a better job offering both comfort and support. Every time Pilar lobbed a sarcastic barb in her direction, Mia reminded herself that this was simply a means of self-protection. She knew she could make things better for Pilar, easier, if she could just say the right thing.

But whenever Mia offered an olive branch, Pil crushed it.

Now Mia met her sister's eyes. Compassion welled inside her. This was the moment.

"Pilar," she began. "I want you to know you can—"

She gasped as Pilar stripped off her shirt—and jumped overboard.

Chapter 3

ANOTHER KIND OF SWEAT

PILAR WAS BETTER OFF alone. Why did she keep forgetting? Her so-called half sister was the perfect reminder. For weeks Mia had tried to force her to talk about things she didn't want to talk about. Didn't *need* to talk about. Pilar had offered to help reroute the halyard, not have a heart-to-heart sob fest with Mia Rose.

The only escape was to go overboard.

"Pilar!"

She dunked her head under, drowning Mia out. The water was bracing. Much better. A jolt of cold ocean to slurp her down.

Her head broke the surface, eyes stinging with salt. Just in time to hear Mia say to Nelladine: ". . . going to get herself killed. Can't you *do* something?"

"Actually, there is one thing," Nell said, and then she was pulling off her shirt, too, and plunging into the water.

Pilar crowed with delight. A moment later, Nell resurfaced, triumphant. Beads of water clung to her thin black braids.

A panicked Mia leaned over the boat's edge.

"I can't sail, Nell!"

"*Maysha* will be fine for a few minutes. There's no wind."

"But what if . . ." Mia motioned helplessly toward the water.

"It's the ocean, Mia, it doesn't bite."

"Except for the thousands of aquatic species that *literally bite.*"

Nell splashed the side of the boat. Mia did not look amused.

"Didn't you grow up on a river?" Pilar asked.

"Not *on* a river," Mia said. "Close to one."

"Why does the water scare you?"

"It doesn't scare me."

"Why do you hate it?"

"Because there are infinite unknowns lurking beneath the surface."

"You don't like that you can't control it," Pilar said. She jerked a thumb toward the sinking sun. "You can't control a sunset. Does that scare you, too?"

She didn't wait to hear Mia's answer. She paddled farther out, blading her hands through the water. Filled her lungs with air. Floated on her back, starfishing her arms and legs. It felt nice to swim, to let her muscles stretch and thrum. You could only bend your body so many ways on a boat. Sit. Stand. Crouch. Lie down—until someone stepped on you.

Mia Rose was that someone. Four weeks and the girl still didn't have her sea legs. Typical.

Pilar had noticed something since they'd set sail. Whenever she thought about what had happened to her beneath the snow palace—trapped in her own Reflections, forced to relive her worst nightmare—she didn't feel a sense of closure. If anything, she felt more exposed.

Mia had seen everything. She'd watched as Orry, Pilar's fight teacher, raped her over and over in his cottage by the lake.

To Mia's credit, she'd said comforting things.

You didn't deserve what happened. It wasn't your fault.

At the time, Pilar had felt seen.

The problem was, sometimes being seen wasn't a good thing. Mia had also seen how desperately Pilar wanted to be loved. At night, trying to snatch a few hours of sleep on the tiny boat, Pilar would remember what Morígna, Orry's wife, had said the day she turned the entire Dujia sisterhood against her. *There will always be girls so starved for attention they must lie to get it. Girls who pretend to be victims when they are anything but.*

Mia had seen that part, too. It gave Pilar a sick feeling. Like she'd sliced open her chest and let Mia Rose root around the slimy guts.

Honestly, Rose would probably enjoy it. She was always yammering on about fibula this and ventricle that.

Pilar hated the feeling of being vulnerable. Needy. Worst of all: weak. She hated the word *rape*, hated everything about it. *Raped.* She didn't recognize herself in those five letters. But she could see them in Mia's eyes every time she looked at her.

Pilar felt herself sealing off again. The same way cuts on her knuckles turned to white-slash scars after a fight. She'd always healed quickly, even when she didn't use magic to speed things along. Her wounds scabbed over within a day or two. The skin scarred up. Got tougher.

Maybe hearts did that, too. Slit them open and they closed up tougher than before. The deeper the cut, the thicker the scar— and the more unlikely the heart would break again.

"You're a strong swimmer," said Nelladine, who'd come up beside her. Pilar stayed on her back, puffing out her chest to keep afloat.

"I did grow up on an island. No shortage of ocean to swim in."

"You all right out there?" Mia yelled from the boat.

"Are *you* all right?" Nell yelled back.

"Yes! I think so?"

Nell shot Pilar a sly look. "To tell the truth, if I had to leave *Maysha* with anyone? Mia wouldn't be my top pick."

Pilar righted herself in the water. "She'd die if she heard you say that."

"That's why I'm only saying it to you."

Why did Pilar feel suddenly protective? She'd done nothing but heap scorn on Mia's bad sailing for weeks, widening the gap between them.

But then she would remember how it had felt to stand beside Mia in their Reflections, hand in hand. The way some torn part of her had begun to knit itself back together. It scared her, how much she wanted to feel that again.

Starved for attention.

In the past her own hunger had made her vulnerable. When you opened yourself up like that, people hurt you.

And then she thought of Quin. Pilar had offered him her body and a good chunk of her heart. He'd offered her the same. But his body and heart were never his to give. Angelyne had broken him, scraped him clean of everything good and gentle.

Pilar saw now what she couldn't see then. She and Quin had never been destined for some epic love affair. He was happiest writing dramatic monologues and correcting her grammar. She was happiest pounding sandbags. They'd found one another because they were desperate, and because there was no one else.

But they had meant something to each other. That part was true. Sometimes when she replayed their history, she felt searing guilt that she hadn't known—or hadn't *wanted* to know—how much he was hurting.

And then she thought of the night underneath the palace. Quin would have burned her alive. She knew it in her core. What a fool she'd been. Still that needy girl, starved for attention. It had almost killed her.

"The water gets warmer the closer we get to Pata Pacha," Nell was saying. "By the time you're in the cove it's practically bathing water. You'll see whole shoals of melonfish."

"Melonfish?"

"They look like halves of orange melons with long trailing lappets, and they're luminous, they create their own light. They're really quite beautiful. My brother caught one once, tried to keep it as a pet. But they don't last long in fresh water."

"Tell me about him. Hardly any girls had brothers on Refúj."

Nell smiled. "He was terrific, such a sweet soul. He looked up to me. He looked up to everyone, honestly, he opened his heart so easily. I worried about him constantly. He trusted anyone who paid him the tiniest bit of attention. He wanted so much to be loved."

Pilar thought about how much she had wanted to be loved. By her mother. By Orry.

"He loved his fight lessons," Nell continued. "They made him so happy. He had a teacher from the river kingdom whom he absolutely adored."

Pilar froze. She felt herself start to sink. Surely Orry hadn't . . .

"My brother was so sad when she left for Prisma. He locked himself in his room for days."

Pilar let out her breath. Relieved.

A female fight teacher. She liked the sound of that.

"You talk about your brother like he's dead."

"Great sands, no! I don't mean it like that. He was only eleven when I left Pembuk, and then he was lost to me, just like everyone else. Sometimes it feels like a whole separate life."

Nell's head sank an inch lower, chin disappearing beneath the surface.

"My brother wasn't just sad about his fight teacher. He was sad a lot of the time, for reasons none of us—including him—understood. Even as a little boy, he was sad."

The water slapped soft against their arms.

23

"I wish I'd taken him with me," Nell said. "I did what I had to do, don't get me wrong. I felt like I would die if I stayed, like I was being crushed from all sides. But I've never stopped feeling guilty for leaving him behind."

They were silent a moment. Pilar watched Mia on the boat, swaying unsteadily. Poor girl with her scientific theories and library books wasn't cut out for sailing the open sea. Despite the multiple daily healings and Nell's fancy fish cream, Rose's white skin continued to turn the color of an actual rose.

Look on the bright side, Pilar had told her. *At least you can't feel the sunburn!*

She was beginning to wonder if her humor could use a little fine-tuning.

"Mia likes you, you know," Pilar said. It was obvious from the way Rose looked at Nell. The way she begged to be touched every day. Even if Mia wouldn't admit it—might not even be aware of it—she clearly felt something for Nelladine.

Nell sighed.

"She thinks she does, yes, I know. She wants me to be the one to save her, to fix all her broken parts. And I'll do everything I can to help her. I think Mia is used to fixing things—her sister, her family, her own body. She doesn't understand some things aren't meant to be fixed. But she's not alone in wanting that. It's why so many people go to Prisma. They'd rather see themselves as who they *could* be, instead of who they are."

"I just wish she'd stop trying to fix me."

Nell shielded her eyes from the sun. "I understand. Believe me, I do."

Pilar gargled salt water. Spat it back into the ocean. It wasn't the first time she'd thought of telling Nell what had happened on Refúj. But whenever she imagined dragging herself back to that dark place, fatigue punched her in the gut. She was tired. Talking about it cost too much. Pilar hated that this was now part of her story. Hated that everyone she would ever meet, for the rest of her life, would fall into one of two categories: those she'd told, and those she hadn't.

"I want you to promise me something," Nell said, keeping her voice low as they drifted closer to the boat. "When we get to Pembuk, will you look out for Mia?"

"Why don't *you*?"

"I want to. It's just, once we get there, things will change."

After growing up with a mother who spoke in riddles, Pilar could read between the lines. Nell was going to leave once she dumped them with the Shadowess. Mia would probably trail after her, abandoning the sisterhood she and Pilar had begun to forge. Proving that even the people who promised to love her always left her in the end.

But Pilar had always been curious about Pembuk. She didn't know much about it—lots of sand, glass cities, ugly animals with humps. And so on. What interested her was that not a single Pembuka had ever come to Refúj. Clearly, the Dujia of the glass kingdom hadn't managed to escape. Or maybe they hadn't needed to.

She set her jaw. She would meet the Shadowess. After that, she made no promises.

As for Mia? Pilar owed her nothing. Rose might be her half sister by blood, but at the end of the day, blood was just another kind of sweat. It leaked out of you in a fight, but you never missed it.

Pilar hardened her voice.

"So what happens after you ditch us in Pembuk? Will you slug some ale in your old haunts? Or turn tail to Luumia so you can make more clay pots?"

Nell was quiet. She treaded water, watching Pilar.

"You don't have to make my life sound small. I've made a home in the snow kingdom. Friends."

"Friends like Ville?"

As soon as the words came out, Pilar regretted them. They had explained to Nell how her friend Ville had never been Ville at all, but Lord Kristoffin Dove, the Snow Queen's uncle, who abducted and enslaved children, wrenching power from their deepest pain.

"How did I not know?" Nell said softly. "It was right in front of me. Ville's lewd remarks, the million subtle ways he undermined me, day after day. I think of myself as a strong woman, confident in who I am, what I'm worth, and even I couldn't see."

Dove had charmed Pilar, too. She'd walked right into his trap.

"Nell, I didn't mean to—"

"Look!"

Something orange swam beneath them. Instinctively Pilar tucked her knees in to her chest.

"What was that?"

Another creature churned past, then another. The ocean was no longer dark. Arcs of gleaming orange light illuminated the water, whirling, spiraling. An eerie chatter cracked the surface of the sea.

"Nelladine?" Mia called from the boat. "Pilar? What's happening?"

Pilar didn't know how to answer. The whole ocean seemed to be rippling orange. The water felt thin and hot, teeming with life.

Nell's face was radiant. "Melonfish!"

They didn't move like any fish Pilar had seen—and she'd seen her fair share. They spun in circles, their orange fins fanning out on all sides. What had Nell called them? Lappets. To Pilar they looked more like flames.

Mia was shouting: *Aretheydangerousdotheybite?* But Nell was lost in her own world.

"You know, it's funny: I thought we were still several days from the cove. But then, you have to remember, four years is a long time! And if the melonfish are here . . ."

"Then we're almost at Pata Pacha," Pilar finished.

"No," Nell said. "We're already here."

Chapter 4

ABANDONED

It didn't take Quin long to find the mark.

It was carved neatly into the trunk of the tree where his cousin had been tethered. Three triangles, one inside another. Quin had seen the symbol before. He'd spotted it above the door of a burnt-out cottage in a deserted river town, a woman's charred body on the stoop. When he'd walked into an empty tavern a few days back, ravenous, he'd found bread crawling with maggots—and the symbol cut deep into the blood-soaked wood floor.

The closer he drew to Kaer Killian, the more triangles he saw.

Quin had a theory. The symbol was carved after some murderous act was committed—or to mark a murderous work in progress, such as Tristan strung up by his neck, awaiting fate.

As if to say, *Violence was committed here.* Or—and this was better—*justice has been done.*

Perhaps, in the end, they were one and the same.

During his long, solitary trek from Luumia, he'd had plenty of time to think. There were different kinds of violence. Violent acts born of hatred and a flair for gruesome showmanship—the backbone of his father's regime—were troubling.

But Quin didn't feel hateful. His mind was sharp and slick and cold, like the stone head of an arrow. The violence he sought was productive, a necessary stop on the path to retribution. He would not hack off the hands of innocent women and dangle them from the ceiling, as had the king. Nor would he stack their bodies in the Hall, as had Zaga.

But if the Twisted Sisters came back to Glas Ddir—assuming Mia, Pilar, and Angelyne had not been digested by a raging sea—he would hold them accountable for their actions. They had used and abused him, wounding him irrevocably. And not just him. Wherever the sisters went, death and destruction followed. In order to resurrect himself as a just and noble king, he would first need to expunge all those whose presence was a threat.

He'd spent the last few weeks composing a letter to the sisters saying as much, continually revising and reshaping the words on a piece of parchment he kept close to his heart.

I once believed that hurting people made you weak. I don't believe that anymore.

Not that he'd sent the letter. You couldn't exactly dispense a courier to the Lilla Sea.

Quin knew the carved triangles were leading him somewhere. Perhaps not him, specifically—he hoped not. His best advantage was the element of surprise. No one expected the little golden prince to resurface in Glas Ddir and reclaim the throne, even if it was his birthright. No one ever expected anything of him. That was the problem.

Needless to say, he followed the symbols.

Violence was his birthright, too.

The brothel stood just outside the borders of Killian Village, which, Quin imagined, meant it was the first place a traveling merchant might stop before entering town. It also meant the women who lived within its walls were beyond the protection of the law, and hence more vulnerable to heinous acts. Though in the river kingdom, heinous acts were all but sanctioned by the state.

Quin traced the three triangles grooved into the knotty wood door. The symbol was so tiny he'd almost missed it. He took a breath. He'd encountered enough corpses in the last month to dread the stench of decaying flesh.

But as the door creaked open, there was nothing. No blood on the floor, no bodies. The brothel was abandoned.

He let the air out of his lungs.

Whoever had been in this brothel had left in a hurry. Quin noted at least a dozen pint glasses, some overturned on tables, others full of flat yellow ale. A lacy black chair had been flipped over, its four shapely legs thrust upward in a way that was almost indecent. On the ground a perfect boot print was stamped into an emerald silk scarf. Whether in mud or in blood, he couldn't tell.

What horrors had befallen the river kingdom in his absence? He'd spent months chasing Mia and Pilar to Luumia, then returned alone. In every village, he had stopped to scrounge food and information. Most towns were deserted. Occasionally he stumbled upon a lone shop or farmhouse with a candle burning in the window, and if he was lucky, the shopkeeper or farmer would share their meager food. No one ever recognized him. He'd grown a scruffy blond beard and left his curls dirty and disheveled. After weeks of uneasy sleep in the forest, dark circles had bloomed under his green eyes.

A few days earlier, Quin had come upon a stone farmhouse. Inside he'd found a crusty old farmer, the lone survivor of a gutted village. The man had offered him a cup of rabbit stew and a thin straw mattress for the night: the greatest kindness he'd been shown in ages.

"I'm a fool to invite you in," the farmer said, watching Quin slurp down his supper. "You'll slit my throat for another cup of stew."

"I won't."

"You wouldn't be the first to try."

Quin wiped his mouth on his sleeve. "Who did this to your village? Was it Angelyne?"

"They said things would get better with the young queen. Another pack of lies." The farmer scratched his gray stubble. "Used to be only women had cause to be afraid. I'm not saying that was right. I lost my wife to the Hunters long ago. But now we men got a taste of it. We all became the hunted."

Quin nodded, his expression grim. In the castle he'd watched Zaga and Angelyne enthrall innocent men like Domeniq du Zol, sending him out into the villages to kill anyone who opposed magic. After promising to end Ronan's reign of hate and murder, they had merely expanded it.

"It's not done, neither," the farmer said. "With the young queen gone, there's a whole new pack of cutthroats rose up to take her place."

Quin set down his spoon.

"Cutthroats?"

"Don't know where they come from. Band of thieves and murderers calling themselves the Embers. Tried to get me to join up—said I'd starve if I didn't. I told them I'd rather starve than spill more innocent blood."

"So the Embers are the ones carving the symbols," Quin said, putting two and two together.

"Don't know about that. But I know the Embers aren't to be trusted." He leaned back in his chair. "I've heard rumors of the young king. That he might be alive in Luumia. If he came back, I think he'd find many of us loyal."

Quin tried to downplay his interest.

"Seems to me the prince never did much of anything for anyone."

"I heard he spent time at the orphanage in Killian Village. He might be a bit wet behind the ears, but I wager he'd grow into a fine king. At least he'd never be his father."

The farmer gathered the stew cups, leaving Quin to unpack his complicated feelings.

"I'll say this for the young queen: at least she opened the borders. People can run to the west, find something better in the glass kingdom. Half the ruins you see around here are the Embers' doing, not the queen's." He shook his head. "When a gap in power opens up, only power-hungry fools try to fill it. My wife used to say that."

"May I ask why *you* have not run west?"

"Because this house is full of her." The farmer's grizzled voice had gone soft. "She's in every room. If I leave home behind, I leave her, too."

He touched the tarnished metal band around his finger.

"Twelve years. I still miss her every day."

Something flickered in Quin's chest. A memory of Mia Rose in the Royal Chapel arose unbidden. A fragment of his wedding vows echoed through his mind.

Flesh of my flesh, bone of my bone,
I give you my body, my spirit, my home.

He'd once thought those words were romantic, even beautiful. What a powerful act: to give yourself so fully to another person.

Now they horrified him. Marriage was a capitulation. Mia had enthralled him, a fateful harbinger of all to come. He had not given his body, his spirit, or his home.

It didn't matter. They'd all been taken from him anyway.

Quin walked deeper into the brothel. He hadn't eaten a real meal since the farmer's stew, and that was days ago. His stomach growled in protest.

In the front parlor, he came to a halt.

A piano stood in the corner.

He felt a powerful urge to touch it, and a commensurate urge to turn away. Music—the piano in particular—symbolized the feeble, mewling part of himself he sought to eradicate. He had no desire to remember his own cowardice.

His gaze lingered on the polished bone keys. He couldn't help it. He thought of his music teacher.

Tobin was barely older than Quin, a musical prodigy with an inimitable gift. The first time Quin saw him play, he decided Toby had the most beautiful hands he'd ever seen on a boy. The most beautiful hands he'd seen on anyone, though to be fair, Quin had seen very few girls' hands ungloved. Tobin's fingers were broad yet elegant, nails cut to the quick. "Any musician who lets his fingernails grow long," Tobin was fond of saying, "loves himself more than his instrument."

Watching Toby's hands fly over the piano keys had stirred something deep inside him. His teacher loved the piano fiercely, the way a drowning man loves the rowboat come to save him. Quin sometimes wondered which he fell in love with first: the piano, or the boy who taught him to play it.

Under the plums, if it's meant to be. You'll come to me, under the snow plum tree.

The image darkened, blood seeping into the frame.

He pushed farther into the brothel. In the kitchens he found salted pork and a loaf of oatnut bread. No maggots this time. His mouth was watering. He carved off a sizable slab of pork—salty and delicious—and devoured three slices of sweet, yeasty bread. He even found a slug of goose milk in a leather flask and swilled it, smacking his lips in pleasure.

With the flask gripped firmly in hand, Quin found a stone staircase in the back corner. He took the steps two at a time—easy with his long legs—and trod lightly down the upstairs corridor, where he passed door after open door. In the brothel's chambers he spied mother-of-pearl screens and sumptuous beds strewn with lush velvet. An array of silks and satins dripped from the walls, garments so pretty you'd never suspect the atrocities that had surely befallen the women wearing them.

Another memory emerged. The night it happened, Quin had been silly enough to fret over what to wear. White linen tunic or blue silk? Jacket or no? He knew the crypt was apt to be freezing. He also knew the royal buttons were a pain in his royal ass. Every night, when all he wanted was to disrobe and go to sleep, he instead had to muscle twelve gold knobs through twelve rigid loops.

Not that Tobin would have any interest in disrobing me, he'd thought at the time. Not that Toby's given any thought to pushing each button through its stiff hoop, one by one, inching slowly down my chest from top to bottom.

Quin exhaled audibly, as if he could breathe the memory out. He pitied the fifteen-year-old version of himself, the boy so preoccupied with buttons he hadn't seen what was coming.

But he was smarter now. Stronger. His powerlessness had

sparked powerful magic inside him. *For the first time in my life*, he'd written in his letter, *I feel no fear. I have always known myself to be broken. But finally, after so many years, I understand my brokenness is a gift.*

In order to reclaim the throne, he would need to prove his new-found power. Especially if a gang of bandits was running wild, savaging what remained of his kingdom. Quin spent hours every day honing his magic, learning to direct his molten streams of fire. The first step was to retake Kaer Killian. If he met with opposition, he would need to perform far better than he had with Tristan.

As for what—or *who*—awaited him in the Kaer itself? Quin had no idea. The farmer hadn't known, nor had any of the beleaguered Glasddirans he'd met. With Zaga dead and Angelyne gone, was the castle empty? Were people like Dom still under the enthrallment? Would Quin be warmly welcomed, or swiftly killed?

A piano note echoed down the empty corridor.

His fingers tightened around the flask. He waited for a second note to warm the air, but there was only silence. Had he imagined it? Sometimes when he closed his eyes, he could hear the melody that had haunted him for three long years. It was the first song Tobin had taught him—and the last song Toby ever played.

Quin had nearly convinced himself it was only in his head when a second note rang out. It lifted into a third, then sank into a fourth.

A chill shot down his spine.

Under the plums.

He descended the stairs with one hand gripping the banister. The brothel was not abandoned after all.

A band of people stood in the shadowy front parlor.

They formed a tight half circle, as if they were guarding something. At least half a dozen of them. They were mostly young, his age or a bit older, both women and men. None was smiling.

Quin's gaze settled on the tallest. He recognized the broad muscular shoulders and close-cropped hair, the smooth brown skin and hint of dimples.

"Domeniq?"

His heartbeat kicked up a few notches. Dom had survived Zaga and Angelyne. He was alive.

Elated, Quin stepped forward—and three others stepped forward, too, fists wadded tightly at their sides.

"It's *Dom* you're excited to see?" said another voice, and Quin realized they weren't guarding something, but someone.

The half circle parted to reveal a boy sitting at the piano. The dim light snagged on his sharp silver eyes. He boasted a shock of black hair, his copper skin lighter than Dom's but not as fair as Quin's, with a smattering of dark freckles. His right hand was splayed over the keys. Still the most beautiful hand Quin had seen, the fingers strong and elegant, though there were now only three.

His music teacher smiled. A smile that fell somewhere between wry and wicked.

"Would you look at that," Tobin said. "The river king has returned."

Chapter 5

SPLIT OPEN

THE BOAT GLIDED INTO the cove as the sun set, a resplendent round peach melting into the sea. Perhaps the last sunset Mia would ever witness from an undulating ocean. She certainly hoped so.

As Nell steered the dhou toward shore, Pilar leapt into the water, drenching her trousers up to the waist. She tugged on *Maysha*'s bow as Nell executed a complicated maneuver with the coconut ropes, rolling the sail and securing it to the gaff with banana leaves.

Once again Mia felt useless. No one had asked for her help. She was left to sit primly on the boat, feasting her eyes on the shoreline.

To be fair, it was a splendid shoreline.

The sand was a ruddy orange, tinged pink by the descending sun. The water was rosy, too, blushing in soft ripples. The coast had a windswept look, sand sloping into mounds and dunes and, farther out, impressive rust-colored bluffs. Mia could make out small towers and turrets on the beach, surely shaped by little hands. Castles.

A sudden memory of Kaer Killian surfaced: how, after loosing the Bridalaghdú with Quin's blade and soaring beside him down the mountain, she had squinted up at the castle they'd left behind. From that distance, it had looked small, laughably so. A minuscule dollhouse perched atop the northern peaks.

Till the northern peaks crumble.

Promise me, O promise me.

The words were too painful. Mia banished them from her mind. It no longer mattered if she and Quin had or hadn't finished the sacred wedding vows. You couldn't be married to a corpse.

She refocused on the shoreline. A row of trees with skinny brown trunks shot high into the sky, then burst into halos of bright yellow leaves. Banked in the sand beneath them were curious gray stones the size of a human skull.

"Lemon coconuts," Nell said. "They fall from the fish trees."

"Fish trees?"

"They don't grow fish, if that's what you're wondering. They're named after their long yellow fronds, which look like spiny fish bones. The lemon coconuts drop from the fronds."

"Do they taste good?" Pilar said.

Nell made a throaty sound of pure yearning. "Like magic."

"That could be good or bad."

"Like *good* magic, then. The flesh of the lemon coconut is a staple here in Pembuk, we bake it into cakes and pies, but also savory dishes. Mix it with a little salt and cold milk and you'll have a frosty yellow crème we call fish ice."

"Fascinating," Mia said at the same time Pilar said, "Disgusting."

Nell laughed. "It's quite tasty, I promise. Again, nothing to do with actual fish."

Mia stood on the boat, unsure what to do with her hands. She watched Pilar wade slowly out of the water, then knot the rope around a fallen fish tree. The same knot Mia had attempted at least half a dozen times. Mia felt simultaneously proud of her sister, and irritated.

"Kind of quiet for a port." Pilar surveyed the empty landscape. "Fine with me. I'm sick of talking."

"Pata Pacha is a cove," Nell countered, "not a port. Keep in mind I ran away under cover of night, it's not like I wanted to trumpet my departure to all of Pembuk."

The boat knocked into the shoreline and Mia lurched forward violently, nearly pitching overboard. Nell grabbed her hand. As she did, her long fingers brushed the frostflower on Mia's wrist. Beneath the moving ink, a new sensation stirred.

Mia gasped.

"What is it?" Nell said. "Are you all right?"

"Heat. I felt heat." Immediately she doubted herself. "I think I felt heat."

"Could be your imagination," Pilar suggested.

"Or it could be Pembuk." Nell cast a reproachful glance at Pilar, then turned back to Mia. "The glass kingdom is known for its restorative properties—arid climate, warm sun. There's something healing about this place, truly. You'll see. In any case, this bodes well, don't you think?"

Mia was still touching her wrist. She wanted so much for the feeling to be real. Every false positive hurt more than the last, a mockery of her former life. She remembered her mother talking about the Pembuka elixir, how she'd briefly tasted licorice and caught the scent of wood fire. Triumphs so small they were almost insulting.

Which was worse? Tasting, smelling, feeling nothing? Or constantly chasing the tiniest consolation prize?

Mia stepped onto the sand, then staggered forward, her land legs buckling beneath her. She fell to her knees, cupping handfuls of shimmering orange sand.

"It smells exactly the way I remember," Nell said, wistful. "Pembuka sand has a distinctive scent. I know this doesn't make sense, but to me it has always smelled *warm*."

Mia took a breath. She sieved sand through her fingers. Tears pricked her eyes.

Warm. She could smell it. *Feel* it.

She buried her arms up to her elbows, pressed her nose to the soft sand. Laid one cheek against it, then the other. It was undeniable. She could feel heat rising off the surface.

Her heart swelled with hope. This place could fix her. It had to.

"Having a moment there, Rose?"

She stared up at Pilar through a film of tears. A few granules of sand clung to her lips. Mia knew she looked ridiculous, but she didn't care.

"I feel something," she said hoarsely. "I feel warm."

Her sister shrugged, turned—and walked away.

If Pilar had struck her, it would have hurt less.

How had things changed so dramatically? That night in the "space between," Pil had stood valiantly by her side. When Mia had confessed her fears that the elixir wouldn't work—that a part of her would always be broken—Pilar had promised to fight *for* her until Mia was strong enough to fight again.

They had escaped the snow palace as allies, not enemies. Since then, Mia had done everything in her power to strengthen that alliance. But the harder she worked, the more guarded Pilar became.

And, as fast as it had come, the warmth died. The sand turned cold beneath Mia's palms.

Fury hissed through her veins. Her first true sensation in months, ripped away from her.

"Who wants a lemon coconut?" Nell said. "I'll find us one that hasn't been eaten. The piglums love them, and they usually get there first."

"I'll try one." Pilar hoisted herself onto the felled tree and adopted her favorite defensive posture: knees pulled to her chest, chin tucked between her patellae.

Kneecaps, Mia thought. Just call them kneecaps. Her obsession with anatomy had become obnoxious even to herself.

Before Mia could ask what a piglum was, Nell raised a lemon coconut above her head and brought it down hard on the tree. The fruit cracked neatly into two halves.

"Flawless," Nell said. "If I do say so myself."

She pierced the coarse gray shell with her knife, then slid the blade until the skin peeled off in curling sheets. She carved thick yellow slabs and handed one to Pilar, one to Mia.

Mia bit down, expecting nothing.

She could taste it.

The flesh melted in her mouth, somehow both sweet and piquant, a sweet citrusy tang softening into a mellow, salty savor. Once again Mia found herself blinking back tears. She wanted to shout, sob, throw her arms around Nell, kiss her beautiful mouth.

She startled. *Did* she want to kiss Nell? Mia had been with a girl only once before, during the long months in White Lagoon when she'd ached so desperately to feel something. Here she was again, aching to feel something. The yearning caught her off guard, yet didn't entirely surprise her. Yes, Mia had grown up in the river kingdom, where loving a woman was a crime punishable by death. But they were no longer in the river kingdom.

Would Nell *want* to be kissed?

"Too salty," Pilar said, interrupting the moment. "Didn't expect a fruit to taste like salt." She cracked her knuckles. "Where to now? The magical mystical Shadowess?"

Nell bit into a hunk of lemon coconut, a contented smile spreading over her face.

"Yes, actually."

"And where might she be lurking?"

"Where all magical mystical sorts lurk," Nell said. "The House of Shadows."

Mia had to laugh at her own naivete. Of course the Shadowess would be at the House of Shadows. How had she failed to put two and two together?

What she knew of the House was hearsay. Her father had spoken of it only twice, the first time when she was a child. She still remembered how his words stoked the flames of her curiosity.

"There's a place called the House of Shadows," he'd told Mia and Angelyne. "People from all four kingdoms go there to seek the truth."

"So they're scientists!" Mia said brightly.

"Scientists are not the only truth seekers, little rose."

"Do they all find the same truth in the House?" Angie asked. "Or different ones?"

"Other people's truths are not the same as ours," their father replied gruffly, effectively ending the conversation. Little Mia did not fail to notice that he hadn't quite answered the question.

The second time was years later, after Wynna was gone. Though Mia didn't know it, her father had begun to think quite differently about magic and magicians. Freshly returned from a voyage to Pembuk, he spoke again of the House of Shadows. This time his whole tenor had changed. He told his daughters how he'd met pilgrims, philosophers, spiritual guides, alchemists, and experts in various fields, as well as people with no illustrious titles or professions. They congregated to converse and question, challenge and argue.

"But why argue?" Angie had asked. "What can they hope to gain?"

"Knowledge," he'd said, and looked knowingly at Mia, whose

cheeks flushed with pride. "The greatest gain of all."

Now a shadow of doubt crept over the memory. Griffin Rose had not turned out to be the most reliable purveyor of information. Nell hadn't been terribly forthright, either; this was the first time she'd mentioned anyplace other than "Pembuk" and "the first of the glass cities."

"What's in the House of Shadows?" Pilar asked aloud, jolting Mia back to her senses. They'd been hiking for hours, trudging through sinking sand, their progress so maddeningly slow she almost wished she were back on the water. Nell had said they would take a caravan to the first of the glass cities. The caravan had yet to materialize.

Pilar kept rubbing her arms, leaving Mia to surmise it was cold, though she couldn't feel it. Above them, the night sky was stained a deep purple, draped with a canopy of stars.

"People," Nell answered.

"Thanks, got that one on my own. How many people?"

"It's constantly changing. There are always a few hundred, at least. Sometimes more like a thousand."

"Sounds crowded."

"The Shadowess would say true spaciousness happens in the mind."

Pilar groaned.

"But who *is* the Shadowess?" Mia asked. She understood Pilar's frustration; Nell had given them precious few details, only that the Shadowess could—and would—help them. Perhaps now that Nell had finally told them *where*, she would fill in the gaps as to *whom*.

"Isn't it obvious?" Pilar groaned. "The Shadowess is their mighty leader."

Mia felt a pang of sympathy. Pil was surely thinking of Zaga, her negligent, backstabbing, murderous mother . . . and the leader of the Dujia on Refúj.

"The Shadowess is a leader," Nell agreed, "but she's appointed to her position. The Manuba Committee selects a number of qualified candidates, votes among themselves, then appoints a Shadowess—or a Shadower—every seven years. The Shadowess can serve two terms, but no more than that. She oversees the work being done at the House, striving to unite all the guests and residents in a common purpose. It's been this way for thousands of years, or quite possibly forever, considering Pembuk was the cradle of human civilization."

Pilar swore. "Everyone knows the first humans were born in Fojo. Our volqanoes spat fire and formed the first islands."

"And here I thought Glas Ddir held that particular honor," Mia countered. "Seeing as how we invented the old language."

Nell laughed. "Yes, every culture wants to believe it was the first. The four gods . . . the Four Great Goddesses . . . even Luumia's Seven Souls. Our creation myths always tell us that the cradle is ours."

Nelladine stopped, squinting up at the star-kissed sky.

"I'm not entirely sure what I believe, or who started what where. But I know in my soul there has to be something more than this." She gestured skyward. "Someone put those stars up there, and it was no mistake."

Mia longed for that kind of faith. She'd always relied on her own intellect and understanding. Knowledge *was* the greatest gain of all. How could she believe in something she couldn't quantify or prove? And why would she want to?

"I stopped believing in the Great Goddesses when I was sixteen," Pilar said. For once there was no vitriol in her voice. "I figured if the Duj existed, they either weren't paying attention or weren't the kind of goddesses anyone should believe in."

Mia saw an opening. She nodded vigorously.

"Makes total sense. What you went through would make anyone lose their faith."

Pilar shot her a dark look. "I don't need your sympathy, Rose."

Mia wanted to bang her own head against a tree until it split open like a lemon coconut. She was trying to offer her sister affirmation. Why in four hells couldn't Pilar just accept it?

"You'll find all sorts of people with all kinds of faiths at the House of Shadows," Nell said. She'd started walking again. "That's one of the things I always liked. That no matter where you came from or what you believed, you were accepted and welcomed, given a seat at the table."

"Then why didn't you stay?" Mia asked.

Nell didn't answer. She gestured toward a haze of orange light in the distance.

"By my estimation, that lovely little beacon is an inn."

Chapter 6

UNCLENCHED

PILAR DIDN'T BELIEVE IN the Four Great Goddesses. But she did believe in a hot meal and a nip of rai rouj. All those times she'd goaded Nell to find a harbor, she'd assumed "harbor" meant food and drink, not an endless march through the desert. It was also freezing. Weren't deserts supposed to be warm?

As they approached the inn, Pilar shot a prayer of thanks up to the sky, just to be safe.

"Kaara akutha!" Nell said as they stepped onto the inn's stoop. She knocked the sand off her boots, motioning them to do the same. "Welcome to Pembuk. You're about to get your first real taste of Pembuka hospitality."

"As long as they feed us," Pilar said.

Nell laughed. "I assure you, you will never go hungry in Pembuk. We are a people who like to eat."

She conversed with the innkeeper in Pembuka, who led them to a long table. Plates of food began appearing from the kitchen. Roasted chicken. Squares of salty grilled cheese. Goop of beans and eggplant.

"Jomos," Nell said, pointing to the goop. "Ah, and you went straight for the piglum!" She nodded toward the greasy meat clutched in Pilar's fist that she'd mistaken for chicken. "I don't eat meat anymore, only fish. But I remember the taste of piglum, I used to dream about it after I left Pembuk. Isn't it delicious?"

Pilar didn't answer. She was too busy shoveling it all in.

"Glad you're taking time to savor it," Mia muttered.

Rose picked at her food. Birdlike. At first she'd bitten into the piglum with relish, and Pilar knew why: she wanted desperately to taste it. But from the way she was chewing on the meat, it was clear she might as well be eating rubber.

Mia stopped abruptly. Her mouth fell open, full of half-chewed piglum.

"Pepper!" she cried. "I taste pepper!" She looked up at Nell, her eyes so full of hope it nearly broke Pilar's heart.

On the beach, when Nell had touched Mia's wrist—and again when Rose practically made love to the sand—Pilar couldn't explain what had come over her. She hadn't meant to be mean. Mia had looked happier than she'd ever seen her. Their conversation under the snow palace came rushing back: Mia confessing she was desperate to feel things, and terrified she never would.

I'm not a fighter like you are, she'd said.

Pilar's own words echoed. *Then I'll fight for you. Until you're strong enough to fight again.*

But now that the sensations were coming back, she wouldn't need Pilar to fight for her. Mia wouldn't need her at all.

So Pilar did what she always did with fear.

Choked it.

The next hour played out like a bad joke. The water in the bath bucket had no temperature, until the moment Mia yelped that warmth had enveloped her feet in silken heat. Those were her actual words: "I feel warmth enveloping my feet in silken heat!"

Maybe Mia really was destined to be a princess. She was as bad as Quin. Like any good royal, she seemed constitutionally unable to say, "The water is hot."

And then Mia's face fell.

"It's gone," she said, all her joy flushed down the drain.

Pilar hated that a part of her felt relieved.

Nell installed them in a room with three hay beds: a welcome relief after weeks on a wooden boat. On each bed sat a white towel twisted into the shape of a miniature elephant. Pilar promptly untwisted her elephant and collapsed on the bed.

Not Mia. She babbled on and on about a large rock near her cottage in Ilwysion—"Angie thought it looked like an elephant, but I never agreed!"—and then, just as Pilar started to drift off to sleep, Rose waxed lyrical about the hay against the down pillow.

"Soft and scratchy! So beautifully juxtaposed!" she moaned, her voice muffled in goose down.

And the fear grew.

At breakfast the next morning—more bean goop with a side of fresh melon—Mia was distraught that she couldn't taste the food.

"It's all right, Mia," Nell insisted. "Even if the sensations are coming back in bits and pieces, they're coming back. Once we get to the House of Shadows, there will be so many people who want to help you, you can't even imagine."

Nell pushed aside her half-eaten soup.

"Now, on to practicalities. I've booked us on a caravan to Shabeeka, the first of the glass cities. Took me long enough to haggle—so many tourists this time of year! The Pearl Moon Festival is in full swing, and more people than ever are making the pilgrimage to the Isle of Forgetting, which seems especially tragic during such a lovely festival, who in their right mind would want to forget that? The House of Shadows sits smack in the center of Shabeeka, so once we've—"

"Are you going to finish that?" Pilar jerked a thumb toward the soup.

Nell shrugged. "Have at it. Just don't eat too much, because the caravan can be very . . ."

Pil had already wolfed it down.

Bumpy. That was Pilar's guess for how Nell would have finished her sentence. The ride to Shabeeka had more bumps than a pox victim.

"Not too much longer," Nell promised.

Pilar grunted. The back of her neck was sweaty, her armpits damp. The cold desert from the night before had thawed into a sweltering desert day.

"You said that hours ago."

"Yes, but now I actually mean it."

Pilar folded her arms. "How are you paying for all this, Nell? Were you hiding gold coins in those banana leaves?"

"The glass kingdom has a strong system of credit. My family's name is well respected."

"They'll know you're here once they get the bill."

"Oh, they'll probably know long before then. That's the problem with family, really: their love becomes a kind of leash."

She shut her eyes, resting the back of her head on the flimsy canvas wall.

Pilar frowned. If love were a kind of leash, her mother had been all too happy to strangle her with it.

She could feel Mia staring at her. Why was Mia always staring? On the boat there weren't many places to fix your gaze. Ocean. Ocean. Ocean. And so on. But here they were, bouncing along in a caravan, Rose giving her that same look. Oozing sympathy. Ready to tell her how she should or shouldn't be healing. Eager to propose a scientific formula to get her back on track.

She knew Mia meant well. That was the story of Mia Rose's life, wasn't it? Trying to do everything right, then doing everything wrong. But Pilar couldn't take Mia looking at her like a piece of broken glass, one that had to be handled gently. She glared back. Ferocious.

"What?" she growled.

Mia shifted on the bench. Opened her mouth like she wanted to say something, then shut it. Turned away.

Pilar felt a stab of guilt. Why was she being heartless? Mia was the only family she had left. The other half of the leash.

But maybe that was why it hurt. In their Reflections, they had understood each other. They'd stood side by side, stronger together than apart. Ready to reclaim their lives. They'd been equals, partners. *Sisters.*

Now when Rose looked at her, it was with sympathy. Or worse, she didn't look at all.

Frustrated, Pilar peeled back a flap of canvas. They were deep into Shabeeka now. Sandy dirt roads, buildings of mud and wood and limestone. There was no glass in the glass city. One more bill of goods she'd been sold.

And then she saw it. The caravan veered down a wide street, and at the far end, an enormous structure appeared. Pilar sucked in her breath.

The building was made of glass. Every wall a different color, cut into a different shape. Her sharp eyes took in spheres, cubes, diamonds, waves. The walls dipped and rose—some smoothly curved, others sliced at sharp angles. One whole surface was blue and rippling. Were those fish swimming inside the glass?

Beyond the fish, she saw bigger blurs. People, she assumed. It seemed laughable, imagining humans in a house of glass. Wouldn't they constantly knock into the walls?

In the front courtyard, a clear staircase led to a massive gold door. The entire building seemed to be hovering a few feet off the ground. Obviously a mirage. They'd been in the desert too long.

Pilar rubbed her eyes.

The building was definitely hovering.

"We're here," Nell said, waking with a start. She hadn't even looked outside, yet somehow she knew.

Mia peered out of the caravan, clearly as awestruck as Pilar.

"Is it . . . ?"

"Floating? Oh yes. That's just one of the many strange things you're about to see, believe me. Remember what I taught you about the Elemental Hex? The House of Shadows was built on an ancient source of power: the Elemental Whorl. All the elements are suspended in perfect balance, no human intervention required. The Whorl is strong enough to hold the whole House, and supple enough to adapt to the wind. The sands here are always shifting. This is why other structures sink, some become totally submerged. But the House hovers, impervious to time."

"Till the glass cities sink into the western sands," Mia murmured. Familiar words, though Pilar couldn't place them.

She felt pulled toward the House of Shadows, and also repelled. It was too open. Too exposed. Pilar thought of Dove's underground torture chamber, where she'd stood, unable to move, staring at her reflection in frosty black ice. Not so different from glass, really.

Of course, the Shadowess didn't torture children to fuel a kingdom. Or so Nell said. You couldn't be too careful.

"Great sands," Nell murmured. "Four years and it hasn't changed a bit."

They stepped out of the caravan, which wasted no time trundling off without them. For a moment they stood in perfect silence, staring up at the House.

"What's that?" Pilar pointed to a coil of glass stones in the courtyard. The path looped in on itself, then looped back, then looped back again. Which was pointless, when she thought about it.

"A labyrinth," Nell said. "It's how everyone enters the House. Sometimes you have to go backward to go forward." She groaned. "Listen to me, I sound just like her! That's the problem with the Shadowess's little sayings: once you've heard them, they're stuck in your head forever."

After a month of silence, Nell was suddenly doling out all kinds of little gems about the Shadowess. It seemed suspicious. Who cared if the Shadowess was appointed to her position? That meant some self-righteous temple of experts gave her power, not the people she served. In Pilar's experience, people with power were all the same. Her mother. King Ronan. Lord Dove. Orry.

No one should have that kind of power. It was too easy to abuse.

"Shall we, then?" Nell started toward the House. "I can't wait to show you the Creation Studio . . . Oh! And the Curatorium, of course. I think you'll love it, Mia, scientist that you are."

When she beckoned, Rose followed.

Maybe Nell *wouldn't* abandon them at the House, Pilar realized. Maybe Nell would stay, and she and Mia would become lovers. Or friends. Or sisters.

Pilar's heart sank. There was more than one way to be abandoned.

She clenched her fists. It wasn't too late. She could leave them before they left her.

"Pilar?"

Mia had stopped walking. Pivoted halfway.

"You coming?"

Pilar's heart lifted. Mia was waiting for her.

"The thing about a labyrinth," Nell said, "is that there's only one place you can end up. Which is exactly the place you were meant to end up all along."

Pilar unclenched her fists. Swallowed. And stepped onto the first glass stone.

Chapter 7

HOME

"Where," said Tobin, rising from the piano bench, "are your manners?"

Quin stood in the not-so-deserted brothel, mouth agape, still trying to parse this unexpected reunion with his music teacher.

"My . . ."

"Not *your* manners. Gods, no." Toby flourished a hand toward his band of unsmiling acolytes, the way an innkeeper might flourish a hand toward a plate of bad cheese. "Don't you remember how to address a royal? All hail the son of Clan Killian!"

"Uncontested king of Glas Ddir," muttered a gravelly voice behind him.

Someone snickered to Quin's left, and it echoed through the

group. He bristled. Was his rightful claim to the throne so amusing? He glanced over his shoulder, hoping it wasn't Domeniq. But Dom was nowhere in sight.

Instead Quin saw a girl of eleven or twelve, with cropped dirty-blond hair and puckish blue eyes. When those eyes met his, she did not laugh. She curtsied. A tiny curtsy—presumably so as not to provoke the others' ire—but a curtsy nonetheless.

"Silence," Tobin reprimanded the others, and the snickers immediately ceased. "Forgive them, Your Grace. We're all in need of a good laugh."

Were these people loyal to Tobin? They certainly seemed to listen when he spoke. Quin winced, remembering the last time he and Tobin had seen each other. As Quin and Mia fled the Kaer, Toby had emerged from the shadows with bread and snow plums—stale and moldy, respectively. Quin knew he deserved far worse. What struck him that night was how old Tobin had looked, how tired. So painfully diminished from the dazzling prodigy he once was.

"What should we do with him, Toby?" said the big fellow to Quin's left, presumably the same jester who'd found his claim to the throne hilarious.

"Take him with us, of course."

"Alive?"

Tobin massaged his temples. "Is that so hard to grasp?"

"But we . . ." The man looked to the others, uncertain. "We don't believe in kings."

"Pinch him, if you must. I'm fairly certain he exists."

This seemed to confound the man, who frowned and folded his arms over his burly chest. The others looked equally uncertain.

Tobin's silver eyes locked onto Quin's, and he did not look away.

"Four gods," Quin said, realizing. "*You're* the Embers."

Toby looked pleased. "Our reputation precedes us! I must admit: I'm surprised you've heard of us. You've been gone quite awhile now. All the way to Luumia, I hear, chasing after your wife." He tapped his upper lip, thoughtful. "Or were you running away from your other wife?"

Quin frowned. His friend had always possessed an acerbic wit, but the line between acerbity and vitriol was growing thin.

"I don't understand, Tobin. You're leading a band of murderers and thieves?"

"Do we look like thieves? We're a band of brothers, sisters, friends, lovers. We are the Embers. The ones the world expected to flicker and die out. Instead we ignited a revolution."

"Remember the Embers," his broad-shouldered acolyte said solemnly. "They remember you."

Quin arched a brow. "Is that some kind of slogan?"

Tobin folded his arms. "Do you not approve?"

"A little grandiose, I think."

"You know what I find grandiose?" Toby smiled. "Tyrants."

The room pulsed with a strange energy Quin couldn't quite read. As if a crust of sardonic laughter had formed on top of something far more malicious.

"You'll come with us," Toby said. "Won't you?"

Quin studied him closely. Was it an invitation or a threat?

He drew himself up, doing his best to sound kingly.

"I've got my own matters to attend to."

"One night, at least. Have a few drinks, a few laughs? Like old times."

Tobin's gaze was steady. Those silver eyes had once sparked delicious heat in Quin's body. To his embarrassment, they still did.

"It's been so long," Toby murmured, in a tone Quin never thought he'd hear again.

A new horror squirmed through him. He had returned to the river kingdom to make his claim to the throne. Any pretenders were his enemy. If Toby led the Embers, would Quin have to fight him? *Kill* him?

"Please." Tobin gestured toward the others. "It would make all of us so happy."

Quin looked from face to face. He did not see happiness. He saw distrust, amusement, and disdain. He wished Domeniq hadn't abandoned him; surely they'd have had at least a glimmer of the friendship they had begun to forge on Refúj.

Again Quin met Tobin's eyes. This time, he understood something. If the lonely farmer was to be believed, the Embers posed the greatest threat to his claim. For days Quin had been following their carved triangles. Not triangles, he realized, in a jolt of epiphany. *Flames.* Those flames had led him, finally, here. The Embers now had a face. A face that Quin had once loved. A face that, he felt certain, had once loved him back.

If he accepted Tobin's invitation, it was tantamount to bedding with the enemy.

What better place than the bed of the enemy to ascertain the threat?

"All right," Quin said. "One night."

Reactions rippled through the group—a mixed bag, from what he could tell.

"Wonderful!" Toby cried. "I'm so happy to hear it. I'll lead the way."

When Tobin turned and walked out of the brothel, Quin did not fail to notice the hitch in his gait. That hitch was a gift from King Ronan. The kind of gift you could never give back.

Killian Village was in ruins. Cottages stood empty, doors ajar or ripped off their hinges. Shops had been ravaged by fire; carts and wagons lay overturned, spilled fruit rotting on the cobblestones. There were carcasses in the streets: rats and dogs and sometimes larger bodies that shook Quin to the core. A mantle of snow covered everything, scabbed over with soot and mud.

As Tobin led the group through the village, Quin fell behind. All the other wrecked towns paled in comparison to Killian Village. Had his father done this? Had he unleashed one last torrent of fury and destruction? Had Zaga? Angelyne? Or were the Embers to blame?

They were passing a corner Quin knew well. On instinct, he looked toward the building that had always lifted his spirits—and stopped dead in his tracks.

What was once a pretty two-story facade had been decimated. The fire-eaten walls were little more than rock and ash; he could see the building's blackened innards. It called to mind a gentle giant, charred down to the very bone.

The orphanage.

Quin could pinpoint exactly when his furtive visits to the orphanage had begun. For years he'd watched his sister ride into Killian Village bringing food, clothes, and other supplies. The villagers invited Karri into their homes, their pubs and taverns, their houses of worship. The princess came ever ready with a kind word or a pint of cold ale. She had a gift.

Quin had no illusions. He'd never been as generous or good-hearted as his sister. But after witnessing firsthand what his father had done to Tobin in the castle crypt—what he was *capable* of doing—Quin knew he could no longer look the other way.

It was too late to protect Toby. He had failed miserably in that regard. But he would do all he could to atone through other means.

The day after King Ronan banished Tobin's family from the Kaer, Quin had slipped out to the stables, saddled a horse, and rode straight to the orphanage. He had stuffed his pockets full of treats: sweet candies in waxy paper he'd pilfered from the kitchens, little music makers constructed of wood and twine, dolls with straw hair. And coins, of course. Tiny discs of Killian gold his father would never miss—but that could feed and clothe a child for months.

Sometimes he wrote them plays. He would bring a pile of costumes, and they'd stomp about the orphanage, performing their roles. Other times he played piano. He'd sit at the rickety instrument and play Glasddiran nursery rhymes, songs the children's mothers might have sung to them. He could guess what had happened to those mothers. Had Quin seen their hands hanging in the king's Hall?

Sometimes when Quin went to the orphanage, he simply sat on the floor with the children, telling stories, laughing at their jokes, and braiding their long, matted hair.

And then he returned to his privileged life. Back to his decadent feasts, his jackets with gold buttons, his cozy canopy bed where every night a servant girl packed smoldering embers into a copper warmer and tucked it between his plush linens.

More often than not, he cried the whole ride home.

And now the orphanage was gone.

What had happened to the children inside?

He wanted to ask Tobin, but by now most of the group had passed him by. His former music teacher walked swiftly at the front, deep in conversation with one of the Embers.

Quin turned back to the orphanage. He strained his eyes to make out the hunk of scorched wood in the corner. *The piano.* He stared at his hands, wondering if he still remembered any songs the children loved. The last time he had touched a piano was in the Snow Queen's music room, when he'd bludgeoned it with a violin.

A sickening thought snaked through him. He could have wrought this destruction himself. With the magic in his hands, he would have needed no torch to set the orphanage on fire.

"Hello!" chirped a small voice.

He looked down to see the puckish blue-eyed girl staring up at him.

"I'm Briallihandra Mar. But you can call me Brialli." She smiled widely. "It's very nice to meet you, Your Grace."

Quin's emotions settled. He began to walk again, Brialli falling in step beside him.

"Did you grow up in the village, Brialli? You speak very well."

"I should think so! My mother was a scholar of the old language, and of the histories, too."

"The histories were always my favorite subject. I begged my tutor to bring me all the books he could get his hands on."

"My mother did her tutoring in private. A sneak-around scholar, she used to say. That was before the Hunters came to our cottage."

Quin steeled himself for what was coming. This girl had every right to hate Clan Killian.

But, to his bafflement, there was no malice in her expression. Only curiosity.

"My mother," Brialli said, "used to say you weren't rotten like your father. She saw you in the village once, when you brought bread and toys to the orphans. Mother said you were gentle with them. She believed you'd make a fine king someday. There are those of us who still—" She stopped herself. "Mother also said you were easy on the eyes."

Quin coughed. Brialli looked up at him, guileless.

"What does it mean, 'easy on the eyes'? She never would tell me. Is it an expression in the old language?"

"And your father? What of him?"

"Mother did that, too. She always changed the subject."

64

Brialli let out a deep sigh, as if she was resigned to adults being evasive. Quin was charmed. The girl reminded him of Karri, so frank and unfettered. Sometimes he missed his sister so much it was physically painful, as if a part of him had been cut out.

"My father was a cook. He died when Queen Angelyne sent her men into Killian Village. I was in the next room, hiding where Father told me to, in an old canvas flour sack. I heard everything. He tried to tell them how much he hated the old regime, seeing as how it was King Ronan who took his wife away, but they . . ."

She trailed off. Quin didn't need to hear the rest to know what had happened. She'd lost her mother to Ronan, her father to Angelyne. How had a girl so young survived much loss?

Quin had stared into the eyes of many orphans; he knew how easily grief could give way to despair, despair to resignation. But, by some miracle, this girl still had hope in her eyes.

Careful, Quin thought. Remember these people are not your friends.

"Tell me, Brialli Mar." He flashed his friendliest smile. "How long have you been with the Embers? Is it quite a large group?"

She shrugged. "Large enough. There was hardly anyone left in the village. They'd all either been killed or run away. When Toby found me scavenging for food, he invited me to join them. We're building a different sort of kingdom, one where the powerful won't use their power against the weak."

"Going to destroy anyone who stands in our way," said a deep voice.

Quin was annoyed to find the big man from the brothel

skulking behind them, shamelessly eavesdropping.

"It appears," Quin said, gesturing grandly toward the remains of the village, "you have destroyed everything already. You Embers roam my kingdom, killing and pillaging, leaving your trail of flames."

"There's naught left to burn." The man waved a meaty arm around them. "This is magic's doing. People with that kind of power are always hungry. Doesn't matter how much they eat."

A trickle of dread dripped down Quin's spine.

"In a perfect world, no one would ever hurt anyone," Brialli said brightly. "Magic or not. But, like my father used to say, sometimes you have to skin a few rabbits to make a good stew."

Quin expected Tobin to take them to a row of cottages, or perhaps a tavern on the outskirts of town. His mouth watered at the thought of a hot meal and a frosty pint of stonemalt. Surely the Embers had some kind of headquarters where they slept and ate.

Only when they started to ascend the eastern road snaking out of Killian Village and up the mountainside did Quin realize where they were going.

They were leading him to the castle.

They were taking him home.

Chapter 8

CELESTIAL

"IT's EXQUISITE."

The word was woefully insufficient. Mia stood at the top of the floating staircase, unable to tear her eyes away from the House of Shadows. Towering over them was a masterpiece of a door, its gilded facade embellished with moons and stars.

"People actually live here?"

"Don't let the fancy exterior fool you," Nell said. "The House is much more relaxed inside."

The door was nested in two curved alcoves, the first a dark, scalloped teakwood that sat atop the golden door like a crown. The larger alcove boasted dazzling mosaics: rust, teal, and sable tiles arranged in intricate patterns.

"Mahraini tiles," Nell explained. "Made by the Mahraini mystics thousands of years ago."

"The door's so pretty I don't want to touch it."

"I'll touch it." Pilar scowled. "Since you won't."

Mia was losing patience. What had she said or done to make Pilar so angry? Granted, anger seemed to be Pilar d'Aqila's default emotion. But something had definitely inflamed it. On the boat Pilar had been guarded. Since arriving in Pembuk, she'd become downright hostile.

And yet. When Mia stepped toward the labyrinth, hesitating on the first stone to look back, she'd seen a flicker of something on Pilar's face. Fear? Hope? She knew how easily those two intertwined. Even now, staring up at the House of Shadows, she felt both emotions. Surely a place this beautiful, this *magical*, would be able to help her. But what if it couldn't?

If even the Shadowess couldn't fix her, who was left?

"There's the Bridge." Nell motioned toward the west. "You can see it from here."

"Bridge to where?"

"Prisma."

In the middle distance Mia saw glinting steel, clean and unsentimental, liquid silver arcing over the water. Beyond the Bridge, the Isle of Forgetting was a white smudge. The color of pale sand. The color of nothing.

Mia turned back to the House. Two brass sconces flanked the door, cradling spheres of green fire. They called to mind the cool green flames from the pinewood sulfyr sticks her father had gifted her after one of his journeys.

She gave a start. It *was* the same fire. Her father had brought the sulfyr sticks back from the glass kingdom. Perhaps even from the House of Shadows, where she knew for a fact he had been. She couldn't explain why, but it soothed her, knowing that some part of Pembuk had found its way to her long ago.

As far as reconciling how Griffin Rose, legendary Hunter— *killer*—of Dujia, had whiled away the hours among peaceful pilgrims and truth seekers? Mia's mind was not up to the task.

"Are we going in or not?" Pilar huffed. She shoved at the door. It didn't budge.

"Funny thing," Nell said. "You actually *pull* it."

Pilar grunted and gave the gold knocker a hard tug. The door swung toward her so quickly she swore and jumped back.

The door was transforming before their eyes. The gold sheen dissolved and became translucent; a glimmering hinge material- ized down the center, splitting the pellucid glass into two perfect halves. Mia watched, spellbound, as the door fell open like a book.

"I've always thought that part was a bit much," Nell said.

Mia didn't hear her. She was already stepping over the thresh- old, drawn onto the page.

The interior of the House took her breath away.

They'd stepped into a cavernous hall. Immense glass pillars stretched from floor to domed ceiling in rich hues of rose and emerald. Crystalline water filled an entire billowing wall, aquatic creatures gliding and drifting. Mia saw fish in every shade of blue:

robin's egg to azure, powder to peacock, rich royal to midnight indigo. And, in their midst, a single orange melonfish, its long lappets whirling bright and brilliant tangerine. Like a coquettish girl at a ball, Mia thought, twirling in place as her skirt spun around her.

She craned her neck, admiring the elaborate mosaics overhead, thousands of Mahraini tiles arranged in dizzying geometries.

"Careful," Nell cautioned. "My mother used to say staring at Mahraini tiles too long could dislocate your eyes, though now that I'm grown I'm pretty sure that's not possible." She laughed. "Mothers say such violent things to their children, don't they?"

In her peripheral vision, Mia saw Pilar flinch.

But there was too much to see, too many marvels to take in, to worry about Pilar. The hall teemed with people. Mia delighted in every manner of attire—smart jackets and trousers; long, flowing garments; veils adorned with jewels—fabrics hugging sharp angles and voluptuous curves, bodies large and small and everything in between.

During Mia's time in Refúj, the Dujia had mesmerized her, their hair and clothes so different from the ones she'd known. Their hands stirred her deeply: countless girls and women without gloves, a glorious display of skin tones she had never seen in the river kingdom.

Here, in the House of Shadows, her awe only grew. She saw not just women, but men. Some covered their hair while others wore it styled in elaborate braids or coils, or lopped off entirely. Countless languages and dialects twined together in a low, resonant hum. The people bustling around her hailed from all four king-doms—including, to Mia's surprise, her own.

She drank in the enthralling blend of sight and sound. A note of music echoed through the hall, followed by another. She followed Pilar's gaze to a group of children holding an array of string instruments: mainly lutes, with a sprinkling of cellos and violins. Pilar was no doubt thinking of Morígna, her violin teacher, who had so devastatingly betrayed her trust. Mia's mind sorted swiftly through appropriate words of comfort.

Pilar seemed to sense her watching. She jerked away from the child musicians and kicked at the floor. Even the ground was a visual feast: as the pale rose glass hovered inches over the orange sand, it mellowed to a deep, sunbaked crimson.

"Blood-colored," said Pilar. "Very comforting. Where's that sheep going?"

Mia blinked. A bearded man was leading a sheep on a rope.

"To the Curatorium, probably, see its hind leg?" Nell motioned to the bandage wrapped around the sheep's femur. "The House is home to many lives, not just human, and the Shadowess has a soft spot for vulnerable creatures. Some people abandon their old or sick animals on the front steps, it truly breaks my heart. But there are always physicians and healers in the House—Curateurs, we call them—who tend to the animals, in much the same way they tend to the elder and ill residents who've traveled long distances, hoping to be healed."

As they watched, the bearded man tugged on the rope. The sheep let out a short, sharp bleat.

"If he doesn't want a hurt sheep," Pilar muttered, "maybe he shouldn't yank so hard."

"Nelladinellakin?"

A woman with pale, cream-colored skin and a long yellow braid stood perfectly still. She had stopped so suddenly that a family nearly collided with her. The father muttered something, then redirected his brood.

"Great sands, Nelladine," the woman breathed. "Is it really you?"

And then she was gliding forward, arms outstretched, kissing Nell on each cheek before pulling her in for an exuberant hug.

"Celeste," Nell said, the name muffled in the woman's thick blond braid. It was hard to tell her age; close up, Mia could detect light creases around her bright blue eyes, but her charming upturned nose made her look younger.

Celeste pulled back, eyes glistening with tears. She cupped Nelladine's face in her hands. For a moment, Mia thought she saw Nell's shoulders stiffen. Then she seemed to relax.

"Let me look at you. You've grown even more beautiful! Can you imagine? You're just glowing, glowing with *it*, truly. She'll be so happy to see you. Stone's here—you have to go straight to him or he'll never forgive you. He's in the Swallow, per usual. That boy can eat!"

Nell smiled. "Some things never change."

Celeste turned abruptly to Pilar and Mia, as if seeing them for the first time.

"Kaara akutha to Manuba Vivuli! Welcome to the House of

Shadows! Forgive me—I'm just so delighted to see Nelladin-ellakin after all these years. I'm Celeste." She beamed at them. Then prompted, "And you are?"

"Pilar d'Aqila."

Celeste leaned forward, hands outstretched. Pilar flinched.

"I don't want—"

But she wasn't quick enough. Celeste kissed one cheek, then the other.

"It's the way we say hello in Pembuk! A kiss on each cheek. It's really quite nice. I'm just so excited to meet you all. The kosmos does provide!"

Mia let her cheeks be kissed, then extended a hand.

"Mia Rose."

"A Glasddiran and a Fojuen!" Celeste clucked. "What a journey you've been on. As the Shadowess says: all those who come to the House of Shadows are those who belong."

"I thought I'd show my friends around," Nell said.

"I'll lead the way! You'll find some parts of the House significantly changed since you left, especially with so many new guests—and the refugees, of course."

Mia raised a brow. Before she could ask about the refugees, Nell interjected.

"That's all right, Celeste. I'm sure we'll find our way."

Something simmered just beneath the surface of the conversation. Mia couldn't quite put her finger on it. Celeste was obviously more thrilled to see Nell than Nell was to see her. Why was Nelladine, normally so effusive about everything, holding back?

She couldn't tell if it was about Celeste specifically, or about the mysterious reasons Nell had chosen to leave.

Celeste waved them off.

"Don't worry, you'll be seeing plenty of me. I'm the House's Keeper, I make sure everything stays in orbit around here. Someone's got to keep the celestial bodies afloat!"

They watched her scurry off, yellow braid swinging.

"So you've met Celeste," Nell said dryly.

"What's a Keeper?" Mia asked, curious.

"Every Shadowess or Shadower appoints a Keeper to help manage the various activities and offerings of the House. Celeste was definitely *not* the Keeper when I left."

"Better question," Pilar said. "Is the Swallow where the food is?"

Mia could say this much for Pilar: she was not constrained by decorum, nor did she ever lose sight of the prize.

When Nell nodded, Pilar smirked.

"The kosmos does provide."

Chapter 9

THE ONE THEY'D COME TO SEE

PILAR'S INSTINCTS WERE SPOT on. A building with glass walls, floors, and ceilings? The House of Shadows was disorienting as hell.

That said, hardly any of the glass was transparent. It wasn't opaque, either, but somewhere in the middle, every hall a different color. They'd round a corner where a green wall met a blue one, casting a turquoise glow. Pretty, she had to admit. Despite the ceiling being one large skylight, the building stayed nice and cool.

Many of the walkways inclined downward or upward, mirroring the strange shape of the walls. She spied dozens of murals: happy scenes painted by children, or possibly adults with zero painting skills. Oceans, forests, flowers. And so on.

Pilar's stomach tensed at a lakeside cottage. Would she ever see a cottage without imagining Orry inside it?

Her boot stuttered on the floor. She caught herself.

"Don't worry," Nell said. "You get used to the glass."

"You sure do know your way around."

"I should, considering how many years I spent roaming these halls. Celeste is wrong, it hasn't changed at all."

"Years? I thought you said residents were always coming and going."

"Look! The Manjala."

Nell was dodging the question. She stopped in front of an egg-shaped door. Annoyed, Pilar peered through the glass.

Inside was a large circular room with curved wooden walls. The Manjala, apparently. The vaulted ceilings reminded Pilar of the sanctuary on Refúj, where Morígna had gathered all the Dujia and turned them against her. Some sanctuary *that* turned out to be.

But whereas the sanctuary was always dark and foreboding, this room was bright and clean. At the front stood a tall woman in a white tunic and short trousers. She balanced on one leg, arms extended in a V. The sole of her left foot pressed against the inside of her right thigh.

Intrigued, Pilar mashed her nose to the glass. A dozen people faced the front, mostly women and a few men. Each stood on a gray wool blanket, mirroring the tunic woman's pose. Some better than others. One bald man wobbled wildly, arms flailing in the air.

"That's jougi," Nell said quietly. "An ancient form of movement and meditation, very calming for the nerves."

"That"—Pilar pointed at the man fighting wildly to stay upright—"does not look calming."

"Is it a kind of athleticism?" Mia asked.

"More of a practice, really. They rotate through different teachers. I liked a couple, some are rotten. I stopped going when I was younger, caused quite the stir, believe me. Oh, and look, there's the Rose Garden! I'd almost forgotten."

She hurried past the Manjala, prodding them farther down the hall. Pilar eyed her warily. What wasn't Nell telling them?

"It's actually a greenhouse. A house of glass inside a house of glass! Over a thousand varietals of roses, every shade in every color you could ever imagine.

Mia wandered through the rosebushes, oblivious to Nell's evasive parries. "Moon Shadow," she said, reading from the name placards. "Lilac Dawn. Kiss of Fire. Vermilion Queen."

With a sigh, Pilar followed. "Since when did roses have names?"

"Look at this one." Mia ran a finger down a black bloom with dark red veins. "I've never heard of a Black Rose."

"Sounds like a bad fantasy novel."

"It's a very rare variety," Nell said, coming up behind them. "Celeste cultivates them. Before she was the Keeper, she used to be the House gardener."

Nell cradled a Black Rose, careful not to tear it off the stem.

"They're wildly expensive. No one takes them out of the House, though if you did, they'd fetch a nice price. Watch this."

She closed her eyes.

A breeze rippled through the greenhouse. All around them, the bushes swayed. Blooms trembled on their stems. Thorns gleamed a little brighter.

The roses were changing. At the heart of each bud, a black stain appeared. It spilled slowly outward, oozing onto the petals like drops of ink. The color spread. One by one, the roses darkened, blackness blotting out the pink and peach and yellow. Red veins wormed over the dark petals. Pulsing. Bleeding.

When Nell opened her eyes, all the roses had become Black Roses. She smiled.

"As the Shadowess says: sometimes it takes only one to turn the tide."

She uncupped her hands. The flowers were already fading back to normal. Pink and peach and yellow, with no sign they'd ever been anything else.

"That was magical." Mia stooped to sniff one of the roses. "You touched them and they came to life."

Pilar's stomach twisted.

Had Nell altered the roses themselves? Or was it Mia's and Pilar's perceptions she had shifted? The whole thing happened so fast. Thanks to Lord Dove—and for that matter, Queen Freyja—Pilar knew your own eyes could deceive you.

But, she reminded herself, that could also be a good thing. In all the times Pilar had relived her past, only when she'd seen her own story through Mia's eyes had she believed it wasn't her fault.

After they'd set sail for Pembuk, Pilar had struggled to hold on to that conviction. But soon the usual feelings crept back. Anger. Shame. She heard Morígna's voice, and her mother's. Two women who'd said they loved her but who had blamed her in the end.

The worst part? They weren't wrong. Awful things happened to girls who opened themselves up to other people. Girls desperate to be loved.

Pilar snuck a glance at her half sister. Whatever was happening between them—or *not* happening—hurt. In their Reflections, Mia's presence had made Pilar feel stronger. But the more Rose tried to fix her, the more broken she felt.

"Did you see what Nell did?" Mia ran her fingers across the peachy roses. "I don't think I've ever seen magic that beautiful."

"Just because it's beautiful," Pilar said, "doesn't mean it's good."

Mia rolled her eyes.

"Could you *try* not being combative, Pilar? Just this once?"

Before Pilar could answer, Nell beckoned. "Come on, you two. There's a lot more to see than just roses."

Eagerly, Mia trotted along beside her. Pilar started to follow, then caught a twitch of movement over her shoulder. She turned.

The original Black Rose, the one Nell had touched, was wilting. The bloom sagged. The petals shuddered, curling toward the flower's heart, and fell, one by one, onto the dirt below.

Pilar was happy to leave the Rose Garden behind. It *was* beautiful, just like everything else in the House of Shadows, or Manuba Vivuli—whatever you wanted to call it. But in her experience, the ugliest things often lurked under the most beautiful. Especially where magic was concerned.

Watching the flower die had filled her with a strange, uneasy feeling. And on that feeling's heels: anger. She'd been right in what she said to Mia. But of course Mia hadn't seen the dead flower, because she'd been too busy chasing after Nell. Pilar could imagine the kind of look she'd get if she dragged Mia back to the Rose Garden to prove her point.

She heard the Swallow before she saw it. Clank of silverware. Roar of voices. They walked into an enormous, echoey hall with high ceilings and colorful tile floors. Children, women, and men crowded around circular tables, eating, drinking, and joking between chews.

A chair screeched over the tile.

"Nell? *Nell!*"

A boy was charging toward them. Pilar knew instinctively who he was.

Nell let out a sharp cry. She opened her arms as her brother tumbled into them.

They both burst into tears. Spun round and round. Hugging. Breaking apart. Hugging again. They were laughing, crying, talking on top of one another. Same fast clip, same high volume. How could they even understand what the other was saying? But somehow they managed.

"Pilar! Mia! Meet my baby brother."

He was still clinging to her neck. Looking at them shyly.

"This is Stone." Nell ran a hand over her wet cheeks. Laughed. "And yes, I know what you're thinking. Who gives their daughter an impossible name like Nelladinellakin and their son a good hearty name like Stone? You can tell who's the family favorite."

There was no doubt Stone was Nell's baby brother. He had the same dark brown skin, though his wiry black hair grew up and out—the same way, Pilar guessed, Nell's hair would grow if she took out her braids. Their round faces were practically identical. Stone would be handsome in a few years, Pilar decided. For now: adorable.

"I've heard a lot about you," she said.

"Look at him," Nell gushed. "He was eleven when I saw him last—now he's all grown up!"

Stone flashed a good-natured grin. "Don't worry, Sis: I still have my baby fat."

"It's part of your charm! But don't get too attached, it'll all melt off by your sixteenth birthday, mark my words. These are my friends, Mia Rose and Pilar d'Aqila, they're sisters, well, half sisters, really, do you see the resemblance? I'm not sure I do! Pilar is a fighter, like you."

"Used to be," Pilar corrected. "I haven't sparred in a long time."

Stone looked at her with newfound respect. "Maybe you'll spar with me?"

It caught her off guard. Before she could respond, Stone turned back to Nell.

"Does Mumma know you're here? She'll be so happy to see you, she thought—"

"Nelladine."

The voice was quiet. Much quieter than Stone's and Nell's. But

somehow Pilar heard it. Maybe because all the other sounds—
clanking, talking, smacking—ceased.

An older woman stood in the doorway of the Swallow. White
linen robe pale against deep brown skin. Curly white hair streaked
with pink. Brown eyes behind wire glasses.

Whatever Pilar had expected the Shadowess to look like, it
wasn't this. But she knew from the way the woman carried herself that this was the one they'd come to see.

"Mumma," said Nell, in a voice Pilar had never heard her use.

Nelladine turned to face them. Gulped some air.

Pilar said it for her.

"She's your mother."

Chapter 10

THE LEADING MAN

THE MOMENT QUIN SET foot in Kaer Killian, the memories cut through his mind like a carving knife.

The castle was a terrifying place. As a boy he'd kept a close eye on the servants—all female, to his father's taste. Quin watched the girls slip silently through the corridors, their hands always gloved. Even then, he recognized their silence as a form of self-preservation: the women were desperate to not attract attention. They yearned to be invisible.

As Quin would learn, invisibility was a gift.

At six years old he had wandered into the Hall of Hands by mistake. He'd befriended one of the more boisterous cooks, who, unlike the other servants, seemed to have no fear of his father. In later years he would come to understand this was not a friendship, but a kindness: the cook had taken pity on him. She never tired of chasing Quin down the castle corridors for animated games of get-the-Gwyrach or hide-'n'-hunt.

But one day he took a wrong turn. He skittered into the dark Hall and froze, eyes wide, transfixed by the hundreds of dangling Gwyrach hands—until he felt an awful wrench in his shoulder. The cook was yanking him out by the arm. She pulled him back into the corridor, swearing profusely, her forehead sweaty and her palms, too.

"Don't you ever go back there! Do you understand me? Never!" She'd slapped him across the face.

At the time Quin was mortified—and righteously indignant at being manhandled by a servant. Only much later did he realize that the cook had been trying to distract him from the horrors he had just witnessed with a smaller, more immediate horror.

He could still recall the look in her eyes as she dragged him back to the kitchens: fear. What he mistook for fear of punishment—she had, after all, just struck the heir apparent— was in fact fear of what it would do to *him*, now that he had seen the Hall of Hands.

She was a good soul, that cook. Quin had always liked her. But even his smarting face could not erase the memory of those hanging, severed hands.

A few years later, King Ronan had concocted some imaginary grievance against the cook. He made a big scene in the Grand Gallery, accusing her of casting a Gwyrach spell on his supper.

Quin pleaded with him to spare her life, but it only made his father angrier.

"Is that why you spend all your time in the kitchens?" the king spat. "Swooning over that old crone?"

It was useless, arguing with his father. Ronan always won.

The cook had shielded Quin, but he could not do the same for her.

The very hand that had tried to protect him from the Hall now hung inside it.

"How long since you've seen the Grand Gallery?"

Tobin's voice drew Quin out of his macabre thoughts. He blinked, waiting for the castle corridors to arrange themselves in his mind.

They had made it quite deep into the Kaer, the other Embers a ways behind. They weren't far from Quin's drawing room in the north wing, where he'd performed many a lonely play on the small wooden stage—and practiced his first kisses on a marble bust. The bust was just face and neck with the barest hint of shoulders; Quin never knew if he was kissing a marble girl or a marble boy. He would have been happy either way, and with that realization came the first prickling of shame incumbent on the son of a bigoted, hateful king.

"Remember the piano?" Tobin asked.

Of course he remembered the piano. Toby had smuggled in an exquisite plumwood piano from Luumia and installed it in Quin's drawing room as a tremendous birthday surprise. Of course, once

King Ronan discovered the instrument, he beat it to a woody pulp. The king would not stand for his son pursuing such a feminine hobby.

But he did *not* destroy the black upright in the library. He had no objection to others practicing piano; he had, after all, brought Tobin's family to court to play the patriotic war songs he held most dear.

And so commenced Quin's clandestine music lessons in the library.

"I remember the clavichord," he said, smoothly shifting the conversation.

Tobin laughed. How Quin had missed the sound of that laugh.

"We filched a whole bottle of rai rouj, didn't we?" said Toby. "Snuck into the buttery and claimed it as our own."

"As the heir apparent, it was quite literally my own."

They'd sat on the edge of the stage that night, passing the rai rouj back and forth between them, until Toby was drunk enough to attempt the clavichord. *I never thought a musical genius could play an instrument badly,* Quin had slurred. *Tonight you have proved me wrong.*

"As I recall," Tobin said, "it was the heir apparent who couldn't hold his liquor."

"Oh, I remember. I got dreadfully sick and retched all night." He flushed. "You took care of me."

Toby smiled. "You would have done the same for me."

Quin could feel himself softening. Was he really so foolish? Whatever sentiment still existed between him and Tobin—if it existed at all—should not be trusted. At best, the Embers were unwelcome guests in the castle. At worst, usurpers.

They were fast approaching the Grand Gallery. The seed of doubt in Quin's chest grew. Was he walking directly into his own execution? At least he knew the Kaer better than anyone. Should his life be in danger, he could disappear down any number of secret passageways.

He was so tired of disappearing.

"Did you want me to find you, Toby?" Quin said quietly. "Were the symbols for me?"

Tobin stared at him, face inscrutable. When he spoke again, his voice had an edge.

"I won't lie. After your father exiled me, I spent months hoping you would come after me. Years."

"You knew my father. You know what he was capable of."

"I desperately wanted to believe you would discover some deep well of courage inside yourself and face what your father had done."

Quin stopped cold. "I know what my father did. I was there."

"Cowering behind a tomb. Yes. I remember."

The words struck Quin like an arrow. No one regretted his cowardice more than he did.

"I don't just mean what your father did to *me*," Tobin said. "If you had come looking for me in the village, you would have discovered there was a movement of people, small but growing, who opposed your father's rule. We oppose all systems of governance that exploit and abuse power. After Zaga and Angelyne took the throne, we opposed their rule, too. Magic relies on a monumental imbalance of power, so you might say we oppose magic most of all."

"I never took you for a revolutionary, Toby."

"I never took you for a king."

The heat crackled in Quin's hands. In that moment, he couldn't believe he had ever loved the boy by his side. He pressed his hand over his heart, the unsent letter to the Twisted Sisters in his jacket pocket. *A weak boy. A scorned son. A used, manipulated lover. Whether prince or king, I have always been the pawn. I have never been the leading man.*

Quin shoved his hands into his pockets, calming himself. He needed more information, and a better sense of what the Embers were planning. He picked up his pace, this time taking the lead, until they stood outside the Grand Gallery.

"Prepare yourself," Tobin said, and reached for the black stone doors.

Chapter 11

POISONED

Mia stared at Nelladine in astonishment. The Shadowess was her mother. The House of Shadows was her home.

"Just what we need," Pilar muttered. "More surprise parents crawling out of the woodwork."

Mia didn't reply. She stood motionless, riveted by the scene playing out before them. The Shadowess moved slowly toward her daughter, almost dreamlike, coming to a standstill a few feet away. Mia sensed the impulses warring inside her: the urge to clasp Nell to her heart, tempered by the desire to give her space.

"It's so good to see you, Nelladine."

Her voice was low and mellifluous. She spoke with a strong Pembuka accent that in Nell only emerged in certain words.

"Mumma," Nelladine said, her voice breaking.

She stepped forward, bundling the Shadowess into a hug so tremendous it swept the woman's feet off the floor. Being a good bit taller, Nell stooped to rest her cheek on her mother's shoulder, her thin braids cascading down both their backs.

"I thought you were lost to us," the Shadowess whispered. "That you had gone to Prisma and I would never see you again."

Her face was obscured by Nell's hair, but Mia could tell she was crying.

"Kaara akutha. Welcome home, my girl."

Nell was never afraid to paint her emotions on a broad canvas. She laughed easily and cried easily, too. So Mia was not at all surprised to see tears streaming down her friend's cheeks. But this reunion felt different from the reunion with Stone. Mother and daughter clung to one another, quietly, almost reverently, as if each were holding the most precious thing.

Mia was deeply affected. She felt happy for Nelladine. Then something oozed through her, green and bilious.

Envy.

It didn't take long to deduce the source. This was the reception Mia had longed for from her own mother. A tender embrace. A warm welcome. What Mia would have given to have her mother wrap her arms around her and tell her she was home.

"Looks like Nell didn't bring us here to save the four kingdoms," said Pilar. "She was homesick."

"It could be both," Mia retorted, though she'd been wondering the same thing. *The only person who can help,* Nell had told them.

Help whom, exactly?

Mia studied the other people in the Swallow. The whole audience was rapt. A few of them had tears in their eyes. One woman cried openly, her hand pressed over her heart.

When Nell finally pulled back from her mother's embrace and began to make introductions, the Shadowess greeted them warmly. Her gaze was intelligent, enlivened by a sparkling curiosity.

"Kaara akutha. You are most welcome here. I am so sorry for all you have suffered."

"Mumma, you're doing that thing you do," Nell chided, drying her tears on her sleeve. "You've only just met and now you're going to scare them off with your mind reading!"

We *have* suffered, Mia wanted to say, but Pilar beat her to the punch.

"She's not wrong."

"It doesn't matter if she's right, it's still a creepy thing to do."

In the Shadowess's eyes, Mia saw a gentleness that moved her. So different from the way her own mother had averted her eyes.

"I've come to see suffering as a kind of shadow," the Shadowess said. "It's fluid and ever changing, and it can reveal things to us we never would have seen if there were only light. But if we honor the work it's doing, if we work *with* it instead of against it, the shadow will lift."

"Sounds like just the kind of thing the Shadowess would say," Pilar said.

Mia winced. Did Pil have to scoff at everything?

But the Shadowess only smiled.

"Please," she said. "Call me Muri."

The next hour passed in a dizzying blur. There were people to meet, cheeks to be kissed.

"We must feed you," Muri said after a while. "You've come a long way."

"Allow me." Stone smiled brightly. "Food is my specialty."

Nell's brother led them to an impressive array of steaming dishes. He went down the line, lifting lids and proudly displaying plate after plate of foods Mia had never seen. Plump little fingers of sticky banana leaves. Thick fava bean soup sprinkled with cumin and dolloped with joguhr cream. Ovals of fried cheese— haloom, Stone told her—melted over roasted onions. Flaky pink pastries stuffed with sautéed spinach. Braised piglum on a bed of soft yellow grains.

"Try the lamb tajin," Stone said, opening an orange clay pot to reveal, with great pride, a salmagundi of pulped brown meat indistinguishable from pulped brown dates. "It's a Pembuka specialty. It simmers for hours. Doesn't look like much, but the flavors are amazing."

"I'll bet they are," Pilar muttered under her breath.

As they piled food onto their plates, Mia studied Pilar. Even holding a serving spoon, she maintained a defensive posture, shoulders tensed as if she might need to wield the spoon as a weapon. *You're safe here*, Mia wanted to say. Though in truth she couldn't provide a rational explanation for why she knew they were safe. She just knew.

Everyone in the Swallow wanted to meet them. As they supped—Mia politely, Pilar greasily, Nell somewhere in between— they were inundated with residents. Some knew Nelladine already, though most did not. Muri sat beside them, graciously offering little personal tidbits to accompany the introductions. "Evange is a brilliant scientist who's here studying volqanoes." "Harith is a wonderful father to two little girls."

In the moments the Shadowess wasn't extolling her residents, she turned her loving attention to Nelladine. Touched her back, squeezed her hand, said how good it was to have her home.

Every time Muri looked at her daughter, a scalding jealousy rose in Mia's throat. She would never see her mother again. Wynna lay crushed under a mountain of snow, along with Queen Freyja, the wife she had chosen, and Angelyne, the other daughter she had left behind.

At least, Mia thought bitterly, her sister and mother had been buried together.

Something the Shadowess said to Nell nagged at her. *I thought you were lost to us. That you had gone to Prisma and I would never see you again.* On the boat Nell had rebuked the poor souls who journeyed to the Isle of Forgetting, choosing to leave their histories behind them. Why would Nell's own mother think Nell wanted that fate? And why *would* she, when in real life she had a family like this?

Mia wanted to be happy for her friend. She cared about Nell.

Cared *for* her. Which of course made it worse when resentment pooled in her belly.

She wanted to feel things again . . . but not like this.

She snuck another glance at Pilar. While Mia had succumbed to the barrage of cheek kisses, Pil had managed to evade them. She was drawing into herself, adding bricks to the wall she'd spent weeks erecting. Mia felt pulled toward her sister, desperate to build a bridge between them, and at the same time hurt that Pilar had no apparent interest in building that bridge.

Can't you see I'm suffering, too? Mia wanted to say. I'm just better at pretending.

"Mia?" Nell's excited voice interrupted her thoughts. "Pilar? How are you two doing, are you all right, are you surviving?"

The Shadowess had stood and moved a few paces from the table; Stone, too. They were redirecting the steady stream of residents to give their new arrivals a moment of peace.

"Not going to lie," Pilar said. "This is a lot."

Nell nodded vigorously. "It's a lot even for me, and I live here! Well, *lived* here. Takes some getting used to, sometimes you need a little breathing room, did you see how happy my mother was to see me? I didn't know if she'd be angry or pleased. And my brother is so grown-up! He's just perfect, I really thought they would have expanded the Swallow by now or at least put in new tables."

Nell spoke at an even faster clip than usual, her mind jouncing from one idea to the next. Mia had a little trouble keeping up.

Pilar licked her spoon, clanking it back into the bowl.

"Why didn't you tell us the Shadowess was your mother?"

"Would you have come so willingly? If you don't mind me saying, you both have rather complicated relationships with your mothers!"

"Last I checked, you were the one who ditched your mother and ran away from home."

"*Pilar,*" Mia scolded, but her heart wasn't in it.

"What? You were thinking it, too."

She *had* been thinking it. Sometimes Mia wished she could be blunt like Pilar, flinging words with wild abandon, not caring how they landed, or whom they hurt.

Pilar was right. Nell had been evasive about the Shadowess, the House of Shadows—all of it. Even if she hadn't actually lied, she had withheld the truth.

But the most baffling thing was how everyone seemed so warm and welcoming, Nell's family most of all. Her brother loved her. Her mother loved her. Nell had everything Mia wanted.

Why in four hells had she thrown it all away?

"Look," Nell sighed. "I didn't want you to think I was running home to my mumma and dragging you along for the ride. I knew you wouldn't take her seriously, you wouldn't have understood that the Shadowess is so much more than just my mother. She *can* help you."

"Help us what?"

To Mia's surprise, it was her own voice asking the question.

"It's easier to show than tell. Let me take you through the House, you can see some of the things people are doing here,

95

some of the ways this place offers healing to those who seek it. The Creation Studio, the Curatorium—there are so many wonders here, things you couldn't possibly imagine. And I'll introduce you to Pappa! He calls himself Lord Shadowess, quite the joker, he's never minded playing second fiddle to Mumma. I'll get you all set up in your rooms, too, we call them sfeeras. Just think how nice it will be to have your own room!"

She gave Mia's hand a squeeze. "And we can talk to Mumma about the elixirs, see what new remedies the House has cooked up, and I know, I feel it in my bones now that we're here, now that I'm back, we're going to be able to help you feel things again, Mia, *all* the things. We're going to bring you back to life."

Mia blinked. There she was, seething with bitterness, while Nelladine was trying to help her. Nell had done nothing but try to help her since the moment they met. Mia, normally so good at helping people herself, hadn't once been able to reciprocate.

And then a new disquieting truth leached into her mind.

Mia had hung every hope on the magical elixir. Now, in Pembuk, things were beginning to shift: a taste here, a scent there.

But along with these sensations came feelings far less pleasant. Mia missed her mother. She was wildly homesick for the home she no longer had. She felt poisoned with envy over everything Nell had, and sad for Pilar—frustrated she couldn't reach her, and increasingly angry that what she was doing wasn't working, that her sister wasn't responding in the right way. She felt guilt-ridden for leaving Quin and Angie to die alone in an avalanche. Or perhaps the guilt was really shame: she hadn't been able to save them. She had failed to save the people she loved most.

Mia was not ignorant enough to think all feelings could be sorted neatly into boxes, as much as she wished that were the case. But she'd been so fixated on restoring her mind and body to its prior state, she'd forgotten the ways that prior state had failed her. What if, even after she could taste things, smell things, *feel* things . . . what if she was still broken?

What if it was better to be numb?

"Rose."

She swiveled in her chair. Pilar's eyes bored into hers.

"We need to talk."

Chapter 12

DIRTY LITTLE SECRET

Pilar stood with feet planted. Arms crossed. Staring at Mia without a clue where to begin. Did the girl have *no* instinct for self-preservation?

"Please tell me you're not seriously considering this, Rose."

"Considering what?"

"Staying here! Going off with Nell to the Curatorium or whatever. Shacking up in a smeera."

"Sfeera."

"We've been here an hour. Don't act like you've got it all figured out." Pilar shook her hair out of her eyes. "Nell hasn't been honest with us. Why should we trust her? Why should we trust any of them?"

"Why shouldn't we? They've fed us and given us a warm

welcome. They're inviting us to be part of their community."

Mia's face changed. Sympathy slid over annoyance. "Of course I completely understand why you'd feel leery, trusting a community of people, after what—"

Pilar smacked her forehead.

"Not everything is about the cottage, Rose! I don't need to be stabbed in the back to know not to waltz into a magical floating castle assuming everyone is my dearest friend."

Mia blinked. Blinked again. Pilar could tell she was dying to say some Sharp Words. But because Rose was Rose, she was currently buffing out the sharp edges to make them the Right Words.

"Just say it. You've been walking on eggshells around me for weeks."

Mia exhaled through her teeth.

"I don't know what to say to you, Pilar. I want you to be able to talk to me about what happened."

"I don't want to talk about it."

"Then I don't know how to help you."

"I thought we were going to help each other."

"Well, *that* certainly hasn't happened. You've done nothing but push me away."

Pilar's stomach churned. She couldn't argue. Yes, she'd pushed Mia away. But only so Mia wouldn't push her away first.

"Do you know how painful it is that I'm starting to feel things again . . . and you don't even care?" Mia's voice was small. "You said you'd fight for me."

"Maybe that's exactly what I'm doing. Did you see the rose in the garden?" Pilar hated how pitiful she sounded. How desperate.

"I saw Nell bring them to life."

"Not the one she touched. It died."

She could tell Mia didn't believe her. And just like that, Pilar was back on Refúj. Stunned by Morígna's words.

There will always be girls so starved for attention they must lie to get it.

"Just go," Pilar growled. "Run after Nell. Get your precious elixir."

Mia's gray eyes glittered. "I don't know if you're angry with me or if you just don't care. I'm not sure which is worse." She straightened. "But they've invited us to stay. You can come or not; it's up to you. If there's one thing I know about you, Pilar, it's that you'll do what you want anyway, regardless of what I say."

She turned on her heel and marched back across the Swallow. Said something to Nelladine, who glanced over her shoulder, concerned. If Pilar had to suffer one more look like that from either of them, she'd stab her own eyes out with a fork.

What now? She had met the Shadowess. After that, she'd made no promises. Should she leave? Desperation welled up inside her. Where would she even go? She had nothing, no one.

Mia wasn't wrong: they *had* been warmly welcomed. Why couldn't Pilar just accept it?

Across the room, Celeste drifted into the Swallow. She greeted the Shadowess, kissing her on the right cheek, then the left. Greeted Mia the same way. Why all the kissing? What was wrong with a simple handshake?

Keeper or not, that woman made her uneasy. Pilar watched as

Celeste offered Mia a plate of red sweets. When Mia shook her head, Celeste laughed, seized a fork, and thrust three sweets onto her plate anyway.

Funny how quickly "welcoming" could become "aggressive."

"Pilar?"

Nell's little brother had snuck up behind her. Impressive. No one snuck up on Pilar d'Aqila.

"Can I ask you something?" Stone said.

"You just did. First lesson of asking: don't ask for permission first."

He looked sheepish. "Can I ask you something else, then?"

"Let me guess. You want me to spar with you."

"How did you—"

"Because I've known you less than an hour and that's been eighty percent of our conversation."

"Well?" His eyes implored her. "Will you?"

"I won't be here long enough to spar with anyone."

"Oh." His face fell. "Because I was going to show you the Gymnasia, my favorite place in the whole House. Where are you going?"

"Not your concern."

"My sister said you came from Valavïk."

"Accurate."

"But you can't go back there. It's been destroyed."

"I saw it, remember? We barely got out alive."

"All four kingdoms are falling apart. The ice is melting in the snow kingdom, forest fires all over the river kingdom. Even the desert here in Pembuk has begun to shift, whole buildings sinking a foot or two into the sand. And the big volqano in Fojo Karação erupted last month."

Pilar tried to keep her face still. To not let this news affect her. But Stone was too quick.

"You're from Fojo, aren't you?"

"It's not my home anymore."

"Soon it won't be anyone's. They say the volqano took out half the big island, and it's been spewing ash on the smaller islands, too. Some people were able to evacuate. Others weren't."

All those islands. All those people. Pilar imagined families fleeing, grabbing whatever they could carry, piling into boats. She heard children screaming as they left their beloved animals behind. Their parents just as scared, but putting on brave faces as burning ash rained down.

For the first time, Pilar realized a part of her had been holding on to the idea of returning to Fojo. Not to Refúj. She would never set foot in that place again. But there were hundreds of islands in the fire kingdom.

Now she saw them as graveyards. Her fellow Fojuen crushed by volqanic debris. Left to starve on the ocean. Their bodies sinking to the bottom of the Salted Sea, taking with them the only home Pilar had ever known.

She willed the tears out of her eyes. She refused to cry in front of this boy.

"We've been getting refugees for weeks," Stone went on, "from Fojo and Luumia. The Glasddiran refugees have been coming a lot longer—running first from the old king, then from the new queen. Mumma says all those who come to Manuba Vivuli are those who belong. But a lot of the refugees don't stay very long."

"Really." She was glad to have something to talk about besides Fojo.

"They're just passing through on the way to Prisma."

She eyed him skeptically. "To get torn apart by a glass terror?"

He cocked a brow. "Who told you that? Glass terrors don't tear you apart. They give you the life you always wanted."

"Terrific," Pilar muttered. Add one more lie to Nell's pile.

"Not necessarily terrific," he said, misunderstanding. "There's a lot of controversy in the House about how much of your real life you have to give up. Some people here embrace Prisma, but most believe it's a kind of self-annihilation. No one's ever come back, so it's hard to know for sure."

"If no one's ever come back," Pilar said, "then how do you know anything?"

"The ancient mystics knew plenty. They saw the Isle of Forgetting in visions, dreams. Now that more and more people are choosing to forget, some believe the end of human history is at hand."

Stone lowered his voice.

"I've heard rumors of what happened in Valavïk. One of the Luumi refugees said an evil old man was working for the Snow Queen and unleashed some kind of magical dragon that breathed fire on all the ice and melted it, then flew over the other kingdoms, which is why there are fires in Glas Ddir and also why the volqano erupted in Fojo."

Pilar snorted.

"That's the fantasy version. No dragons in real life. An evil old man using stolen magic, yes, but in the end he was just a pawn. It's the cute freckled ones you have to watch out for."

"Like Mia?"

She frowned. "No. Not Mia."

Pilar looked back at the table. Mia, Nell, Celeste, and the Shadowess were gone.

Her breath hitched. Why did she care? Hadn't she told Rose to go? Pilar hated how she'd become one giant contradiction. She craved Mia's attention, then spurned it. She wanted community, then rejected the one she'd walked into.

"Fine." Pilar cracked her knuckles. "You win."

Stone looked confused. "Win what?"

"Take me to the Gymnasia."

"Right now?"

"You really do ask a lot of questions."

He grinned slyly. "And look at that. It worked."

The Gymnasia was not a short walk. As Stone led Pilar down one hall after another, she began to suspect him of taking the long way around.

"Not sure how much Nell showed you on your way in," he said, "but she's been gone for years. I'm a much better guide."

"I don't need the full tour," she said, knowing it was futile.

The more Pilar saw of the House of Shadows, the more it

confused her. She felt the same impulse as when she'd first seen it: an almost magnetic tug, met by a strong repulsion. Not so different from the contradiction in herself, honestly. Push me, pull me. Stay away—and hold me close.

If the House looked massive on the outside, the inside was even bigger. Stone paraded her past dozens of room-sized glass spheres clustered together. Like bubbles in a giant bath.

"The sfeeras," he said.

Some of the sfeeras had curtains. Others didn't. She spotted beds, hammocks, and simple straw mats. Tables, chairs, bookshelves, bathtubs. She saw one pale-skinned woman *in* a bathtub.

Stone's skin flushed a shade darker. He looked away.

"Some residents like to be sky-clad. Up to them, of course. I just wish they'd do it more . . ." He coughed. "Privately."

"How long do people stay here?"

"As long as they need. We always find room."

He took her past lecture halls crammed with important-looking people droning on about who knew what. Past a sweet-smelling chamber Stone called a "chocolate kitchen," where two cooks argued passionately about cacao beans. Past a long, skinny room filled with children in capes screaming and chasing each other. She felt a sharp pang, thinking of all the families who must have tried to escape Fojo Karação.

"Here's the Creation Studio," Stone said, ushering her inside a big airy space with easels, pottery wheels, and fat orange octagons she was pretty sure were kilns. People sat around the studio painting. Drawing. Slapping wet lumps of clay. And so on.

"Do you practice any art?" Stone asked.

"Not this kind."

"What kind, then?"

She shifted her weight. "Music."

"Then I'll take you to the Orkhestra! A troupe of traveling musicians arrived a few days ago from Fojo. They're amazing. And just children! I'm sure they'd—"

"Won't be necessary," she said curtly. "I don't play anymore."

He nodded, taking this at face value. A note of sadness echoed in her chest. She'd thought Stone would try harder to persuade her. The last thing she needed was a bunch of doe-eyed children butchering their violins. But she'd seen those children when she'd first walked into the House, and they didn't seem like butchers. They'd touched their instruments with love and care.

She thought of Quin at the piano. How gently he'd touched the keys. She remembered the notes humming through her bones, stoking her desire. Now, with a little distance, she saw she had been more in love with the way he made her feel than with Quin himself. The Doomed Duet of Pil and Kill had been doomed from the start.

"See that?"

Stone pointed to a muscular, sandy-haired woman in the back corner, running her bare hands over a hunk of pearly white stone. From across the room, Pilar saw the stone crumble, dropping in chips and curls at her feet.

"Fire sculpting," Stone said. "Annabeth carves the stone using the heat from her hands. She says it melts away like butter.

Annabeth is from the river kingdom, actually. Her hands were always burning through her gloves. For years she managed to hide it, but then someone tipped off the Hunters. She escaped moments before they arrived."

Pilar swallowed. "You know about the Hunters?"

"Everyone knows about the Hunters. That kind of evil spreads through all four kingdoms."

How long before Stone found out the leader of the Hunters was her father? Considering Nell knew, it was only a matter of time.

"Like I said," Stone continued, "we've been getting refugees from Glas Ddir ever since Ronan became king—back before I was born. Whole families take everything they can carry on their backs and start trekking west. It's a monthlong journey, and a hard one, mostly desert. Many don't survive. When Mumma was appointed Shadowess for her second term, she started sending caravans to our eastern borders to find people and bring them here safely."

Pilar watched the white stone spall under Annabeth's sure hands. The steadiness of her fingers filled Pilar with a calm, peaceful feeling. Those hands had been liberated. Now they were shaping something beautiful. As the sculpture began to emerge from the stone, Pilar detected one large, drooping ear. Then another. The nose was long and skinny, almost trunk-like.

"An elephant!" she exclaimed.

Stone smiled. "She makes all kinds of animals. You'll see them stationed around the House."

Pilar started to smile back. Then she remembered Mia chattering about the rock shaped like an elephant. Chattering to Nell, not to her.

Pilar's mood darkened. Where was Rose now? Strolling through the House of Shadows, stroking the stone elephants? Chugging magical elixirs? Fawning over Nell?

A part of Pilar wanted to protect her half sister. Save Mia from herself.

Another part wanted to punish her.

Something had shifted. Now when Pilar looked at Annabeth and her elephant, she felt only sadness.

She gave Stone a hard look.

"The Gymnasia," she said.

It was stuffed into the far back corner of the building, making Pilar wonder if the Gymnasia was the House's dirty little secret. It certainly lacked polish. Clamped to the walls and floors were thin, shiny cushions, streaked with sweat or spit. Maybe blood.

She loved it.

"Hardly anybody comes here anymore," Stone said. "I've got the whole place to myself." He toed a floor mat. "Now if only I had someone to spar with."

Pilar pressed her lips together to keep from grinning. There'd been a chance the Gymnasia would bring back her worst memories. Orry in the cottage, teaching her to fight. Quin using her own moves against her.

But she didn't see Quin or Orry. She saw sandbags hanging

from the ceiling. Straps for wrapping hands and wrists. This place was worth a hundred Rose Gardens. It was *real*. No magic. No lies. The Gymnasia was the first place in the House of Shadows where she'd felt at home.

In the absence of another home, where else could she go?

Pilar felt Stone watching her, his round face hopeful. She thought of what Nell had told her: that her baby brother trusted people too easily.

"Why do you want to spar with me, Stone? You don't even know me."

"But I'd like to."

She studied him. If she detected even a seed of infatuation, she would root it out before it ever had a chance to grow.

But that wasn't what she saw in Stone's face. She saw a boy eager to worship people he'd only just met. A boy dying for someone to follow. A boy willing to trust anyone who paid him the smallest bit of attention.

She saw a child who would keep slicing his chest open until someone broke his heart.

It scared her, how much he reminded her of herself.

"All right," she said. "I'll spar with you."

His brown eyes lit up. "Fantastic! Let me get my—"

"No. Not now. I'll meet you here in the morning, six o'clock sharp. Wrap your wrists ahead of time. We'll train every morning. Afternoons, too, depending on how bad you are." She sniffed. "I'll also teach you how not to go around asking people you've never met to teach you things. You get that lesson for free."

"You're going to stay at the House, then?"

Pilar made a decision. She didn't trust these people—but she'd give them a chance to prove her wrong. She'd focus her attention on Stone, while also keeping an eye on Mia. Best of all, she'd eat good food cooked by other people while hammering out her plan for what came next.

She didn't owe anyone anything. But she would give Stone one week.

"Seven days," she said. "That's how long you have to impress me."

"And if I don't?"

Pilar stretched her neck to one side, then the other. Her spine gave a satisfying crack.

"Then find someone else. I'll be gone."

Chapter 13

INK

THE FIRST ASSAULT WAS the noise.

Under King Ronan's reign, the Grand Gallery had been draped in fraught silence, everyone frightened of the king. Quin had endured many a meal beside his parents without a single word passed between them. Even if his sister came to supper—and she rarely did—her lively banter would eventually peter out, powerless against the oppressive quiet.

But the Gallery was quiet no longer. Musicians strolled through, crooning ballads and war songs as the Embers laughed and caroused. The black feasting table where the royals once sat had vanished; the smaller gray slab tables had tripled in number, and at least a hundred women and men gathered around them. At a makeshift bar of wood planks resting on large barrels, a barkeep poured pints of stonemalt. A few inebriated Embers reclined on piles of furs and animal skins by the giant stone hearths at either end of the Gallery.

Instinctively, Quin searched for his dogs. Wulf and Beo had always loved curling up on the fire-warmed stones. Every time Quin trudged in for another insufferable supper, the sight of their furry golden heads, ears pricked, was the one thing that sustained him.

But they were not there.

He forced himself to look away. Zaga was not one to protect the small creatures under her care. Nor was Angelyne.

He didn't want to know what had happened to his dogs.

"What do you think?" Tobin said, gesturing toward the hall.

"It's transformed."

"Yes, I decided it could use a dose of cheer. And a dose of strong spirits. Though, to be honest with you, not everyone agreed. Some thought we should burn Kaer Killian to the ground."

As Tobin spoke the words, a ripple moved across the Grand Gallery, laughs swallowed and sentences left dangling, as one by one every head turned toward Quin.

That was the second assault. The eyes.

Quin had known his return to the river kingdom would be controversial. He was, after all, son of King Ronan—and husband to Queen Angelyne, in a spurious, nonconsensual sort of way. But from what the old farmer had said, and what Brialli Mar had hinted at, there were still some Glasddirans loyal to the crown. Quin had hoped he might be met with pleasure, even gratitude.

He had returned to his people after a long, arduous journey. Their orphan-loving king had come home.

Indeed, he saw a smattering of kind, open faces. But on the whole, the Embers greeted him with pure, unadulterated loathing. If looks could kill, he would have collapsed to the stone floor in a heap of human rubble.

And it was this thought—that his own people would murder him in his own home—that flooded him with fury. Didn't they understand he'd been a victim, too? The Kaer had always been the site of his victimhood, in one form or another.

Quin had returned to claim his rightful place on the throne, which was another way of saying he sought the power he had always been denied. Yet here he was, just as weak and humiliated as ever. And hated, too.

"Care for a drink?" Tobin said with a smirk.

Quin eyed the barkeep, who looked eager to serve him a pint of arsenic.

"I'm all right."

"Not the warm reception you'd imagined?"

Tobin turned to face the group.

"Friends!" he shouted. "Embers! Do not be alarmed. The prince is our guest."

He needn't have shouted. In the absence of other noise, his words were perfectly audible. Quin could not help but feel the presence of his father, King Ronan's ghost lurking still. As if the moment a Killian walked into the Grand Gallery, the shroud of silence fell once again.

"Guest?" A woman's shrill voice rose from the sea of stony faces. "You expect me to share my bread and wine with the son of a slaughterer?"

Someone hushed the woman—"sins of the father" or some such—while two new voices joined with hers. Dissension in the ranks, Quin thought. If the Embers were divided, it could only work in his favor.

In the far corner he noticed a distinguished older man and a tall white-haired woman conversing in low voices, their heads bent close. Quin squinted, then gave a start. The man used to be his father's head guard. How had Sylvan survived Zaga and Angelyne's regime?

Unlike the rest of the Gallery, Sylvan had his gaze firmly locked on Tobin, as did his companion. They did not look pleased. For the first time, Quin realized that his former music teacher was not the only leader of the Embers, or perhaps not a leader at all.

The woman narrowed her eyes. She began walking toward them, Sylvan a few steps behind. Was it Quin's imagination, or did Toby blanch?

"M-Maev," Tobin stammered. "I thought you and Sylvan were . . . I'm glad you're here, actually. I . . . I thought we might—"

"I told you," Maev said, making no attempt to lower her voice, "that the only sovereign I care to see in this hall is a Killian head on a spike."

Quin's throat tightened. His fingers twitched with pent-up heat. In a closed space like the Grand Gallery, his aim wouldn't matter. How easy it would be to set them all ablaze.

He restrained himself. There were innocent people in this room. The Embers might be pretenders, false claimants to the throne, but others, like Brialli, were clinging to the only option they had left. There were more Glasddirans in the Gallery than all the other survivors he'd met put together. Did he really want to burn what was left of his people?

Besides. At the moment, Maev's ire seemed to be directed entirely at Tobin.

"Who else have you invited into our midst, Toby? Is Angelyne next?"

"Maev." Sylvan laid a hand on her arm. "There's no need to make a scene."

"A *scene*?" She shook her head bitterly. "We've worked so hard to get here, Sylvan. We've given up so much. And now this"— she sneered at Quin—"threatens to upend everything we've been working toward. Has it not occurred to either of you he's here as Angelyne's spy?"

Quin shook his head fiercely. "I'm here of my own accord."

"'Accord,'" she spat. "You're a son of Clan Killian. You know nothing about *accord*. Nothing about harmony, or what is just and fair."

Fair. Quin mulled the word. His father had never been concerned with fairness—though his aunt had. It was Queen Bronwynis who'd created the Council of the Kaer, surrounding herself with eight councillors to advise her on the finer points of governance.

And what was her reward? Murdered by Ronan, her own brother, who blamed the Gwyrach for the assassination—and promptly commandeered the throne.

What kind of Killian did Quin want to be? A queen like Bronwynis, or a king like Ronan? His gaze swept the Grand Gallery. He saw anger and mistrust, grief and despair. Where was the rest of Glas Ddir? Had they really all fled to the glass kingdom?

They were a broken people. They deserved him, a broken king.

Quin felt a stirring of pity. And, just as quickly, he stamped it out.

Pity had no place in the heart of a king.

"I know this much," he said, choosing his words carefully. "We have a common enemy. Angelyne is no friend of mine."

Maev eyed him charily. The entire room was eyeing him the same way. Here, Quin thought, was an opportunity. He'd been given a chance to disarm the Embers—and win their trust.

Seized by sudden inspiration, he angled his body toward the stone tables. If he was going to make a speech, he might as well address them all.

A chill swept down his neck. Here, standing in the Grand Gallery, he had what he had always craved: an audience.

"I've come all the way from Luumia," he began, pleased at how his voice echoed off the Gallery's black walls, "where Angelyne's magic has grown even more powerful."

A murmur swept through the crowd. Quin thought of what Tobin had told him: that the Embers opposed magic most of all.

"Angelyne's magic thrives on the imbalance of power. With her sisters by her side, she will bring death and destruction to all four kingdoms. Her dark reign has already begun."

Quin cleared his throat.

"I know the Embers oppose all exploitative systems of governance. You have suffered at the hands of those who abused their power.

"Under my father's rule, you lost your wives and mothers, your sisters and daughters. You lived in abject fear of a cruel dictator, powerless against his every whim.

"Under Angelyne's rule, those losses did not abate. With Zaga by her side, the queen murdered your husbands and fathers, your brothers and sons. She destroyed your families and set fire to your villages. You no longer had autonomy over your own bodies, your own minds. I know this nightmare, because I, too, have lived it."

Quin took a breath.

"I cannot give back what was taken from you. But I can eat beside you, sleep beside you, march into war beside you. We are fighting the same battle. I stand against the tyranny of magic, and any tyranny constructed on the bones of the helpless and the weak."

He reached into his jacket pocket. Someone gasped, as if Quin might draw a dagger and plunge it into an unsuspecting heart.

Instead he withdrew the letter.

"I have in my hand a missive to the Twisted Sisters. I will order them to return to the river kingdom to face the destruction they have wrought—and pay the price for their crimes."

Quin brandished the letter overhead, the parchment worn and soft like a white handkerchief. But this was not his surrender. Rather, it was his greatest triumph.

"If the Embers stand against kings," he said, savoring his final coup de grâce, "then I stand with the Embers."

The Gallery erupted into cheers.

Quin had never been applauded by a roomful of people, not once in his life. Gone were the empty silences and the lonely stage. Breathless, he let his ears drink up the sound. He wanted to bathe in it.

I choose to return to the people of the river kingdom.
I choose to take my rightful place as king of Glas Ddir.
I choose to never be enthralled, enkindled, or controlled again.
And if these choices throw me into conflict with any one of you, so be it.

It really was an excellent letter. He'd always had a way with words.

As Quin smiled beatifically at the Embers, he assessed their leaders in his periphery. Maev was fuming as Sylvan tried to calm her down. But he could see in their faces they would not fight the popular opinion. Quin would stay in the Kaer.

Tobin stood a ways apart. Curious, and a little defiant. Did he want to see the letter? Fine. Quin had nothing to hide. He did plan to embellish the last bit to make it more forceful. He was not merely *requesting* the return of the Twisted Sisters to Glas Ddir; he *commanded* it. And though it would take the courier a month to cross the desert and reach the glass cities of Pembuk, it would be well worth the wait.

A flash of movement caught his eye. Domeniq du Zol stood outside the kitchens. In the firelight, Quin detected a glint of cerulean: the blue uzoolion pendant Dom always wore around his neck. A stone meant to protect against magic. Some good it had done him, once he'd been rendered helpless under Zaga's and Angelyne's enthrall.

Three scullery maids poured out of the kitchens, drawn to the commotion, and when Quin looked again, Domeniq was gone.

Twice now Dom had avoided him. His brooding presence was a puncture wound, deflating Quin's good mood. Had Dom sniffed out his secret? That Quin, too, had dark magic?

He shoved the thought out of his mind. He would deploy subterfuge, play the guest in his own castle, and flatter the Embers—but only as long as it took to learn how to defeat them. He knew he could burn them alive this very instant. But that was no way to win hearts and minds.

So he would be clever. Charming. A man of the people. He would pretend, just as he had done on the stage in his drawing room—only this time with the benefit of applause. And when it came time to show his strength, he would not hesitate to destroy those who opposed him. The Embers. The Twisted Sisters. Anyone who had ever called him weak.

But first things first. On the morrow he would dispense a courier to the glass kingdom to deliver his letter. Mia, Pilar, and Angelyne had thought him gentle, *good*. He was going to prove them wrong.

It was impossible to rewrite the past. But the future was a story waiting to be told. Blood was merely the ink.

Quin would make it spill.

ACT II

Once upon a time, in a house cut from glass,
a girl plotted escape.

Chapter 14

BLOODBLOOM

PICTURE THIS: MIA ROSE in her tidy sfeera at the House of Shadows, wearing a borrowed green dressing gown, hugging a porcelain chamber pot.

Vomiting.

Vomiting.

Vomiting some more.

And utterly delighted.

"Garden-variety stomach bug," Nell said from her chair beside the bed. She had effortlessly assumed the role of nurse. "Mumma says there's a bug going around the House, what a shame you had to catch it on your second day!"

She leaned over and pressed the back of her hand to Mia's forehead.

"Too warm, I think. You haven't filled your pot in a while, do you still feel nauseated?"

Nauseated: affected by nausea. Not to be confused with *nauseous*: *causing* nausea. In the old language, *nau* meant "boat," and *sea* meant "sea." To feel nausea was to be seasick, to sense the waves billowing in your body, the water swelling in your stomach.

To feel nausea.

To feel.

"I do," Mia said, elated. "I feel nauseated."

Nell laughed. "I've never seen someone so happy to throw up."

Mia was likewise amused. She'd never expected to enjoy the taste of half-digested lamb tajin spiced with stomach acid, or the painful heaving of her chest.

But everything felt so deliciously *new*. She hadn't experienced nausea since she stood in the castle crypt, watching an enthralled Quin kiss Angelyne. Even when she'd spewed bile in White Lagoon after drinking too much, she hadn't tasted the silver death coming back up her throat.

The first day in Manuba Vivuli had passed like a dream. Nell had led her through the glass halls, unmasking wonder after wonder: a laboratory full of scientists scuttling about, proposing theorems; a light-kissed studio where artists created beautiful things; and, best of all, a Curatorium where sick creatures—birds, beasts, even humans—were mended and tended to. From everything Mia had seen, the House encouraged a fluid interplay of magic and non-magic: the two blended seamlessly together.

"Remember what I told you," Nell had said, as they stared through the glass wall of the Curatorium, watching an older gentleman heal a blond puppy with a hurt paw. "An imbalance of power isn't intrinsically harmful. Life is full of counterbalances, as the Elemental Hex attests. What matters is *how* you strike a balance, or even an imbalance—and to what end."

In truth Mia hadn't been thinking about magic. She'd been thinking about Quin's golden dogs. She had grown quite fond of Beo and Wulf at the Kaer. Whenever she'd spied them trotting down the corridors, their pricked ears and gently curling tails always lifted her spirits.

What had happened to them? Were they alive?

Come illness, suffering, e'en death,
Until my final breath I will be yours.

She didn't understand why her wedding vows kept trailing through her mind. *I will be yours.* What did that even mean? Why would she want to abdicate her personhood and belong to someone else?

It didn't matter. Quin was dead. She belonged to no one but herself.

"Mia! Hello!" Nell snapped her fingers. "Have you been listening? I'm going to the Swallow for a bite to eat, though I shouldn't talk about food with you, you'll lose your whole stomach!"

"I won't," Mia said, desperate to keep Nell a little longer. She conjured the game Quin had taught her long ago, as they'd wandered famished through the Twisted Forest.

"If you could eat anything right now, what would it be?"

Nell looked at her blankly. "Whatever's in the Swallow, why are you asking?"

Mia felt a pang. She missed Quin's games. And now she would never play them again.

Nell stood.

"Rest up, Mia. Isn't it funny how all the science and all the magic in the world can't cure a trifling stomach bug? Sometimes the body will do as the body will do. I told Pilar I'd meet her for supper, I'll be back to check on you."

She squeezed Mia's hand. Nell's skin wasn't as smooth as usual; Mia detected something dry and grainy in the creases of her palms.

Clay. Nelladine was making pottery again.

"Can I bring you anything from the Swallow?" Nell asked. "Fish ice? Hot chrysanthemum tea? It helps settle the stomach."

"I don't need a thing," Mia said, burying her loneliness. "Give Pil a hug for me."

After their quarrel over whether to stay in the House of Shadows, Mia had been sure Pilar would leave. And, in the heat of the moment, Mia had wanted her to.

As Mia stormed out of the Swallow, she'd been angry and hurt. Angry at herself, perhaps, for giving Pil the power to hurt her, for believing they could ever waltz into some kind of idyllic sisterhood. Mia wanted to connect the way they had in their Reflections. But, more and more, that seemed the exception to the rule. A flawed experiment with unrepeatable results.

She had lost another sister. She had failed again.

And yet: Pilar had stayed. She just hadn't come to visit.

Mia sank lower into the bed. Her brain was tired from trying to make sense of everything. She laid her cheek on the pillow and peered out her sfeera window. She'd spent a good deal of time gazing through the glass, savoring her view of Prisma.

The island seemed to have its own atmosphere, distinct from Shabeeka. Usually it was swathed in white fog, though sometimes the air was so clear and vivid she could make out the lemon coconuts swaying from the fish trees. The sand shimmered, pale as chipped ivory, so different from the rusty orange sands around the House of Shadows.

"Why is the House so close to Prisma?" she'd asked Nell earlier that morning. "If people come here because they're suffering, aren't they terribly tempted to cross the Bridge and leave all their pain behind?"

"You've got cause and effect mixed up," Nell told her. "The House isn't here in spite of Prisma, it's here *because* of Prisma. The ancient mystics knew what a great temptation the island would always be, so they created a resting place for pilgrims headed to the Isle of Forgetting. It was always meant to remind people their lives were worth living, that when it came to the things they had suffered, there were many different ways to heal. To *survive*."

Now, as Mia drifted off to sleep, the island slipped away, like grains in an hourglass.

She stood in the Royal Chapel, her gloved hands clasped in Quin's as she said her wedding vows. She stared into his eyes, a scintillating green, his gaze burning a history of fire and ashes beneath her skin.

And then, in the strange, fluid way dreams move from place to place, the Chapel vanished. Mia stood under the snow palace, clasping Quin's bare hands in hers. She stared into his eyes, a hateful green, as his fire scorched her palms, burning her flesh down to bone.

Flesh of my flesh.

Bone of my bone.

"Knock-knock." A woman's voice jolted her from the dream. "Are you up for a visitor?"

Mia sat upright. She blinked as the sfeera took shape around her. Through the window, night had cloaked the Isle of Forgetting in a dark purple cloud.

The Shadowess stood in the doorway.

"Did I just talk out loud?" Mia said.

"Yes. Something about flesh and bones."

"I don't even remember falling asleep." She rubbed her eyes. "You can come in."

"Lucid dreams are strange, aren't they?" Muri lowered herself into Nell's chair. "I like to write from that place. I wake up, grab my notebook, and let the words spill. It feels like I'm channeling something far deeper than anything my conscious mind could create."

"So you're a writer?"

"I don't know if I'd call myself a writer. But writing does feed my soul. I've spent some long, painful years searching for the things that sustain and nourish me. Writing is one."

Mia had never heard someone describe a hobby in those terms. What sustained and nourished *her*? Reading science books? Sketching human anatomy? It seemed puerile to imagine her Wound Man anatomical plate as "feeding her soul."

She did miss Wound Man, though.

"Would you like to write something?" the Shadowess asked. "We have a whole stack of beautiful hand-bound journals in the Creation Studio."

Mia thought of her mother's journal, lost to her so long ago. The brown leather book had stored all of Wynna's truths, when in life she'd told only lies.

"I wouldn't write in it," Mia said. "But I might sketch."

"Wonderful! I'll bring you one." The Shadowess smoothed a crease in her tunic. "I know you've been suffering, Mia. I am so sorry."

There was an ambiguity to the way she said *suffering*. Did Muri mean the recent vomiting, or the preceding numbness?

"Your daughter's taken good care of me," Mia said.

"Nelladine has shared some of your story, but I'd like to hear more from you. We may have elixirs that can help you. Before we go there . . . are you game for a little experiment?"

She'd spoken the magic word. Mia the Scientist leaned forward, overjoyed to be summoned.

"I want you to take a deep breath and roll back your shoulders. Like so."

The Shadowess took off her wire spectacles, inhaled, and set her shoulders, drawing her scapulae down her back. Funny how such a simple gesture could revolutionize one's posture: Muri had grown at least an inch taller.

Mia found this an odd way to begin an experiment. She would have preferred a scalpel and a dead bird. But she mirrored the movement.

"Have you ever felt yourself breathe, Mia?"

"Is that a trick question?"

"What I mean is, have you ever turned your conscious attention to the breath flowing in and out?" The Shadowess put a hand over her heart. "Much of my personal journey has been in learning to work *with* my body instead of against it. There is great healing to be found in our own hands."

She placed her other hand on her abdomen, her mahogany skin dark against her pale peach tunic. "Every time we inhale and exhale, the diaphragm contracts and expands."

Mia tried to swallow her annoyance. "I know."

"Nell tells me you know a good deal about the human body. Far more than I do, I'm sure. I'll only offer you this: sometimes knowing *how* something works is different than letting it work *through* you."

In the sense that breathing was a physiological process, it quite literally worked *through* you: the nose took in air, nostrils sifting out dangerous particles, and then the lungs expanded, filling with breath. When the lungs contracted, they shunted the air back out.

But none of this was conscious. That was the whole point.

"Is this the experiment?" Mia said, growing impatient. "To analyze my own respiratory system?"

"No need for analysis. Just observe."

Mia shifted. She thought again of her mother's journal. Wasn't this what Wynna had tried to teach her? To sit quietly, place one hand on her heart and the other on her belly, and breathe?

What good had that done either of them?

"In through the nostrils," the Shadowess prompted, "out through the mouth. It's a way of centering, of calling yourself back home. All you have to do is breathe."

Mia watched Muri's abdomen rise and fall, rise and fall.

Fine. The sooner she did what the Shadowess wanted, the sooner she could be done. She slapped her left hand on her chest and right hand on her stomach, ivory skin pale against the green dressing gown. Her abdomen hardly moved, even as the breath came in and out.

"So often our breaths are shallow," Muri said. "They only reach our chest. But when we breathe from our diaphragm, we flood the whole body with rich, sweet air."

The only thing flooding Mia's body was her own irritation. But when she looked into Muri's brown eyes, she saw no judgment, no impatience over Mia's failure to absorb this lesson. The Shadowess simply sat calmly, hand on belly, asking her to breathe.

Mia's shoulders had sunk, her chest drawing in and down, as if her heart were protecting itself. She closed her eyes. Drew her shoulder blades down her back once more and felt her spine lengthen. This time, she sipped in more air through her nostrils.

131

It went farther, deeper. Beneath her left hand, she felt her lungs broaden. Beneath her right hand, her diaphragm bloomed.

When the breath rushed out of her open mouth, she heard herself make a "haaa" sound.

Hot tears pricked her eyes.

The tide of feeling came out of nowhere. Months of betrayal and heartbreak, grief and anger, slammed into her. The wave crashed through the wall of numbness, and, to Mia's astonishment, her own hands were the flumes.

She gasped. The act of breathing had quite literally taken her breath away.

"How does it feel?" the Shadowess asked gently.

Like everything, Mia wanted to say. *Like it's too much and I'm going to crack wide open.*

"Terrible," she said.

"Let it go." Muri's shoulders dropped. She shook them out, loosening her posture. "When it gets to be too much, you can always, always let it go."

Mia's hands were glued to her body. She wanted to undo what she had done, to put whatever was coursing through her veins back into its box before it was too late.

But she also wanted this ocean of unbearable feeling to swamp the room so that the Shadowess could feel it—drown in it, even—because at least then Mia wouldn't drown alone.

She felt her shoulders inching back up toward her ears, rhomboids tensing. She inhaled one last gulp of air, then let it go.

"I want to give you something, Mia. It helped me a great deal when I was first learning to connect to my breath."

The Shadowess reached into her pocket and pulled out a wooden disc burnished to a dark, dewy sheen.

"Are you familiar with the bloodbloom tree?"

Mia shook her head.

"Thousands of years ago, the Mahraini mystics came to Pembuk after the great land divide. It was the mystics who first discovered the Elemental Whorl. They cultivated the ancient windwood, a genus of tree that holds wind and wood in perfect balance, soothing both breath and bone. Thus the bloodbloom was born."

The Shadowess centered the wooden disc on her own palm. As she inhaled, it transformed. The wood grew upward, reshaping itself into an elegant tree with curving limbs. Mia heard the hollow creaks of branches, a sound she knew well from Ilwysion. She'd always thought of the oaks and elms of her childhood as stately elders with creaking bones.

Then the Shadowess exhaled. The limbs of the tree sprouted tiny, delicate green leaves. They rustled and sighed, as if Muri's breath were a cool breeze sweeping through them.

And so it continued. With every inhalation, the creaks and groans of wood; with every exhalation, the whispering of wind through the leaves. The little tree grew larger with each round of breath. The rhythm was profoundly calming, the magic mesmerizing.

"I used to have so much trouble breathing," Muri said. "A strange thing to say, perhaps, considering I took thousands of breaths every day. But the more obsessively I thought about the process, the more my mind spun out of control. The bloodbloom helped ground me."

She offered it to Mia.

"I hope it does the same for you. Your own healing magic will activate the magic inside it. The more comfortable you get with your own breathing, the bigger the tree will grow. We cannot heal the world until we heal ourselves."

Mia accepted the bloodbloom. As she held it on her palm, she spied a red bird peeking out from the branches. She started. In her mind's eye she saw Angelyne under the snow palace, clutching their mother's fojuen wren in one hand, her black gemstone in the other. And Quin, seizing both stones, slamming them together—and unraveling the very fabric of their world.

She lifted the tree to eye level. Not a bird, she realized. Just a tiny scarlet bloom.

"The flowers have healing properties," the Shadowess explained. "We use them in the Curatorium to excellent effect."

Mia's fingers closed around the tree. She felt it shrink back into an unassuming wooden disc.

"I'd love to see that."

"You're most welcome in the Curatorium. I'm sure Nelladine would be happy to take you. We'll plan for it." The Shadowess smiled. "As soon as the vomit abates."

Chapter 15

MUSCLE AND BONE

QUIN HAD LONG BEEN a student of human nature. As a boy he had scrutinized his mother's face, her violet eyes growing crueler, and had come to understand that this was how the queen had chosen to survive her husband's hate. He watched his sister, marveling at how Karri's ferocity of spirit and pureness of heart seemed to emerge unscathed from the battlefield of their family.

But, most vitally, he learned to predict his father's violence. Every nerve in Quin's body was finely calibrated to the tone of Ronan's voice. The king knew how to throw a fiery tantrum, but he was most dangerous when he went still and quiet. The cold, smoldering blue of his eyes was a harbinger of much, much worse than his rages.

If Quin was exceptionally gifted at the pretending arts, his true gift lay in his ability to perceive—and adjust to—the subtle nuances of human emotion, often by concealing his own. From an early age, the young prince had learned not only how to mimic, but also how to hide.

Now, as he paced the corridors of his own castle, Quin did what he had always done.

He observed.

After more than a week in Kaer Killian, he had learned many valuable things. He knew, for example, that the Embers were divided. Some felt the food coming out of the kitchens was rank and unsatisfactory; others were grateful for it. Most believed magic of all types should be condemned, but a few maintained it could be used for good.

Quin's revelation that Angelyne had torn the four kingdoms asunder had caused quite the stir. He heard nervous whispers about the devastation in Glas Ddir and whether the young queen's dark magic was to blame. Quin wondered how much the rest of the Embers knew about Tobin's raids on the surrounding villages. How horrified would they be to discover that more violence was being committed in their name?

Quin sat and drank and made merry with them, listening diligently to their hopes and fears. He could feel himself winning them over, Ember by Ember. Many now smiled at him when they passed in the corridor. Especially the women. He took a little extra care each morning to shave his face and comb his golden curls. It never hurt, he reasoned, to be easy on the eyes.

But wherever he sensed an opening, he planted small seeds of discord. While pretending to be united with the Embers, he quietly endeavored to exploit every fissure. He knew a fissure could be coaxed into a crack.

"Your Grace?"

Domeniq stood at the threshold of the drawing room, where Quin sat on his stage, a ream of parchment balanced on one knee as he jotted down observations. When Tobin had invited him to stay in his old quarters in the north wing, it had infuriated him. He did not need an invitation to sleep in his own chambers. But he had forced himself to smile graciously and accept.

Only later did he discover that Maev and Sylvan had taken the queen's suite, and Tobin the king's.

"Please, Dom. I told you to call me Quin. And you don't have to lurk outside like that."

"I didn't want to intrude."

"You're not intruding. You're a welcome change of pace." He set the parchment aside. "Ink and paper are a lonely man's game."

Dom took a step into the drawing room. His ever-present blue stone rested comfortably against his broad chest. He clasped two icy tankards of stonemalt; the sight of the sweating pewter was enough to make Quin's mouth water.

"No shortage of games for lonely men," Dom said.

"Something only a fellow lonely man could know." Quin smiled. A real smile this time. "I'm glad you came. I was beginning to think you were avoiding me."

Dom shook his head. "Just had to get a few things squared away."

Quin's curiosity was piqued. After Domeniq vanished into the kitchens the night of Quin's grand declaration, he hadn't seen him all week—until earlier that morning, when Dom had practically collided with him in a corridor. They'd greeted each other hesitantly, muscling their way through a clumsy embrace and the subsequent strained conversation.

"I brought you a pint." Dom set one of the tankards on the stage. "Thought you could use a drink."

Quin raised a brow. "Not trying to poison me, are you?"

A shadow passed over Dom's features. "I've killed enough people for ten lifetimes."

"Fair. I'm happy you're not one of the Embers who would prefer me dead."

Dom looked around the room, his gaze coming to rest on the clavichord.

"What kind of instrument is that?"

"Clavichord. Believe me, it sounds just as ugly as it looks."

"Can you play it?"

"I'd rather compose you a sonata with brass spoons and a chamber pot."

To Quin's surprise, Dom laughed. At the sound, something that had been locked in Quin's chest for months unlatched. Not completely, but enough to feel it loosen.

He remembered the first time he saw Domeniq du Zol. The night before his ill-fated wedding, Quin had sat beside Mia in the Grand Gallery, his gaze inexplicably drawn to the handsome young Hunter at a table below. Dom's brown skin stood out in a sea of freckled white faces, his crooked smile illuminating the room.

Of course, once Zaga and Angelyne began stacking corpses in the Hall of Hands, they had forced Domeniq to do unspeakable things. As a fellow prisoner, Quin had seen Dom roaming the castle corridors, eyes glazed, mind and body not his own. But who was Quin to judge? He had done unspeakable things himself.

"Maybe you can answer a question for me." Quin set his quill neatly at the edge of the stage. "When did the Embers occupy the Kaer? I've tried to trace the general timeline, yet find myself at a bit of a loss."

Dom sat heavily on the clavichord bench. He rubbed the back of his head.

"I don't know. When I shook the last of Angie's enthrallment a couple of weeks ago, they were already here."

"And then you joined their ranks."

Dom shifted on the bench. "There aren't many places left to go."

"I'll drink to that." Quin raised his pint, downing a healthy mouthful. "Now that's a fine ale. If the Embers brewed this, I have sorely underestimated them."

He leaned back, careful to keep his tone casual.

"I take it they'd been gathering steam in the village for a while."

"I guess so. Your father was good at making enemies. No offense."

"None taken. It was only a matter of time before a group like the Embers came to be. What's the official slogan?" He rubbed his temples, as if he were struggling to recall. "Ah. 'Remember the Embers. They remember you.'"

"I don't really go in for slogans."

"It's quite catchy. As are the little flames you carve wherever you commit an act of violence. You've got a catchphrase *and* a symbol. Why not have some tunics custom-sewn?"

Quin had meant it as a joke, but his friend didn't smile. Once again Dom rubbed the back of his head. Was he fidgeting from habit or nervousness? Quin hadn't spent enough time with him to know. Though in the brief time they *had* spent together, he'd found du Zol to be remarkably relaxed. It was partly why Quin liked him. As they'd danced on the tavern bar, sweaty and drunk, he had marked the easy way Dom moved, the warmth kissing the air between them.

"Tobin says you knew each other pretty well," said Domeniq. "Before all this, I mean."

"He was my music teacher."

"Just your music teacher?"

"Also my friend."

"He told me what happened in the crypt."

Now it was Quin's turn to shift his weight. "It's not a night I like to remember."

His father had been mercilessly violent, but then, his father was always violent. It was Quin who'd made the unforgivable mistake. No one knew better than he what Ronan was capable of.

Quin knew how to hide. He was, after all, a master of the pretending arts. And the very first time he'd tried to come out of hiding, the worst possible thing had happened.

"Toby asked me to come here, you know," Dom said. "To your drawing room. He and Maev and Sylvan want to know what you've been doing in here."

Quin folded his arms over his chest. And here he thought *he'd* been doing the interrogating.

"What do you plan to tell them?"

"That if they want to know what you're doing, they can come see for themselves. I'm sick of doing other people's dirty work." He toed the bottom of the clavichord. "It's a funny thing having leaders, when leaders are what you're fighting against."

"But there have to be leaders. Otherwise the world erupts into chaos."

"Maybe. But not every leader has to be a tyrant." Dom picked up his tankard, frowning at the stonemalt inside. "Or maybe they do. Even the volqanoes in Fojo are tyrants now. Big monsters blowing their lids."

Quin studied him. He'd heard rumors among the Embers of the volqanoes erupting, but it was only hearsay. Domeniq— Fojuen by birth—spoke as if he knew for sure.

Before he could press the point, Dom swore.

"Faqtan. The whole world has gone to hells."

Quin felt the anger radiating off his friend. It was an anger he wore, too, invisible but always present, like a film of sweat over his skin.

"What was it like?" Quin said quietly. "When Angelyne was enthralling you."

"Like shards of glass in my skull." Dom tugged at the blue stone around his neck. "She was too strong. Even my father's uzoolion was useless. Maybe I didn't have enough."

"For me it was cobwebs. My mind felt so dark and dusty I couldn't see my own thoughts."

"At least she and Zaga didn't make you kill anyone. They sent you after Mia and Pilar, sure, but you never murdered innocent people. You didn't have to drag their bodies back to the Kaer."

Dom's wide shoulders folded in, more like paper than muscle and bone.

"I still see their faces. All the people I hurt. The people I killed."

"Dom . . ."

"I know what you're going to say. 'It wasn't your fault, Dom. You were being enthralled. Your actions weren't your own.' But those people are still dead. And I'm the one who killed them."

Domeniq clanged his tankard down and stared at his own hands.

"I should have found a way to stand up to the enthrall. I should have fought it."

Quin had thought the same thing many times. *If only I were stronger*, he'd told himself. *Braver.* Even after Angelyne stopped enthralling him, he'd been so weak that the mere echo of her magic was enough to render him powerless.

He raked a nail down the pewter tankard, scraping off the

condensation. The wetness cooled the heat in his fingertips. Now he *was* stronger, and braver, and—best of all—powerful. He was the one with magic. According to the Embers' creed, that made him the enemy.

"How is your family, Domeniq?"

"My family?"

"Your mother and little sisters. Your grandmother, too. With the volqanos erupting, I take it they're no longer in Refúj?"

Dom bristled. "What difference is it to you?"

"I was just wondering, since the Embers have taken such a strong stand against magic, what they would think of your family of Dujia?"

Dom rose. He could be quite formidable, his large shadow stretching over the stage.

"Are you threatening me?"

"Of course not," Quin said smoothly. "I was simply curious."

Dom took a menacing step forward. Quin flinched.

But Dom only bent and swiped the tankard off the stage.

"I'll leave you to your ink and paper, *Your Grace.*"

"I wasn't done with that ale."

"I'm sure you weren't," Dom said, and took it anyway.

Chapter 16

STARVING

PILAR'S DAILY ROUTINE WAS simple. She got up before the sun rose. Threw cold water on her face. Laced her boots. If she timed it right, she could make it to the Swallow before the morning rush—meaning she wouldn't have to talk to anyone or dodge their hello kisses. She'd scarf down a few hard-boiled eggs with jomos and head straight for the Gymnasia.

Stone was always waiting. No matter how early she got there, he got there first. He'd greet her with a giant grin and hand her something hot. Black tea. Strong coffee.

"You don't drink enough fluids," Stone said one morning. "You have to hydrate more, now that you're in the desert."

"Maybe the desert suits me."

"Maybe you're going to choke on those eggs."

He was good at making her laugh.

Stone wasn't a great fighter, but she liked sparring with him. He never got tired, never gave up. Still, she worried her attempts to toughen him up weren't working. His stance was improving, as were his jabs and blocks. But the trust-bordering-on-worship he'd shown her from day one was only getting worse.

"Where's your head this morning, Stone?"

"Sorry, I'm a little distracted. Celeste was leading the circle yesterday, and she said I wasn't breathing deeply enough. That I was chest breathing, not belly breathing."

Pilar knew all about the circle. Stone wouldn't shut up about it. Different teachers led the circle, and the residents who went always seemed to walk out looking happier. Lighter.

She found it highly suspicious.

"Chest breathing?" Pilar snorted. "What does that even mean? Don't let her get inside your head, Stone. Why do you look up to someone like her?"

"She's the Keeper."

"Doesn't mean she walks on water."

Pilar threw a light punch. He didn't duck in time. Her fist caught him on the chin.

"*Awg!*" He rubbed his jaw. "You didn't have to punch me."

"We're sparring. That's the whole point."

"Be honest. I'm not bad for a big fellow, am I?"

"Your size is a strength, I'll give you that. But your confidence, well . . ."

"I'm very confident!" he cried.

She grinned. "That's the problem. If you want to be confident, don't let people in your head. Tell them to mind their own."

She came at Stone again. This time he matched her, blow for blow.

Half an hour later, they both collapsed onto the mat, panting.

"Better." Sweat dripped into her eyes. She grabbed her leather-skin and gulped down water. "Who taught you that left hook?"

"I used to have a fight teacher from the river kingdom."

Nell had told her this before. Even so, the water caught in Pilar's throat. She saw the cottage by the lake. Orry.

"She taught me a lot," Stone went on. "I was sad when she left for Prisma. We've lost so many residents to the Isle of Forgetting. Are you all right, did you just choke on your water?"

She swallowed. "Went down the wrong pipe."

Pilar could go hours without thinking about the cottage. She no longer saw the rafters, the violin bow, or even Orry's face. The memories that came now were from after. The coldness in her mother's eyes when Pilar told her she'd been raped. Morígna's calm voice as she stood in the sanctuary, giving her own version of events. The entire sisterhood of Dujia craning their necks to see which girl was the liar.

Honestly, sometimes she missed the rafters.

You didn't deserve what happened. It wasn't your fault.

Those were Mia's words. At first they'd brought Pilar comfort.

But then the doubt crept in. What did Rose know? She'd seen pieces of the story, not the whole thing. Pilar had been infatuated

146

with Orry for years. She liked being his favorite. She had smiled at him the first time he pressed his hand to her back to correct her fighting stance.

Morígna's words vied with Mia's. *There will always be girls so starved for attention they must lie to get it. Girls who pretend to be victims when they are anything but.* Zaga's voice joined the chorus: *Even if what you say is true, you have no one to blame but yourself.*

Pilar had wanted Orry's attention. And she'd gotten it.

In their Reflections, Mia had said pretty things. But since leaving Luumia, she'd only made Pilar feel *more* starved. Frankly, she was relieved Mia had spent the last few days spewing chunks.

"You in there?" Stone waved a hand in her face. "It's like you left your body for a minute."

She eyed Stone. He wanted attention, too. Differently from how she'd wanted Orry's, thank the Duj—she'd seen her young pupil drooling over a pretty blond girl in the House. But it concerned her how hungry he was for her approval.

She crouched. "Come at me again."

"You sure you're all right? We can take a break if you—"

She pivoted, redistributed her weight on her back leg, and landed a solid kick to his stomach.

He *oof*ed and stumbled back. Tried to stay upright. Failed, landing on his ass.

"Guess *I'm* the one who needs a break."

"How about a snack?" Pilar yanked him to his feet. "You've earned it."

She'd given Stone one week to impress her. One week to show up at the Gymnasia and spar with everything he had. She assumed he would get tired after a day or two, muscles sore, pride bloodied. Then she'd be free to go. Leave the House of Shadows and strike out on her own.

Problem was, Stone had exceeded her expectations. He showed up every morning, wrists wrapped, raring to go. Absorbed her lessons like a bread roll absorbed gravy. He was a good pupil— and she was a good teacher. It made her happy, watching him improve.

But the more he learned how to defend his body, the more frustrated she became that he couldn't—or wouldn't—defend his heart. The boy was an open book. He'd tell her every single thing he was thinking and feeling, or gush about some new teacher or guest he adored.

What if his next teacher saw that hunger—and exploited it? Pilar had been fifteen when Orry and Morígna came to Refúj: Stone's age. So trusting, so naive. She'd left herself vulnerable to attack.

How could she teach him to protect himself from the people who would try to hurt him?

In other words: How could she keep Stone from turning out like her?

"Oh, hello!" Nell waved from a nearby table as Pilar and Stone strode into the Swallow. "It's my two favorite fighters. Come join us! We're just finishing breakfast, we got a late start today."

Mia sat beside her. Still pale from all the vomiting, but otherwise none the worse for wear. Pilar felt happy to see her. The feeling came as a surprise.

But it clearly wasn't mutual. Rose had suddenly become very interested in chasing pulped eggplant around her plate with a piece of flatbread.

Fine. Pilar shoved her warm feelings aside. She jerked a chair from the table and spun it around, straddling the seat.

"Welcome back to the land of solid food, Rose."

"Thanks."

Silence. Not that Pilar was angling for a conversation about food and vomit. But Mia's curtness still hurt.

Stone whipped a chair around and sat backward, too.

"We've been sparring for hours. Sorry if we smell."

"I can tell, you're both glowing! How's my brother, Pilar, is he giving you any trouble?" Nell hesitated. "Thank you for what you're doing. I haven't seen him this happy in a long time."

"You haven't been here in a long time," Stone countered.

Pilar swiped a golden shrimp from Nell's plate and dipped it in tangy garlic sauce.

"It helps pass the time."

Mia stood. "I don't mean to be rude, but I was actually on my way out. I don't want to be late for the circle."

"What's so great about the circle?" Pilar munched loudly on the shrimp, well aware that Mia did not approve of her table manners. "You sit on pillows chanting and humming."

"It's not about humming and chanting!" Stone cried. "I mean, that's not *all* it is. I told you, it's one of those things you have to experience to understand."

Pilar shrugged. "I'd rather eat Nell's shrimp."

Stone rolled his eyes. "I won't force you. Mumma says you can't make people go to the circle, they'll find their own way when they're ready."

"Everything's your choice in the House of Shadows," Nell chimed in. "That's the Shadowess's creed! From the way you like your eggs, right down to how you heal."

"Then why don't *you* go to the circle?"

Nell laughed nervously.

"Great sands, I've been to enough circles to last a lifetime! Might as well let other people have a go."

"Goodbye, then," said Mia. She picked up her plate, scooped a strange wooden disc off the table, and hurried out the door.

"Can't get away fast enough," Pilar muttered, watching her go.

"I'm sure it's not personal. She's thriving here, she really is, I'm happy for her."

There was a slight shift in Nell's voice. Subtle, but Pilar caught it. Their cheerful hostess didn't seem as chipper as she had that first day.

"Hello, Stone!"

They all turned.

A skinny pale girl with wavy blond hair and a cute button nose stood beside the table, wearing a white dress that frilled at the knee. Stone's age, but an inch or two taller. The one Pilar had caught him swooning over.

The girl smiled. Waited. After a moment: "Won't you introduce me?"

"Oh, right, yes. Right." Stone swallowed. "Shay lives here. Her mumma is Celeste."

That explained the button nose. Pilar braced herself, waiting for the onslaught of kaara-akutha kisses. But Shay only smiled.

"And you're Pilar. Stone's told me all about your sparring sessions. He said you've brought the Gymnasia back to life! Maybe I can come sometime?"

Pilar sized her up. If someone as much as breathed on Shay, she might keel over.

"Not to spar!" Shay said, cheeks flaming. "Just to watch." She smiled at Stone again. "If that's all right with you."

He looked panicked. "I'm not very good."

"I'm sure you're better than I would be." The smile was permanently stuck to her face. "I'm going to the circle. Maybe I'll see you there?"

"I . . . I . . ."

Pilar took pity on him. "Sadly, Shay, we've got a sparring session this afternoon."

"Oh." For a moment the girl looked crestfallen. But she recovered quickly. "Maybe next time?"

Stone nodded, a little dazed.

"I'll save a seat for you!" she said, beaming, then practically skipped away.

Nell and Pilar exchanged a look, each fighting back a smile.

Stone glared at them.

"What?"

"Don't *what* me, baby brother. You like each other!"

Pilar slugged him in the arm. "Look at you, charming the ladies of the House."

"She isn't . . . I'm sure she wouldn't . . . it's not like that."

Stone blushed fiercely like the liar he was.

"Well *I* think it's sweet," Nell said. "She's certainly less obnoxious than her mother, don't you think, Pil?"

So she wasn't the only one who found Celeste unbearable.

"Sure," Pilar agreed. "But it's not hard to be less obnoxious than Celeste."

Nell laughed, delighted. Pilar felt a flicker of camaraderie. She'd been at the House long enough to trade inside jokes about its Keeper. It gave her a warm buttercup feeling.

"I'm starving," Stone said.

He got up from his chair, spinning it back around the right way.

"While you two make jokes about my love life, I'm going to get food."

Chapter 17

YOUR OWN BLOOD

Mia was bleeding.

She had never been enamored of her menses. She disliked the aching throb around her lumbar spine, the irritation that made her quick to bicker, and the inevitable stains on her undergarments and the rags she used to catch the flow. Still, she knew the blood needed out. So when she woke to find dark red smears on her inner thighs, she grudgingly accepted it.

"Mia?" Nell rapped on her sfeera door. "Are you in there, are you awake?"

"Don't come in!" she cried, waddling over to the bath bucket. "I'm . . . indisposed."

"Are you all right, did you get sick again?"

The door to her room swung open. One thing Mia had learned during her tenure at the House of Shadows was that Nelladine did not abide the implications of a closed door.

Mia stood poised between bed and bath bucket, fingers sticky with blood. Face red-hot with humiliation.

"Oh, I see! You're bleeding—why didn't you just say so?" Nelladine flopped down on the bed. "Do you have bloodmoss?"

"Is that the same as bloodbloom?"

Mia glanced at the wooden charm beside her bed. She'd been breathing with it several times a day, though to her disappointment she had not yet mastered the magic. The Shadowess's tree had grown to the size of a human skull. Mia's was no bigger than an eye socket.

"Your mother said the flowers on a bloodbloom tree have healing properties."

"It's not like your monthly bleedings need to be healed! The moss that grows on the trees is different from the flowers, it's remarkably absorbent. Women use it during their moon cycles, keeps their undergarments clean. We have loads in the Curatorium, would you like me to bring you some?"

Mia envied her friend's insouciance about bleeding. She could still recall how frightened she'd been the first time she bled. She ran to her mother, who held her close and stroked her hair. *Your body is a woman's body now, my red raven. You have nothing to fear from your own blood.*

Oh, Mother, Mia thought with a heavy heart. There were so many things for us to fear.

"I'd love some bloodmoss. If you don't mind."

"Bloodmoss and clean rags, coming right up."

Mia leaned over the bath bucket, splashing water on her hands. Once Nell left she could splash a little lower down.

She chastised herself. Mia had spent years studying the human body. Why did menstruation embarrass her? Was it because, in the river kingdom, a woman's menses was shrouded in shame? The prevailing theory was that women emitted a vile vapor while bleeding, so noxious that jam would not set and bread would not rise. Why had she not interrogated this superstition?

Mia felt a fierce, sudden longing for her anatomy sketches. She missed Wound Man. Or perhaps she missed the girl she used to be. Delighted by tibiae and fibulae. Engrossed in the way veins shunted blood through the body.

"Wait, Nell?"

Nelladine paused in the doorway. "Yes?"

"Do you think I could go with you to the Curatorium? I know we walked by it that first day, but your mother said maybe we could—"

"Why didn't you say so? Of course we can! Now I'm remembering, Mumma told me to take you, there's just been so much going on, I . . ."

Nell waved away the thought.

"Come with me. We'll stuff your undergarments full of moss and have ourselves a grand adventure."

As they made their way through the House, Mia's chest swelled with excitement. She'd been wildly curious about the Curatorium. She often took the longer way back to her sfeera just so she could steal a glimpse through the glass. But she'd been too shy to go in, for reasons she didn't fully understand.

"Important question," Nell said. "Have you been taking the elixir?"

Mia nodded. Since her first breathing session, she'd gone to see the Shadowess twice a day. She would walk to the House's westernmost wing and wait in a room where a cerulean tank teemed with live fish. Across from it were seven doors: one for the Shadowess, one for the Keeper, and the others for the five members of the Manuba Committee, an exclusive group of highly esteemed scholars who appointed the Shadowess or Shadower every seven years—and whom Mia had never seen.

Once ensconced in Muri's working chambers, Mia spoke with a frankness and lucidity that surprised even her. The Shadowess was easy to talk to. She had a wry, disarming sense of humor. At their third session, Mia described the elixir her mother had tried to give her.

"I know that tincture," the Shadowess had said. "It originated here, in fact. Nell tells me you're a scientist. At the House we welcome and encourage experimentation. That tincture shows a lot of promise, but the truth is that it's relatively new and has not been widely tested. When it comes to the health of the mind, I prefer to err on the side of caution."

Mia appreciated this approach. Every hypothesis deserved a set of controlled variables.

The Shadowess opened a drawer and handed her a vial. The viscous liquid was a deep, ocean blue; when Mia tipped the bottle from side to side, it coated the glass.

"We'll start with two drops. One with breakfast, one before bed. From there we'll go up as needed. This tincture is one of my favorites. They've been fine-tuning the formula far longer than I've been the Shadowess. It's helped a good many people."

Muri handed Mia a notebook with a bright orange melonfish on the cover.

"Feel free to use this however you like. Sketch, scribble, daydream. I encourage you to track your progress. The science of the mind is like any other science: we must measure and adjust. Just don't expect immediate results. It can take several weeks before you feel the effects."

But Mia *had* felt the effects. At least, she thought she had. The sensations were still intermittent, but they lasted longer. She had savored the tart lemon tang in a bowl of jomos and the sweetness of fig-pistachio cake drenched in almond syrup. She'd smelled the smoky aroma of roasted piglum and the woody, floral scent of her bloodbloom charm.

If she couldn't attribute these things to the elixir, then to what? The House of Shadows? Nell?

Now, as they walked past the Rose Garden, Mia explained to Nell how the elixir had made it easier to sustain certain tastes and smells.

"I'm glad to hear it. Though in light of where we're headed, that could be a good or bad thing, depending." Nell gave her a curious look. "You know I tried some elixirs myself."

"Really?" Mia said, surprised. "You've never mentioned it."

"It was years ago, before I left Pembuk. I was fourteen, my emotions were hard to control, so volatile! Sort of the opposite of you—you want to feel more, and I felt too much."

"Did it work?"

Nell shrugged, but Mia saw the muscles tighten in her jaw.

"Not really, no. I wanted it to, I wanted that so much. I've been really hopeful it would work for you, so I didn't say anything, didn't want to taint your hope. As Mumma says, it's different for everyone." Nell imitated Muri's thick Pembuka accent, *"You get to choose your own elixir, and it may not be the kind in a bottle. We all find our own path to healing."*

Mia laughed. "You sound just like her."

"Yes, well, I've had some practice. She can be terribly irritating, can't she? Just imagine what it was like growing up with her, imagine having the Shadowess for a mother!"

A bitter seed of envy settled in Mia's stomach. She *did* imagine it, every time she met with Muri. She loved their sessions. Sometimes they breathed together with the bloodbloom, sometimes they talked, but whatever they did, she always left feeling more centered than she had before. What would it have been like to have a mother that honest, that *real*?

Deep down Mia knew it wasn't her mother's fault. Wynna had simply been trying to survive. But it still stung that once her mother *had* survived, she had not chosen to come back.

"And here we are," said Nelladine, as they approached the Curatorium. "I warn you, you may soon wish you had *not* recovered your sense of smell. The Curateurs do their best to clean up after the animals"—Nell smiled mischievously—"but they are animals, after all."

Nell wasn't wrong. The Curatorium had a distinctive odor, an earthy cocktail of sweat and bile and blood, and perhaps a few less savory humors.

Mia did not mind one bit.

The space was far vaster than it appeared from the outside, revealing whole miniature topographies: grassy enclosures, small sand dunes, and a modest grove of bloodbloom trees no taller than Mia's hip. Other than the transparent glass facing the corridor, the walls were pearly white, casting an opaline glow that felt somehow familiar.

In the foreground, the Curatorium was partitioned into neat surgical stations stocked with bandages, knives, and bottles of dwayle, taxonomy tables and anatomy plates hanging from the walls. But there were also gemstones glowing in every imaginable color and elixirs smoking and churning of their own accord. Mia was struck by how science and magic coexisted happily, no division between them.

"Noisy, isn't it?" Nell asked. Mia was so mesmerized by the sights she'd been oblivious to the sounds. Now she heard brays, bleats, howls, and growls. She took in the menagerie of patients around them: furry dogs and house cats; harlequin birds in aviaries; reptiles and amphibians in gigantic vivaria, sunning themselves under orbs of magic-breathed light.

She saw other animals, too, genera she hadn't even known existed. Giant wildcats with serpentine tongues. Sea creatures boasting wolf heads. Four-legged equines with yellow stripes.

"Queen zybras," Nell said. "Aren't they beautiful? I've always loved them. Here, this is for you."

She held out a handful of spongy brown fibers she must have collected while Mia was staring slack-jawed at the wonders around them.

"Thanks."

Shyly, she stuffed the bloodmoss in her pocket.

"The human patients get a little more privacy." Nell gestured toward the back of the Curatorium, where the white walls tapered into a corridor.

"This is incredible, Nell. Did you come here all the time when you lived in the House? I could spend hours here. Days."

"No, I spent most of my time in the Creation Studio. There was less . . ." Nell hesitated. "When the animals first come here, they're in pain, they're suffering. The people, too. I found it all a little overwhelming."

If this was overwhelm, Mia decided, let her never be underwhelmed again. She watched as Curateurs in midnight-blue robes moved deftly between the creatures, wielding various tools and tinctures. Sometimes the injury was obvious—a broken leg, a cut gone septic. Other times a wound was not readily apparent, and the Curateurs would gather to discuss.

In one such station, a small pink creature crouched on its muscular back haunches, wriggling its black nose. A corresponding anatomy sketch hung from the wall. Mia vaguely recognized the animal's shape, though she didn't know why; she was quite sure she'd never seen one in Glas Ddir. Three Curateurs crowded around the sketch, pointing, arguing.

But this was no ordinary sketch. It was as if her beloved Wound Man had come to life. At the Curateur's touch, ink became blood,

blood flowed through arteries, and skeletal muscles contracted. She realized the Curateurs were testing a hypothesis. Conducting an experiment on the creature's effigy before operating on the creature itself.

Mia gave a start. She'd seen this kind of magic before. Lord Kristoffin Dove had shown her a moving map on the wall of his laboratory. Meanwhile, beneath their feet, he'd milked the suffering of seven innocent children to fuel the kingdom. Well, *six* children, plus Pilar.

Did the Curateurs, too, deploy their magical science to nefarious ends?

"See that little piglum?" Nell said, pointing to the pink creature.

Mia pulled herself back. Now she understood why she recognized the animal. She'd eaten one.

"Piglums are prone to infection," Nell explained, "especially when they haven't been well cared for."

"But don't you eat them?"

"*I* don't. Most Pembuka do. We strive to give all animals a good life, regardless of where they end up. Every creature deserves to be healed when she is suffering.

"Pappa!" Nell cried, waving to an older gentleman in a blue robe who, despite his age, boasted a fine crop of wiry white hair.

Mia waved, too. Nelladine's father had eaten with them several times in the Swallow. Whenever Lord Shadowess saw Stone and Nell around the House, he stopped what he was doing and gave them his undivided attention. So different from Mia's own father. Nell's whole family was so different—in all the best ways. And yet, for some reason, Nell had chosen to leave.

Lord Shadowess ambled toward them. Nell hugged him, pecking him fondly on each cheek.

"Pappa, would you show Mia the work you and the other Curateurs are doing? You'll explain everything so much better than I can, and you two speak the same language, science and all, and I ought to . . ." She glanced toward the door. "I have some things to take care of."

Mia was confused. "I thought we were going to—"

"You'll be fine! Pappa will take good care of you, won't you, Pappa? Mia is a gifted healer, she's got quite a knack for it, I think she'd be a big help if you need a pair of hands."

Lord Shadowess smiled. "We can always use an extra pair of hands."

Before Mia could argue, Nell was sweeping past. At the door she took a moment to press both palms against the pearly white stone. Then she pushed open the door and disappeared through it.

Mia gazed after her, perplexed. Nell's entire demeanor had changed, for no reason she could ascertain.

"Have you had any experience with the lloira stone?" asked Lord Shadowess.

A chill dripped down Mia's spine. No wonder the pearly white walls looked familiar. She envisioned the moonstone clenched in her sister's hand, Angelyne twisting their mother's healing magic into something hateful.

She turned to face Lord Shadowess.

"Not good experiences, sad to say."

"I'm sorry to hear that." He gestured toward the opalescent walls. "Here in the Curatorium, we have found it to be very useful. The Curateurs are gifted healers, and the moonstone augments their natural gifts. The lloira has helped heal many creatures within these walls, both beast and human." He gestured toward the grove of small trees. "As have the scarlet blossoms of the bloodbloom. At the House we're interested in the healing properties of the natural world. My wife likes to say we cannot heal the world until we heal ourselves."

He smiled. "Muri is right. She's right about most things. There's a reason she is the Shadowess. But I believe the opposite is also true: we cannot heal ourselves until we heal the world. A paradox."

Mia looked into his deep brown eyes. Here was another lord, in another laboratory where science and magic collided. She had been wrong about people before. *Most* people. But somehow, in the core of her being, she knew this man was not Kristoffin Dove.

"I ask about the lloira," he said, "because stones have great power. We are stewards of that power, and we must use it well. Would you be willing to give the moonstone another try?"

Mia thought of her mother. How her quiet trips to the river towns to heal sick and dying Glasddirans with medicine had been a pretense for healing them with magic.

How the moonstone had helped Wynna make her own heart beat again and, three years later, had done the same for Mia.

How tenderly her mother had stroked her back during her

monthly bleedings, and how, afterward, Mia's lumbar spine had always ached a little less.

Tears sprang to her eyes.

Her mother had been healing her. Even then.

"Yes," she said to Lord Shadowess. Even though in her mind she saw Quin and Angelyne under the snow palace, black and red gems clutched in a desperate power play; even though it frightened her to know that the magic pumping through her own blood could twist the magic inside a stone; even though she didn't know if she deserved to be a steward of anything, after so many mistakes, so many failures.

Your body is a woman's body now, my red raven. You have nothing to fear from your own blood.

"Yes," she said again, and meant it.

Chapter 18

UNCOMFORTABLY FAMILIAR

NAVIGATING THE KAER WAS not for the faint of heart. The castle comprised hundreds of tunnels, each meticulously hacked from soulless black stone. The labyrinthine corridors had both delighted and frightened Quin as a child. But unlike a true labyrinth, there was always more than one way to reach your destination. Consequently, he knew how to avoid the Hall of Hands.

He would not avoid it anymore.

As Quin skulked through the bowels of the castle, his thoughts fixated on Domeniq. He'd spent the last week weighing the cost of their conversation. Had he turned a potential ally into a potential enemy? And for what? He had not gleaned any substantive new information about the Embers, though he did know one thing: Dom was hiding the truth about his family. If Quin needed to force an alliance, he now had the right ingredients for extortion.

How far I've come, Quin thought darkly. From dancing shirtless with a handsome boy to plotting how best to blackmail him.

Finally, he stood outside the Hall of Hands. He thought of the cook who had tried to save him from the horrors therein. As if not seeing something meant it did not exist.

Perhaps if he had not been so coddled, he would not be so weak.

Quin took a breath—and walked inside.

The Hall was empty.

King Ronan's ghastly hands had been cleared, along with Zaga's collection of corpses. Had the Embers removed them? Absent the gory trophies, the room struck Quin as impressively large—with its vaulted ceilings and iron candleholders, it could have been the Royal Chapel's twin. In a way, that seemed fitting: both Ronan and Zaga had used the Hall as a kind of shrine.

What would *he* use it for, Quin wondered, when he reclaimed the river throne?

"Your Grace?"

Brialli Mar stood in the corridor behind him, her blue eyes wide. He hadn't seen her since his first day in the Kaer. Hadn't seen any children the last two weeks, come to think of it. Where were all the Glasddiran girls and boys? What had happened to them? He did not want to imagine how the orphans might have met their grisly end.

"Was this where your father kept the hands?" Brialli asked quietly, as she came to stand beside him. "I wonder where my mother's hand hung."

Quin hated that he felt responsible. He had known what his father could do, what he *was* doing. And how had Quin responded? By handing out sweet taffies to destitute orphans. What a pathetic excuse for a future king.

He could do so much more now. With his magic, he could do virtually anything. Yet here he was in his own castle, ingratiating himself with the Embers, charming the women and chumming around with the men. Pretending, always pretending. Hiding the truth of who he was.

It was all uncomfortably familiar.

"I need to ask you something, Your Grace," said Brialli, and he heard a note of uncertainty in her voice. "If one of your subjects were, say, keeping something from you . . . but for your own good . . . would it be treason?"

"I take it you're the subject?"

She paled. He adjusted his approach to one of clemency.

"Treason would be an act of betrayal," he said mildly, "if I were in fact your king. But I stand with the Embers now, remember? We fight against all tyrants."

Brialli drew herself up tall. "My mother always saw the truest parts of people. Even when everyone else said someone was bad, she could tell if their heart was good. She saw how you were at the orphanage. She said you were gentle."

Quin's throat tightened. On the bare walls of the Hall of

Hands, he saw a vision of his younger self: playing piano for the orphan children and crying as he rode back to the Kaer.

Even now, as he so diligently plotted his path to the throne, telling himself he was powerful, strong, he was nothing but a tragic character in one of his plays. A sniveling little boy doomed by his fatal flaw. *Gentleness.*

Why did he continue to let himself be coaxed back into what he was?

Quin hardened his jaw. He stared down at Brialli. Eyes cold.

"Your mother was wrong," he said. "She was foolish. And now she is dead."

He left Brialli alone in the Hall and did not look back.

Chapter 19

LYING SLUT

Today's the day.

Pilar walked to the Gymnasia, wrapping her wrists. She'd given Stone one week—and now two weeks had passed.

Today's the day I leave.

But every day, he got better. Punched harder, fought smarter. They sparred in the morning, noon, and night. Stone was shedding his baby fat. His mind was getting tougher, too. He drew into himself more now. Didn't divulge his whole life story to strangers.

Sometimes Stone seemed almost sad. Once or twice she'd opened her mouth to ask him what was wrong, then clamped it shut. He was learning to protect himself, wasn't he? That was the reason she'd stayed. After he learned that lesson fully, Pilar would go.

Maybe today's the day.

She grimaced. She was stalling and she knew it.

Why couldn't she leave the House? Was it the good food? The nice bed? It sure wasn't the female bonding. Mia and Nelladine were always off somewhere, breathing or chanting or playing with sick dogs. Didn't matter. She was perfectly happy punching sandbags with a fifteen-year-old.

But when she got to the Gymnasia, it was empty. Sandbags hung from the ceiling, eerily still. She never beat Stone to their sparring sessions. Her pulse quickened. Had something happened?

"Sorry!" Stone called out, and relief whooshed through her as he hustled in. "Sorry I'm late. I lost track of time."

He handed her a mug of hot rice tea, then started lighting the torches.

"I was talking to this new sandologist in the House, he's amazing! He was telling me how the glass cities are sinking even faster than normal, so much that people are worried. He told me he'd take me to his laboratory if I wanted to see it, he has a house on the Pearl Peninsula, and—"

"When did you meet this scientist?"

He shrugged. "An hour ago?"

Pilar fought the urge to shake him.

"You met him an hour ago, he offers to take you to his home half a kingdom away . . . and you're considering it?"

"This is the House of Shadows, Pilar. Bad people don't come here."

She let out a strangled laugh.

"Bad people come everywhere, Stone. They come to giant glass houses in the desert. They come to little islands in the middle of the sea."

He gave her a curious look.

She'd said too much. Pilar was always very careful not to share her personal history with Stone. Every time he tried to tease out pieces of her past, she told him to mind his own. She didn't air her own foul laundry. Neither should he.

"Are you going to leave?" Stone asked.

"What?"

"Are you going to leave the House because I talked to that sandologist?"

Pilar saw fear in his eyes. It made her chest ache.

"You're getting better every day, Stone. But you should be taking these lessons off the mat. When are you going to realize you can't give people that kind of power?"

"Maybe you should stay," he said, "until I get that lesson through my thick skull."

Pilar sighed. Set down her tea. He'd won.

"I won't go anywhere with the sandologist," he said, chastened, "if you think it's a bad idea."

Pilar rolled her eyes. Terrific. He'd simply moved the power back to her.

"Enough talking. More fighting."

She positioned herself on the mat.

"Today we work on pins. Don't just block. You have to counter-attack. Defend yourself, but don't hesitate to hurt your opponent."

"Hi, Stone. Hi, Pilar."

They both turned to see Shay at the door in a ruffled pink skirt.

For the past week she'd been showing up daily at their sparring sessions. She loitered in the hallway, hesitant. Like she was afraid of what might happen if she stepped over the threshold.

"Are you a vampyr, Shay?" Pilar said wryly. "I always have to invite you in."

The girl turned bright pink.

"Come in, then."

Shay scampered into the Gymnasia, long blond hair streaming behind her.

"Don't mind me! I'll just sit right here." She situated herself on a padded mat off to the side. Her face contorted. "This one's kind of sticky." She got up and moved one mat over. "I'll sit right here, if that's all right?"

Pilar felt Stone tense. He was always distracted when Shay was there. At first it had galled her. Then she realized it might be useful. Stone was too willing to give other people power. To let them get inside his head.

If she could train him to focus on his *own* power? That was a lesson worth teaching.

"Sit anywhere you want, Shay. We're doing pins."

"Oh. Actually . . ." She smoothed out a wrinkle in her skirt. "Can *I* try?"

Pilar blinked. Had she heard right? Shay only ever sat on the sidelines in her frilly skirts, watching.

But Shay wasn't sitting now. She stood at the edge of the mat. Smiling. Shaking a little.

"Since when do you fight?" Pilar said.

"Since now, I think?" Shay paused. "I've been paying really close attention. I want to see if I can do it."

Pilar shrugged. "Fine by me. Stone?"

"Sure," he said, staring at the floor.

Stone stepped clumsily to the side. He always lost his base when he was nervous. Pilar made a note to work on that later.

She beckoned Shay to the mat.

"What you have to remember is that a fighter like Stone has size on his side. You're the opposite. What you *can* use is speed. Being small has been one of my biggest advantages. I'm light on my feet. Of course, that won't help when you're on the ground. The trick is to be fast. Keep moving. The minute you stop moving because you're afraid, your opponent will sense it."

"I know." Shay smiled sweetly. "I've been watching you all week. That's why I wanted to try. It seems like the scariest thing to me, being trapped underneath someone."

The words hit home. Pilar had spent years trapped under Orry. Only later would she realize that the one thing he had never taught her was how to escape a pin.

Even if he had, would she have been brave enough to do it?

She felt a fierce and sudden urge to protect Shay at all costs. Maybe if she taught this girl how to escape a pin, she could save her from the same fate.

"Let's give it a go." Pilar dropped to her knees and patted the mat. "Your attacker has the advantage, being on top of you. But if you can throw him off balance, you can use his own weight against him."

Shay nodded. "I'll do my best."

She stripped off her pink skirt. Underneath she was wearing snug black tights. Pilar blinked. How long had she been sitting there with tights under her skirt, waiting to spar?

"Nice and slow," Pilar said as Shay lay on her back. "Remember, you're trying to reverse the move and pin *me*. If you feel uncomfortable at any point, just slap the mat and say stop."

She climbed on top of her new student, pinning her down.

"Whenever you're—"

Shay bucked up with her hips. Her sharp hip bones slammed into Pilar's stomach, and Pilar fell forward, catching herself with her hands. In a flash, Shay wrapped her arm around Pilar's arm, yanking it toward the inside of her body. Then she hooked Pilar's leg with her own shin, using the momentum to pull her off balance—and roll them both over.

The back of Pilar's head slammed into the mat. Exactly the way she'd taught Stone, only he'd never done it as cleanly or as well.

In a flash, Shay straddled her. Tightened her knees. Bony knees. And strong as hell.

"Pinned," Shay said, triumphant.

Pilar stared up at her, stunned. Shay smiled. Not the same smile she flashed constantly at Stone, trying to be coy. This was different. A new light sparkled in her blue eyes.

"That," Stone said from somewhere above them, "was amazing."

"See?" Shay grinned. "Told you I'd been paying attention."

In that moment, Pilar felt wildly happy. She couldn't remember the last time her chest had flooded with so much joy. She'd given this girl something.

No. Better. She'd made space for something that was already there.

"Shay?" called a voice from the doorway. "What is this?"

Instantly the weight lifted from Pilar's chest. Shay shot up so fast her foot got caught, walloping Pilar in the ribs as she stumbled forward.

"Mumma."

Celeste stood at the door, arms akimbo.

"What are you doing in here, Shay? I thought the Gymnasia was closed."

When Shay didn't answer, Celeste turned on Stone.

"Does your mumma know you're here?"

Pilar sat up, rubbing her side. "Why would the Shadowess care? We're just sparring."

"Yes, I can see that. I'm sure I don't have to tell you this isn't in line with what we believe here at the House. You're teaching them violence."

"I'm teaching them self-defense." Pilar could feel her voice rising. "How to protect themselves *against* violence."

"By having them beat each other to a pulp? I know you come from a troubled background, Pilar, and clearly those experiences have left their mark. Violence breeds violence. But I'm the Keeper of Manuba Vivuli. I can't have you set a poor example for our residents and guests. And certainly not for my daughter." She looked at Stone. "I'll be talking to the Shadowess as well."

"Mumma, please." Shay had tears in her eyes. "Please don't do this."

"Out," Celeste ordered. *"Now."*

For one tense moment, everyone was rooted in place. Pilar on the mat, Stone off to the side, Shay and Celeste locked in a stand-off, staring each other down.

Celeste won. Pilar had a feeling she always did. Shay said nothing. Just stomped out of the Gymnasia.

Once she was gone, Celeste softened. She fixed her blue eyes on Pilar. Shay's eyes.

"Please understand. I'm not trying to be harsh. It's just that there are healthier ways to heal."

She brightened suddenly.

"Now that I think of it, I haven't seen you at the circle. I'm leading a session this afternoon. Why don't you join us?"

Pilar cracked her neck.

"Why would I do that?"

"Because if you are going to be a part of this community, Pilar, you should try actually being a part of it."

Pilar unwrapped her hands, taking her sweet time. Tilted her fists frontward, then backward, then in circles. Stretched the muscles in her wrists.

This wasn't about Celeste. To go to the circle was to get comfortable.

She didn't want to get comfortable.

"If you come," Celeste said, "perhaps we can discuss a way to keep the Gymnasia open."

Pilar was about to tell Celeste to go dangle her carrots else-where when Stone said, "Please."

He was looking at her, not Celeste.

"Please do it, Pil. Sparring has made me happier than I've been in . . . I can't even remember. I don't want to give that up." He took a breath. "I'll come to the circle, too, if that makes a differ-ence. So you won't be alone."

Pilar could feel herself caving. Stone looked so expectant. So trusting.

"Fine." She turned back to Celeste. "Just this once. But you better not sit my ass on a cushion and make me chant."

Celeste smiled serenely. "See you there."

Pilar sat her ass on a cushion, chanting.

More of a hum, really. Not that that made it better.

She'd come to the Manjala two minutes late to find ten black cushions arranged in a circle, graced by ten asses. One of those asses belonged to Stone. Another to Mia Rose.

For some reason, Rose being there made it that much worse.

"Kaara akutha!" Celeste beamed. "Welcome to the circle. Can everyone please make room?"

A bald man gave Pilar his cushion and went to get another for himself.

"Now let your eyes lightly close," Celeste instructed, once they were situated. "We always start the circle by lighting the candle to anoint the sacred space. Take a deep, cleansing breath. Stay with your nostrils. *Be* with your nostrils."

Pilar, who had never given a single thought to her nostrils, kept her eyes open. She watched Celeste light the candle.

"Now together we will make the sacred sound."

Like clockwork, everyone opened their mouths and let out the strangest sound Pilar had ever heard. Half dying animal, half mating call. She stifled a laugh.

Across the circle, Stone opened his eyes and shot her a pleading look.

Please.

Fine. She opened her mouth. Made the sound. Like eating a hummingbird that got stuck in your throat.

Pilar thought she'd do it once and that'd be it. But people kept sucking in more air for another round. Over. And over. The room was alive with dying hummingbirds.

"This can all feel very new and uncomfortable," Celeste cooed. "I urge our newer residents to relax into what their conscious mind may not understand. Our job is to be empty vessels and let the kosmos, in its infinite wisdom, provide."

Pilar closed her eyes to see if it was less strange. No. Stranger. She could feel the vibrations knocking things loose in her head.

She felt someone watching her. Looked up, expecting to see Stone. But everyone's eyes were closed.

Except Celeste's.

"There is great healing to be found in this community," she said smoothly. "But some of us fight it. Can you imagine? The kosmos offers us infinite abundance, yet we fall back on our bad habits and behaviors. We retreat into our wounded selves. In so doing, we drag others down, especially younger souls who look up to us. We thrive on their adoration because it feeds our insatiable need to be loved. Today I invite you to ask yourself: Are you hungry for connection? Or are you hungry for attention?"

Pilar's mouth went chalk dry.

She wasn't in the House of Shadows anymore. She was back on Refúj, in the circle of Dujia. Morígna's words piercing her heart.

Starved for attention.

Her shame burned a hole in her chest.

She was on her feet before she knew it. Bolting for the door.

"Pilar! Wait."

She didn't look back. She was halfway down the turquoise hall. After that, peach, then green, then yellow: the path out of the House.

"Please!" a voice called after her. Mia's.

You didn't deserve what happened. It wasn't your fault.

Was Mia saying the words now, or were they only in her head? Pilar could feel her feet slowing. She must've stopped running, because suddenly Mia was by her side.

"What happened in there, Pilar? Are you all right?"

"What *happened*?" She pointed back at the Manjala. "That little show was for me. She only wanted me to come to her precious circle for a public shaming."

"I don't think that was her intention. Celeste can be a little much sometimes, but she's the Keeper. She was trying to offer you a place in the community. That's her job."

Pilar's laugh could have cut glass.

"Do you know what it's like to have a community, Rose? To have your sisters stab you in the back?"

"I know a little, considering my little sister wanted me dead." She hesitated. "Both sisters, actually."

Pilar stood there, fuming. She couldn't argue.

"But I know it's not the same," Mia added quickly. "I saw what Morígna said to the Dujia, and what your mother said to you. I'm so sorry. What they did was—"

"You saw pathetic little slivers. Everyone looked at me like I was a lying slut. *Everyone*."

"But you're not. There's nothing you could ever do that would have made it your fault." Her gray eyes softened. "*They* were wrong, Pilar. Not you."

Pilar clenched her fists. Unclenched them. Tears welled in her throat. She wanted to believe this. *Needed* to believe it.

She choked the tears back down.

"'Be with your nostrils'?" She coughed. "Look me in the eye and tell me that isn't a heaping pile of swan shit."

Mia's face was perfectly still. Then the faintest smile crept into her eyes.

"Perhaps a small pellet of swan shit," she allowed.

They held each other's gaze. Pilar wanted to laugh. Wanted to cry.

Mia cleared her throat. "How about we go to the Swallow and get lunch? I have no idea what you've been up to, or how you're feeling about the House. And, well, you are my sister, even if it's been a rather rocky road. We haven't talked in days. I'd . . . I'd really like to."

Mia exhaled. Only then did Pilar realize she'd been holding her breath.

"You're the only family I've got left, Pil. Surely that's worth fighting for."

Rose was being gentle. Kind. Pilar could feel herself leaning toward Mia, wanting to tell her how Stone had all but perfected his right hook, how Shay had surprised her in the best possible way. She could feel the words on the tip of her tongue, everything she'd been thinking and feeling. The things about the House she hated, and the things she loved.

It terrified her.

"I want to be alone," Pilar said, turning on her heel.

Today's the day, she thought. *Today's the day I leave.*

In the Gymnasia, she punched a sandbag until her knuckles bled.

Chapter 20

AN IMPOSSIBLE LIFE

"MIA, SOMETHING'S HAPPENED."

Mia stood in the Shadowess's doorway. She'd arrived early for their session—she liked watching the fish swim through the walls, especially now that she'd been spending more time in the Curatorium, helping Lord Shadowess and the other Curateurs tend to the animals. She was excited to tell Muri everything she was learning: how she now took the melonfish notebook with her every day, jotting down notes and making anatomical sketches of the different creatures under her care. In the Curatorium, her healing gifts were not only welcomed, but admired.

Instead she found the door to the Shadowess's working chambers ajar as Muri sorted frantically through parchments, wire spectacles at risk of sliding off her nose.

"I'll have to cancel today's session. I apologize."

Mia's heart sank. She didn't only want to share her progress in the Curatorium. She wanted to tell Muri she had once again offered an olive branch to Pilar, and had it once again rejected. The only family she had left wanted nothing to do with her.

"Maybe tomorrow?" Muri offered. "Or the following morning? I can't quite predict my schedule at the moment."

She'd never seen the Shadowess so flustered. "Is everything all right?"

"Everything's fine. We've had some unexpected visitors arrive from the snow kingdom."

Muri paused. Mia sensed she was choosing her words carefully.

"I want to be transparent with you. The visitors are Queen Freyja of Luumia and her lady."

Mia's heart stopped.

Her mother.

Impossible. It couldn't be. She gaped at the Shadowess, trying to process what she'd just been told.

"I'm sure you have questions," said Muri.

"My mother is *alive?*"

"Yes. They both survived the avalanche. Apparently there were more survivors than we thought, which is good news. Freyja and Wynna have journeyed a long way to the House of Shadows."

"For me?" Mia's voice was painfully small. "Did my mother come for me?"

Muri's eyes shone with compassion.

"I don't know, Mia. I wish I did."

Mia was reeling, her thoughts racing too quickly to hold on to. *Breathe*, she told herself, reaching instinctively into her pocket, where the bloodbloom charm was waiting. She marshaled all the Shadowess's training, calling on the breath work they'd done together.

But her breaths remained shallow. Sharp.

The little tree did not bloom.

"You don't have to see her, Mia. It's entirely up to you. You've been doing so much good work here. I'm proud of you. If you feel you're not ready to have that conversation, you don't have to. It's your choice."

Mia nodded, only half hearing the words. In theory she knew she could say no.

But theory was worthless in matters of the heart.

The unexpected visitors were gathered in the Swallow. The heart of the House, the place where residents and guests alike ate, talked, and laughed together. Just like our kitchen in Ilwysion, Mia thought. She conjured up the square wooden table, the simple meals of potato cakes and sweet brown mustard.

The memory ached.

Her feet slowed as she neared the Swallow. Each emotion was more unsettling than the last. For three years Mia had believed her mother dead. Then she'd found her in the snow kingdom—alive, but cold and distant, having chosen a life with Queen Freyja above all else. Then Mia had lost her again, the same night she'd lost Angelyne and Quin.

Now she and her mother were together in Pembuk. Both escaped from Luumia and, before that, from Glas Ddir. Both chasing their physical sensations, and their emotional ones, too. Both fighting so hard to feel alive.

What if her mother had come to the House as her last stop on the way to Prisma, the Isle of Forgetting? What if she and the Snow Queen were only passing through, soon to forget everything, everyone, from their lives before?

"Mia?"

And then she was there. Stepping over the threshold, luminous red waves tumbling down her back. Hazel eyes smiling. Arms reaching for her daughter.

"My red raven," she whispered.

Mia's knees buckled. All her plans of remaining calm and reasonable shattered as she fell into her mother's arms. An embrace she hardly remembered, but that instantly felt like home.

"You're here," her mother murmured. "When the Shadowess told us you'd come to the House, I could hardly believe it. I prayed to the Duj to keep you safe, Mia. I hadn't prayed in such a long time, but I fell to my knees every morning and every night. I couldn't bear losing you again."

Mia held her closer. This was everything she'd wanted and hadn't dared to dream. She buried her face in her mother's hair, inhaling her unique scent, a little sweet and a little wild, like fresh flowers and woodsmoke. Mia could smell all of it. That alone was enough to make her cry. She flooded her nostrils with the beloved fragrance, succumbing to a heady rush of memories—moments from their cottage, their long forest walks, their lives before.

She caught something new in the aroma: a slight tinge of snow plum. A note of Luumia.

Mia would have been happy to keep her mother clasped to her heart forever, breathing her in, both their cheeks damp with tears. In that moment she could have forgiven Wynna anything. What did it matter if she'd left? They were together now. They didn't ever have to be apart.

But of course they did. Wynna pulled away first. She wiped her cheeks, then Mia's, laughing.

"We're a mess, aren't we?"

Before Mia could respond, she saw movement behind her mother. A large woman stood quietly, snow-fox cloak draped over her broad shoulders. She had cool silver eyes, tawny skin, and black hair shaved close to the scalp.

"Mia," Wynna said, taking a breath, "I want you to meet my wife."

The Snow Queen stepped forward. She had a regal bearing, though not in the way of King Ronan. Whereas he always seemed to be looking *down* at you, Freyja's gaze was somehow level, in spite of her height and girth. As if you were not her subject, but her equal.

"Your Grace," Mia said, dipping her head.

"Please. Freyja."

The queen enveloped Mia's hand in a hearty grip.

"I'm sorry I wasn't able to welcome you to my palace."

"I'm sorry you no longer have a palace."

Was that the right thing to say? Mia had never met the queen her mother had fallen in love with, leading her to subsequently abandon her daughters, one of whom went on to destroy said queen's palace and a sizable part of her queendom.

They were clearly in uncharted terrain.

"Who else made it out alive?" she said softly. "Did Angelyne?" She swallowed. "Quin?"

Gently, her mother took her hands.

"We looked for them. We thought perhaps they . . ." Her eyes were tear bright. "That we could at least put them to rest. But everything was buried. We couldn't reach them."

She touched Mia's cheek.

"They're gone, my raven girl."

Mia felt a sob rise in her throat. She didn't know why. She had already grieved the loss of her sister and the boy she could have loved. Why did it hurt so much to have that loss confirmed?

She thought her mother might fold her into another embrace. She wouldn't have fought it.

Instead Wynna reached for Freyja's hand.

As a child, back when she knew everything, Mia's knowledge of love was unassailable. Love existed between one man and one woman, marriage the holy consummation of that bond. A wife could take her gloves off in the presence of her beloved husband, and only then.

To know how love manifested, Mia had only to look at her

parents. Their love was a comet whirling through the sky. They lived and breathed one another, sometimes sharing a single plate at supper, each with their own fork. In the cottage, whenever her mother walked out of the room, her father's eyes trailed after her, as if he couldn't bear to have a wall between them.

Of course now Mia knew the truth. Griffin was being enthralled. Wynna's doting affection was a fiction. The price she paid to sleep next to an assassin, working quietly and fervently to save the women he aimed to kill.

But this? Now? The tenderness in her mother's face? The way her eyes sparked when Freyja lifted her hand to her mouth and kissed it?

Mia knew, in the fiber of her being, that this was love.

She thought of Quin. Not the tableaux that so often came to her: their witty banter in the hot spring, their bodies intertwined in the Natha River. Now a bevy of smaller moments sprang to mind. Quin brushing a stray curl from her eyes as they sat beside the lake in Refúj. *Your hair is wilder here. I like it.* How he beamed with pleasure in the Twisted Forest as she raved about his delectable hare stew. The way he kissed her fingers on the red balloon, saying her hands were even more beautiful than he'd imagined.

What a precious soul he was. Someone to be treasured. Why had she not done everything in her power to protect him?

Till the ice melts on the southern cliffs.

Promise me, O promise me.

"We will rebuild," said the Snow Queen, dragging Mia from her reverie. "But we cannot do it alone. For thousands of years Manuba Vivuli has offered refuge to pilgrims. My lady and I have come to seek counsel from the wisest minds in the four kingdoms. The Shadowess has promised us whatever resources we require."

"And your uncle?" Mia's voice came out sharper than she'd intended. She felt a dull pain in her wrist where the fyre ink flowed. "Lord Dove was interested in resources, too."

Freyja looked stricken.

"If I had known what he was doing to innocent children . . . in my own palace . . . under my own feet . . ."

A strange, terrible sound came from her throat. Wynna gripped her hand more tightly.

"It's all right, my love. You didn't know. How could you possibly have known?"

She stroked Freyja's back. Mia could almost feel the warmth of her mother's fingertips, her healing touch when Mia's back had ached during her monthly bleedings. She never imagined one day she would see her mother touch another woman with such tenderness and devotion. A thing so blasphemous in the river kingdom, it had not even been a figment in her mind.

Mia thought of Nelladine. She felt something when she looked at Nell; she could not deny it.

They weren't in the river kingdom anymore.

In Pembuk, everything was possible.

Now she watched her mother trace gentle circles on Freyja's back. Such a small thing, and not small at all. Her mother seemed happy.

Did that mean Wynna's elixir was working? Logically speaking, did it follow that if Mia kept taking her tincture, she, too, might feel this kind of love?

The Snow Queen exhaled. When her eyes met Mia's, there was fire in them.

"I failed my people. But I will not fail them again. I will fight every day to make reparations. I believe it was my uncle's greed and lust for power that led him into an alliance with . . ."

She and Wynna exchanged a heavy, painful look.

"An alliance with others who shared his greed," Freyja finished. "That power lust is the black heart beating around us." She straightened. "Each of us stands at an unprecedented moment in history. Now is the time for us to put aside our differences and fight side by side to save the four kingdoms. We must work together if we want to survive."

The truth hit Mia with astounding force.

Her mother had not come to the House for her. She'd come for Freyja.

Mia turned slowly to face her mother. "You didn't even know I was here," she said. "Did you?"

Wynna held her gaze.

"But I'm so glad to find you, my raven girl." She glanced at Freyja. "*We're* so glad."

"What changed?" The question left a bitter aftertaste in Mia's mouth. "Last time we saw each other, you said you were tired of fighting. That you'd found quieter places to put your heart."

"You are right to call me to account. I struggle with my part in all of this. It has been such a long fight to feel anything again, even the good things. My own mind felt so fragile. I thought . . . I feared . . . that if I opened myself up to others' pain and suffering, it would consume me. So I stepped back. I looked away."

She shook her head. "I will not look away any longer. I will fight with my queen."

Wynna took a breath.

"You have always demanded the truth, my raven. You ask questions and challenge assumptions, pick and prod at things until you make sense of them. We desperately need truth-seekers like you. We want you to come back with us, Mia. You have a home with us."

"The snow queendom is not my home."

"You have a family."

The word rocked the room.

Family.

What made a family? Was it the name Clan Rose? The blood coursing through Mia's veins? The kinfolk she'd known as a child? By that measure, she had no family: her mother, father, and sister were all strangers masquerading as people she knew.

Was Pilar d'Aqila her sister simply because they shared a father? Or did something else tie them together? Mia knew they had forged a bond beneath the Snow Queen's palace, even if Pilar continued to deny it: they had made a choice. They had promised to fight for one another.

And now Mia's mother was promising to fight for her.

Only, she wasn't. Not really. She'd come to Pembuk to fight for

191

Freyja, the woman she loved. Her daughter was an afterthought. A pleasant one—Wynna had believed her dead, and was surely glad to see her. Mia did not doubt her mother loved her. But Wynna hadn't *chosen* her. Not for a long time.

Mia caught the sound of voices in an adjacent hallway. She heard the punch line of a bawdy joke, followed by the low, husky laugh she knew so well.

Her heart lurched toward Pilar and Nelladine. She was astonished by how much she wanted to be where they were, strolling down a corridor, sipping a cup of fish ice.

Pilar had rejected her countless times. But Nell was different. Nell had opened her heart, offering healing, laughter, and companionship. Mia yearned to give her something in return. She had so much to give.

Maybe a family wasn't the one you were born into, but the one you chose.

Maybe Nell would want to be chosen.

Maybe Mia could give her love.

"It's so good to see you happy, Mother. I mean that."

Mia's eyes warmed with tears. She had not expected empathy to well inside her. But when she looked at the woman who had given birth to her, fed and loved and held her every time she cried, she was overcome by compassion. Wynna Rose had been forced to live an impossible life. She had done the best she could with what she had.

"I love you," Mia said softly. "I will always love you. You once told me that love is all that matters in the end. You also told me to trust my heart. And in my heart I know I want to be chosen. You've found a new family. I want to find mine."

Her mother reached out for her. Hands trembling.

"Oh, little raven," Wynna whispered. "My wise girl. My Mia."

The words crashed into a sob. Mia stepped forward and cradled her mother's face. Pressed her forehead to Wynna's.

"Fidacteu zeu biqhotz, Mother." *Trust your heart.* "Thank you for teaching me to trust mine."

Chapter 21

ESPIONAGE

QUIN HAD ALWAYS LOVED the kitchens. Though he found solace at his piano, the library was shrouded in fear and silence. Only the domain of the cooks vibrated with joyous noise. If Kaer Killian touted itself a mausoleum of the dead, the kitchens promised the opposite. They were boisterously, deliciously, unequivocally *alive*.

As a lonely boy, Quin had spent years shadowing the cooks. He was delighted to discover they were among the more loose-lipped servants. They knew Ronan would never darken the doors of the kitchens; thus emboldened, the cooks aired their grievances. They swore constantly, colorful expressions little Quin learned, then parroted with immense pleasure. The swats and scoldings he earned felt more like affection than anything either of his parents bestowed.

He discovered something else, too. The cooks were intimately acquainted with the royals' preferences—not just how burnt they liked their toast or how sweet they liked their tea, but what time they breakfasted, snacked, and supped, and with whom they shared each meal. The subtlest shift in a pattern was hotly debated: If Princess Karri left even the smallest scrap uneaten, she was clearly unwell. King Ronan, on the other hand, hardly ever touched his food; if by chance his plate returned empty, it was a cause for alarm.

Quin was no longer an impish kitchen waif, spouting swear words and conspiring to filch a caramel off the cooling table. But since arriving in the Kaer, he'd dredged up a half-forgotten truth: the cooks held within themselves a glut of information, whether they knew it or not.

"Come to steal our sweets again, have you?"

A pretty brown-eyed girl stirred a saucepan leaking steam. She swept the dark blond hair off her sweaty forehead, scowling at Quin as he tied his apron.

"Don't you have better things to do?" she said.

"I think I'm winning you over, Phoebe. Even if you won't admit it."

After hearing multiple Embers complain about the deplorable food, Quin had devised an ingenious plan. He would offer his culinary talents, endear himself to the cooks—and glean valuable information about the Embers.

That was nearly a month ago. He'd been shocked how quickly

195

they'd said yes. The kitchens were short-staffed and eager to accept his help. He didn't have to work very hard to charm the scullery maids; they were a willing audience, laughing easily at his jokes. Of course his true purpose was to pilfer not sweets but knowledge, to gain a deeper understanding of the Embers and their intentions.

True to form, he had learned a great deal. Maev wanted him dead. Sylvan, on the other hand, argued that the Embers had taken a shine to Quin, and if anything happened to him, they might revolt. "I know you don't want to believe it," Sylvan had said, in a conversation overheard by a maid sent to retrieve dirty plates, "but there are people in this kingdom still loyal to the crown."

When Quin fantasized about the moment he would seize power, he imagined killing Maev first. Or perhaps the greater punishment would be to make her watch as he set fire to any Ember who refused to swear fealty, eaten alive by the knowledge that she had been right all along.

As for Tobin? He was a bit of a mystery. The Embers seemed to both fear and respect him, but no one knew him very well. If Maev wanted Quin's head on a spike and Sylvan insisted they keep it firmly attached to his neck, where did Tobin fall on the question?

"I don't know how anyone can stay out of the kitchens," Quin said, reaching for a wooden mixing spoon, "with such toothsome aromas wafting through the Kaer."

"Others manage," said Phoebe. She was the lone holdout, the

one member of the kitchen staff he hadn't been able to win over. It vexed him.

"As a boy I'd catch a whiff of honey cake rising in the oven, raspberries and sugar and lemon juice melting in a saucepan for the glaze, and I'd trot right into the kitchens like a dog begging for a bone. My favorite cook always let me dip a spoon into the batter."

Phoebe grunted, immune to his charms.

"You'll get sick that way."

She wiped her hands on her apron and went back to stirring.

"Let's play a game," Quin said. "If you could eat anything right now, any dish in all four kingdoms, what would it be?"

She shrugged, tapping her spoon on the steaming pot. "This one."

Quin leaned over the saucepan of white slop, inhaling dramatically. "You'd choose a pot of creamed wheat?"

"It suffices."

"I'm offering you anything in the world, Phee. Any meal you could possibly imagine! Succulent black truffles drenched in a roasted walnut crempog. Or do you prefer sweet? Buttermilk toffee pudding dusted with nutmeg and rimed in pink salt. A chocolate cinnamon mousse served inside a butterfel flambé. This isn't fantasy: I'll actually cook it for you."

"I don't need to be cooked for. And I don't want your fancy food." She handed him the spoon. "I've got vegetables to chop."

She wiped the sweat off her brow and left him to stir the pot.

Quin watched her cross the room. It was late, the kitchens

empty save for the two of them. A moment earlier, he'd felt magnanimous—kingly, even, in his munificence. He really would have cooked her any dish she wanted. Who wouldn't say yes to an offer like that?

As Phoebe reached into a basket and lined up a row of cheerful orange carrots, Quin felt a sharp stab of fury. She should thank him for his kindness. He'd been generous, more than she deserved. He wanted—*needed*—her to look at him with something other than disdain.

Could he enthrall her?

It wasn't the first time he'd asked himself that question. He'd wondered a thousand times on his trek from Luumia if he had the power of enthrallment. The query had been purely intellectual; to his knowledge, he could only conjure fire. Not until now had he felt a physical craving to bend someone else's will to his own.

He stiffened. If he enthralled this scullery maid, he was no better than the men who had bent the will of women for thousands of years, including his own forebears. He felt a burst of pity for the Twisted Sisters. Even Angelyne. She had enthralled him, yes, used her dark magic against him. But enthrallment had arisen as a response to the abuse of power.

And yet. He, too, had suffered abuse. Why should he not also be granted the power of enthrallment to right previous wrongs?

Edgy heat coiled in his fingers. He touched the outside of the saucepan. The metal should have blistered his fingertips, but it felt cool to the touch. It took him a moment to understand why:

his own hands were hotter than the pot.

Quin set the spoon aside. He pressed both palms to the metal. The pan grew warmer, and warmer, every bit of coolness dissolving as the contents churned to a savage boil. A caustic stench pocked the air.

"Your wheat is burning," he called to Phoebe, drawing his hands back into his pockets. "Did you have the heat too high?"

By the time she stood beside him, the creamed wheat had charred completely black, a shroud lying at the bottom of the pan.

Quin walked back to his quarters from the kitchens, his mind alive with revelations.

For the past two months, he had assumed it would be impossible to mask his magic. He couldn't exactly hide an arc of flame, especially if he didn't know how to control it. But in the kitchens, he had performed a subtler kind of magic. Instead of fire, he had transferred heat through a gentle touch.

The look on Phoebe's face had been intoxicating. She knew he had somehow burned her precious wheat, yet had no way to prove it. Glasddirans were taught that only women could be Gwyrach, a lie Zaga and Angelyne had chosen to perpetuate, perhaps because they did not want men to know their own power. Give little boys their fists and their swords—but never magic.

History reshaped itself in Quin's mind. He imagined a kitchen full of boys like him who preferred cooking and the pretending arts to hunting and swordplay, their magic swelling secretly inside them, along with their pervasive terror of looking or acting or loving differently from the way King Ronan believed men should look or act or love.

"I wondered when you'd be back."

He looked up, startled. Tobin was leaning against the door-jamb of Quin's drawing room.

"I almost gave up and went to bed. Maev said you've been spending hours each day in the kitchens. Trying to curry favor with the cooks, I imagine."

"And you've been sending Dom to spy on me."

"Dom is free to do as he likes. As are you."

"Yet evidently you've been watching my every move."

"You're a son of Clan Killian. You were born to be watched." Tobin smiled. "You and I have each been seeking information, in our own ways."

"And here I thought you loved music," Quin muttered, "when your real talent was espionage."

Instinctively they both glanced toward the clavichord—and caught each other doing it. Embarrassed, Quin looked away. It was too easy to imagine Tobin as he'd looked that night, cheeks ruddy from the rai rouj, plunking out the melody they both knew by heart.

Under the plums, if it's meant to be. You'll come to me, under the snow plum tree.

Tobin sighed. "I didn't come here to fight. Truly. Will you walk with me?"

"Where? Has Maev ordered my public execution?"

"She would like nothing better. Lucky for you, I don't answer to Maev."

Quin appraised him. "Where would you have me, then?"

The question kindled the air between them, bright and hot. Just as he'd intended.

Toby's silver eyes gleamed.

"Where I always had you," he said. "In the library."

Chapter 22

SOMETHING TO PUNCH

PILAR HAD NO GREAT love of books. She'd grown up surrounded by her mother's, all disappearing ink and dark magic. Words written by people who were long since dead.

But lately she'd been poking around the House library when she wasn't sparring. Stone still came to the Gymnasia—and now Shay came too. "Mumma thinks I'm in the Creation Studio," she said, gleeful. "I told her I can't channel my full creative abundance if she's watching. She'll believe anything if you put it the right way."

Stone and Shay had started bringing friends. Day after day, more new recruits piled into the Gymnasia, eager to learn to fight. Some loved the House. They met all kinds of interesting people. Others hated it. They'd been dragged there by their parents, forced to give up their friends. They resented being told how to heal, or that they needed to be healed at all.

Pilar liked those pupils best. She understood them. Her students' hunger made her want to do better. *Be* better. Teach them to protect themselves not just with their fists, but with their minds.

The problem was, her recruits were rapidly outpacing her. Especially Shay. That girl was born to fight. So Pilar had started going to the library to dig up new tricks, new techniques. Even when she wasn't sparring, she was thinking about sparring. She loved it.

She was also tired as four hells.

Sometimes she thought of going to the Orkhestra. Picking up a violin. Blowing off steam. But she always talked herself out of it. If that troupe of child lute players was still hanging around, they'd ask her how long she'd been playing or where she learned. No one deserved to know those things. It was easier to hole up on a ratty library sofa and read about how to break someone's nose.

"Oh. I'm sorry, I . . ."

Pilar looked up to see Mia Rose lurking in the doorway, a satchel slung over her shoulder. Blinking like a startled deer.

"I just . . . I was looking for Nell. I never thought you'd be in the library! I can go."

"No. Stay." Pilar dropped her book. Rose winced as the spine hit the floor. "If you want."

To Pilar's surprise, she meant it. Training the recruits—her brood, as she sometimes thought of them—had put her in a good mood. She knew she hadn't been kind to Mia. But maybe they could start over. Maybe it wasn't too late.

Rose sat uneasily at the other end of the sofa, placing her satchel beside her. After a moment, she said, "What are you reading?"

"A book on fighting. You wouldn't like it."

"I tend to like most books."

Mia scooped it off the floor. Turned to a random page and pretended to read.

Pilar found it endearing. She was trying, at least.

"Nell told me your mother was here."

"Still is, last I heard."

"Did you see her?"

"Yes." Mia gave up on the book and set it aside. "She and the Snow Queen came to the House to enlist help and gather resources. When I saw my mother in the palace, she had no interest in saving the world. I guess that's changed. They're going back to Luumia to rebuild."

"Who would want to rebuild that hellshole?"

"My mother and Freyja, I guess. I think the queen really is trying to set things right." Mia shook her head. "Listen to me, defending the woman who stole my mother."

"Maybe your mother needed to be stole."

Mia coughed. Said something under her breath.

"What was that?" Pilar said.

"Nothing."

"Tell me."

"It's really nothing."

"If you don't—"

"It's *stolen*. Not *stole*. *Stolen* is the past participle of *steal*."

Pilar groaned. Rose really was impossible.

"Quin did that too. Corrected my speech with his princely grammar."

"Yes." Mia smiled sadly. "I teased him about that myself."

They were both quiet. Quin was uncharted terrain.

"Do you ever think about him?" Pilar asked.

Mia shifted on the sofa. "All the time. I think about things he said or his clever little turns of phrase. He could be quite funny. Don't *you* think about him?"

"No," she lied.

"You spent more time with him than I did. You . . ." Rose blushed bright red. "You did a lot more things with him than I did."

How could Pilar make Mia understand? Sure, she and Quin had been intimate. And she wouldn't lie: it had felt terrific. But now when she thought of their time together, she realized she hadn't really known him. She'd been so busy mooning over him she hadn't seen him at all.

"Neither you or me knew him all that long," she said. "Or that well."

"He was a victim of Angelyne, just like we all were."

Pilar frowned. "You forget that he did try to kill us."

"Are you going to keep being angry with him? Even though

205

he's dead?" Mia let out a long, frustrated sigh. "You're stubborn, Pil. So am I. But there's a difference between stubborn and recalcitrant. My father used to say that when a donkey—"

"He's my father, too."

Mia stared at her, surprised. But not as surprised as Pilar. The words had appeared on her tongue with no warning. *My father.* Almost wistful. As if she'd ever want a father like that.

Griffin Rose, the Snow Wolf. Assassin of Dujia.

"So." Mia rearranged the pillow behind her. "What do you think of Nell's father?"

An obvious segue to a safer topic. Pilar shrugged.

"He's nice."

Stone had dragged her to the family sfeera on her second day, thrilled to introduce them. Lord Shadowess was the spitting image of Stone, just older. Pilar had never seen a family look so much alike.

In her periphery, she studied Mia's curly red hair, freckled white skin, gray eyes. Thought of her own straight black hair, olive skin, brown eyes. No one would believe they were half sisters.

"Lord Shadowess is a gentle man," Mia said. "I've been getting to know him in the Curatorium. He treats every creature with kindness. He says when he's entrusted with the care of another living soul, they all become his children."

Pilar folded her arms over her chest. "I heard plenty about fathers on Refúj. Girls either hated them because they were violent, or missed them because they were kind."

She picked at the scabs on her knuckles. They were still healing from when she'd beaten the sandbag to a bloody pulp. Once she got back to the Gymnasia, she'd rewrap them.

"Either way, fathers did more harm than good. I survived just fine without one."

She could feel Mia staring. Judging. Probably not believing.

"The thing about my father," Mia said slowly, "*our* father, was that he set impossibly high standards. He'd get cross when I was slow to absorb a concept. Once during a history lesson, he said, 'You're smarter than this, Mia.' Not 'little rose.' He called me Mia when I disappointed him. I still remember how fiercely my heart palpitated. '*You're smarter than this, Mia.*'"

"You?" Pilar shuddered. "Slow to absorb a concept?"

"I'm trying to be vulnerable, you know, and you're not making it any easier."

Pilar squirmed. Why was it so much easier to jeer than to sit quietly and listen?

She uncrossed her arms.

"You're right," she muttered. "Sorry, Rose."

"What I was going to say is that Father could also be tender in unexpected ways. I know you never knew him, but on our birthdays he would slip chocolate sparrows beneath our pillows. Once he surprised Mother with a picnic. He told Angie and me stories from his most recent trip to Fojo, a real treat. He so rarely talked about his travels."

Because he was off killing Dujia, Pilar wanted to say. *Off murdering women like me.*

207

"When I saw my mother in the snow palace," Mia went on, "she told me Father was racked with guilt over what he did. That he'd been trying to make reparations for years."

"He said as much to me on the Snow Queen's ship."

"You're so lucky you got to see him." Mia smiled sadly. "I like to imagine he's sailing the four kingdoms at this very moment, helping the people he used to hurt. And that someday, the three of us will meet again."

Pilar said nothing. For all her posturing, she wanted to believe it, too.

But she only shrugged. Such a handy reflex. A shrug said, *Whatever you are telling me can't hurt me. I refuse to let it in.*

"And now my mother wants to make reparations. She invited me to come back to the snow kingdom. Said I had a home with her and Freyja. A family."

"Why didn't you say yes?"

Mia smiled. "Because I'm making a new family. Right here."

Hope rose in Pilar's chest. What would it be like to have a sister? A *real* sister, bound by blood, not magic. She used to dream about it. Even before Orry came, she'd never fit with the other girls on Refúj. She'd been lonely. So lonely. After she started picking fights with different Dujia in the merqad, they went out of their way to avoid her.

Maybe that was why none of her sisters had stood by her after Morigna lied. Maybe if Pilar hadn't been so prickly, so hard to love, they would have believed her.

You didn't deserve what happened. It wasn't your fault.

"I'm learning so much here," Mia said, glowing. "The sort of work we're doing in the Curatorium? It's magical. But not *just* magical. That's the thing. The Curateurs integrate science and magic. And the Shadowess is teaching me how to use breath to calm my mind, which helps control my magic. I healed Quin twice in the forest. But his sister . . ." She swallowed. "I tried to heal Karri. But I didn't know enough about my own magic. It left me susceptible to . . ."

"My mother," Pilar finished. "It's all right. You can say it."

Mia nodded. "Zaga was able to twist my ability to heal into an ability to kill. Just like Angelyne twisted the healing magic in the moonstone. They turned something beautiful into something ugly. I want to turn it back."

"Where are you going with all of this, Rose?" Pilar asked, suspicious.

"Remember how Nell told us the House was built on an ancient power source with all the natural elements in perfect balance? That's why magic works differently here. It sort of . . . levels things out. It makes it harder to hurt people. Of course it also makes it harder to heal people, which is why we use stones. Magic essentially becomes a system of checks and balances. That way no one abuses their power."

"People like Celeste abuse their power."

Mia sighed. "Celeste isn't so bad once you get to know her."

"I don't *want* to get to know her. I've known women like that."

"I wish you'd stop thinking every place is like Refúj," Mia

said, an edge to her words. "You're not on the island anymore. Move past it."

Pilar went completely still. Rose clearly didn't want to wade yet again through Pilar's troubled past. As if she weren't sick of wading there herself.

"Pilar, you're bleeding!" Mia said, aghast. "What did you do to your knuckles?"

Pilar looked down. She'd been picking her scabs again.

"I used them to punch things."

"That blood is fresh. It looks painful. Hold on." Mia fumbled something from her satchel. "I'm going to make it better."

When she opened her fingers, a pearly white orb sat in the center of her palm.

Pilar jumped off the sofa. Palms sweating. Heart racing. All she could see was Quin's pouch with Angelyne's moonstone inside.

"Where did you get that?" she hissed.

"From the Curatorium," Mia said. "It's lloira. We use it to heal—"

"I know what it is. I've obviously seen a moonstone before."

"It's all right, Pilar. I'm not Angie. Look."

Mia stood. With her free hand, she probed at the moonstone— and it changed shape. It wasn't stone at all. A cone of white cream clung to Rose's fingertip.

"It's ointment," she explained. "It can stop bleeding almost instantly. We grind the lloira down to a fine powder and blend it with two other elixirs."

Mia reached for her bleeding hand.

Pilar reeled back.

"If I wanted to heal my knuckles," she spat, "I'd heal them. If I wanted to use magic, I'd use magic. You don't get to tell me all the ways I'm broken."

"I wouldn't have to," Mia shot back, "if you'd admit it yourself."

"Look at that," said a voice behind them. "Two sisters, studying quietly together in the library. Who'd have thought?"

Nelladine stood in the doorway. From the look on her face, she'd heard everything.

"I came in here looking for *you*, Nell," said Mia, and Pilar felt her twist the blade. "I know your hands get dry and cracked from throwing clay all day. So I've been blending lloira powder with various tinctures, and your favorite fragrances, until I finally got it right."

She held out her palm. Gray eyes dewy. Full of hope.

Pilar kicked herself. Mia's "new family" had nothing to do with her. Rose didn't want to be a sister. She wanted to be in love.

Nell paused a second longer than Pilar expected.

"That's very sweet, Mia, that's lovely. Thank you for thinking of me." Nell reached out tentatively and dipped a finger into the ointment. Brought it to her nose. "It does smell nice. I was actually on my way to the Creation Studio, maybe later we could—"

"I'll join you!" Mia cried.

Nell hesitated, then turned to Pilar.

"Would you like to come, too?"

Rose laughed. "Have you *met* Pilar d'Aqila? She doesn't want to come to the Creation Studio! She'd rather go punch things."

"Even clay needs a strong, steady hand. How about it, Pil?"

There was a note of desperation in Nell's voice. Pilar had no idea why.

Frankly, she didn't care.

"No thanks." She wiped the blood off her knuckles. "Better go find something to punch."

Chapter 23

THE PRETENDING ARTS

THE KAER SEEMED SOMEHOW emptier with Tobin by his side. Quin couldn't explain it. Perhaps it was the knowledge of how freely their banter had once flowed, so different from the heavy silence enrobing the space between them.

He slowed his pace. Through the loop windows he could see the grove of snow plum trees, silvered by the first frost. He wondered if, when the late Luumi queen bequeathed a thousand trees to King Ronan, she had ever imagined he would plant them above the crypt to "grow fat on the flesh of the dead."

Quin grimaced. Even his father's gardening was predicated on subjugation.

You'll come to me, under the snow plum tree.

He glanced at Tobin. The memory chafed.

The day it all ended had started like any other day. He'd walked into the library for his morning music lesson to find Tobin already at the upright piano, a slice of sunlight glinting off his unruly mop of hair. He was so beautiful it made Quin ache.

"Do you remember," Tobin said, hearing him approach, "the first song I taught you?"

"As if I could forget."

"Play it for me."

For weeks the air between them had crackled with tension. Quin knew Toby felt it, too. In the past he had often entered the library to find his music teacher pacing, fingers drumming a soft rhythm against his thighs. Tobin's sharp silver eyes always shone a little brighter when he was composing a new song, teetering on the cusp of some fresh, sweet melody—and now they shone the same way when Quin walked into a room. It made his knees go soft.

"Remind me of the chords?" he asked innocently.

"You've played them a hundred times!" Toby teased.

"I suspect I might need a hundred more until they stick."

"Then come." Tobin patted the bench. "I'll show you."

They always had to be so careful, so painfully careful, not to touch each other. But at the piano they had a reason to be skin to skin.

Quin eased himself down on the bench, their arms pressed close. He forced himself to breathe. Toby slid his left hand over Quin's right.

"Like this. Remember?"

The gooseflesh pricked from wrist to shoulder, a symphony of tiny bumps sweeping over his nape. Tobin leaned in, his mouth an inch from Quin's ear.

"You'll come to me," he whispered, pressing both their fingers into the keys as the chord thrummed beneath them. "Under the snow plum tree."

Every part of Quin's body sprang to life.

Abruptly, Tobin withdrew his hand.

"Keep practicing," he said quickly. "I have no doubt you'll find your way."

He rose from the bench and hurried out of the library.

Quin was trembling. He knew, instinctively, that this was more than a song.

It was an invitation.

Three years later, Quin and Tobin entered the library side by side. In the eastern alcove, the upright stood like a quiet sentinel, its satiny black veneer bathed in silver moonlight. Quin had avoided the library since his return to the Kaer—had avoided this whole wing, in fact. But the sight of the piano comforted him.

"It was remarkably dusty," Tobin said, "and regrettably out of tune. It's been a while since you played."

Quin heard the note of reproach in his former teacher's voice.

"I've been fairly preoccupied. Nearly dying, being enthralled, discovering a band of insurgents in my castle—that sort of thing."

"Any musician who lets his instrument go out of tune—"

"Loves his own vanity more than his music. Yes, I know."

Tobin walked toward the piano. He brushed off the bench before easing himself onto it. Dust motes spun into a shaft of starlight.

"Sit," he instructed. "Like old times."

Quin's heart was pounding. He couldn't tell if he was frightened or aroused.

"You and I both know the old times are over, Toby."

"In some ways, yes. In others, no."

Tobin lifted the fall board, the hinges squeaking, and propped it up gently. His right hand hovered over the keys. Three fingers where there had once been five. It hurt to see the damage Ronan had wrought. He had stripped Toby of his greatest gift—and Quin had let him. He had watched his father mutilate the boy he loved as he cowered, craven, behind a tomb.

A deep, rich E-flat reverberated through the library.

Quin did not expect what came next.

Tobin's hand burst into fluid motion. His three fingers stretched over the keys, crossing over one another in a wild and elegant dance. Swiftly, confidently, he wove the notes into a triple arpeggio that flourished into a cadenza, a solo so virtuosic it rivaled a sonata. The melody echoed through the dark, neglected room, swirling life into the dust motes. Out of tune, the notes made for an eerie, atonal melody. As if a sanguine love ballad had been transposed to a minor key.

Quin remembered how he'd felt the first time he watched Tobin play, not coincidentally the first time he suspected the

216

expression *falling in love* might be more than just a turn of phrase. It struck him as a movement more than a feeling, the sensation of falling from a hard place into something softer.

A conversation with his favorite cook came back to him. "Careful," she'd told him, when as a boy he'd pined for yet another servant girl. "You've a tender heart, love, but don't offer it so freely. Every time someone breaks that sweet heart of yours, they'll take a piece with them."

How right she'd been. Quin fell in love with everyone, and each time hurt worse than the time before. They always left him in the end. And yet he learned nothing.

Even now, standing beside the piano, his hope mingled with the rising notes. Would he ever stop wanting someone to love him?

The cadenza ended on the note where it began. As E-flat slowly faded, Toby's hand came to rest in his lap.

"Does it surprise you?" he said. "That I can still play?"

Quin hesitated. It *did* surprise him. After what his father had done, he'd assumed Tobin would only ever be able to plunk out a few meager notes—or, devastated by the butchery, would never play again.

"I've never needed pity, Quin. Not yours or anyone's. When someone takes something from you, you adapt. That's the only way to take it back."

Quin thought of the Twisted Sisters and all they had taken from him. He had adapted, too. Not just the magic in his body, but the fury in his heart.

He sank onto the bench beside Tobin. It was muscle memory more than anything. Or so he told himself. He left a healthy space between them, careful their arms did not touch.

"I'm sorry, Toby."

"Sympathy is a worthless fuel."

"On that we're agreed. No king has ever built a kingdom on sympathy. There are times violence must meet violence if justice is to prevail."

"Are you ready to stand by that, son of Clan Killian? Because I know what you've been playing at. You've been observing us, gathering information, ingratiating yourself with the Embers. You're pretending, just like you always have."

The muscles in Quin's jaw tautened. He willed himself calm. What did it matter if Toby guessed the game? He had still succeeded in teasing out the pressure points and weak spots among the Embers.

"Let me ask you this," Tobin said. "I know you think that once you have what you need, you will strike. But are you *really* ready to use violence?"

Quin set his jaw. "I am."

"Even against those of us who oppose you?"

"From where I sit, the opposition diminishes every day."

"You have found loyalists among the Embers, true. But you will also find dissenters. And once your duplicity is revealed, you will find even more. Are you prepared to kill people to reclaim the throne? Domeniq? Me? Your darling little Brialli Mar, who loves you so?"

Quin hesitated. Tobin saw it.

"Forgive me, but I don't believe you. I don't believe *you* believe you. You've summoned the sisters back to Glas Ddir with threats of violence, but you'll never harm them. I think you loved Mia and Pilar the same way you loved me, and your heart will always succumb to love before it succumbs to hate. You will never be your father's son."

"I don't want to be my father," Quin growled. "I want to be better."

"Your sister was better. Karri would have been the kind of ruler you could never be. She was better at swords and war games. But she was kinder than you, too. She knew how to listen to her people. To *truly* listen, not quietly feed their fears and longings into some manipulative scheme."

It was a low blow. Tobin had inflamed Quin's grief—and used his dead sister against him.

"Have you wondered why we've kept you alive, Quin? Why we have allowed you to saunter about the castle the last month, fervidly taking notes, cooking soup and eavesdropping?"

Quin's pulse kicked up a notch. "Because I vowed to fight against tyranny."

"Do you think we are so easily misled? To believe a tyrant when he vows to fight tyranny?" Tobin's laugh was sharp and brittle. "Some of the Embers bought into your deception. They're clinging to the belief that the last heir of Clan Killian might be worthy of their loyalty. That he might *not* uphold a reign of death and terror. On that last point I do not disagree. I think you are

219

incapable of inspiring terror. Those of us in charge never once considered you a threat."

Quin swallowed. "But Maev—"

"Maev despises you. She told me to slit your throat the night you arrived, before any of the Embers grew too attached. But Sylvan and I convinced her you were more useful to us alive. You are a bargaining chip. The more the kingdom loves you, the more leverage we have."

Toby straightened.

"Since the moment I found you in the tavern, you have been our prisoner, not our guest. With every attempt you've made to woo the Embers, you've only given us more power. Our revolution is far stronger than you could ever be."

Quin's blood boiled.

"This isn't a revolution," he spat. "It's a bunch of drunkards pretending to have power."

"If anyone has mastered the pretending arts, *Your Grace*, it's you."

Quin hated that Tobin was right. Hated that, after a lifetime of hiding in Kaer Killian, he was once again mincing about, trying to be liked, wanting to be loved—and repressing who he truly was. He finally had real power, and he was too frightened to use it. No matter how hard he tried to eradicate his weakness, it clung to him like a second skin.

He stood, shoving the piano bench back so forcefully Tobin sprang to his feet.

"I don't have to pretend anything. This is *my* castle. I am not a prisoner. I am a king."

"No, Quin. You're still the soft and spineless prince you always were. Last I checked, you had neither the grit nor the prowess to reclaim a kingdom, let alone lead it."

In one swift motion, Quin snapped the fallboard shut. The wood landed with a hollow thud, sealing the keys inside. He pressed his hands to the glossy black veneer. Then he summoned every smoldering spark of hurt and rage and shame.

The piano burst into flames.

Tobin stumbled back. Mouth agape, eyes asking the inevitable question.

"Yes," Quin said. "I have magic."

His cheeks blazed from the heat. The piano made for perfect kindling: the wood popped and crackled as smoke coated the air. Soon the library's books would catch fire, igniting thousands of years of history, page after page of hate and death and tyranny. All the finest jewels of his inheritance.

"I've seen your symbols in the woods, Toby. *Remember the Embers*. Your desperate attempt to leave your mark. I know you carve your sad little flames wherever you commit violence."

Quin smiled.

"I, unlike you, do not require a knife."

Chapter 24

FREELY GIVEN

MIA COULDN'T SLEEP. SHE turned and tossed, unable to get comfortable. Outside her sfeera window, she could hear the streets of Shabeeka pulsing with energy from the Pearl Moon Festival. Surely someone was awake in Manuba Vivuli, too.

She threw her green dressing gown over her shoulders and wandered out into the hall.

Mia loved the House at night. The moon sent fulgent beams through the domed glass ceiling, planting a forest of shadows on the walls. She found herself thinking, as she so often did, of Nelladine.

They had yet to kiss. Yet to do anything, really. But Mia didn't mind. Every moment they spent together was precious, and she wanted to savor them. Nell had given her more than anyone ever had. She'd taught Mia about magic and brought her to the House, then shared her parents so generously. Nell was always there to offer a word of encouragement or a warm embrace.

Whenever Mia wasn't in the Curatorium or the Shadowess's working chambers, she was with Nelladine. Watching her throw clay. Eating the delicious new Pembuka foods Nell introduced her to. Imagining how Nell's lips would feel against hers.

Now Mia glided down the corridor, slippers swishing softly over the glass. She knew where she was going. Her pace slowed outside the Creation Studio, where she heard a low, whirring hum. She peered through the open door.

Just as she'd hoped, one of the potter's wheels was in motion, a mound of wet clay at its heart. Nell's head bowed over the wheel, her black braids pulled back at her nape. Moonlight spilled over her hair and bare shoulders. Although the room was cool, her brown skin glistened with sweat. The muscles in her arms were lean and sculpted, biceps curved into a neat figure eight.

Mia inched closer to the wheel, hoping to go unnoticed. She'd whiled away countless hours sitting in the Creation Studio, watching Nell's strong hands deftly shape the clay, coaxing it up into a cone, then smoothing it down into a disc, her long fingers stained a pale liquid gray. It reminded Mia of how her bloodbloom charm expanded, then shrank back down.

Nell's version was better. As she pulled and pressed, a bowl emerged from the clay.

"So you couldn't sleep, either," Nell said, without looking up.

"And here I thought I was being so furtive."

"You can hear everything in here, it's always echoey. Pull up a stool."

Mia claimed the stool to Nell's left. It came with its own pottery wheel, which lay still and quiet.

"These stools are rather short, aren't they?"

"You want your hips at the height of the wheel. It's easy to strain your back muscles when your posture isn't right, that took me a long time to learn." Nell pushed a pedal with her foot and her wheel stopped spinning. "You want to sit like this."

She planted her feet on either side of the wheel, a wide, bold stance. Then she dug her elbows into the spots where her groin met her hip bones, leaning over the wheel with her back flat, forearms resting comfortably on her thighs.

"You need to be strong to throw. Nobody ever thinks that. They assume it's all about making something pretty, and I want to make beautiful pieces, of course I do. But I want to make strong pieces, too, ones that will survive a long time, and to do that you have to be strong yourself."

Again Mia's eyes were drawn to the elegant curve of Nell's biceps. Or were those her triceps? Mia's pulse quickened. Had she really just conflated basic anatomy?

"Throwing makes me feel powerful. I love *Maysha* more than life itself, but I feel powerless on the ocean, and that's the charm of it, the fact that I don't know what's coming. The sea is a goddess and I serve her whims. Throwing makes *me* feel like the goddess, like I'm breathing life into something that was dead."

She smiled. "You know a bit about that."

Mia stared at the empty wheel in front of her.

"The elixir has been amazing, Nell. I feel so much more now. But there are still times . . ." She hesitated. "Times I think I'm not entirely alive."

Nell took her hand, sending a thrill up her arm. She pressed a fingertip to the frostflower on Mia's wrist. The fyre ink pulsed and churned.

"There," Nell said. "A sign of life."

She removed her hand, leaving Mia's wrist smudged with wet clay, her skin vibrating.

Nell had touched her, just like she wanted. Mia felt most alive when they were skin to skin. Even Nell's presence was intoxicating. But it also left Mia with a growing desperation; Nell had given her so much, and she'd given Nell so little.

"How are you liking the lloira ointment?" she asked. "Is it keeping your hands soft?"

"It's very nice, thank you. You didn't have to do that."

"I wanted to. You've shared so much with me. I don't know how I can ever repay you."

Nervous, Mia smoothed a fold in her dressing gown.

"I've been working on a muscle cream, too. I just thought, on the days you're in here for hours . . ."

"I appreciate it, Mia."

Nell straightened, twisting her torso one way, then the other. She tipped her head toward Mia's wheel.

"Want to take it for a spin?"

"Gods, no! I wouldn't even know where to begin."

"You've spent so many hours in here, countless hours, watching me. I think it's time *you* try. I know you have an artistic eye, I see you drawing in your notebook."

"I'm a scientist, not an artist. My sketches are anatomical in nature. I can render a human heart with excellent precision, but that's another thing entirely."

"Think of clay as a heart, then. It's just as malleable"—Nell smiled—"and just as easy to break."

The log of clay was heavy. When Mia hoisted it onto the butcher block, Nell wielded a thin, sharp wire, slicing a hearty slab off the loaf.

"You want to get out all the air pockets so it doesn't explode in the kiln. Have you heard of clay memory? You can have a ball of clay that looks absolutely perfect, not an air pocket in sight. But there are things *inside* the clay, little flaws and impurities no one can see. Clay remembers everything."

She slammed the clay down hard, shoved it roughly forward, then lifted it off the block. Slam, shove, lift. Slam, shove, lift. The movement was mesmerizing. On it went, until the clay looked vaguely like a ram's head.

Nell reshaped the ram's head into a perfect round orb, then handed it to Mia.

"Now we throw."

A fringe of sweat had broken out at Mia's hairline. On the boat when Nell had tried to teach her to sail, she'd done nothing but humiliate herself. Now here was the other thing Nell loved, one she so clearly wanted to share. What if Mia bungled that, too?

"Throw your clay in the middle of the wheel. It'll spin counterclockwise, and your hands go clockwise. Always keep them nice and wet, that's important. If it gets too dry your hands will stutter, and you don't want to fight the clay. You're on the same side."

Nell had restarted her own wheel. She dipped her fingers into a blue bucket of water. Newly wet, her bowl turned from light gray to dark. She demonstrated how to glide her hands clockwise over the slippery surface, fingers curled loosely around the top.

Mia threw her ball of clay and felt a flush of pleasure: it landed at the wheel's perfect center. Maybe this wouldn't be so hard. She wet her hands and cupped her fingers.

And thus began her embarrassing attempt at bowl making.

Her first lump of clay went flying off the wheel. Her second lasted longer, but when she tried to "draw up the walls," the clay rose with frightening alacrity into a hideous, lopsided bowl.

"It's all right." Nell slid her wire around the top of Mia's monstrosity, peeling off a sad, limp ribbon of clay. "There you go, a clean slate."

Ten seconds later, the clean slate had turned once again into a hideous, lopsided bowl.

"You're holding on too tight. Press down with the heels of your palms, but keep your fingers loose. The clay doesn't like to be constricted, remember, it wants to breathe."

Mia tried to hold her clay the same way Nell did: like an

extension of her own hands. But just when she thought she'd mastered it, the bowl would collapse on itself, or she'd forget to add water and her dry hands would trip along the rim, the flesh of her palms burning. For months she'd missed feeling pain. Now she wasn't so sure.

"Mia." Nell had stopped her own wheel. "It's all right, it's your very first time."

Mia's cheeks were hot with humiliation. The fact that Nell was being so damn *nice* somehow made it worse.

She had a sudden flicker of memory: trying to make a lean-to in the Twisted Forest, failing miserably, while Quin sat on a tree trunk making acerbic asides. She missed his sarcasm. Nell was many things, but sarcastic was not one of them.

Mia's bowl collapsed. Naturally.

Nell pulled her own stool up behind her, slid her arms down Mia's arms and her hands over Mia's hands.

"Like this. Press down harder until you've centered it. Only once it's centered will it become what it's meant to be."

Mia held her breath. Nell's curves pressed against her back, soft and warm, the inside of her thighs brushing the outside of Mia's. For all the bodily sensations returned to her, she only felt this kind of melting heat when they touched.

How was she supposed to think about clay bowls? She could smell the shea butter in Nell's braids. The sweetness of Nell's sweat.

Mia wanted to kiss her. She'd wanted to forever. She turned her body, leaning into Nelladine—and heard the screech of metal as Nell shoved her stool back and stood, abruptly.

"Mia."

She didn't understand the look on Nell's face. Was it exasperation? Anger?

"I—I'm sorry," Mia stammered. "I thought—"

"I can't fix you, all right? I know that's what you think, that I'm some kind of . . . elixir."

"No," Mia said vehemently, though in a way she *had* been thinking it. "That's not true. It's just, when I'm with you, the way I feel . . ." She searched for the perfect words to make Nell understand. "I feel whole. Like I'm alive again."

"That doesn't mean I feel the same way."

Mia's mind was spinning faster than her wheel. Nell tapped the pedal and the wheel came to a stop.

"Do you even see me?" Nell said. "Or do you just see what you need me to be?"

Mia faltered. "I . . . I'm not sure what you mean."

"Have you noticed anything different about me since we got back to the House?"

"You seem . . . happy? I can tell you're glad to be back with your family. And you're making pottery again, spending hours each day creating beautiful things."

"Has it occurred to you I might spend hours a day throwing clay as a way to escape?"

Mia was dumbfounded. It had not occurred to her.

"It's too much, being back, coming home after all these years. It's overwhelming. And I knew it would be, I expected that. But

I thought it would be different, that *I* would be different, and the problem is, I'm exactly the same. And no one's even noticed."

Nell took a deep breath.

"When I was a little girl, I felt *everything*. Big things, small things, happy, sad. But I felt them differently from other people. The littlest things broke me. Once I went to visit Pappa in the Curatorium. He was trying to heal a kitten who'd been abused by her owners, starved and left for dead. But he couldn't save her. She died in his arms. I started sobbing. I sobbed for two days straight."

"So you're empathic. There's nothing wrong with that."

"There *is* something wrong with that, when you're drowning in your own empathy. Mumma said emotions are like waves: they ebb and flow, and we can learn to ride them, to breathe through them until we arrive safely on the other side.

"But I couldn't ride them. For me they weren't pleasant waves rolling in and out to sea, they were storms that left me on some distant shore, gasping for breath. I started absorbing other people's feelings, too. I'd sense their anger or sadness, and that became all I could see. Their feelings were unbearable, and I felt somehow responsible, like I could save them, and then all I could think about was making them feel better. Even if it made me feel worse."

Nell stared at her hands. The clay was already drying, encrusting her fingers in pale gray.

"Then my brother started struggling. He was so little, and so sad, and no one could figure out why. He'd be fine one minute, and then the light would just . . . go out of his eyes.

"I was angry. Angry at Mumma and Pappa, that they couldn't help Stone. I stormed into the circle one day when Mumma was leading it and shouted, 'Aren't you supposed to heal people?' After that the other residents gave me a wide berth. I heard Celeste in the Rose Garden once, talking to two residents, back before she was the Keeper. 'Can you imagine?' she said. 'Someone like the Shadowess having a daughter like *that*.'"

Nell let out a long, shuddering sigh.

"During my worst episodes, the ones where I truly felt out of control, I fantasized about what it would be like to go to Prisma and forget everything. To forget how much pain I took on, both my own and other people's. Once I even packed a bag and got as far as the Bridge. I didn't go any farther, because I couldn't leave my brother. I didn't want him to feel alone.

"But then, after a while, I knew I couldn't stay at the House, either, with everyone tiptoeing around, judging me, waiting for me to fall apart. My brother was doing better, he was thriving, and I knew he could survive without me, while I was growing less stable by the day.

"So one night I took the bag I'd packed for Prisma . . . and I went to Pata Pacha instead. I steered *Maysha* all the way to White Lagoon. I found a potter's wheel. My pieces were good, it didn't take long to find patrons. I did what I loved, and I was happy. I had romances, friends. Away from the House, I felt like I could hold on to who I was, maybe because I got to *re-create* who I was. No one knew me. In Luumia I had a fresh start. I could make space around me, which I'd never done. If someone needed too much, I could take a step back. But since being here . . ."

She shook her head.

"I thought I was stronger. That I would be able to maintain my own boundaries and, if I needed to, pull back, step away, take care of myself. But the opposite has happened. It's like I've turned into the person I always was. Worse, maybe, because now the four kingdoms are crumbling down around us, everyone is so afraid. I can't hold on to myself, can't feel my own emotions anymore, because I'm too busy feeling everyone else's."

Mia struggled to process all this. "But Stone seems so happy. They all seem so happy."

"I know you think we're this big, happy, perfect family. But there are no perfect families. We have wounds and failings and betrayals, just like you. But also . . ."

Nell took a breath.

"I'm not just talking about them, Mia. I'm talking about *you*."

All the saliva in Mia's mouth evaporated. She stared at Nelladine. Stupefied.

"Since the moment you stepped onto *Maysha*," Nell began, "I've done nothing but take care of you. I'll admit it's partly my fault. I'm always so ready to take on someone else's suffering, to make myself responsible for their pain. So I brought you to Mumma here at the House. To Pappa in the Curatorium. I tried to help you taste and smell and feel all the things, even let you come in here and watch me throw. It made you happy, and it made me happy that you were happy, even though sometimes I just wanted to be alone. I didn't need the ointment, Mia, my hands are fine.

I've been throwing clay for a long time, I know how to take care of myself. But I took it from you, because you needed to give it to me. I've taken all your joy and hope, but also your fears and disappointments. And somewhere in there, *I* stopped existing."

Nell's brown eyes filled with tears.

"I'm tired, Mia. So tired. I just can't do it anymore."

"Please." Mia groped for the right words, panic rising inside her. "Please don't go to Prisma. I'll be better at listening to you, *seeing* you. I know I've been selfish. But I promise I won't fail you again, Nell. It's what I'm best at: taking care of the people I love."

The word had come out in spite of herself. *Love.*

"Great sands, Mia. It's not about failing me! It's not about failing at all. That's part of the problem, how you see everything in terms of failure or success. I don't want to hurt you, but I don't want to lie to you, either. I should have said all this weeks ago. I'm sorry I didn't."

Nell forced the air out of her mouth.

"You say you take care of people, and in a way, you do. You threw yourself into protecting Angie, but you never really saw her. Now it's happening again with Pilar. You think if you can fix her, *save* her, then it'll give your life purpose. But in saving them, you expect it to save *you*. It's not really about the person: it's about being needed by them. You don't recognize yourself unless you're 'saving' someone—which means you don't really know who you are."

Nell's eyes locked onto Mia's.

"That's not love, Mia. Not *real* love. If I'm being honest, I'm not entirely convinced you know what love is. At least not the kind that's freely given, freely shared. Love is what happens when two people come together as equals, each with their own painful history and gifts and failings, neither of them needing to be saved."

Silence clotted the air between them. Mia was folding in on herself. Soon she would collapse onto the wheel, flattened. Cracked.

The sound of footsteps echoed through the Creation Studio. Someone was running down the corridor.

Fine. Let them come. Anything would be better than this.

"Rose?"

Pilar materialized in the doorway, silhouetted against the glass. She was panting.

"I ran all the way to your sfeera. Should've known you'd be here instead. A courier just came from the river kingdom."

She held out a piece of parchment, clenched tightly in her fist.

"He brought a letter for you and me. It isn't good."

Mia stood. Heart racing.

"A letter from whom?"

"Quin."

Chapter 25

DISAPPEARED

In the end, it was shockingly easy.

"Tell everyone what you've seen here," Quin told Tobin, as they left the library. The acrid reek of scorched piano filled the castle corridors: burnt wood, burnt ivory, burnt books. "I want all the Embers in the Grand Gallery within the half hour."

Tobin nodded stiffly. He'd said nothing since Quin ordered half a dozen Embers to douse the raging flames. The piano was ruined, of course, reduced to a pile of smoldering ash, as was a considerable portion of the Kaer's library. It gave Quin a perverse satisfaction to know that the plays he'd devoured, not to mention the histories he'd once found comfort in, were gone. Vestiges of a life he'd rather not remember. A *self* he'd rather not remember.

"Do not defy me," Quin said to Tobin, his voice low. "Or you will pay the price."

"Liar."

Maev accosted Quin as he strode into the Gallery. Tobin had gathered the Embers; he now sat among them at the low slab tables. They were silent, watchful, so different from the raucous horde Quin had met when he first returned to the Kaer, carousing around their makeshift bar.

Maev, however, was not seated. She stood in the center of the Gallery, fuming. Strands of thin white hair had come loose around her face.

"Tell them," she said, pointing at the Embers. "Tell them how you lied."

"I am not the one on trial."

"I should never have let you come here. We fed you, treated you like one of ours." She shook her head in disgust. "I swore on my mother's grave that if I ever met a Killian face to face—"

"You will be silent." He looked coldly out at the room. "The Kaer is my home. The crown is my birthright. I am Quin, son of Clan Killian, the uncontested king of Glas Ddir."

"We don't want your bloody crown," Maev spat. "It's crowns we're fighting against!"

"You will be *silent.*"

With a flick of his fingers, a red flame appeared in Quin's palm.

A chorus of gasps rippled through the room. It sent a bolt of lightning straight into his veins. How often he had wished for a captive audience, a crowd to gape and shiver at his performance.

He pooled all his attention into his fingers—and sent a sphere of crimson fire into the makeshift bar. Instantly it ignited. Flames licked the wood plank, spewing sparks onto the barrels below. The bottles heated up, spirits seething inside, a dozen paroxysms waiting to explode.

From the farthest table, he heard a whimper. He turned his head.

Brialli Mar.

He hadn't seen her in days. She was watching him intently, unsmiling, a small black dog tucked under her arm. It was not Brialli who had whimpered, he realized, but the pup.

For a moment, Quin's love for Wulf and Beo knocked into him so fiercely his breath caught. They had been a comfort to him during his darkest days. His dogs had reminded him of his humanity, even when humanity at large seemed brutally bleak.

He swiftly cauterized the wound.

His dogs were lost to him. And rightfully so. Only when a man was free of love was he free to do what he was meant to do.

"I trust you will not need another demonstration," Quin said.

Maev had gone lily white. She shrank backward, fumbling her way to one of the stone benches without ever taking her eyes off his face.

"My forebears would punish you all for gathering here in Kaer Killian. For plotting treasonous acts within my walls. I would be well within my rights to kill you."

He turned to face the rest of the Embers.

"But I am not my forebears. If you swear fealty, I will forgive your transgressions. I order you to return to your homes. Rebuild. Focus your efforts on resurrecting Glas Ddir from the ashes. But if you oppose my rule?"

He let the threat linger.

"Then you are a traitor, and therefore not welcome in the river kingdom. If you stay within our borders, you will live to regret your choice."

"And what of the sisters?"

It was Tobin speaking. His silver eyes glittered with scorn.

"Did you not say that you had invited the Twisted Sisters back to the river kingdom so you could 'stand against the tyranny of magic'? Evidently that was never your plan. I assume you will join them in tyranny and dark magic?"

"I will not join with the sisters. Not for anything."

"Why not? They'd probably be more effective."

Tobin rose from the stone bench.

"I believe, of everyone here, I have known the prince the longest. I have seen the full extent of his fear and his cowardice. I bear the marks of it."

He held up his right hand.

"These are also the marks of his father's hate. Every person here paid the price for Ronan's tyranny. We lost our families. Our bodies. Sometimes our lives."

"I am not my father," Quin said angrily. "I seek justice. Peace. And I will do what needs be done to achieve it."

"Peace." Tobin laughed. "You seek the power you have always been denied. The power you now believe your magic has granted you."

He gestured toward the fire blazing in the corner.

"But even this is a performance. At heart you are still a coward, unable to commit any true acts of violence. Admit it. You're desperate for the love and admiration of your people. So you, son of Clan Killian, are doing what you have always done. You are playing a part."

He straightened. "I, too, have been playing a part. But it is time I step off the stage."

Tobin stooped. Pressed his fingertips to the black stone floor. Closed his eyes.

A deafening crack echoed through the Gallery.

The room erupted.

The gray slab tables jutted up, then split apart, fracturing down the center. Onyx floors ruptured like glass. The Embers were screaming. People staggered and fell as the earth shifted beneath them. Walls and ceiling splintered. Quin watched as a giant shard plummeted from above, crushing a girl and a small black pup beneath it.

Brialli.

"Did you really think," Tobin shouted over the din, "that it was only *your* suffering that bred magic? That after what your father did to me, my body would not rise up in mutiny?"

Quin's heart was in his throat. He stumbled toward Brialli Mar. But he couldn't reach her. He was back under the snow palace, facing the Twisted Sisters. Cave cracking open, snow rushing in. And the avalanche, the endless white, drowning him, suffocating him, ravenous for his useless body, hungry to make him disappear. As if he had not disappeared long ago.

"Quin."

A voice rose from the chaos. He spun, unsteady on his feet.

Domeniq du Zol stood behind him.

"I'm sorry to do this," Dom said.

In one swift move, he clapped manacles of blue uzoolion around Quin's wrists.

"This, too."

And then Dom's fist was moving quickly, *too* quickly, a blur of knuckles coming straight for Quin's face.

The world went thick and black.

Chapter 26

EVERYTHING YOU TOUCH

"WE HAVE TO GO back," Pilar said.

Mia stood in the Creation Studio, blinking at her half sister. Trying desperately to wrangle her spinning thoughts.

Dear sisters,
Let me tell you a story.

Quin was alive. Angelyne was alive. Quin thought Angelyne was with them. Quin had, in no uncertain terms, threatened them all.

The boy she had tried so hard to save.

The boy she had loved.

I'm not entirely convinced you know what love is. At least not the kind that's freely given, freely shared.

The words lingered, even though Nell herself was gone. "I'm going to leave you now," she'd said after Pilar appeared with the letter. A statement that left a painful, deeper echo. Nelladine was not just leaving her in the Creation Studio, Mia knew.

"I should've known he was still alive." Pilar swore. "I just couldn't imagine how he survived! But if he survived, Angie did, too. No wonder the volqanoes are erupting in Fojo. She's out there picking the four kingdoms apart piece by piece."

"Volqanoes?" Mia said numbly. The only word she'd managed to speak.

"Have you even been paying attention, Rose? It's not just the Luumi glaciers that are collapsing. Here in Pembuk the glass cities are sinking faster than ever. Fires in your kingdom, volqanoes in mine. The smaller Fojuen islands have been completely wiped out. There were innocent people on those islands. Children. It's the end of the fucking world."

Till the glass cities sink into the western sands,
Till the eastern isles burn to ash.

Mia's wedding vows to Quin mingled with the words from his letter.

Only when a man is free of love is he free to do what he is meant to do.

She felt a burst of anger. She wanted to be happy Quin was alive. But with his cold, hateful words, he had stripped that joy from her in the same moment he had offered it.

Mia was ashamed how wounded she felt by the letter. Maybe her feelings for him were not as inert as she'd assumed.

Pilar was right. Mia had been blissfully naive, floating on air between the Shadowess's chambers and the Curatorium, feeling again, healing again. Oblivious to everyone but Nell, whom she had followed around the House like a lovelorn puppy. And in the end, oblivious to Nell, too. She had misread, misinterpreted, misunderstood.

"We have to go back," Pilar repeated.

"What could we possibly do?"

Pil's features twisted with disbelief. "We fight. What else?"

"Fight *Quin*?"

"Either that or we save him. Maybe those are the same thing. If we can get to him, we might be able to talk some sense into him. This?" She brandished the letter. "This isn't who he is."

"Maybe we don't know who he is." Mia's voice was low. Resigned. "You said yourself we never really knew him."

"And *you* said we couldn't blame him for being enthralled. I don't understand the sudden change of heart. You're the one who told me to stop being angry at him!"

"I know you cared about him, Pilar. You're letting that keep you from accepting the truth."

"Trust me, I'm not going back so I can ride in on a white horse and confess my undying love. I'm going back because Quin's hurting and needs help. If I had understood that sooner . . . if I'd been a better friend to him . . ."

243

"Maybe he's gone too far off the edge for us to pull him back."

Pilar kicked the potter's wheel. It jerked, spinning halfway around before going still.

"Typical. Mia Rose refuses to get her hands dirty."

"It's not about getting my hands dirty. It's about knowing when you're defeated before you've even begun. Some fights you can't win. I thought you of all people would understand that."

Mia slipped a hand into her dressing gown pocket, searching for the bloodbloom tree. But her pocket was empty. She'd left the charm in her sfeera.

"That's right," Pilar muttered. "Rub your little wooden tree. 'Cause that'll solve everything."

Mia's eyes flashed. "You don't even know what that tree is."

"Sure I do. It helps you belly breathe instead of chest breathe. Or whatever they're feeding you here at the House."

"You should try it sometime. See if it helps with your chronic rage." Mia could feel herself growing fangs. She inhaled, reminding herself that the bloodbloom was nice, but she could still breathe without it. "The Shadowess says we can't heal the world until we heal ourselves."

Pilar let out a half-mangled cry. "Please don't tell me you believe that."

"Why not?"

"Do you have any idea how selfish you sound, Rose? You're in there with the Shadowess every day, breathing, chanting—whatever it is you do. Or you're fawning over Nelladine. Meanwhile, people are dying. The whole world is crashing down around you, and you're hiding from it all. Have you ever thought of standing up and taking responsibility?"

"Is that what *you're* doing, Pilar? Taking responsibility? By teaching children how to punch sandbags?"

Pilar flinched. "At least I'm helping people."

"Keep telling yourself that. Because I think you're hiding, too. You're doing what you've always done: using your fists to seal your heart off from the world. You think if you can be cold and cruel, flinging barbs at anyone who tries to get close, you'll never get hurt."

She glared at Pilar, readying her ammunition. Preparing to say everything she'd held back for the past two months. Mia had tried so hard to be patient and kind and understanding. What a colossal waste of time and effort. She was done.

"Maybe you're right," Pilar said.

Mia's eye twitched. Had she missed something? Pil wasn't the type to give anyone the upper hand.

But now Pilar sank onto a stool, dropped her head in her hands.

"It's my fault," she said, words garbled against her palms. "I was so angry at Quin for betraying me. For being weak. I wanted to punish him for it. So I left him behind."

Mia had been more than ready to unleash all her pent-up anger and frustration. But this? Pilar being vulnerable? She had no idea how to respond.

"I left him first," Mia conceded. "I abandoned him in the Kaer when I stopped my heart. Abandoned all of you. I had planned to come back for him. I thought if I could find my mother and we neutralized the magic in the moonstone, maybe we could coax Angelyne back from the brink, and then I'd be able to save her, Quin, you—everyone."

"But you didn't come back," Pilar said.

Again Mia heard Nell's words.

In saving them, you expect it to save you.

"No," she said. "I didn't."

It struck her then, how much she was like her mother. Wynna had left her family behind. At first it was out of necessity. She'd been forced to stop her own heart to survive. But then, once she arrived in a far-off kingdom, she began to forget the old ties. She built a new life. Found a new love.

Wynna could have come back to Glas Ddir. The Dujia of the river kingdom needed her. Her *daughters* needed her. But when Mia had asked her to come back and take responsibility, her mother had refused.

And here was Mia. Refusing to go back to the river kingdom. Throwing herself at a woman in a far-off land, sure this would save her. Always the wild-eyed hope that *this* person, *this* love, would finally make her whole.

The difference was that Mia's beloved did not love her back.

"Maybe Quin's right." Pilar stared at her hands. "About hating the three of us. He thinks we broke him. Maybe we did."

A torrent of memories swamped Mia's mind. Every word Quin had ever spoken, from the beginning to the end. His icy formalities in the castle. His growing warmth in the Twisted Forest. She remembered the softness of their conversations on Refúj, their whispered intimacies in the river the night everything went wrong.

"It's *my* fault," she said, her voice so quiet she could barely hear it. "Quin has lost everything because of me. His family. His autonomy. I enthralled him without meaning to. I led him out of the Kaer and into the forest, where he almost died. I killed his sister when I was trying to save her. I said I would come back for him. And then I didn't. You're right. I *have* been selfish."

"Then face the truth—and do something about it. It's better than sitting around fondling a tree."

Mia fixed her with a penetrating gaze.

"Every time I've tried to save someone, I've failed."

"You're smart, Rose. Too smart for your own good sometimes. You could do so much more than you're doing here. *Be* so much more. Do you remember what I told you in the Reflections?"

"That you'd fight for me until I was strong enough to fight again."

"I think we've both been fighting our own battles—just in different ways. But each way was the opposite of what the other person needed. I needed to feel strong. Not sit around, talking endlessly about what happened to me."

Mia started to interrupt, but Pilar cut her off.

"I'm not saying you were wrong. Or maybe I am saying that. But I was wrong, too. The thing you needed was to talk and feel connected. I couldn't do that, either. The more you tried to engage with me, the more I fought it. I got angry. Shut down. I didn't want to feel broken. Didn't want to be your latest experiment, just another animal in the Curatorium you needed to fix."

Pilar stood. Cracked her knuckles, then her neck.

"You're right, Mia. I *have* sealed my heart off from you. I don't want to do that anymore. I'm trying so hard not to. The truth is, I don't know if Quin is beyond saving. But we have to try. And I say we do it together. As sisters."

She held out her hand.

"Come with me?"

Hot tears rushed to Mia's eyes. She'd been waiting so long to hear those words.

But now that they'd arrived, they landed all wrong.

For the last seventeen years, Mia had diligently, painstakingly crafted her impeccable sense of self. Even the childhood game she'd played with Angelyne reflected it: she was Mia Rose, Lover of Science, Knower of All Things. But also—and perhaps more vital—she was Mia Rose, Protector of Sisters, Savior of Lost Souls.

In a matter of minutes, Nell had deftly unraveled the threads of that delusion. Now the truth slid into Mia with brutal precision.

She needed to be needed. She gravitated toward broken people because she herself was broken. She was no better than her Wound Man sketch, pierced in a dozen different places, doomed in a dozen different ways. What a mockery she'd made of herself, doddering around the Curatorium. How could she heal anyone else's wounds when she could not even see her own?

No wonder she destroyed the very people she tried to save.

She knew nothing about love. Nothing about sisterhood. Her whole life had been a farce, a thin, gossamer skin wrapped around a shattered skeleton. She had failed. All the time she had spent breathing with Muri, chanting in the circle, caring for creatures in the Curatorium—meaningless. Expendable variables in an unsolvable equation.

Mia Rose, Fixer of Damaged People, was unfixable.

She would never be whole.

The grief came so quickly it stole the breath from her lungs. The pain of her failure crushed her. She lay pinned beneath the enormity of it, powerless. Decimated by every hurt she'd ever felt, every loss she'd ever suffered. She wanted nothing more than to forget.

And in that moment, she knew exactly where she was going.

She met Pilar's eyes. But she did not take her hand.

"I'm not coming with you, Pilar. You're on your own."

The change was immediate. Pilar yanked her arm back. Clenched her jaw. The pain in her sharp brown eyes was scorching.

Mia could read her sister like a book. Pilar had tried to open her heart, thinking this would finally bridge the gap between them. She'd been wrong.

"Fine. Don't come. I'm better off alone anyway."

Pilar hugged her arms to her chest. A gesture Mia knew so well.

"You're right, Rose. You really do break everything you touch."

Chapter 27

ONLY LIGHT

THE WALK THROUGH SHABEEKA was long. At night the Pearl Moon Festival was in full swing, revelers clogging the narrow passageways, vendors hawking their wares. The smells of smoked meats and raw fish were an assault to Mia's senses. She could smell everything now, even though she no longer wanted to.

On the shore, Mia stared up at the Bridge. It was bigger than it looked from her sfeera window, stretching on for an eternity. But when she squinted, she could make out the white smudge of island on the other side.

A sense of peace poured through her. Once she'd made up her mind to go to Prisma, she'd felt an almost eerie serenity. As if she had always known she would end up at the Isle of Forgetting. It was only a matter of time.

Mia had taken nothing with her. No bag, no possessions. She walked onto the Bridge freely, unburdened by her former life.

At the apex, she stopped. Above her the cables were pulled taut, glimmering in the moonlight like the vertebrae of a giant silver spine. She stared over the edge. A shoal of melonfish swam beneath the bridge, chattering, illuminating the ocean with trembling orange light. She thought of the notebook the Shadowess had given her, now filled with dozens of Mia's sketches—wounds and how to dress them, formulas for healing tinctures. She wouldn't need any of it now.

She fixed her gaze on Prisma. For just a moment, the fog cleared. Mia could see the tall fish trees, yellow fronds swaying in the breeze. The sand was pristine white: a pleasant balm after the endless jarring orange of Shabeeka. Everywhere she looked in Pembuk, she saw fire and scalding heat. It had seemed so invigorating when she first arrived. So *alive*.

But that was precisely the problem. To be alive was to hurt. To live was to be broken, failing the people you loved, failing yourself. Every child was born a blank slate on which other people inscribed their pain, until the child learned to inscribe her own. That legacy could not be undone. The markings were indelible.

Except on Prisma. On the Isle of Forgetting, even the darkest marks could be erased.

The ivory beach unfurled like a blank piece of parchment in the distance. Beckoning. A chance to rewrite all her previous mistakes.

For a moment, Mia craned her neck to look back. She saw children skipping rocks on the shore of Shabeeka. Musicians and dancers strolled the streets for the festival. In the middle distance, the House of Shadows glinted in the starlight. She could make out a row of round glass windows, some glowing a warm rose, others black. One of them was hers.

Her gaze dropped to her feet. She had stopped precisely at the zenith of the Bridge. Right foot on one side, left foot on the other. What was it Quin had said that day on the red balloon? *We're always in some liminal state, moving toward something or away from something else.* That seemed so very long ago.

A honeyed sweetness drifted through the air.

She could still go back. Run after Pilar, beg her sister to take her to Glas Ddir. She could save Quin, or stop him; perhaps those two things really were one and the same. She could find her mother, accept her offer of a home and a family, travel to Luumia and invent herself anew. She could stay in the House of Shadows, licking her wounds, giving Nell the space she needed. Mia knew Lord Shadowess would welcome her back to the Curatorium with open arms. So would the Shadowess. *Suffering is a kind of shadow,* she'd say. *It can reveal things to us we never would have seen if there were only light.*

Mia took a step toward Prisma.

Funny how so much could be decided in a single step. She was no longer at the apex, suspended between worlds. She had transported herself both closer to the future and farther from the past.

In the end, the choice was not difficult.

She would forget them all.

ACT III

Once upon a time, on an isle made of sand,
a girl stopped plotting.

Sand is a forgiving mistress.

She molds herself to your whims,
your craters and depressions,
your pinnacles and peaks.
Stomp your foot into her skin and she
shapes every grain around you.
The faithful holder of your prints.
The keeper of your story.

Ask a question and sand will echo.
An echo is a kind of answer, no?
Insofar as every ear wants to be
pressed against its
own
mouth.
Drinking words it knows already.

My whole life I have been little.
A speck so small
no one
sees
or even cares.

A grain of sand can rage against the ocean,
but the ocean has the final word.

Perhaps the sea is the forgiving mistress.
Twice a day she sweeps over the shore,
frees the sand from its memory.
Every footprint,
every violent echo,
fades upon the tide.

To forget is to forgive.
To forgive is to forget.

I suppose this is what I do now,
on the warm white sands of Prisma.
Write bad poetry.

Soon I'll forget that, too.

Chapter 28

THE LAST DROP

IT WAS A GOOD thing Rose left. If she hadn't, Pilar might've killed the girl herself.

After their fight, she'd gone straight to the Gymnasia. Re-bloodied her knuckles. Thought about everything Mia said.

The more Pilar replayed their conversation, the surer she felt that she was in the right. Instead of shutting down, she'd opened up. All those weeks of Mia trying to connect had finally worn her down. Either that or her time in the House had shifted something.

She didn't want to go back to the river kingdom, either. She liked training Stone and Shay. Liked the steady trickle of girls and boys who came to the Gymnasia. Liked hearing their stories, their fears, their dreams.

But then she read Quin's letter. She'd never felt so simulta-neously relieved and horrified. Relieved to know Quin was alive—and horrified he was apparently still trying to kill them.

She had searched her heart. Was she still pining for her former lover? No. She'd never been one for epic love stories, and this was most definitely not that. Their romance had run its course.

What she felt was compassion. The kind she should've felt all along. Pilar knew what it was to suffer from the abuse of power. She and Quin were both survivors. If she could speak to that side of him, maybe she could pull him back from the brink.

And if she couldn't, so be it. She would do whatever she had to do to stop him. She refused to let him do to other people what had been done to him.

It was up to Pilar and Mia to set things right. They were the only ones who could. So Pilar had left the Gymnasia, marched straight to Mia's sfeera, and pounded on the door.

"Rose? You awake?"

Silence. She'd pounded harder.

"Get up or I'm coming in."

She didn't have to kick the door down. It was unlocked.

The second Pilar stepped inside, she knew. There was a kind of emptiness she couldn't put into words. Mia had stripped the lin-ens off the bed. Stacked all her books. Left an orange melonfish notebook on her pillow, her wooden charm placed neatly on top.

The truth struck with savage force. Rose had made her sfeera easier for someone to clean out.

Pilar clutched the charm in her fist. She stumbled back into the hallway, stunned.

Mia had left her. She had gone to Prisma.

There was no note.

Pilar sprinted all the way to the Bridge. She kept seeing Mia everywhere—in a crowded street, stooped over a food stall, standing on the shore. But every time she spun a new redhead around, she found herself peering into a face she didn't know.

She ran onto the Bridge. The moon made everything too bright. Pilar shielded her eyes.

There. At the other end she saw Mia. A tiny red-haired speck moving toward the island.

Pilar yelled. Waved her arms. Ran faster. The Bridge was much longer than it looked. She soared past the middle, then the three-quarter mark. She was so close to the end. Heart exploding. Lungs shrieking. She doubled over, gasping for air.

"Mia!" she screamed. Pilar held up the tree charm, one last desperate attempt. "MIA!"

She watched her sister disappear into the white fog.

Rose never once looked back.

Pilar sank. Her kneecaps slammed into hard metal. She'd have bruises in the morning, no doubt. She hugged her chest, pulse crashing in her ears.

She knew she should go straight to the Shadowess. Tell her what had happened. Nell, too. Beg them to bring Mia back.

But in her heart, she knew their answer. The leaders at the House were happy to counsel people *before* they went to the Isle of Forgetting. Once they'd crossed the Bridge? There was no turning back.

Pilar walked back to the House alone. Angry. So angry.

She had opened herself up to Mia.

And Mia had left.

The Orkhestra was pitch-black. How could anyone see their instruments? Pilar knocked down a music stand as she stumbled through the room. Swore. Flicked the cap off the flask of rai rouj she'd drunk half of in the Swallow—and downed the rest in one gulp.

The spirits burned. She'd missed that punch to the throat. She remembered giving Rose her first nip of rai rouj on Refúj. The girl had taken one sip and nearly fallen on her ass.

Did Mia remember that moment?

Didn't matter. If she did, she wouldn't for long.

The tears raged behind Pilar's eyes. She fought them back. She wanted to be angry, *stay* angry, but she kept smacking up against her own guilt. Had she pushed Mia over the edge?

Pilar's last words ripped through her bleary brain.

You really do break everything you touch.

She didn't want to think anymore. She had to occupy her hands—and not by punching. She needed something that would make her feel not so alone.

She needed a violin.

"Pil?"

She squinted into the dark. Saw the silhouette of wiry black hair. Groaned.

"Why are you here, Stone?"

"I thought you might be up late, sparring. When you weren't in the Gymnasia I looked a little farther afield. Not in a million years would I have thought I'd find you here."

Pilar swept her arm across the empty chairs and music stands.

"Come in! Private concert. Now if I could just find the violins."

"Are you . . . drunk?"

"Maybe a little." She moved forward and knocked over a music stand, which knocked into another. A whole row went down like dominoes.

"Maybe a lot." Stone pointed to a line of wooden cabinets. "They keep the instruments in there so they're not exposed to direct sunlight."

Pilar staggered toward the cabinets, still holding the empty flask. She stared at it.

"How did *this* get here?" she slurred.

"I'm guessing you put it there. Is something wrong, Pilar?"

"What could possibly be wrong in the House of Shadows? Everyone here is so happy!"

"You don't seem happy."

"Really? Because I'm breathing through my belly! I can hum, too. Watch."

She threw back her head and crowed like a dying rooster.

Stone didn't crack a grin.

So he wasn't amused. Fine. Pilar shrugged and swung the cabinet open.

"Listen, Pil . . . now might not be the best time, but I was wondering . . ."

"You call this a violin?"

She pulled out the closest instrument and brandished it overhead.

"No," Stone said. "I call that a piccolo."

"How do you get two piccolo players to play in unison?"

"Make them practice?"

"No! You stab one." She guffawed. "Get it? Then there's only one!"

"I wish you'd tell me what was wrong."

She chucked the piccolo off to the side. Slammed the cabinet shut. She couldn't play violin if Stone was here. She hated him for taking that away from her.

"Why do you trust me, Stone?"

The question hung in the air a moment. When he answered, he sounded uncertain.

"Why wouldn't I trust you?"

"Let's see. Maybe because I'm a complete stranger who arrived from a foreign kingdom at the end of the world with a certain murderous Dujia for a sister?"

He was quiet. Surely he'd known about Angelyne. Pilar figured Mia had spilled their whole twisted history to the Shadowess, and that Muri had in turn spilled it to her children.

"But *you're* not a murderer," Stone said.

"You have no idea the things I've done. The things I've survived."

"I would if you told me." He hesitated. "You know everything about me. Or, well . . . almost everything. I'm an open book. I want to know where you come from, what your life was like. But you're a brick wall."

"And you, my friend, are a piece of straw."

She waited for him to argue. He didn't.

"Did you know I had a fight teacher from the river kingdom, Stone? Just like yours. Well. Not *just* like yours. I liked him. Liked him a *lot*. He understood me better than anyone. We'd spend hours sparring. He gave me attention. So much attention! He told me I was his favorite."

Tears jammed her throat. Why had she invoked Orry? She'd beaten him back for so long. But there he was, in the House. In the Orkhestra. His hand pressing into the small of her back.

"Come here," she said to Stone. "I have a new move to teach you."

"Right now?"

"When do you think?"

He trotted eagerly toward her, weaving through the music stands. The look on his face—so trusting, so hungry for her approval—infuriated her. She'd spent a solid month teaching him how not to leave himself vulnerable to attack. He had learned nothing.

"Come close," she said, as he got into his fighting stance. He took a step. "Closer."

He stepped forward again. His face was inches from hers.

"Lean in a little more," she said.

He leaned toward her. Tilted his upper body. Lost his base.

It was too easy.

She swiped her foot behind his left ankle. Stone fell backward—and went down hard. He crashed into a music stand. Let out a whimper.

"Why did you trust me just now?"

"I . . . you said . . ."

"You let me get into your head. You didn't just let me—you practically begged me. You've been begging me for weeks."

"I thought you said I was getting better," he said quietly.

"Sure, you're better at jabs and hooks. I was good at jabs and hooks, too. But your fists are useless when someone really wants to hurt you. You have to defend your mind."

"Defend it from what?"

"From anything! Anyone who tries to hurt you. Or people who pretend to love you. I've tried to teach you to stand on your own two feet. But you keep leaning. If you lean into someone, they're going to pull away. People always pull away. I promise you that."

She was thinking of Mia now. How Rose had painted such a pretty portrait of sisterhood, promising to stand by her side. And then, when Pilar was finally ready to open her heart—Mia had jumped ship.

The Orkhestra was so quiet she could hear her own breath. She tried to imagine it during the day. Noisy with music.

She couldn't imagine it.

"What is it, Pilar?" Stone said finally. "What aren't you telling me?"

She took a breath.

"Mia is gone. She left for Prisma. Decided to forget us all. I'm leaving, too. There's a new king in the river kingdom, a boy I used to know. He hates me. He probably should. I have to stop him. I've already packed a bag."

She hadn't, but she might as well have. When you owned nothing, there was nothing to pack.

"Don't go," Stone said, and the raw pain in his voice stopped her cold. "You didn't see me before you came here, you don't know what it was like. How sad I was all the time. It's the one thing I haven't told you. Because . . . because I'm ashamed."

Pilar leaned forward. Stone had never mentioned being sad. He showed up every day in the Gymnasia, jolly and good-humored.

"Sometimes there were whole days I couldn't even leave my sfeera. No one knew what was wrong with me. *I* didn't know what was wrong with me. But I'm so much happier since we started sparring. We all are. Things are better for us, a lot better than before you came to the House. I'll work on not trusting people. I won't lean on them. I promise. I'll learn to defend my mind the way you have. But please don't go, Pilar. We need you. *I* need you."

The picture of him as a sad little boy made her want to wrap her arms around his shoulders and pull him close.

But she didn't. She couldn't. All she heard were his last three words.

I need you.

She picked up the flask of rai rouj. Shook the last drop onto her tongue.

"Congratulations, Stone. That was your last lesson. You failed."

Chapter 29

BRIALLI MAR

Quin awoke to the smell of hot coffee.

The scent wafted into his nostrils slowly, easily. His face felt delectably warm, and when he blinked his eyes open, the morning sun poured in, melting onto the quilted blanket he was tucked beneath.

He sat up sharply.

This wasn't his room. He was no longer in the Kaer.

"Are you awake, darling?"

A woman sat in the corner. It took him a moment to place her. Black corkscrew curls. A kind, open smile. Her skin the same mellow brown as her son's.

"Lauriel du Zol," Quin murmured. Domeniq's mother.

The memory of his last moments in the Grand Gallery came rushing back. Tobin putting his hands to the floor, rupturing the stone. Walls crashing down around them. The embers screaming. And a piece he was forgetting, some vital fragment his foggy mind couldn't quite grasp.

Quin frowned. Groggy or not, he still remembered the punch to the face.

"Dom is sorry, darling," said Lauriel, correctly reading his expression. "He wasn't sure you'd come of your own free will, or who you might hurt along the way. And he had to act quickly."

"Is the whole Kaer destroyed?"

"We'll talk about everything, I promise."

When Quin tried to touch his throbbing nose, his arms were wrenched roughly back into his lap. He looked down to find his hands swallowed by a monstrosity of blue stone—half manacle, half glove.

"I asked Dom to remove them, but he insisted we keep the uzoolion on. Just for now."

Quin glowered. He had been stripped of his magic and taken here against his will. Had Dom tasked his mother with playing warden? Was he back at the Kaer with Tobin, plotting the Embers' next move?

Was Quin really so impotent that even with the power to create fire, he had failed to reclaim his own castle?

"Where's Domeniq?" he said gruffly. "We have unfinished business."

"He'll be back soon."

"Then he's with the Embers."

"Duj katt! I hope not." Lauriel shook her head. "They'll be the death of him. Of us all."

Intrigued, he studied her. She clearly had no love for the Embers. Quin had never been able to justify Dom's allegiance to the group, seeing as how Dom came from a family of Dujia. Then again, Domeniq du Zol had once been a Hunter, swearing a vow to *kill* Dujia. He seemed to have a knack for infiltrating enemy camps.

Quin took in his surroundings. He was in a cabin of some sort, perhaps a trapper's, in light of the sheer density of animal skins: bear, wolf, deer, and rabbit pelts hanging from the walls and piled on the floors. Several dishes lined the small wooden table where Lauriel sat. He noted the washing strung across the far wall, the long white cord bowed from the weight of freshly laundered socks and women's undergarments.

Embarrassed, he looked away.

"Where are we?"

"A little plot of land between Ilwysion and Killian Village. Would you like some coffee?"

She held up a copper coffeepot.

"I make it very strong. Come, sit with me."

Quin knew he should say no. He was a bound prisoner in enemy terrain. For all he knew, the coffee was spiked with poisonous chokecherry pits, a trick he'd used himself.

But he saw no malice in Lauriel's brown eyes. Her presence was strangely comforting.

"What am I doing here, Lauriel?"

"I'll explain everything, darling. Vuqa. Come, come."

When was the last time he'd had a proper cup of coffee? Perhaps not since he last saw the du Zols, when he and Mia had breakfasted in their cottage. It seemed impossibly long ago.

Quin's mouth was watering. If a strong cup of coffee would be the death of him, so be it. He kicked off the quilt—uncomfortably, without the use of his hands—and stumbled out of bed. Lauriel gestured toward the other chair, which he flumped into.

She poured him a generous cup. Steam curled off the top. He stared at it ravenously, as if he could will the dark liquid into his mouth.

Lauriel sighed.

"My son does enjoy being right. But sometimes, he is wrong."

She reached out and unclasped Quin's uzoolion gloves. They dropped to the floor.

"You'll be good, won't you?"

Good. A perilous word. Quin stared at the discarded gloves, bending and straightening his fingers, waiting for the blood to recirculate. Was this how it felt to be a woman in the river kingdom? Your hands always gloved, your blood flow always constricted?

He studied his own hands. They looked unexceptional—yet he'd burned down half a library with a single spark. He would have done worse in the Grand Gallery, were it not for Tobin.

Surely the Kaer was still standing. No matter how great the damage, they could repair it. Kaer Killian had withstood far greater attacks in its long, bloodied history.

Ah! He almost had it. The sliver of a memory hovering just out of reach. Something he'd seen in the moments before he lost consciousness.

Then it was gone again.

Warily, he regarded Lauriel. She, too, had magic. With a brush of her hand she could unblood him or, worse, enthrall him. As he'd told the Twisted Sisters in his letter, he swore never to be enthralled, enkindled, or controlled again.

"You must eat something," Lauriel insisted. "You look famished."

He *was* famished. Even more so than usual. He felt weak with hunger.

Very well. He would replenish his strength, then decide how to proceed with the du Zols.

Quin slurped down half the coffee Lauriel offered him and reached greedily for the closest dish: warm slices of crusty bread and a dollop of purple jam.

"Zanaba jam," he murmured, remembering how Lauriel had proudly presented each dish in her kitchen. He never forgot the names of foods he loved.

"Yes! You remember. There's minha zopa, too. I believe you liked that quite a bit when you last ate with us, no?"

She nudged a steaming bowl of soup across the table. He inhaled the spicy-sweet aroma of onions and tomatoes, garlic and wine.

"Not my finest effort," Lauriel conceded. "I have not been able to find chouriço, and the tomatoes aren't as fresh as I'd like. But the river kingdom never did have the right ingredients for minha zopa, even before everyone fled for their lives."

Quin didn't want to think about the gutted villages of his kingdom. He lifted one lid after another, carving off flaky pink pieces of salmon, dipping potato wafers into cheese gravy, and scooping up heavenly spoonfuls of buttermilk pudding. The meal was more modest than their breakfast on Refúj, but still outrageously good, a blend of Glasddiran and Fojuen cuisines.

Yet the more he ate, the heavier the silence between them. Lauriel, so boisterous and larger-than-life, had fallen quiet.

Quin patted his mouth with a napkin. Cleared his throat.

"When did you leave Refúj?"

She nodded, as if she'd been waiting for him to ask.

"After Zaga betrayed us, we knew we were no longer safe. And when I learned what she and Angelyne had done to Domeniq . . ." She pressed a hand to her heart, as if it hurt to remember. "I took my mother and my daughters and came straight to the Kaer. I knew I had to save my son."

"Your son seems perfectly fine."

"In body, yes. In soul, I worry." She refilled Quin's coffee cup, then her own. "These are strange, uneasy times. And not just for us Dujia."

The "us" included him. To his surprise, he felt moved.

Lauriel gestured toward the east. "If things were different, I would take my family back to Fojo. But the volqanoes have made that impossible."

"Has there been an eruption?"

"Duj! You haven't heard? *Dozens* of eruptions. The sleeping giants have come back to life, screaming gray plumes of smoke into the sky. One by one the islands burn to ash."

Till the eastern isles burn to ash.

Promise me, O promise me.

"The elements are out of balance," Lauriel said. "Whether the cause is natural or unnatural, we are all suffering for it."

Quin's wedding vows to Mia dissolved into Angelyne's menacing words.

She who can tip that fragile balance is a mighty queen.

Minutes later Quin had slammed the two stones together, and the snow palace had collapsed.

Was it the stones themselves that had tipped the fragile balance? Angelyne's magic? His own? After all this time, he still didn't know. Sometimes he wondered if this was simply what happened when two broken people collided. Two Dujia with nothing to lose—and everything to gain.

And then Quin saw another castle crumbling down around him: his own.

The food soured in his stomach. How had he not suspected Tobin's magic? He'd been ruinously naive. If magic bloomed inside a body that had been ruthlessly abused, of course his former lover's blood and bones held a powerful strain.

Quin thought of the Grand Gallery, the walls fracturing and falling, smashing into the frightened Embers below.

He choked on his coffee. The memory came searing back.

Brialli Mar.

He saw her being crushed under a giant stone.

He saw himself, unable to save her.

Had he even tried?

A knot rose in Quin's throat. His kingdom was ravaged. Countless Glasddirans dead. Why did he care so much about one little girl? She was not the only innocent. He thought of all the children from the orphanage, who had no doubt suffered equally terrible fates. Perhaps even worse.

"There was a girl with the Embers." He fought to keep his voice even. "Lithe and fair. Her parents both dead."

"Yes, darling. You knew her as Brialli Mar."

Knew. The past tense landed hard. His cup trembled as he sat it back in the saucer.

"What was done with her body?" he asked, but a noise outside the cabin devoured his words.

"Mamâe!" shouted a girl's voice, followed by a burst of laughter. The cabin door swung open, banging into the wall so hard it shook the laundry line. A pair of ladies' undergarments leapt to an ignoble death on the floor below.

"Mamâe, where's breakfast?"

A girl charged into the cabin. She had Lauriel's vibrant spiral curls; her skin was a dark, dewy umber. Quin knew her immediately. Junay, one of the du Zol twins.

"Duj katt." Lauriel massaged her temples. "Must you enter every room like it's a castle under siege, Jun?"

"Apparently she must," said a voice at her heels.

273

Sach'a, Junay's twin, rolled into the cabin, one hand expertly maneuvering the wheels of her wicker chair, the other resting on a furry black creature in her lap. Quin gave a start. He recognized the dog. The puppy had been in the Kaer, tucked under the arm of Brialli Mar.

"Nanu's coming," said Sach'a. "Callaghan is with her. They're going very slowly, because Nanu tripped and almost fell—" Her eyes landed on Quin, then widened. "Your Grace!"

"I told you he'd be awake." Junay surveyed the table. Her eyes narrowed. "And now he's eaten all our food."

Lauriel sighed. "Be kind, Jun. I can always make more."

"Because there's so much food lying around an empty village."

"You could try cooking yourself," Sach'a suggested. "Instead of waiting for Mamãe to feed you."

Her sister brandished a hand at the puppy. "*He* waits for you to feed him."

"His brain is the size of a walnut, Junay."

Quin felt a pang. He missed Wulf and Beo terribly. But it was more than that. Seeing the sisters griping and swiping at each other brought back the cozy morning he'd spent with Mia in the du Zols' kitchen. Quin was no stranger to the coziness of kitchens; he knew they engendered a special kind of bond. But he'd never felt that warmth in his own family. Not once.

Was it possible to miss something you never had?

"Hello!"

A cheerful voice came from the doorway.

"I've got Nanu!"

The twins' grandmother stepped shakily over the threshold, helped by a girl of eleven or twelve. Cropped dirty-blond hair. Puckish blue eyes.

Her smile faded when she saw Quin.

Quin's jaw dropped halfway to the floor.

"Bri—Brialli?" he stammered. "I don't understand."

He glanced at Lauriel, then at the twins, then back at Brialli Mar. No one else seemed shaken.

"But I saw the Kaer come down around you. You were pinned under a stone."

"I'm fine. So is the Kaer."

She stared him down. Challenging. Defiant.

"And I'm not Brialli Mar."

Chapter 30

NO MARK

THE WEATHER WAS MARVELOUS. Balmy, never hot. Brisk, never cold. Every day on Prisma had a dreamlike quality—swaths of alabaster clouds pitched against cerulean skies, stately fish trees jangling lemon coconuts, air so crisp and sharp she wanted to frame it. In Ilwysion, those sorts of perfect days only happened when spring thawed into summer, or under the harvest moon.

On the Isle of Forgetting, they were eternal.

Mia found it odd. When she had gazed out at Prisma from her sfeera window, she'd seen everything from clear skies to snow flurries to raging thunderstorms. The climate rarely corresponded to the mainland. More often than not, the island was cloaked in a thick white fog. The night she crossed the Bridge, she had felt it reach hungrily for her body, warmer than she expected, an angel draped in white rising up to greet her.

But the moment she'd set foot on the Isle of Forgetting, the fog had evaporated.

In Prisma, there was always sun.

Would you like some shade?

She was accustomed to it now. The lingering voice, nibbling at the fringes of her mind. Pleasant, agreeable. Never anything but polite. It had arrived when she had, the second she'd stepped onto the soft white sand.

At least, she thought it had. She wasn't entirely sure. Sometimes she thought the voice had been there longer. Other times she mistook it as her own.

At first she hadn't engaged. The voice would fade to a mild hum in the back of her brain, as if it didn't want to bother her and would rather return, amicably, whence it came. But it would soon resurface, posing another question in its hushed, dulcet tone.

Do you need a rest?

How about some fish ice?

Would you like there to be?

It took her a while to realize the questions came in direct response to her thoughts.

I'm tired.

My throat is parched.

Is anyone else here?

That last question was pivotal, because the one thing she had *not* expected when she came to Prisma, the one fact that seemed theoretically improbable, if not impossible, based on the sheer quantity of people who traveled across the Bridge every day to leave their worldly woes behind them, was that the island would be empty.

And yet, it was.

How many days had she spent on Prisma? Sometimes she thought one or two. Then she'd reconsider and come up with a quite different number. Two months, maybe. A year.

The fog had returned. She could see now that it wasn't fog at all, but a kind of white mist. The mist seemed to pour in from some mysterious inland source, though whenever she wandered toward the island's heart, she found herself miraculously back on the beach, staring out at the ocean. As if she'd been walking straight into her own reflection, ending back where she began.

She wasn't sure when she'd started answering the voice. It couldn't have been long after the moment she set foot on the Isle of Forgetting. It started simply enough: a tacit admission that, yes, she *would* like some fish ice—her throat was awfully dry.

And then the mist would clear as her foot struck something hard: a lemon coconut with the top hacked off. Inside she'd find a frosty yellow crème mixed with frothy milk.

So it went. When she was thirsty, the island brought forth fish ice, ginger mint juice, pulped papaya. When she was tired, the voice led her to a hammock strung between two trees, or a silken beachside pallet with an exquisite sunset view. When she was hungry, it produced spits of fish roasting over a crackling fire.

At the beginning, she remembered Nell, Pilar, Quin, the Shadowess, the animals in the Curatorium—all of them. When the thoughts came, they were rich, drenched in color, full of rough spots and sharp, painful edges.

But then the color would seep out of them. They grew harder to hold on to, like a painting held under a stream, colors swirling into the water, parchment weakening, until finally the whole thing dissolved.

The strangest part was not that the memories disappeared. It was that she didn't mind.

Those early days, out of sheer curiosity, she'd conducted a series of experiments, in which she would attempt to etch a particular memory into the sand. She started with a simple shape, more straightforward than a human face: a bloodbloom tree. It was easy enough to draw—a thick trunk and tiny flowers nestled among the branches.

Only, once she'd drawn the trunk, she couldn't quite remember how the branches looked. Were they graceful, supple limbs twisting around each other? No. She was thinking of the swyn trees in the Twisted Forest, where she'd walked with Quin. She could still remember the moon shining against the creamy white bark like candlelight on naked skin.

The memory peeled away. It wasn't painful. Nothing was painful anymore. It simply sifted through her mind like grains of sand.

Or perhaps the branches of the bloodbloom were angular, weighed down by thick spruce needles? She'd seen trees like that outside her childhood home, in a forest she couldn't quite recall the name of. She'd woken up in that forest once. Stared up into a lush green canopy of leaves as she climbed out of a wooden box.

Had she really climbed out of a wooden box?

That seemed a trifle histrionic. Surely she'd misremembered.

And then that memory was gone, too, along with the misremembering, because you couldn't misremember a memory you no longer had.

The experiment always ended the same way: with her standing on the beach, staring blankly at the sand, the blank sand staring back.

The island was hers. She knew that now, knew that it was meant for her, and had been since forever. Her mother had told her so. She'd written the words in a brown leather book and drawn a map to this very place. *The path to safe haven will reveal itself to she who seeks it.*

She had sought, and she had found.

She watched the birds fly over the ocean. Her name was a kind of bird in the old language. Or her mother had called her a bird. Or perhaps her mother was the bird? *Trust your heart,* her mother had told her, *and you will never die.*

More and more memories rolled in by the hour, waves curling into shore. She remembered walking through a forest with a green-eyed boy who loved her, a boy she had married and grown old with. She remembered laying her hands on a woman dying, watching the color come back into her cheeks, until she rose from the snow, healed. She remembered dancing through a cottage on a bluff with her little sister, twirling in fancy lavender gowns.

She held each memory close to her heart, these precious jewels from her life before. The gifts she been given by the Isle of Remembering.

She began to hear other voices.

At first, they were distant. A woman laughing, a boy talking, a girl singing. Music floated through the mist. Words washed over her in languages she didn't recognize, vowels weaving around consonants, consonants pressing into vowels. She found it soothing. And comforting, too, because the one thing the voice had *not* provided was other people.

She didn't mind that, either. She didn't mind much of anything. From the moment she set foot on the Isle of Remembering, she'd felt a bewitching lightness in her soul.

The voices were stronger now. One in particular—sweet, mellifluous. She followed it. Her feet left no mark on the sand as she moved deeper into the white mist, pushing toward the heart of the island. This time, the mist let her pass.

And that was how she found her sister.

Chapter 31

COMPLETELY GONE

PILAR AWOKE WITH AN arrow embedded in her forehead.

At least that was how it felt. Like someone had lodged a pointy chunk of fojuen between her eyes.

She sat up in bed, massaging her throbbing temples. The sun was already high in the sky. She'd forgotten how mornings went after a bottle of rai rouj. Even healing magic was useless. The only thing that helped was to sweat it out. A good spar should do the trick.

Then the memory of last night knocked into her. The letter from Quin. Her fight with Mia.

Pilar let out a low moan. She'd been cruel. Now Rose was gone, and it was too late to say sorry. *Was* she sorry? She was too hurt and angry to tell.

She thought of her drunken slog through the Orkhestra. And of Stone.

She'd been cruel to him, too. That was one apology she *could* still deliver, before setting out for the river kingdom.

But first: this headache. She'd have to beat it back without sparring. The thought of going to the Gymnasia one last time hurt too much.

She hobbled over to the bath bucket and splashed water on her face. The room came slowly into focus.

How many weeks had she lived in this sfeera? Except for a few dirty clothes balled on the floor, it looked as barren as the day she'd moved in. Other than a few stacked plates—lightly crusted with food she'd snuck out of the Swallow—there was no evidence she'd ever been there.

She eyed Mia's charm lying on the bed. Why had she kept it? It was broken anyway. She'd seen Rose turn it into a tree. Now it was just a sad wooden disc.

A rap on her door.

Pilar bristled. Then relaxed. Only Stone came to see her. At least now she wouldn't have to track him down.

But when she swung open the door, she found not Stone, but his mother.

"I hope I didn't wake you," the Shadowess said.

"I was on my way out."

They stared at each other. Pilar shifted her weight.

"I'm so sorry about Mia," said Muri.

Stone must've spread the word. Good. That meant Pilar wouldn't have to.

The Shadowess removed her wire-rimmed glasses, wiped the lenses on her sleeve. Pilar couldn't help but think her brown eyes had lost some of their sparkle.

"We haven't spent much time together since you arrived at the House, Pilar. I know my son is grateful for everything you've taught him. Your friendship has been a tremendous gift. I would welcome the opportunity to get to know you better myself."

"Sorry. I'm headed for Glas Ddir."

Muri looked surprised. Stone must not have told her that part.

"I'm sad to hear that. Is there anything we can do to persuade you to stay?"

Pilar cocked her head, curious in spite of herself. The Shadowess hadn't taken much interest in her. She was always dealing with more important people—fancy guests and residents, fancy members of the Manuba Committee, fancy Mia Rose.

"What you can do," Pilar said, "is stop ignoring what's happening in the river kingdom."

"I agree. I've spent the last few weeks organizing a caravan of ambassadors to journey east. The recent spike in Glasddiran refugees has been alarming. Truthfully, we've been troubled by news from the river kingdom for some time."

Pilar blinked. This was unexpected.

"In general we try not to intervene in other kingdoms' affairs. But when a tyrant threatens to commit war crimes and atrocities against his people, we pay attention. Now that Glas Ddir's western borders are open—perhaps the one good thing the young queen did—we have more leeway. I assure you, you are not alone in your eagerness to bring King Quin to account."

King Quin. Pilar wanted to laugh. Also throw up. The rai rouj was sloshing around her skull. Maybe she'd go to the Swallow. If she couldn't sweat it out, a hot meal was the next best thing.

"Something else you could do"—she was making this up as she went along—"is spend less time on chanting and breathing, and more time giving people actual tools. Like, oh, I don't know. Teaching them to protect themselves."

Muri smiled.

"Again, I agree with you. My great desire for the House is to give people tools they can take with them out into the world. Those tools look different for everyone. We all find our own paths to healing. There are ways of protecting yourself that do not require your fists. And there are other times the work lies in learning to leave yourself unprotected."

Pilar frowned.

"You disagree," said the Shadowess.

"I think your beloved Keeper would disagree. Celeste seems to know an awful lot about how people should heal."

Muri's eyes narrowed. When she opened her mouth, Pilar interrupted.

"I really don't have time. I'm eating. Then leaving."

The Shadowess said nothing for a moment. Then she replaced her glasses, pushing them up the bridge of her nose.

"The caravan to Glas Ddir will be leaving soon. I wish I could go myself. Unfortunately, I am needed here." She paused, thoughtful. "Would you be interested in accompanying them?

285

You would have companions on the journey, and I know they would appreciate your knowledge of both Kaer Killian and the river king."

Pilar was taken aback. She had to admit, the offer was tempting. People from the House would have access to things she didn't. Coins, for starters. Places to stay along the way. Animals for trekking through the harsh desert.

But if she went with them, she'd be dependent. Her words to Mia echoed through her head.

I'm better off alone.

If she learned anything from Mia's sudden departure, let it be that.

"I don't think so," she said. "Thanks anyway."

"The offer stands if you change your mind. And I do hope you'll find Stone. I know he would want to say goodbye."

Pilar braced herself as she walked into the Swallow. She liked to eat alone. But now that she had so many sparring students, someone from her brood always waved her over.

She didn't want to say goodbye. Didn't want to answer their questions about where she was going and why. She needed to be stealthy. Grab something quick to knock out this headache.

"Pilar!"

So much for stealthy.

"Pilar! Over here!"

Shay was sitting at a table, nervously fidgeting with her turquoise skirt. She was alone. Shay was never alone.

Pilar trudged over.

"I'm sorry about your sister," Shay said.

"Half sister. And I went the last nineteen years without one. I'll survive."

It occurred to her that this wasn't posturing. She *would* survive. And the thought that life would go on—that she'd go back to how she was before Mia—was surprisingly painful.

"Pilar." Shay leaned in, eyes wide. "Have you seen Stone this morning?"

Ah. So this was the real reason Shay had called her over. Pilar shook her head—and regretted it. Any sudden movement above the neck was a mistake.

"He always comes by my sfeera," Shay said, worried. "But today he missed breakfast. It isn't like him."

"Maybe he had a rough night."

"I hope not! We went into Shabeeka yesterday for the Pearl Moon Festival. We had the most amazing time. At least *I* thought so. Now I'm scared he's avoiding me."

Pilar plucked a foggy memory from the haze of last night. Stone had wanted to ask her something. Was it about Shay?

"Great sands, I'm anxious. I can't think clearly! I'm going to go to jougi, try and calm my mind. Do you want to come?"

Pilar had managed to avoid jougi, just like she'd avoided the circle and all the other "paths to healing" the House hawked. Why give up her crusade now?

"No."

"You're so stubborn, Pilar. I don't know why you won't just try it. You're a physical person! You might really enjoy it. I promise you'll work up a sweat."

Sweat.

Pilar chewed her lip. If she wanted to lose this headache before she left, sweating wouldn't be the worst thing.

But from the jougi she'd glimpsed through the Manjala's glass doors, she wasn't convinced.

"I really doubt I'm going to work up a sweat standing on one foot."

Shay rolled her eyes. "It's not like that's all you do! You go through different movements, different poses. Some of them are impossibly hard."

She folded her arms over her chest. Sized Pilar up.

"I dare you to come with me," she said.

Pilar grunted. She knew when she was beat.

"Fine. But if I don't work up a good sweat, there'll be hells to pay."

She had never sweat so much in her life.

The hour started easily enough. Ten or so people gathered in the Manjala. Shay greeted several of her friends, then laid a thin wool blanket on the floor. Pilar followed her lead.

The teacher, a short blond man with a pointy beard, kaara-akuthaed everyone to today's practice. He instructed them to lie on their backs and drop their knees to one side, then the other. They came to their hands and knees, arching and flattening their backs. Pilar's spine felt nice and tingly, but it wasn't exactly sweat-worthy.

288

After that, she changed her tune.

They lay on their stomachs, mashed their palms and toes into the blanket, and lifted their bodies off the floor in one straight line. The teacher reminded them to breathe. They pressed their thighs back and stuck their asses in the air. The teacher reminded them to breathe. They bent their knees, squatting for an unbearably long time. The teacher reminded them to breathe.

Pilar was so out of breath, for once she appreciated the reminder.

She had no idea what she was doing. She tried to force her body into the same shapes Shay was making, but Shay had a fifteen-year-old, bendy body. Pilar knew from their sparring sessions that her student was flexible, but she'd had no idea how much. When Pilar tried to balance on one leg and twist the other leg around it, she could not for the life of her stay upright.

At one point the teacher came to stand beside her.

"May I offer you an assist?" he said quietly.

Pilar stiffened. The thought of his hands on her body scared her. She shook her head.

He nodded respectfully. Smiled. And walked away.

A few minutes later, when everyone crouched, bent their elbows, crammed their knees into the backs of their arms, and levitated, bodies hovering a few inches off the floor, Pilar felt a surge of hope. She was both small and strong. This should be easy.

She crouched, pressed her knees into her arms, tilted forward— and fell flat on her face.

"Are you all right?" Shay whispered.

Pilar rubbed her forehead. She was sweating so much her hand slid right off.

"How are you even doing this? You're like a human flamingo."

Shay giggled. "I told you it's hard. It just takes practice. Now shh."

Pilar guzzled water from her leatherskin and sat the next one out.

They ended where they began. On their backs, tipping their knees from side to side. Then they stilled their bodies like they were sleeping. Or dead. She was so tired she felt halfway dead. The teacher walked around the room with sweet-smelling oil, flapping a towel over them. The cool breeze felt delicious.

Pilar stared up at the ceiling. There were wood rafters.

She flinched. Waited for Orry's cottage to drag her back. Her body stiff and numb.

But her mind was strangely calm. Her body relaxed and open. Instead of the cottage, she was in the Manjala, surrounded by a circle of sweaty strangers lying quietly on their backs. Overhead, cheerful square flags dangled from each rafter.

Only then did she realize her headache was completely gone.

"See?" Shay whispered from her blanket. "I told you you'd like it."

"I wouldn't say I *liked* it."

The truth was, she loved it. Even if her pride had taken a drubbing, her body thrummed with energy. She felt both grounded and vibrantly alive.

Shay reached out and squeezed her hand.

"Thank you for being here. I feel much calmer now. I hope you'll come with me again."

Why hadn't Pilar come to jougi before now? Why hadn't she done so many things in the House? If she'd felt this grounded, this calm, maybe she would have been kinder to Mia. Gentler with Stone.

Pilar tried to smile, but tears blurred her vision. She blinked them back before Shay could see.

Her head was no longer hurting. Only her heart.

Chapter 32

BACK FROM THE DEAD

"I'M NOT BRIALLI MAR," said the girl Quin knew as Brialli Mar, her eyes boring into him. "My name is Callaghan."

"Callaghan's been indispensable," said Lauriel, leaning over the breakfast table and dividing the leftovers between three small plates. Junay was actively gobbling as much as she could while Sach'a looked on disapprovingly. "As we find more Glasddirans, her work becomes all the more important."

Lauriel waved them over. "Callaghan, Sach'a. Come. Vuqa. You've earned a hot meal."

Sach'a installed her grandmother on the bed and deposited the black puppy in Nanu's lap for safekeeping. After they were both situated, she wheeled her chair to the table.

Brialli—or, rather, *Callaghan*—didn't move. She was staring at Quin. It took him a moment to realize she wanted his chair. He stood clumsily, and she sat without ceremony. When she turned her attention to the food he breathed a sigh of relief. He didn't think he could bear the ferocious intensity of those blue eyes for one more second.

Quin tried to make sense of these new revelations. Brialli was, first and foremost, not dead. She was also not Brialli. And while Brialli Mar had seemed to adore him, Callaghan unmistakably did not.

"You're not one of the Embers," he said.

Callaghan shook her head vehemently. "Dom and I move freely between here and the Kaer, gathering what news we can of the Embers' plotting, and bringing it back to the others. Dom's been doing it longer, but I've got the advantage. No one suspects a little girl of being a spy."

Including me, Quin thought.

He had so many questions. Who were the "others"? And how long had Callaghan been a spy?

But what he asked was, "Did you really lose your mother to the Hunters and your father to Angelyne?"

She looked up, mouth full of minha zopa.

"Why would I make that up?"

"You lied about your name. Why not your parentage?"

"Briallihandra Mar is the name my mother gave me. But since the day she died, I've gone by Callaghan: the hero in an old fairy tale my father read to me. Sweet little Brialli would never have survived this long."

She shot him a withering glance.

"If you act like a decent person, I might let you call me Cal."

He felt irritated. Why did he care about being liked by a little girl? He was a *king*, for gods' sakes.

"Your Grace." Sach'a set her spoon down neatly beside her plate.

Quin turned, pleased to be properly addressed. Though even he had to admit the title felt out of place in this humble trapper's cabin. In the Kaer he'd been all might and glory; here he was a toy soldier who didn't know what to do with his hands.

"I know all the things you've said about the sisters." The girl's clear, knowing gaze unnerved him. "But I think your decision to group them together is flawed."

Quin crossed his arms. Then uncrossed them. He had long feared this was true. Even in his darkest moments, he would see Mia's gray eyes, or Pilar's strong jaw, and his rage would soften.

"You can't deny they've all caused harm," he argued.

The puppy slid off Nanu's lap and toddled over to Sach'a, curling himself protectively against the wheel of her chair. She reached down to scratch his ears.

"Everyone causes harm at some point," said Sach'a. "Whether they mean to or not. I think you're probably right about Ange-lyne. She's beyond saving. But you're wrong about Pilar and Mia."

"Sometimes you have to skin a few rabbits to make a good stew." Quin leveled his gaze at Callaghan. "Isn't that right, Cal?"

The girl spooned up minha zopa, thoughtful, then let it dribble back into the bowl.

"Sometimes it's better to just not make the stew."

This time, it was Quin who looked away.

"Magic should only be used in the direst circumstances," he said tersely, aware of the irony.

"You have magic, too," said Cal. "You could use it to help people."

"Also, have you seen your kingdom lately?" Junay brandished a fishbone toward the window. "It's pretty dire."

"Give him time, Jun," her mother chided. "He's still recovering from Tobin and the Kaer."

Quin turned on Callaghan.

"Didn't you just tell me the Kaer was fine? How could it be, when I saw the whole thing crack wide open?"

Lauriel and Callaghan exchanged glances.

"The thing is," Cal said slowly, "that didn't really happen."

Quin blanched. *"What?"*

"You are a Dujia who can manipulate Fire." Lauriel had begun to collect the washing from the line, bundling the clean clothes onto the bed. "Tobin is a Dujia who can manipulate Stone. His gift lies in shifting the aether to change what the eyes see. He used head magic to make you believe you saw something that wasn't real."

Quin thought of the Snow Queen's Reflections. In the space between, he'd seen things that weren't real. Then he thought of Mia and Pilar journeying there together, and how abandoned he had felt. That was the moment he had realized the sisters would choose each other every time.

Now Tobin was practicing the same dark magic. He had made a mockery of Quin—in his own castle, in front of his own people.

"It wasn't just you," Callaghan said. "Tobin made all the Embers see the same thing. Dom and I had our uzoolion, so we weren't fooled. But in the ensuing chaos we were able to get you out."

"Tobin had no right." Quin could feel his blood igniting. "I am the king."

"Do you remember what I told you on Refúj?" Lauriel set the laundry on the bed. "Kings are just men in paper hats, darling." She touched his cheek lightly. "Even if your hat is made of gold."

Quin froze. Why had she touched him? Was she using magic?

Forcefully he shoved Lauriel's arm away. A shower of sparks arced from his hand, falling to the floor below.

"I could cut off your hand for that," he growled.

The room went dead silent.

Quin's words hung, suspended in the air. Even *he* couldn't believe he'd said them. They dangled, raw and bleeding, like the hands in his father's Hall.

On the floor, the puppy began to cry.

Sach'a reached down and pulled him onto her lap. "You could have hurt him," she murmured, combing her fingers through his fur, checking for embers. Junay stamped out a smoldering spark on the bearskin rug, glaring at Quin.

His rage leaked out as shame oozed in. He couldn't meet their eyes. His gaze fell to the dog, though that was no good, either.

All he could see were Wulf and Beo as puppies. Their sweet, cold noses pressed into his hand.

He did not want to set this family on fire. He did not want to hurt them at all.

It was Callaghan who spoke first.

"Do you want the rest of my soup, Jun?" She pushed her bowl away, the iron scraping over the wood. "I've lost my appetite."

She stood. Faced Quin, fists clenched at her sides.

"My mother believed you were different. She saw you visit the orphanage. She said you weren't rotten like your father, that you had a kind heart. But right now you're just like any other Killian. Or any royal, for that matter. You're as cruel and heartless as Ronan. And you're as angry and vengeful as Angelyne."

Callaghan turned to face the others. She had reminded Quin of his sister before, but now, standing proud with her blue eyes blazing, she was the spitting image of Karri.

"I want to show him."

"Tell me you're not serious," Junay scoffed. "He'd set them all on fire!"

"It might be our last chance to make sure he doesn't set fire to anyone. Tobin will be looking for him. For all of us." Callaghan nodded toward the uzoolion gloves on the floor. "He can wear those. And Dom will be there if anything goes wrong."

"For once I agree with my sister," Sach'a said. "I don't think it's wise."

Callaghan threw up her hands in frustration. "None of this is wise!"

"Mamãe?" Sach'a looked to her mother. They all did. "What do you think?"

"Duj katt." Lauriel sighed. "Just because it isn't wise doesn't mean it isn't right."

Callaghan nodded, satisfied. She reached for the gloves.

"We're going on a little trip," she said.

Quin appraised her. The former Brialli Mar, this devious girl spy, who had far more layers than he'd ever suspected.

He was still suspicious. But he was curious, too.

"And why do you think I'll go anywhere with you?"

"Don't tempt me," Callaghan said. "Or *I* get to punch you this time."

Ilwysion was beautiful. The fresh alpine air, the susurrant rustle of leaves, the majestic oaks and elms reaching as far as the eye could see. Even with his hands behind his back, Quin was happy to be outside. It made his heart light with possibility.

"Junay told me the Roses lived not too far from here," said Callaghan, leading him through the woods with a walking stick in her hand. At least she had the decency not to prod him with it. "In a big cottage on a bluff."

"I wouldn't know. I've never seen it."

Quin envied Mia for having grown up in this place. So different from the cloistered Kaer, where the air was always stale, the corridors dark and narrow.

How would his life have been different if he'd been born in Ilwysion? He felt a deep longing as his eyes took in the green peaks and valleys, the elegant Natha River a piece of black thread stitching everything together. He had never been given a decent chance to love his kingdom, but here, in nature, he felt it call to him.

As a common boy in a river town, would he still have had to pretend to be someone he was not?

"It's not much farther," Cal said, and prodded him with the stick.

At first blush, the lodging house looked deserted. Heaps of snow piled on the roof, icicles dripping from the eaves. But then Quin saw it: a thin coil of smoke snaking into the sky.

As his gaze fell to the front door, his blood ran cold.

A symbol was carved into the wood. Three triangles, one inside the other. Quin recognized the hallmark of the Embers. A mark of violence.

Death.

Callaghan had lied to him. They were part of the Embers after all. There was no time to run. The door creaked open, and a man stepped out onto the porch, his face cloaked in shadow. He folded his arms over his burly chest.

"So it's time, then," he said.

"It's time," said Callaghan.

The man turned his head, calling through the open door.

"He's here! The king is here."

Quin heard a shriek from inside, then a shout. The sounds of many pairs of feet rumbled through the lodging house, so many it shook the walls.

He flinched, feeling Callaghan's grip tighten at his back. She was fumbling with the uzoolion. To his astonishment, his hands lightened as the gloves dropped to the ground.

Quin did not have time to coax fire from his palms. They were pouring out of the lodging house, coming so fast, girls and boys barreling toward him, shouting, laughing. They had come back to him, back from the dead.

The orphans of Killian Village.

Chapter 33

GWYRACH

"Mia?"

It startled her. Not her little sister, sitting in the mist. The sound of her own name, which she had almost forgotten.

"Angelyne?"

That word, too, felt strange in her mouth—but also sweet. As if she'd forgotten the taste of a sun-ripened peach, then sunk her teeth into its flesh.

"I knew you'd come, Mi. The *real* you, not the one I've been imagining. I could never get the freckles quite right, no matter how hard I tried to remember."

The mist moved outward, enshrining them both in a white halo.

"We didn't know when to expect you," Angelyne said.

She sat beside a burbling stream, trailing her fingers through the water. Mia's heart flooded with joy. Her sister's strawberry hair tumbled down her back, full and lustrous; her complexion had recovered its smooth, peachy glow. The last time they'd met, Angie's face had been drawn, her body emaciated.

The memory jarred. Mia saw glittering shards of ice and dead-eyed children, though she couldn't quite recall how they fit together.

"Come." Angelyne beckoned. "Sit with me."

Mia felt a twitch of warning. Fragments of a memory pressed at the edges of her mind.

"You don't have to remember," Angie said. "At the very least, you don't have to remember right now."

She patted the soft sand beside her. Angelyne's blue eyes were piercing, vivid in a way nothing else on Prisma had been.

Mia sat. She mirrored Angelyne, trailing her fingers through the crystalline stream, the water surprisingly warm. Something pleasant bubbled just beneath the surface, another time she'd submerged herself in water like this. A hot spring?

"I just saw you," Mia said, struggling to remember. "I think we were dancing. Yes, that's right. In our cottage. We were much younger. And we were wearing . . ." She lost hold of it.

"Mother's gowns?" Angie smiled. "Yes. I have that memory, too. It'll get easier to pluck out specific ones, don't worry. The mist can be disorienting when you've just arrived."

"Have I only just arrived?"

Angie didn't answer. She stretched, drawing her arms overhead. Yawned. Unbent her legs, flexing and pointing her toes. Angie had always had small, dainty feet with fine arches. They used to hurt her, Mia remembered, whenever they walked in the forest for too long.

Now she dipped her bare toes in the water. Shook her ginger tresses off her shoulders.

"Would you like to see my island?"

Mia cocked her head. "I thought it was mine."

"You must have wanted to share it. Otherwise you wouldn't have found us."

"Us?"

"The island and me. We're in constant dialogue. As are you."

"Is that what's been speaking to me? The island?"

"Yes and no. The voice is the island, but the voice is also you. I like to think of Prisma as a kind of ship. The voice provides the parchment, and the mist is the ink. But the map is of your own making. You are the one charting your course."

In the mist, Mia saw a pale yellow coracle shaped like a walnut shell. Then a varnished black teardrop bobbing on the ocean. Then a dhou with long coconut ropes rigging a triangular sail. So many boats, for a girl who hated boats.

They blended together, one dissolving into the next.

Mia felt the twitch in her chest again. She should say no to her sister. Fade back into her own mist, her own island.

"Ange?"

"Mm?"

"It's so good to see you. I just . . . I feel like there are things I want to say."

Angelyne reached out and touched Mia's wrist.

"You've still got your fyre ice frostflower. Beautiful."

Mia blinked at the indigo mark. She'd forgotten all about it.

"You'll see the magic I've worked with fyre ink," said Angie, "a little later on."

She squeezed Mia's hand. The skin of her palm felt different than Mia remembered. Grooved where it used to be soft.

"Don't worry, Mi. We have time."

Her rose-petal lips curved into a smile.

"We have all the time in the world."

Had her sister been wearing a green dress by the stream? Mia didn't think so. But she wasn't sure. As they walked side by side along the beach, Angie's emerald gown swished against her delicate ankles, the bodice cinched severely at the waist.

"Are you wearing a *corset?*" Mia asked in disbelief.

"Why not? I like corsets."

"How are we related?" Mia muttered, and despite everything— or perhaps because of it—they both burst into laughter. It had always been that way with Ange: ready to kill each other one moment, then shrieking with glee the next.

"Now I *know* you're not a figment of my imagination," Mia said, once their laughter had subsided. "Not in one million years would I have thought to conjure you in a corset."

She leaned in impulsively and kissed her sister on the cheek.

304

"This feels nice."

"It does, doesn't it?"

Mia's misgivings evaporated like a puff of steam. She hadn't known how much she missed Angelyne until she had her back. Now she couldn't imagine the island without her.

"Look," Angie said, pointing to a place in the distance where the ocean met the shore.

Mia stopped short. A magnificent structure rose out of the sand. A castle nestled atop a wooded bluff, graced by a sweeping balcony and an iron door with a rose-shaped knocker.

Mia knew it instantly.

"Home."

Angie nodded. "In the beginning I spent all my time here. We don't go so much anymore."

She waved her hand. All at once, the cottage crashed into sand. Gigantic clumps of balcony broke apart on the shoreline, followed by the door, the rose knocker, the mountain itself. Every trace of the Rose family home disintegrated into sea foam.

The pain was visceral. Mia cried out.

"Why did you—"

"I told you. We don't live there anymore."

Angelyne started walking again, faster this time. Mia had won every race she'd ever had with her sister. Now she struggled to keep up.

"Do you know what *Prisma* means?" Angie asked.

"Of course."

"I bet you don't."

"It comes from the word *prysm*, which in the old language means 'something seen.'"

"Mia Rose, Scholar of the Old Language, Knower of All Truths." Angelyne tossed her strawberry hair over her shoulder. "Not *all* truths. You were always the better student. But all those hours Father spent teaching you, I spent lying in bed, listening. *Prysm* doesn't mean 'something *seen*.' It means 'something *sawn*.'"

She stopped and spun around so quickly Mia nearly collided with her. Their eyes locked.

"A prism saws the world into a new shape," Angie said, "distorting your view. It creates a kind of fragmentation. The cutting requires an act of violence. Only then can you bend the light."

Angelyne pivoted away from the ocean—and drew her hand across the mist.

Mia saw the four kingdoms.

Or, rather, she saw their dissolution.

In the snow kingdom, glaciers fractured, avalanches crushing towns and hamlets, sealing them in ice.

In the glass kingdom, the desert sun whipped the sand into sharp and shimmering cyclones. Cities sank as the earth tore open at the seams.

In the fire kingdom, volqanoes shivered to life, spewing ribbons of lava. The ocean seethed as enormous blue ramparts engulfed whole islands.

And in the river kingdom, Mia's beloved Glas Ddir, scarlet flames reduced whole villages to cinder. Proud trees, ripped from their roots, slid down hillsides, as the hills themselves crumbled.

Mia gasped. She knew some of these things had already happened. Others she hoped never would. Was she watching an illusory performance, Angelyne's cruel fantasies playing out in the space between? Or had her sister rendered a dark magic on Prisma that was being inflicted on the four kingdoms in real-life?

In an instant, the fog in Mia's mind cleared—and the memories came screaming back. Her *real* memories. Angelyne's betrayal. The hopefulness in Pilar's eyes. The rejection in Nell's. Quin lifting his hands, his fists full of fire.

"Do you know how much I wanted to kill you, Mia?"

Angie's words made her blood run cold.

"I was so sick of feeling powerless. My whole life I've been little. A speck so small no one sees or even cares. You thought you saw me, but you never did. I was your delicate little sister who couldn't possibly survive without you. I went half mad just to prove you wrong."

Mia stared into her sister's bright blue eyes, wondering who this stranger was. This half girl, half demon. *Gwyrach.*

"Is that what you're doing, Angelyne? Destroying the four kingdoms so you'll finally feel powerful?"

"No," Angie said quietly. "Not anymore."

"Did you get tired of murdering innocent people?"

"You have the order wrong. I didn't come to Prisma to destroy the four kingdoms. I came to Prisma because I already had."

Angelyne extended her arm, palm facing up.

Mia's stomach twisted.

Under the snow palace, Angie had gripped the seven-pointed gem in one fist, their mother's ruby wren in the other. Now a jagged black wheel was seared into her flesh.

Mia cradled her sister's hand. To say the black stone had left a mark would be inaccurate. It had left *itself*. The entire wheel was embedded in her palm, marred only by pink ridges of scar tissue, her skin's failed attempt to heal.

"Do you remember my little monologue," Angelyne said, "about the Elemental Hex? I said there were seven elements, not six."

"The seventh is death," Mia murmured, touching the seventh spoke.

"You don't deserve to die, Mi."

Slowly, Mia looked into Angelyne's eyes. She was prepared to see brutal hatred, or savage calm.

She was not prepared to see her sister's face crumple.

"*I* deserve to die," Angie said, and began to cry.

Chapter 34

TWO SPIKES

QUIN HAD NEVER BEEN so happy.

He knelt with the orphans on the floor of the lodging house. The children fought over who would sit closest, shoving and arguing, until finally he organized them into a circle and placed himself at its heart. They were as raucous as he remembered, and as delightful.

But there were new faces, too. Quin had not visited the orphanage since before his wedding to Mia, and months had passed since then. It grieved him, knowing these were children for whom the loss of their parents was still fresh.

"Your Grace?"

Quin turned to see the man from the lodging house porch.

Now that he no longer stood in shadow, Quin recognized him. Here was the grizzled farmer who had so kindly shared his rabbit stew with Quin during his long journey back to the Kaer.

"Stoddard," the man offered, in case Quin had forgotten.

"Of course," Quin said a little too quickly, ashamed that he had.

"The children come from all over," Stoddard explained. "We've been searching the villages day and night, hoping the cutthroats didn't find them first."

Quin had a thousand questions. For Stoddard, and for Callaghan, too, who sat at a nearby table, watching the joyous reunion. One thing he did know: the fear he'd felt staring at the carved symbol on the lodging house door—and in the du Zols' cabin—had vanished the moment the children looped their arms through his and tugged him happily inside.

They wanted to tell him jokes and stories, climb onto his back, run their fingers through his curls. One little girl begged him to play a song. "Like the olden days, Your Grace." When no piano could be found, he sent them on a hunt through the lodging house, promising to play whatever instruments they dug up. They brought him tin cans, spoons, and a violin so out of tune it was laughable. Quin made a great show of it, flapping his imaginary tailcoat and bringing the bow to the strings—only to play hideous, screeching tunes that made the children shriek with laughter.

As he strutted and performed, Quin slowly became aware that the lodging house held not only children. Women and men were streaming in. More reticent than the children, but no hostility in their faces. Only curiosity. And perhaps a dash of hope.

"All right, children, all right. All eyes and ears on me, please!"

Stoddard clapped his hands, calling for order. Quin marveled at how easily the crusty old farmer had transformed into the jovial, avuncular fellow who now stood before him.

"Time to share King Quin for a bit, children. Do your chores and I reckon he'll play with you again."

There was one elated squeal, and a good bit of groaning, and then the children began to file out in separate directions. Quin felt sad to see them go.

"Your Grace." Stoddard nodded toward the table where Callaghan sat, now with two steaming mugs in front of her. "I hope you like butterfel."

Quin's whole face lit up. "You wouldn't believe how fervently I've longed for a hot mug of butterfel."

He slid into the seat and took a sip. It was just as good as he remembered. Heavenly, even.

"You're a man reformed, Stoddard."

"What do you mean?"

"Only that when I saw you last, you were determined to stay in the farmhouse forever, missing your wife."

"Still miss her, Your Grace." He touched the metal band around his finger. "I figure she'd want me to help the living, is all."

"Did you always know who I was?"

"I suspected. We'd all heard rumors you were coming back. We hoped very much they were true." He beckoned to the other adults, who were waiting shyly around the room. "Come meet the river king. He won't bite."

They came to Quin, one by one, each with a bow or curtsy. He met farmers and innkeepers; merchants and sailors; potters, bakers, blacksmiths. There were women who had worked in taverns and brothels; men who had led houses of worship before those houses were destroyed.

Here were the subjects Quin had so dearly sought, whom he had feared all dead or fled to Pembuk. For all his sweeping proclamations, he had failed to find them—until a puckish girl had taken him through the forest to a lodging house packed with Glasddirans ready to swear fealty as he claimed the throne.

The question was, did he deserve it?

"They all seem to believe in you."

Callaghan sat across the table, sipping her butterfel, watching him.

"*You* don't," he said. "Evidently."

"You're great with the orphans, don't get me wrong. That was a sight to see. But in the castle? It's like you became a different person." She shoved her mug away. "Maybe the Kaer is cursed. No Killian can set foot inside without turning into a soulless tyrant."

"Is that what you think I am?"

"Maybe." She scrunched up her nose. "I reserve the right to change my mind."

Quin regarded her, thoughtful.

"You remind me of my sister. Have I told you that?"

She brightened. "I loved Princess Karri. We all did."

"As did I. She had the biggest heart of anyone I've ever met. Karri was a Killian, but she didn't fall victim to the castle's curse, as you say. She would have loved"—he motioned around them—"whatever this is. What *is* this, exactly? If you're not Embers."

"We're the resistance to the resistance."

"I see. And do you have a name?"

She rolled her eyes. "No. We don't have a slogan, either."

"Then may I ask why you have the symbol of the Embers on your front door?"

Callaghan looked confused. "The Embers?"

"The triangles. The three flames."

She burst out laughing.

"Those aren't flames! And the Embers have nothing to do with it. Dom and I carved those."

Quin sat back. Trying to make sense of this.

"Did you leave them for me to find in the forest?"

"Not everything is about you! We didn't even know you were alive. We thought you might come back, but unlike some"—she lowered her voice—"we weren't convinced that would be a good thing. We worried you might try to claim the throne by show of force."

She stared pointedly at his hands, then skewered him with another of her withering looks. He was almost starting to like them.

"But to be honest, you weren't our main concern. The du Zols and I had been watching the Embers for a while. We saw the way Tobin was sweeping the countryside, promising a new kind of rule, then killing anyone who didn't agree. The symbol was meant to warn people. Whenever Dom or I got a whiff of where Toby was headed, one of us would slip away from the group and run to the village to carve three triangles in the places he intended to do harm."

"You were trying to protect people," Quin said, stunned.

"Sometimes we even succeeded. That's how we found the children. We brought them all back here to give them food and shelter." Her face fell. "But we failed many, many times."

Now Quin understood why the symbol always marked sites of death and destruction. He had assumed the triangles were carved after the violent deed was done, when in fact they'd been intended to prevent it.

"Not all the Embers are rotten," Callaghan said. "Most of them are innocent. They're just people trying to survive. And Sylvan and Maev were never as cruel as Tobin. If they were, I never saw it. I think they truly believe they're creating something better than Ronan or Angelyne."

A blade appeared in her hand. So deftly Quin startled.

"Don't worry," she said. "Not for you."

She pressed the tip of the knife into the wooden tabletop.

"That's the thing about power. It corrupts even good people. My mother taught the histories, remember? She said it's always the same cycle: first there are the monarchs."

Cal scored three sharp lines, etching a small triangle.

"Then, after the kings—or queens, they can be rotten,

too—come the ones who overthrow them." She engraved another, bigger triangle around the first. "But they're often just as bloody and violent as the kings and queens themselves. That's the second wave. It's up to the next wave of people to overthrow *them*."

She drew a third triangle around the first and second. Then set the knife down, satisfied.

"The third wave is the biggest. That's because we have the people on our side. The power is shared among all of us. We're the ones who balance things out again."

Quin peered intently at the triangles. With his fingertip, he traced the first, then the second, then the third. How could someone so young be so wise? He mulled it over, the idea that power was by its very nature corruptive. It had certainly corrupted his father. King Ronan had been drunk on his own might—and the river kingdom had paid the price. Same with Zaga. Then Angelyne.

Would power corrupt Quin, too? Or had it done so already?

"And then I came back," he said. "Just as desperate and hungry as Tobin."

She nodded. "We were eager to see what the Embers would do with you. We wondered if they'd put your head on a spike to prove a point."

He grimaced. "Thanks for the concern."

"Your head would look nice on a spike." She shrugged. "Easy on the eyes."

Did he detect the hint of a grin? He caught a glimpse of Brialli Mar, the girl he'd found so charming.

"You know, you really had me fooled. I never thought to look past the sweet, wide-eyed girl skipping through the woods with the Embers. You'd do well in the pretending arts."

"Not as well as you." She sniffed. "The thing is, I still can't tell if you're a tyrant pretending to be a good person, or a good person pretending to be a tyrant."

Neither, Quin realized. He was failing at both.

The door swung open with a bang. Quin and Callaghan looked up sharply as Domeniq stormed into the lodging house.

Cal sprung to her feet. "What's happened?"

"It's Maev and Sylvan."

She went ashen.

"Did they find us? Do they know we're here?"

"They didn't find anyone. Their heads are on two spikes outside the Kaer."

Quin's stomach pitched. Before he could respond, Dom turned to him.

"Tobin wants yours next."

Chapter 35

CHOKED

PILAR COULDN'T FIND STONE.

He wasn't in his sfeera. Wasn't at the circle, either. When she poked her head into the Manjala, she got nothing but a scowl from Celeste and the stink of incense in her nose.

Pilar hated herself for stalling. She knew exactly where Stone was. She just couldn't bear to say goodbye to that dirty, sweat-soaked room she loved so much.

But she owed Stone an apology for the way she'd treated him the night before. She didn't want his last memory to be her knocking him on his ass before he had time to defend himself. She couldn't let her last words to him be *You failed.*

There was another reason she needed to apologize. When it came to last words, she couldn't get the ones she'd said to Rose out of her head. *You really do break everything you touch.* She had called Mia a failure. And for someone like Mia Rose, failure was the worst possible thing.

Pilar didn't doubt Mia had crossed the Bridge to Prisma for a million reasons she would never understand. But she would always, for the rest of her life, wonder if her words had dealt the final blow.

So Pilar trudged to the farthest wing of the House of Shadows. Down the hallway she'd walked so many times—and into the Gymnasia.

At least, that was the plan.

The first thing she noticed was the sign.

Someone had nailed a large piece of parchment to the closed door of the Gymnasia. The message screamed in bloodred ink.

Kaara akutha! Here at Manuba Vivuli, you are warmly invited to explore modes of healing and self-expression that do not hinge on physical violence and aggression. We encourage all guests and residents to attend the circle, try jougi, or spend time in the Creation Studio!

To facilitate a better, safer, healthier experience at the House of Shadows, the Gymnasia will be permanently closed. We appreciate your understanding.

Blessings,
Celeste, the Keeper

Furious, Pilar ripped the sign off the door. It came loose in damp strips, the ink still wet. Parchment stuck to her palms and gummed up her fingernails. She wasn't going to let Celeste take this away from Stone, Shay—any of them. They deserved a place they could gather. Joke and laugh and learn how to protect themselves. They deserved to feel safe.

Once she'd peeled the last scrap of parchment from her hands, she looked back up.

The sign was still there.

What in four hells?

She ripped it off again. This time she kept her eyes glued on the door. Forced herself not to blink. And watched the sign regrow itself.

It happened again. And again. Pilar had seen some dark magic in her day. But watching Celeste's sanctimonious sheep shit reappear on the door over and over took the cake.

And then she spotted what she'd missed. The door had been sealed shut with some kind of caulk—also red, probably also magic. But when she traced a finger down it, she saw it had been slit down the middle with a blade.

A dagger was plunged into the side of the door. The hilt studded with blue uzoolion.

Someone had broken into the Gymnasia—and she had a feeling she knew who.

Silently, she nudged the door open.

At first she didn't see him. The room was pitch-black, and he was in the far corner, hunched over on the floor. Only the outline of his hair gave him away.

Stone's head was buried in his hands, his shoulders racked with sobs.

Pilar stood helplessly in the shadows. Groping for the right words. A joke to make him laugh. A kind word to console him. But what could she say? She'd taught him the Gymnasia was not a place for jokes and kindness. You went there to be hard, not soft.

And then her eyes adjusted to the darkness.

Her mouth fell open.

The Gymnasia had been stripped bare. Gloves, wrist straps—even the mats on the floor—all gone. The room had been scrubbed clean. Instead of sweat and blood, it reeked of lemon and sage.

Pilar imagined Celeste burning sage to clear out the evil spirit of violence.

In other words: the evil spirit of Pilar.

Her gaze snagged on a giant mound. Large, lumpy objects were piled carelessly on top of each other, like bodies lying in the dark. *The sandbags.* They hadn't just been cut down from the ceiling. They'd been gutted. Sliced open to ensure no one could ever punch them again.

The pain was physical, a blow to the solar plexus. All the things that made the Gymnasia a safe haven had been taken from them.

"Stone?"

Pilar froze. Shay's voice was coming from just outside the door.

"Are you in there, Stone? Please don't ignore me. I'm just as upset as you are. Please let me in."

Stone stayed hunched on the floor, though his sobs stopped abruptly.

Pilar's stomach dropped. Stone and Shay were the first of her brood. She should comfort them. Share their grief. And it was true grief she felt, standing in the ravaged Gymnasia. Knowing Celeste had stolen something precious from them all.

She should face them.

But she didn't. She hid like the coward she was.

Pilar ducked behind the sandbags. Crouched catlike on the floor. She could still hear herself bragging to Shay. *Being small has been one of my biggest advantages. I'm light on my feet.*

What a bill of goods she'd sold them. Acting like she was tough, courageous.

Shay slipped into the room.

"Stone. Please."

He didn't look up.

"I've been searching for you everywhere. I didn't know my mother would do this, I had no idea. It's so hurtful. This is too much, even for her."

"Your mother disgusts me." Stone's voice was low. Raspy. "*You* disgust me."

From her hiding place, Pilar watched Shay go completely still.

"I do?"

"Things were fine before *you* started coming. I felt happy sparring. I've spent years looking for something that makes me feel happy and strong. And now it's gone, thanks to you."

"I'll talk to Mumma. I can make her listen. She just doesn't understand what we do in here, how good it is for us." Her voice wavered. "Would you come walk with me, Stone?"

He laughed. A nasty sound that cut Pilar to the core.

"Why would I walk with you?"

"We could . . . talk about how you're feeling. I know you're angry. I'm angry, too. I want to be there for you. If you lean on me, you won't have to be alone."

"I don't need anyone to lean on, Shay. I know you want me to like you. You'd do anything for people to like you. It's pathetic."

"But . . . yesterday at the festival, I thought . . . I thought you liked being with me? You said you couldn't remember the last time you'd felt so happy."

"I was happy to get out of the House. It had nothing to do with you."

He stood. In the dark room Pilar could only see their outlines. Shay was so small next to Stone. But she was trying so hard to be tall.

"Let me make this easy for you," Stone said. "Whatever you thought was happening between us? You were wrong. I know we'll both be at the House for as long as my mumma is the Shadowess and yours is the Keeper. But I wish I never had to see your face again."

Pilar's blood was on fire. Why was Stone doing this? Why was he *lying*? She'd seen the way he looked at Shay. He was as smitten by her as she was by him.

"Thank you for being honest."

Shay's voice had lost all its light. She turned and walked slowly toward the door. Trembling. Even in the dark room Pilar could tell how hard she was fighting to stay upright.

Shay stopped in the doorway.

"I'll talk to Mumma. I want you to have the Gymnasia, Stone. You deserve to be happy."

And with that, she left.

The room went terribly silent. Pilar didn't know how to accept what she'd just seen. She sure as hells couldn't make sense of it.

"So." Stone's voice echoed off the empty walls. "How'd I do?"

Pilar swallowed. Her throat was bone dry.

"How long have you known I was here?"

"Since the moment you came in. You forget how much time I spend in here. I know every place the floor creaks."

Pilar took a step toward him.

"What the ___ was that, Stone?"

They stared each other down. His face was swollen, his cheeks tearstained. After what he'd said to Shay, she thought his eyes would be hard. Angry. But what she saw was pain. And something more complicated. It took her a moment to place it.

Hunger. That was it. The hunger of a student eager to please his teacher.

"I did it," he said. "What you taught me."

Pilar heard her breath catch.

"What do you mean, what I taught you? You were an ass to a girl who cares about you. A girl you care about yourself."

"Exactly." His gaze was fierce. "Why are you acting like this isn't what you wanted?"

He kicked one of the damaged sandbags. Red sand oozed from the wound.

"I came to find you last night because I needed your help. Yesterday, in Shabeeka, Shay and I had an adventure. We spent all day together, just eating and talking. Sometimes she would say something I was thinking before I did. She understood me. I've never felt that way with anyone."

He shook his head.

"It was exhilarating—and also terrifying. I didn't know what to do. So I came to ask your advice. You were drunk, but you answered my question anyway. You said not to trust people. That I shouldn't leave myself vulnerable to attack, because if I open myself up, people will hurt me."

"Shay?" Pilar shouted. "I didn't mean *Shay!*"

"Yes you did."

They glared at each other. Pilar clenched her fists. Stone clenched his at the exact same time.

"Tell me," she said, enunciating very slowly, "exactly what you mean."

"You were obviously too drunk to remember. But *I* remember. You said if you lean into someone, they're just going to pull away. I don't want that. I've felt lonely for so long. Everyone says I'm lucky to have the Shadowess and Lord Shadowess as my parents, and they're good people. Even I can see that. But they don't understand me. I thought maybe, if I found someone who understands me . . . who likes me for who I am . . . someone who might even love me . . ."

His voice broke.

"But you said even the ones who pretend to love you will abandon you in the end."

Pilar's heart was beating fast. Too fast.

"I thought you'd be happy, Pilar. I promised to work harder to learn everything you've been teaching me. And I'm trying, I really am. I won't let Shay into my head. I won't let her into my heart, either, so she'll never have a chance to break it."

Stone was full-on crying now. She wanted to reach out. Take his hands in hers.

"I didn't fail your lesson, Pilar. I did exactly what you told me." He choked on a sob. "I just didn't think it would hurt this much."

Chapter 36

THE SMALLEST

TOBIN'S DEMANDS WERE SIMPLE. Quin would come to the Kaer. His hands bound in uzoolion behind his back. Alone.

Tobin was holding the Embers hostage. All except Maev and Sylvan, whose scorched heads now graced the castle's southern parapet. For every hour Quin did not comply, Tobin would burn another body, adding a new head to the balustrade.

"He's baiting you," Domeniq said.

Dom paced the lodging house as Quin and Callaghan sat tensely at their table. Stoddard and a handful of others stood around the room, their faces grave.

"I don't disagree," said Quin. "But it's bait I have to take."

"You really think he'll free all the Embers in exchange for you?"

"It's me he wants. He doesn't care about the others."

"That's just it." Dom rubbed the back of his head furiously. "He'll slaughter them without a second thought."

"I'm going to get them out before he hurts anyone else. I do have magic, remember."

"So does he. He'll bend your mind the moment you set foot inside the Kaer."

"And if you're wearing the gloves," Callaghan added, "your magic will be weak."

Quin had a burst of inspiration. Uzoolion weakened magic, but other stones augmented it. He thought of Mia's fojuen wren. The same wren he had held himself under the snow palace, crashing it against Angelyne's black stone—and promptly shattering the known world.

"Fojuen," Quin said. "What if we balanced the uzoolion with fojuen?"

Domeniq rubbed his hands together. "It's worth a shot."

He waved over two men.

"Gather all the fojuen charms you can get our hands on," Dom instructed. "Amulets, runes, pendants—anything goes."

As the men hurried away, Dom turned back to Quin.

"We'll stuff as many as we can inside the gloves."

"I imagine Tobin will be ready for that," Callaghan said. "Stone is his specialty, remember? And anyway, he'll use head magic to manipulate the aether before you even get close."

"It's not like I'm going to waltz up the eastern road, Cal. I know the Kaer far better than he does. There are passageways he's never even seen. I spent my whole childhood skulking through them."

He stood.

"I'll go up the cliffside, then through the crypt. I'll be breathing down his neck before he even knows I'm inside."

Callaghan stood, too. "I'm going with you."

"Out of the question."

She stared him down, fierce and unwavering. The most Karri-like he'd seen her. He missed his sister more than he missed anything.

"You have to take me with you." Cal stepped closer, lowering her voice so only he could hear. "There's someone else in the castle."

He frowned. "Someone other than the Embers?"

"They're going to need our help to escape. But only I can take you to them."

She straightened.

"If you won't take me, then I'll find my own way in."

Against all odds—and despite the fear pulsing through him—Quin felt a smile rise to his lips. Callaghan was still keeping secrets. A fine mistress of the pretending arts.

He couldn't bear the thought of something happening to her. But he saw in her blue eyes that she would go to the Kaer with or without him.

He turned to Dom and the others.

"Pool all the uzoolion. The gloves, too. She's going to wear all of it. I want her protected from Tobin's magic." He met Callaghan's gaze. "And from mine."

They took two candles. Small and easily concealed. In the clunky uzoolion gloves, Callaghan clutched hers clumsily—but refused to let Quin take it from her.

"I know how to hold a candle," she hissed, and he stood down.

They had already passed the gilded carriage of the Bridalaghdú, dangling at the end of its cable. What a preposterous ritual, to lower a royal bride over the village draped in fine silks and jewels. Thank the four gods Queen Bronwynis had abolished it during her short-lived reign. One of his aunt's rare rulings that his father let stand.

Quin still remembered how it had felt, soaring down the cable with Mia by his side. Like flying. Like finally being free.

"A new head every hour," Cal reminded him, and he stopped gaping and took the lead.

As they edged along the cliffside, creeping ever closer to the crypt, the only sound was the guttering of two flames. A soft, uneven rhythm.

You'll come to me, under the snow plum tree.

The night of his secret rendezvous with Tobin, Quin had waited until the whole castle was asleep. He'd paced his drawing room so long that by the time he donned his jacket, his stomach was in knots. He crept silently past the grove of snow plums— and down into the crypt.

Tobin was there already. Pacing between the mausoleums, fingers tapping a nervous beat on his thighs.

You came, he said simply.

Of course I came.

"I wanted to tell you from the very beginning," Callaghan whispered, knocking him out of the memory. "But you were quite awful, so I kept it a secret. A secret from everyone. There was too much at stake. If Toby found out I was harboring members of your family . . ."

That brought him up short. "My family?"

She held a finger to her lips.

Quin's mind was spinning. His family was all dead.

Except for his cousin, he realized with a jolt. Had Tristan ridden to Kaer Killian and sought refuge? And why, of all people, would Callaghan be the one to give it?

"Are you harboring the duke?" he asked, keeping his voice low.

Her eyebrows arched. "Is that his name? 'The Duke'? It suits him!"

Quin began to sweat. He had sworn to himself that if he ever saw Tristan again, he would not fail to kill him. But was he prepared to take his cousin's life in front of Cal?

"This is it," she whispered.

They were on the precipice now, the ledge where Mia had shoved Quin into the laghdú for their death-defying descent. If he closed his eyes, he could see the wind whipping her curls around her face. She had looked wild, untamable. He'd been afraid of her. He'd been afraid of everything.

"Now or never," Cal said.

"Wait." He hugged his candle to his chest, cupping his hand around the flame. "If something goes wrong . . . if it comes down to the Embers and me . . . save the Embers. Get them out of the Kaer and take them somewhere safe."

She nodded, and together they ducked into the crypt.

It took a moment for their eyes to adjust. Quin's candle had flickered out; now only Callaghan's burned. But the moon bled light through a fissure, and the crypt revealed itself. He saw mausoleums and charnel houses, row after row of oppressive stones inscribed with names of Killians he had never known, and never wanted to.

Someone stirred behind the tombs. Quin's stomach clenched.

"Do you see them?" Callaghan whispered. "They see you."

Slowly, tentatively, two creatures emerged from the shadows.

Quin let out a cry.

He was looking at his dogs.

Wulf and Beo stood before the tombs. He would have known them anywhere. Their dusky yellow fur a burnished gold in the moonlight. Tails that curled into question marks when they were happy. Baleful brown eyes that had always seemed human.

"Beo." Quin held out his hands. "Wulf."

The dogs did not move. Had they forgotten him? But they forgot nothing. Especially Beo. Quin could hide a beef bone in a particular corner of the Kaer, and years later she would return to the exact same spot, licking her chops.

His hands were shaking. Did they smell it on him? The hateful things he had done? The things he'd *wanted* to do?

Or was it that he had abandoned them?

Quin loved his dogs more than anything. But he had left his own castle. Abandoned them at the mercy of cruel, violent people. They would not forgive him for it.

He did not deserve to be forgiven.

And then they caught his scent. Their brown eyes lit with recognition. Wulf yelped and loped forward, scrambling so fast his paws skittered across the stone. As Quin fell to his knees, Wulf barreled into him so hard with his cold nose they both fell backward.

Beo trotted forward, then hesitated. She had always been more sensitive than her brother, closely attuned to Quin's every emotion. When his father hurt him, she knew to lick away his tears. On the nights Quin ached with loneliness, she would jump onto his warm bed and wedge her body next to his, letting him wrap his arms around her.

"Beo." His voice was cracking. If she backed away, he did not think he could survive it. "Beo, my love."

And then she was coming toward him, climbing into his arms, licking his face, nuzzling her head into the space between his chin and collarbone. She pawed his face, whimpering, and Quin was crying, too, burying his face in her soft fur. She smelled of dirt and must and Beo. He had never loved her more.

"Wulf and Beo. That's perfect." Callaghan crouched beside him on the floor. "This whole time I haven't known their names."

She rubbed Beo's head, then scratched Wulf under his chin. He licked her hand.

"I've never seen them so happy," she said.

332

Quin was crying too hard to say anything.

"I hope you can forgive me for keeping them down here," Cal said. "I had seen them around the Kaer, begging for scraps. But then I heard some of the nastier Embers talking about what they'd like to do to the prince's dogs, and . . ."

Her voice dropped an octave lower.

"I decided the crypt was the safest place for them. I bring them raw meat and bones whenever I can. But I know they're lonely. Every time I tried to take them to Ilwysion, some Ember was always prowling about. And truthfully, your pups were just as impossible. Even when I tried to lure them out with treats, they refused to leave the crypt."

She leaned into Wulf, who rested his chin on her knee.

"I think they were waiting for you to come home."

Quin couldn't find the words. Cal had given him the greatest gift. How could he ever express what this meant to him?

His eyes roamed the crypt, noting a bowl of water, two piles of blankets, and a chewed-up wooden ball.

"You've taken good care of them," he said hoarsely.

"My father used to say that if we don't do right by the smallest creatures, there won't be any rightness left."

"I wish I could have met your father," Quin said.

Cal leaned her head against the tomb.

"I wish that, too."

They lingered in the crypt, perhaps because they did not know what would come next, or how painful it would be. The silence was broken only by the dogs' yawns and nuzzles. Later, when

Quin turned those precious final moments over in his mind, he would wonder why he hadn't heard the footsteps.

An object rolled gracelessly across the cold stone floor. Another wooden ball, Quin thought. Though much bigger.

"Your cousin missed you," said Tobin, stepping out from behind a mausoleum.

Only then did Quin realize the ball was Tristan's head.

Chapter 37

AGLOW

THEY SAT TOGETHER IN the surf. Mia with her trousers cuffed to the knee, auburn curls dancing at her cheeks. Angelyne with her emerald gown pooled around her, bare toes dug into the wet sand. The two Rose girls leaning toward one another, at the lip of an ocean, the cusp of a world.

"It's all right," said Mia, stroking Angie's back. Her sister's sobs were finally beginning to subside. "It's going to be all right," she said, though she wasn't sure it was.

Nothing had gone the way she expected. But then, nothing ever did. Just when she'd been absolutely certain Angelyne was going to kill her—as the phantoms of the four kingdoms crumbled like sandcastles—her sister had collapsed in her arms.

I deserve to die, she'd said, and those four words struck more fear into Mia's heart than all the other words put together.

"I tried to save you," Angelyne whispered, her slender chest heaving. "You and Pilar."

Mia fought to remember. No easy feat on the Isle of Forgetting. She struggled to parse the real memories from the unreal, holding each one up to the light.

"The snow palace," Angie pleaded. "Remember?"

It was coming back to her, in shadowy slivers. Quin in the underground cave, lunging at Pilar with fire between his fingers; Mia leaping into his path, hands closing around the flames; her skin blistering, though she couldn't feel it; scorched flesh melting away to reveal her carpals and metacarpals, hamate, capitate, scaphoid—in other words, her bones.

And then the piece she had somehow managed to forget. A piece so pivotal it astonished her that it had fallen into the recesses of her memory, though she had a theory, a hunch, that her mind had filed it away as too painful. She was never any good at feeling pain.

Go. Take Pilar and leave before I change my mind.

The last words Angelyne spoke before the ground fractured beneath them. Her final gift.

Mia's head reeled. Angie had wanted her dead. Angie had saved her life. She had brought the four kingdoms to their knees—and here she sat, weeping at the end of the world.

Did she deserve to die? Angelyne had hurt and killed, decimated and destroyed. She had built an empire on the bones of death.

But *deserve*? Since when was Mia Rose the arbiter of who deserved to die or live?

"I still don't know how I survived," Angie murmured, tugging her gown tight around her knees. She looked for all the world like a little girl at the seaside, soon to shape sand into towers. "It was only Quin and me, the cave falling down. I knew he was going to kill me. I didn't blame him. But when I looked into his eyes . . ." Angie pressed her fist into the sand. "I saw it."

Mia studied her sister. "Saw what?"

"What I had always seen in mine. There's a kind of knowledge you carry inside you when you've been stripped of every kind of power. Deep in your soul, you know you're weak." She shook her head. "No, worse than weak. You're *nothing*."

Angie whisked a fresh tear away. A few granules of sand clung to her cheek.

"It was like looking in a mirror. I don't know how else to describe it. I saw his pain and his rage. His whole life people had thought him a pitiful coward, and he was desperate to prove them wrong. I was like that, too. How could I not be? I grew up in the river kingdom, where girls were treated as less than human. They held us captive in our own homes, watched and restricted us—and we were the lucky ones. Other girls were tortured. Murdered. We all lived in fear."

"You didn't have to be afraid," Mia said quietly. "I would have protected you."

"That was part of the problem."

Angelyne gazed up at the impeccable blue sky.

"My whole life I looked up to you. I lived for the days we'd play dress-up and dance around the cottage. But you were always happiest out in the woods with the maps and curios Father brought you. Mia Rose, Explorer of Worlds, Hoarder of Treasures. You were never afraid like the other girls. You were Father's favorite. Mother's, too. And so blissfully unaware.

"Of course, everything changed the day Mother died. When she stopped her heart because I'd threatened to expose her as a Gwyrach, something died in me, too. But something also awakened."

Angie freed her right foot, then her left, brushing the sand off her toes.

"How did it feel when you first bloomed, Mi? What was your magic like?"

Mia considered it.

"I'd get those atrocious headaches, remember? Especially once Father gave me Mother's ruby wren. It was awful."

"For me it was extraordinary. At least at the beginning. I'd never experienced anything that powerful. I knew it made me wicked. I was a Gwyrach. Our own father had sworn to kill women like me. But I felt so alive. My mind was fierce, my heart courageous. For the first time, I felt like *you*."

Angie's pale blue eyes took on a fervid sheen.

"I had never kept a secret from you. And suddenly our mother was dead, all because I'd been afraid of her magic—unaware that *I* had magic. Of course, you changed that day, too. You swore your life to the Hunters, determined to kill the Gwyrach who'd murdered Mother."

The light in her eyes faded.

"My heart and mind had never felt stronger. But my body was a different matter. I got the same headaches, and worse—fevers, numb hands and feet, those terrible hacking coughs. You made it your mission to take care of me. The sicker I got, the more obsessed you became with healing me—which only made me feel more weak."

Mia winced. Pilar had said much the same thing. Another sister she had been ruthlessly determined to heal.

"It wasn't until Quin smashed my stones together that I understood where I'd gone wrong. I sensed the rift as soon as it happened—and not just because the glacier was collapsing. I could feel all four kingdoms torn asunder. It was what I'd thought I wanted. To be the mighty queen, the only one who could tip that fragile balance.

"But then I saw the emptiness in Quin's eyes. A hunger for power that could never be sated, because the more he tried to seize it, the emptier he would feel. That was the moment I understood that death is a kind of emptiness. And emptiness will never make you powerful. True power is the ability to create."

Angelyne exhaled all the air from her chest.

"Of course, by then it was too late."

They were quiet a long while. Mia had a million things to say. But for once, she said nothing. She let the words rest as the tide rolled in.

"And then you came to Prisma," Mia said finally.

"And then I came to Prisma. I was running from the magnitude of what I had done. But even here, I couldn't let go."

She held out her hand, showing Mia her palm. Fused with Angie's pink skin, the black gemstone had a virulent gleam.

"Death was with me always. I had excruciating visions of each kingdom being destroyed, people screaming in pain and terror. I knew it was all my fault. In the morning I'd walk the beach for hours, conjuring the images from my nightmares, forcing myself to watch the whole world die."

Now Mia understood what she had seen on the shoreline: echoes of her sister's nightmares, some true, some not. Angie needed only swipe her scarred hand over the horizon and a host of atrocities would rise from the sand.

Mia wanted to comfort her sweet baby sister. Angie had done horrible, unthinkable things—and she clearly regretted them. Mia imagined their mother bundling them both into her arms. *My little raven. My little swan.*

But even now she was falling back on old habits, infantilizing Angelyne. Her sweet baby sister hadn't asked for comfort. She had asked Mia to remember she was not a sweet baby at all.

Angie rose, shaking her dress free of sand.

"I only showed you one part of my island. The most painful part. It's getting harder to hold on to these memories, I think because I'm getting closer to being able to let go."

Mia stood. The way Angie said *let go* worried her.

"Let go of the memories, you mean?"

"You'll see. It's a part of what comes next."

Angelyne took her by the hand. Mia felt the cold stone embedded in her sister's palm. She tried not to shudder.

"I want to show you my island, Mi. Before it's too late."

Angelyne's island was beautiful. Magnificent waterfalls crashed into shallow green pools. If you looked to the very top, the sun's glare slashed a pink star through the water.

Angie took her to a valley blanketed with a patchwork of brilliant squares, one bleeding into the next: coral to vermilion, vermilion to violet, violet to ochre. They were blanketed with poppies, narcissus, clover—and fruit trees, too, apple and wolf peach and snow plum. Buttery sunlight scraped over the hills, turning each square into combed velvet.

Why, in the midst of such stunning beauty, did dread coil in Mia's stomach?

"Look," said Angelyne.

Above them, a modest castle nested in the cliffside, carved from pale-green stone.

"Aventurine," Angie said. "I always thought it was so pretty. Certainly prettier than the ugly black Kaer. I'm glad I don't ever have to go back."

"Is this where you live now?"

"Yes." Angelyne beamed. "Would you like to come inside?"

In every room of the castle, Mia recognized her sister's touch. Tapestries graced the walls, bursting with silk ribbons and peacock feathers. A spacious courtyard revealed a well-tended topiary and an orangery with garlands of scarlet stoneberries woven through the trees. Every embellishment was elegant without being ostentatious—regal, but tastefully so.

"You must see my chambers," Angie said, leading her upstairs to a room with a sweeping balcony that reminded Mia of their childhood home. Beside a canopy bed smothered in fluffy pillows was a vanity glittering with jewels, brooches, combs, skin greases—and a moonstone pendant that looked exactly like their mother's. Mia felt both comforted and alarmed.

She inhaled the scent of lilacs and lavender soap. Even here, on the Isle of Forgetting, her sister's scent had not changed. Mia reached out and touched a braided strand of swan and raven feathers twirling from a hook. The whimsy hurt her heart. In spite of everything, all the death and destruction, Angelyne was still a fifteen-year-old girl.

"This is how I always wanted to decorate my room at home," Angie said wistfully. "I imagined one day I would live in a castle like this."

"It's lovely," Mia replied, unable to shake the nameless fear that had curled into her belly.

From a nearby room, she heard a cry. The tendons in her neck tensed.

"What was that?"

"Oh, it's all right. Fin's just hungry for her breakfast."

She walked under an archway entwined with pink roses, beckoning Mia to follow.

They had stepped into a nursery. Here was the fyre ink Angelyne had promised: cheerful scenes played out on the walls in moving ink, raccoons gobbling plump cherries, a scarlet bear peeking out from the snow. In the corner, a small red bird peeked out of a miniature birdcage.

A white-haired woman sat beside a cradle, rocking it gently.

Mia gave a start. She looked like an older version of their mother. A ghost version.

"It's about time you came back," scolded Wynna's ghost. "She's hungry."

Horrified, Mia turned to her sister—and was transfixed by her face.

Angelyne had never looked so happy. On the beach she'd been crushed under the weight of shame and regret. But here, in the nursery, she was aglow.

Angie reached into the cradle and lifted a bright-eyed baby into her arms. She turned to Mia, cheeks flushed, eyes dewed.

"Mi, I want you to meet my daughter."

Chapter 38

NOTHING

"Is it real?" Quin asked.

He gestured toward the charred head on the crypt floor.

"Did you kill Tristan? Or is it only in my mind?"

Tobin stepped into the light, amused. He tapped the severed head with his boot.

"I suppose you can't know for sure, can you? You'll just have to take my word."

The head was hard to look at. Even so, Quin forced himself not to look away. His cousin was irredeemable. A rapist. A traitor. Quin had wanted him dead.

And now here he was. Burned beyond recognition. Dead.

Why was it that Quin felt no satisfaction, only fear?

"It's real," Callaghan confirmed, her voice small but brave. Cal was ensconced in enough uzoolion to sink a small ship—and neutralize any head magic. What she saw was true.

"You were to come alone," Tobin said coldly. "Now I've found not one traitor, but two. Four, if you include the dogs. It seems little Briallihandra Mar has been keeping secrets."

"Let her and the dogs go, Toby. We can settle this between you and me."

"On the contrary. Brialli has been harboring these beasts without my knowledge. She appears to also have been harboring *you.*"

Tobin took a menacing step toward them. Quin tried not to flinch.

"Remarkable," Tobin said. "You went right to it."

"I—I'm not sure I follow."

"Why would you? You had your eyes squeezed shut the entire time."

Tobin slammed his palm into the nearest tomb. Wulf's yelp echoed through the crypt.

"Stop cowering, son of Killian. Take note of where you are. Where you're sitting."

A sick feeling crawled through Quin's stomach.

"I don't—"

"Want to remember? I don't want to remember, either. But I don't have the luxury."

Tobin lunged. Callaghan shouted, veering around Tobin, then bolted out of the crypt, the dogs at her heels.

Good. At least Cal had escaped.

Quin willed the fire into his hands, summoning the power of the fojuen stones around his neck, stuffed into his trouser pockets, lining the inside of his jacket.

But the fojuen did not augment his magic.

It augmented Tobin's.

"Remember," Toby said, wrapping his hands around Quin's skull.

And the memory came.

Under the plums, if it's meant to be. You'll come to me, under the snow plum tree.

Quin crept through the corridors, past the grove of snow plums, and down into the crypt. Tobin was pacing between the mausoleums, fingers tapping a nervous beat on his thighs.

"You came," he said simply.

"Of course I came."

He didn't know who stepped toward the other, or if they both stepped forward in perfect harmony. But suddenly their bodies were pressed together so naturally Quin wondered how they'd ever been apart.

His whole life he'd felt soft. Helpless to escape his father's rages, helpless to evade his carefully scripted future. But when Toby wrapped his arms around him, Quin thought for the first time that perhaps softness was a kind of strength.

Tobin kissed him. Quin kissed back. The tension drawn taut between them melted into a melody longing to be written. His music teacher touched his chest, fumbling feverishly with his gold buttons.

"You unbutton these every day?" Toby said, tugging so hard

that one button popped off its threads and rolled across the floor.

"My life is fraught with hardship," Quin said.

Tobin's laugh was so beautiful he wanted to eat it, to move it from Toby's mouth to his, and so he kissed him more deeply, their tongues lightly touching, until the tombs dissolved and there was only them.

And then there wasn't only them.

Quin felt his father's presence before he saw him. The hairs prickled on his neck. He'd always sworn every room grew colder once King Ronan stepped inside it.

Tobin pulled his hands out of Quin's curls so quickly Quin winced. *Hide,* Toby mouthed, and tugged him behind the closest tomb.

Ronan didn't see them. He charged into the crypt barking orders at his men.

"There," he said, pointing to the long stone slab. Only then did Quin realize the guards were carrying a body.

From his hiding place, he recognized her. Wynna Rose, wife to Lord Griffin Rose, leader of the Circle of the Hunt.

Griffin stood in the shadows, his face sickly gray. He took a step toward his wife's body.

"Leave her," Ronan commanded.

"Let me take her home, Your Grace. I beg of you. Let me bury her."

The king's blue eyes smoldered with silent rage. Quin knew the look well.

"She stays here. You may choose her stone. A gift far more

munificent than you deserve."

Griffin's eyes were blank. A practiced blankness, Quin thought.

"Thank you, Your Grace."

"Keep your gratitude. When your eldest daughter comes of age, she will marry my son. Keep my Hall of Hands well fed and no harm will come to her."

Quin's eyesight blurred.

She will marry my son.

In those five words, his fate had been decided. The happiness he'd felt only moments ago lay dead at his father's feet. The king's latest victim.

"What's this?" Ronan said.

He pointed, his shadow shifting across the catacombs. The breath caught in Quin's throat.

"Bring it to me."

A guard stooped and plucked something off the floor. Quin saw a familiar glint. A chill swept down his spine.

"A button, Your Grace," the guard said, handing it to the king. "A gold button."

Ronan held it in his palm for only a moment.

"My son is here."

For years after, Quin would wonder how his father knew so quickly. As if he kept a catalog of all the gold buttons in the Kaer and knew exactly which were Quin's. He did keep catalogs of other things: imported liquors, grain stores, names of the women whose hands he took.

"Reveal yourself," Ronan commanded.

Quin was trembling so hard he couldn't feel his feet.

And then he felt Tobin's hand on his arm. Toby gave a gentle squeeze.

"It's all right," Toby whispered, and stepped out of the shadows.

"Please, Your Grace. This isn't what it looks like."

Quin followed, shamefaced, a few steps behind.

"It's entirely my fault," Toby continued. "I thought we could explore the Kaer as a way of finding music in unexpected places. But I assure you, your son—"

"Say another word and I'll cut out your tongue." Ronan turned to Quin, sneering. "Considering where it's been, I should cut it out regardless."

The king was many things, but he was not a fool. He had a knack for sniffing out a person's true crime.

Ronan set his cold blue gaze on his son.

"I've always known you for what you were. I prayed to the gods I would never have to see it."

He had the knife in hand before Quin could blink.

The moment his father's blade sliced into Tobin's finger, blood spurting from the wound, Quin fell to his knees and vomited. He crawled behind the closest tomb, retching, as inhuman screams shredded the air.

For months he had sat on the piano bench, lovestruck, as Tobin's beautiful hands played the most exquisite music. Now he covered his ears, desperately trying to seal out the sounds of metal hacking into flesh.

It didn't matter. He heard them anyway.

349

"You will watch," Ronan roared, dragging Quin out from behind the tomb by his hair. "You will see what you have done."

So he watched. He saw. And he did nothing.

Nothing.

Nothing.

He simply wept.

Chapter 39

THE WAY WE SAY GOODBYE

Pilar had never seen Celeste's working chambers. She'd done everything in her power to avoid the woman, and now here she was, seeking her out.

She had paced the House for hours, thinking. Not about her conversation with Stone. She refused to think about that. Instead, all her rage and fury settled on Celeste. The woman claimed to want to protect the children of Manuba Vivuli from harm. But she was *causing* harm. Closing the Gymnasia and stuffing her own self-righteous belief system down people's throats.

Keeper. Pilar had to laugh. Keeper, her ass.

But she had to be careful. As much as she wanted to punch the Keeper in her cute little nose, she knew that wasn't the right tactic. It would only prove Celeste's point.

So she would do her best to play nice. Appeal to Celeste's infinite wisdom and the abundance of the kosmos. Talk about what model citizens the students were, Shay most of all. Pilar would even cry if she had to. She was prepared to do whatever it took to win back the Gymnasia for her brood.

Even if she had to pry it from Celeste's cold, sage-infested hands.

The hallway dead-ended in an empty room, in a wing she hadn't even known existed. Pilar thought she knew the House pretty well by now. But it was still keeping secrets.

The room was a giant fishbowl. Not just the shape—half of it was an actual fishbowl. Dozens of fish swam through the glass wall at her back. In front of her: seven doors.

One was open.

"Pilar d'Aqila."

Celeste stood in the doorway. A curious smile on her face. Like she'd been waiting.

"I'm glad you found me. I was on my way to find you."

Pilar cocked a brow. "Really."

"Really. Kaara akutha. Please! Come inside."

Pilar tensed as she walked through the doorway, bracing herself for the cheek kisses. But for once Celeste kept her hands and mouth to herself.

Her working chambers were simple—two chairs, a wooden desk, and a single Black Rose in a vase. Walls mostly blank except for a few parchments with trite messages Pilar guessed were meant to be inspiring.

When Celeste motioned her toward a chair, she sat.

"Thank you," she said, forcing herself to be polite.

"You're most welcome!" Celeste sat, too. "I understand the Shadowess has extended an invitation for you to accompany the caravan to Glas Ddir?"

Pilar shifted, uncomfortable.

"If you're wondering how I know, it's because she and I had previously discussed it. She felt it was a good idea to expedite your departure from the House of Shadows. I agreed."

Pilar frowned. From her conversation with the Shadowess, she'd gotten the sense that her presence was actually *wanted* on the expedition.

"Are you saying she was trying to get rid of me?"

"She was trying to do what's best for the residents of the House. Your presence here puts vulnerable populations at risk. You don't belong here, Pilar."

Pilar was staggered. Celeste wasn't even trying to be nice. The niceties were clearly a show she put on for other people.

To hells with politeness. Pilar opened her mouth to say some choice words—but different words came out.

"You said all those who come to the House of Shadows are those who belong."

"Great sands, no! *I* didn't say that. The Shadowess did."

She leveled a cool gaze at Pilar.

"Did you tell Stone to hurt my daughter?"

"No. Never. That's not what I—"

"An hour ago Shay came in here absolutely distraught. My daughter has a tender spirit. She's fragile, and for some reason she looks up to you. But thanks to your 'teachings,' that boy broke her heart."

"I didn't mean to teach him that," Pilar said weakly. "Mia had just left, and I . . . I wasn't in my right mind."

"Is it really any different from what you've been teaching them for the last month? You've shown them a variety of ways to hurt and wound one another. These are children."

"I was trying to teach them to protect themselves. I want them to be safe."

"And did these lessons keep *you* safe, Pilar? On Refúj?"

Pilar froze. She forced herself to breathe.

"Correct me if I'm wrong," Celeste went on, "but wasn't Orry the one who taught you how to fight? And in the end those lessons proved quite . . . ineffectual."

Pilar's hands went numb. She hadn't talked about her past to anyone at the House. Not a soul.

She stared into Celeste's icy blue eyes. Realization dawning.

"You can see . . ."

"Your memories?" Celeste was fighting back a smile. "Yes. I simply have to touch you first. A quick peck on the cheek works just fine."

Pilar's stomach twisted. In her mind she saw Celeste greeting everyone who came to the House of Shadows. *It's the way we say hello in Pembuk. A kiss on each cheek.*

"I'm the Keeper. It's important I know what kind of history our guests bring with them. Some people's memories are easier to see than others. Yours, for example. So raw! Poor thing."

Pilar shrank. She was back in the snow palace, Lord Dove prying into her head. Feeding off her most private pain.

"You used my own memories against me." She choked down the bile rising in her throat. "You invited me to the circle so you could say Morígna's exact words."

Celeste let out a long sigh.

"I feel for you, Pilar. I do. Orry harmed you, as did Morígna, as did your Dujia sisters. It wasn't right. But I can't have you damaging the young, impressionable souls here at the House, all because you haven't worked through your own damage. What kind of Keeper would I be? Can you imagine?"

Fondly, she reached out to stroke the Black Rose. The petals curled inward at her touch.

"I've given you so many chances to do the work," Celeste said. "But you seem uninterested in doing so."

Pilar's world was spinning. She reached out to steady herself on the desk.

"I don't like to use my magic unless it's absolutely necessary. But the kosmos has granted me certain gifts. There are times when, for the good of the residents and guests here at Manuba Vivuli, I am called upon to use them."

Pilar couldn't look at her. She was afraid if she did, she'd see Morígna looking back.

"Don't misunderstand me, Pilar. It's not your fault you are the way you are. Each of us is formed by our unique experiences—our parents, our childhoods, the things we've suffered. But some people are so sick, there's nothing we can do to heal them. Not even at Manuba Vivuli."

Celeste rose. She stepped around her desk, smiled—and cupped Pilar's face in her hands.

Pilar jerked away. She didn't want to be touched. Not now, not ever.

But Celeste held on tight, bending down to kiss one cheek, then the other.

"It's the way we say goodbye in Pembuk."

With a look of smug satisfaction, Celeste released her.

"Goodbye, Pilar. Salu karaa. May you find abundance. I trust the kosmos will provide."

Chapter 40

EXPLORER OF WORLDS

THE BABY SAT ON Mia's lap. Burbling, cooing, nibbling on Mia's fingers, now sticky with spit.

"I've never been good with babies," Mia said, afraid that any minute the child would slip and hit the floor.

"You're good with her," Angie countered.

Every few seconds, it would wash over Mia anew: that she was in a castle, with Angelyne, holding her sister's daughter.

And none of it was real.

Even as Mia held on to the baby's wiggling legs, she could feel the wrongness of it. The little body was too light to be made of flesh and bone, the skin so pale it was almost diaphanous—yet there were no veins beneath the surface, no blood being shunted to and fro. The girl's hair was feather fine, but far too long for an infant, blond curls already spilling halfway down her neck. She smelled of lavender and sweet roses. It was as if Angelyne had imagined the way she thought a baby would look and feel and smell, then conjured this fantasy child from the aether.

"It took me a while," Angie explained, "to understand how the island worked. At first all I did was take long walks on the beach and watch all the horrific things I'd done. There were more intimate memories, too: Mother stopping her heart, or the day I sent Quin to follow you and Pilar. I got used to the pain. I even came to enjoy it. It was no less than what I deserved."

She squeezed her eyes shut, slowly releasing her breath.

"But the longer I spent here, the more the memories began to shift. The mist was transforming them. I never killed anyone. Mother didn't die; we watched her grow old. I set Quin free. But he came back and chose me, because he loved me. I was a good queen."

The baby hiccoughed, then let out a cry. She reached for Angelyne.

"But I didn't just want to be a queen. I wanted to be a mother. I've always wanted to be a mother."

She scooped up her daughter, then unclasped the bodice of her gown, bringing the infant to nurse. Her breasts were fuller than they'd ever been, plump with milk. Something Angie had said long ago drifted through Mia's mind. *What I wouldn't give to have a porcelain swell of breast.* How hard they'd laughed.

"Her name is Fin Morwynna. I named her after Mother. And after you."

Mia's chest ached. She could see what was happening. Her sister had done unconscionable things, and when she wanted to punish herself, she held up her black gemstone and walked the shore of death. When it hurt too much, she faded back into the fantasy world she'd created. Back and forth she cycled between them, an endless cycle of attack and retreat.

But Mia's chest ached for another reason. Angelyne looked so happy, sitting there. Like she was always meant to be exactly where she was, in this pretty castle, a *good* queen, not a wicked one. Angie in a green gown with a baby cradled in her arms.

"Angelyne Rose," Mia murmured. "Queen of the Castle, Mother of Fin."

"I always wanted to get married and have children. You thought those things made me a failure as a woman. But that was *your* failing, deciding for all women what we were allowed to want."

The indictment landed hard. Her sister wasn't wrong. Mia had proclaimed herself the savior of women, in a world where she felt confident women needed to be saved. She was only now beginning to understand that she had merely prescribed her own belief system. As if women were a monolith. As if they should all want the things Mia wanted.

"Here," Ange went on, "in this place, I didn't have to feel ashamed of wanting these things. My life was mine to design. I could live however I wanted, with whom I wanted. You saw Mother already."

So the white-haired woman was indeed their mother—or, rather, an echo of their mother. Mia scanned the nursery. Wynna had either left the room or simply faded away.

"She was a tremendous help when the baby was born. The king is around here, too, probably out in the orangery. Quin loves the orange trees this time of year."

Mia's heart lurched.

Quin was here.

Only, he wasn't. None of these people were. They were ghosts, mere shades of the real thing.

And suddenly Mia understood why her sister had chosen Quin as her companion in this strange, dreamlike place. It ran deeper than some girlhood crush. As the snow palace fell, Angelyne had found her own fury and suffering reflected in Quin's eyes. In that moment, she had seen him, *known* him, and, perhaps more important: she had felt known herself.

And rightly so. They had both felt powerless to change their stories. The world had tried to crush them—and had, in many ways, succeeded. Quin and Angie had paid close attention, then done the only thing they knew how to do: crush others to survive.

"Come back with me, Ange."

Mia hadn't known what she was going to say until she said it. She hadn't even known she wanted to go back herself. More than that, she wasn't sure she *could*. No one had ever returned from Prisma. Was it really as easy as stepping onto the Bridge and returning to her old life?

She heard the echo of Pilar's voice in the Creation Studio.

We have to go back.

Pilar was right. It wasn't even Pil's kingdom, and yet somehow she'd known what they had to do. As opposed to Mia, who had run in the opposite direction, wanting only to forget.

"Come with me to the river kingdom, Angie. We can save Quin from turning into his father. I know we won't be able to undo everything that's been done. But we can still set things right."

For a moment, Angelyne held her gaze. Silent. Unmoving. Then she drew a finger over her nipple, unlatching Fin's small, hungry mouth.

She placed her daughter softly back in her crib. Turned to face Mia.

"We're so tired of being angry, Mi. Tired of waking every day to shame and regret."

A trickle of unease slid down Mia's spine. Her sister had shifted again from *I* to *we*.

Angie strode across the nursery. She rearranged the cushions on the checkered window seat, then situated herself, motioning Mia toward the glass. Outside, the orangery was in bloom.

Mia crept closer. For just a moment, she saw him, wending his way through the orange trees. A flash of golden curls glinting in the sun. Ghost or no, she could feel herself leaning toward Quin.

"Oh, Mi," Angie said softly. "Do you think I haven't wished a thousand times that I could go back and undo what I did? I meant what I said. I deserve to die. It's better for everyone if I let go."

"No." Mia shook her head furiously. "I refuse to believe that. You're not evil, Angie. You understand the things you did were wrong. You can still atone for them."

"People come to the Isle of Forgetting to let go, Mi. It's why you came, too, remember?"

"I was wrong. I thought I wanted to leave my life behind, but I don't. Because this?" Mia waved her hand around the nursery. "This is beautiful, Ange. It's magical." She gestured toward Fin. "*She's* beautiful. But it's make-believe. If you come back with me, you can have these things in the real world. You can still be a mother."

Angie looked wounded.

"Maybe it's make-believe to *you*. But it's real to us. And once we let go of the rest, we'll have it forever. I won't be the sister you remember. We'll be unrecognizable to you. But the world will be better for it. *I'll* be better for it. We are not afraid."

Angelyne's smile was beatific, with no trace of bitterness.

"If you want to leave, Mi, leave. But you have to let me go."

Mia's heart flailed in her chest.

"I'm not leaving you behind."

"Maybe I want to be left behind. That's the part you always got wrong. You wanted to save me. Now I get to save you."

"Please don't do this, Angelyne. We can get through this. We'll find a way. You don't have to sacrifice yourself for the things you've done. I forgive you."

"I don't deserve to be forgiven."

"Then I forgive you all the same."

Angie's smile was sad around the edges.

"I want to give you something, Mi."

She laid her hand on her lap, revealing her ravaged palm once more.

"Under the snow palace," Angelyne began, "I said that the Elemental Hex was a feeble human attempt to understand a complicated world. I stand by that. You cannot reduce humanity to six tidy elements on three perfect poles. There is a seventh axis. But I was wrong about what that axis was. It isn't death."

Angelyne's other hand was balled into a fist. She offered it to Mia, who hesitated.

"She's yours," Angie said. "But don't let her fly away."

Intrigued, Mia held out her hand, Angie uncurled her fingers—and the ruby wren strutted onto Mia's palm.

The bird tilted its head, calmly assessing her, as she assessed the bird. Mia felt as if she'd been reunited with a long-lost friend. She remembered the night her father gave her Wynna's journal, back when the bird was just a fojuen key. Both she and the ruby wren had survived quite a lot since then.

"The seventh element is life," Angie said gently. "Remember that. Take it back with you to the river kingdom. That's what Mother tried so hard to teach us. Love is always the stronger choice. Hatred only leads you astray. It's led me so far astray I can't find a way back."

Fin cooed in her cradle. Ange smiled.

"And life is *always* more powerful than death."

Mia sank onto the window seat beside her sister. She was tired, too. She wanted Angelyne to choose life. *Real* life, not the kind in an imaginary cradle.

She rested her forehead against the windowpane. Stared into the orangery, reshaping the orange trees into bloodblooms in her mind. Mia imagined the charm in her palm, the sound of creaking wood as she breathed in, the hush of rustling leaves as she breathed out.

Maybe she could teach Angelyne what Muri had taught her: how to calm her own breath. If Mia coaxed her sister back into her body, would she be able to convince her to come home?

"Angie," she began. "I'd like to . . ."

Angelyne was peering intently out the window. Mia followed her gaze. The mist hovered thickly above the orangery. It stretched as far as the eye could see, seeping over waterfalls, pouring through valleys, masking the entire island in a soft white cloak.

From this height, Mia saw what she'd missed. The mist wasn't stagnant, as she'd assumed. It churned in a rapid spiral. She peered more intently. There was something odd about the way it caught the light. Almost like it wasn't droplets of water. Which would mean it wasn't mist at all.

She heard the voices whispering. Calling to her. Some were new. Some she recognized.

And then, unmistakably, she heard Nell's words.

The wind whips up the sand and the sun melts it into a glittery glass cyclone, and when you look into it you see your life . . . only it isn't really your life. All the grief and sadness are gone, along with the mistakes you made, the

*people you lost, so you're looking at the life that might have been, the better one,
and you don't just see it, you're inside it.*

Startled, Mia pushed back from the window.

"It's not mist," she said. "It's glass."

"Beautifully done." Angelyne looked pleased. "A million tiny
shards, to be specific. They call it a glass terror on the mainland,
though. I don't much care for that name."

She lifted herself off the window seat to perch on the sill. Mia
fought the urge to grab hold of her. To make sure Angie didn't
plummet to the ground below.

"Do you see now? It's not like we stop existing. We've been
sawn into a thousand pieces, yes. You might call that an act of
violence. But our hopes, our most precious longings, our very
souls—the mist holds them all. And when we are ready to let
go of what came before . . . to let the mist rewrite the pain and
suffering of our past . . . once we choose to move into the final
stage of our life on Prisma . . . it invites us into a warm, eternal
embrace."

Instinctively Mia traced the six petals inked on her wrist, conjuring the Elemental Hex in her mind. Glass was a kind of Stone,
and Stone was bound to aether. A shard of glass could twist what
the eyes saw and what the body understood.

A thousand shards of glass could make it so there was no longer any body at all.

Mia stared out the window, heart pounding in her ears.

"That's what a glass terror is," Mia said, realizing. Her words
thick with horror. "And that's why there aren't any people on the

island. The bodies of everyone who came to Prisma have been sliced apart."

Angelyne's eyes shone like glass.

"Not apart, Mi. We've finally come together. This is the last choice I must make. The last choice for anyone who comes to Prisma: the moment we decide to truly let go. The mist is a million souls freed from a million bodies, liberated from all pain and suffering. Now that they've surrendered the lives they had, they are finally able to give themselves—to give all of us—the lives we've always wanted. A life without illness or death. We vow to give our bodies and our spirits to this island. In return, we are given only love."

The words skulked through Mia's mind with an eerie familiarity. She had once said something similar herself. Standing in a chapel that felt more like a tomb. Quin's hands in hers.

I give you my body, my spirit, my home.

Come illness, suffering, e'en death,

Until my final breath I will be yours.

No. The Glasddiran wedding vows had it all wrong. Had she really expected otherwise, from a kingdom as backward as Glas Ddir? Love was not meant to be an abdication of your personhood, a capitulation of body, spirit, and home.

She summoned Nell's words.

Love is what happens when two people come together as equals, each with their own painful history and gifts and failings, neither of them needing to be saved.

That was the kind of love Mia wanted. That and only that.

That was the kind of *life* Mia wanted. A life of painful histories, and gifts, and failings. Perhaps failings most of all.

She had spent the last seventeen years doing a kind of accounting. On one side of the ledger was every theory or hypothesis she was able to successfully prove, every time she'd been unequivocally, unmistakably *right*. She had forced her need to be right on other people—bludgeoned them with it, really—treating them as equations that needed to be solved. As long as they needed her, she must be worth something.

Mia had run from her mistakes. Run from suffering, both other people's and her own. In truth she had treated all pain as an ailment in search of an antidote, not a natural course of body and soul. She had fled from all her failures, sure that they would stack up on the wrong side of the ledger, chipping away at her perfect armor—and proving just how broken she was.

She was beginning to see it differently. Her failures were what made her whole.

When Mia spoke again, her voice was quiet.

"I tried to take care of you, Angie. But I failed. I never saw what you needed. I saw you as our pretty little swan. A delicate rose, tragically sick, unable to survive without her big sister."

"Sweet baby sister was the role you gave me. And it was the role I played."

"You shouldn't have had to play any role. You weren't a pet. You were wild and beautiful. You deserved to have magic, and have babies, and be anything you wanted to be."

Angelyne stared at her scarred palm. Then closed her fingers around the wound.

"Girls don't get to be both wild and beautiful."

"They should," Mia said resolutely. "They *will*."

She cleared her throat. She could already feel the tears building behind her eyes.

"I am so sorry, Angelyne. Sorry for everything you have suffered, and for the ways I have deepened those wounds. I love you. You will always be my sister. And I wish you'd come back with me. I wish that more than anything. But I won't pretend to know what is best for you, or try to mold you into the shape I want. You get to choose."

Angelyne turned away from the window. She gazed toward Fin's cradle, her blue eyes soft.

"I already have."

The grief Mia felt then could not be named. She had known this would be her sister's answer. But for maybe the first time in her life, she had wanted so desperately to be wrong.

She reached out and touched Angie's cheek. Mia's hands were steady, even as her voice shook.

"Goodbye, Angelyne Rose," she said. "Explorer of Worlds. Sister of Mine."

Chapter 41

REMEMBER ME

EVERY PART OF PILAR hurt. Outside, inside. Scabs on her knuckles. Holes in her heart.

She dragged herself back to her sfeera, unaware of anything but the pain. Celeste had abused her position and her power. She had stripped Pilar's history for parts and made them into weapons. Lord Dove had done this, too. So had her mother. Morígna. Orry.

The same questions looped through her mind.

Why does this always happen? And why does it always happen to *me*?

But she knew why. These people, these predators, hunted her like a wolf hunts a dying deer. They smelled it on her. Her hunger to be loved.

Pilar had amassed a whole brood of recruits because she needed to be loved. She'd found joy in teaching them. Pride. But she'd taught them the wrong lessons. Or maybe the right lessons, in the wrong ways. In trying to keep Stone from being hurt, she'd only hurt him—and then he had hurt Shay in return.

Pilar wanted to cry, scream, break something. She'd wanted to give Stone a set of tools to protect himself against people trying to hurt him. Not people trying to love him.

She kept smacking up against her own hypocrisy. She drew a circle in her mind around everyone she had ever loved. Or *almost* loved.

Her mother. Orry. Morígna. Quin. Mia Rose.

It was a small circle.

She drew a second circle around everyone who had ever hurt her.

Her mother. Orry. Morígna. Quin. Mia Rose.

Not two circles. There was only one.

Then she thought of Stone. Shay. All their funny, eager friends, young women and men searching for something they couldn't quite describe. Pilar loved her students in a different way, of course, but that love was no less valid. No less true.

But when it came to opening *herself* up to love? No. She'd blocked it at every turn. She'd refused to share anything personal. Rebuffed Mia. Stone. Her brood. They didn't need to know anything about her. She deflected every question they asked about her life, her fears, her dreams. She was teaching them to be strong. How to defend themselves.

Or so she thought. Because what had she taught them, really?

How to be lonely. How to hold themselves apart from everyone and everything. And she'd modeled it so well! Don't go to jougi. Don't join the circle. Don't share meals. Answer vulnerability with sarcasm. When someone wants to connect, laugh. Shrug. Always shrug. Build a wall around your heart so tight, no one can ever break it.

Build the wall so tight, your heart can't even beat.

Celeste's words haunted her. But they were true.

Pilar didn't belong in the House.

The reek of roses knocked her back. She was passing the Rose Garden. She thought of Celeste, the gardener with the touch of death.

Then Pilar thought of Mia. Where was she right now? She pictured Rose sitting on white sand. Sipping pulped papaya. Blissfully unaware of everyone's suffering. Including her own.

Honestly, pulped papaya didn't sound so bad. Even a glass terror would be child's play compared to how Pilar felt.

Maybe Rose had it right. Maybe the only way to survive loving people was to leave them.

When Pilar reached her sfeera, her key didn't work. The locks had already been changed.

She felt a mounting panic—for a reason that surprised her. Mia's wooden charm was locked inside.

Then her hand flew to her trouser pocket. The charm was there. Relief surged through her. She had something of Mia's after all.

Pilar dropped the sfeera key. When the metal struck the glass floor, it let out one shrill, sad note.

It wasn't her sfeera anymore.

But then, it never was.

Food. Bed. Coins.

Sandbags. Sparring.

Sisters. Brothers. Broods.

Laughter.

Music.

Love.

How could a single person need so much—and then pretend she didn't?

The violins were exactly where Stone said. In the Orkhestra, stacked inside the cabinets.

"Who are *you*?" asked a girl with curly blond hair, hard at work murdering a violin. "You're not one of the players."

"You're not holding your bow right," Pilar tossed over her shoulder. She was eyeing a pretty silver case. When she opened it, the violin inside was even prettier.

"You can't take instruments out of the Orkhestra," protested the girl as Pilar cut a path through the music stands, case tucked under her arm.

"You can't murder them, either," she replied. "Though you seem to be doing just fine."

Light leaked out from under Stone's sfeera door.

Pilar's heart ticked up a notch. She saw his shape, hazy through the frosted gray glass. He was inside.

"Stone?"

She didn't expect him to answer. That was all right. She'd come equipped.

"I brought you something," she said.

She slid to the floor. Pressed her back to the door. Opened the violin case.

The memories came in one heady rush. The sweet ones from the early days, when she didn't know how to hold a bow herself. Morígna had been a patient teacher. Gentle. Forgiving.

Pilar remembered the first time she'd played a song well. It had felt like magic flowing through her fingers—the good kind.

There were bad memories, too. Of course there were. The violin would always be bound up in what happened. Pilar had lost so many precious things that night.

But there was comfort to be found in music. That much she knew. A song could be a gift. And if this was the final gift she could give Stone, then she'd better make it good.

She nested the violin in the crook of her chin. Brought the bow to the strings.

Froze.

What was she doing? Music couldn't save someone. It had certainly never saved her.

A sound came from the sfeera.

"Pilar?"

The voice was muffled. Soft. Had she imagined it?

She lowered the violin.

"Stone?"

Shuffling inside the door. Was he about to open it?

No. She heard a heavy slide, then a thud. She could see it so clearly. Stone slumped on the other side of the door.

"Can you stay with me for a little while?" he said. "I don't think I can open the door."

"You don't have to. I'll be right here."

"Are you crying?"

She was. Funny how she hadn't known until he asked.

"Yes."

For once she didn't fight the tears. They welled in her eyes. Spilled down her cheeks.

"I've done everything wrong, Stone. I taught you to shut people out. I told you not to trust anyone because they'd only hurt you. It scared me how easily you opened yourself up to people, how much power you gave them. But the reason it scared me is because I used to be just like you."

She took a breath.

"You wanted to know my story, what happened to me. What happened is that the person I trusted most—the person I *loved* most—betrayed that trust. He hurt me so badly it almost destroyed me."

Stone was quiet. She could feel him hanging on every word.

"I didn't want you to get hurt like that. So I tried to teach you how to protect yourself. I thought the only way to do that was to close yourself off completely. And then . . ."

Her voice wavered.

"Then I saw you with Shay. Someone who so clearly adores you. Someone who understands you and likes you just the way you are. And you rejected her, all because I taught you to. Of course I taught you to. I've been rejecting everyone who's tried to understand me, too."

She heard a soft sound against the door. Imagined Stone pressing his palm to the gray glass.

She pressed her palm to the other side.

"You taught me how to fight," came his muffled voice.

"I'm not saying fighting is bad. Celeste is wrong about that. Knowing how to protect yourself *is* powerful. It lets you take ownership of your own body. But there's a difference between hardening your fists and hardening your heart."

She tasted salt on her lips. Tears dripped off her chin. She let them fall.

"I'm sorry, Stone. I should have known better than to try and teach you things I hadn't learned myself. I'm lonely, too. I've always been lonely. My whole life I told myself it was better that way. That I was better off alone. But I was lying. I don't want that for you."

"I don't want it for you, either." His voice was soft. "Stay in the House, Pilar. Let us in. Don't shut us out."

"I can't stay."

You break everything you touch, she'd said to Mia.

But she'd been talking about herself all along.

The violin was getting wet. She wiped her face on her sleeve.

"Besides," she said, trying to joke, "Celeste is a demon from four hells. I'm not going to stay in a place where the Keeper gets to kiss your cheek and read your mind."

Stone was quiet. Neither of them said anything for a while. Just sat together, with only a door between them.

"I wanted to give you something before I go," Pilar said finally. "One last gift. Probably the best one I've given you—though considering the others, that's not saying much."

Her arm shook as she clutched the bow. She willed her hands steady.

"When you remember me, Stone? Please remember me like this."

She kissed the bow to the strings.

And played.

Chapter 42

THE LAST SON

WHEN QUIN CAME TO, he was no longer in the crypt.

He knelt on the Kaer's southern parapet, the river kingdom unfurling at his feet. His cheeks wet with tears.

For so long he had tried to outrun it. But a part of him was still cowering in the crypt, locked forever in that gruesome night.

"You remember now," said the voice behind him.

The wind tore through the balustrade, stinging Quin's cheeks.

"I hadn't forgotten, Toby. How could I ever forget?"

He turned, wincing when confronted with the row of heads. He saw Maev and Sylvan; Tristan had joined their ranks. A fourth, too, which he feared might be Phoebe from the kitchens. She had never liked him, and now she was dead, all because he had taken an hour too long.

"Our little Brialli is quite the revolutionary," said Tobin. "Quite the spy, I should say."

Quin's heart dropped into his stomach. He saw the wet knife in Toby's hand.

"If you've hurt her—"

"Then what? You'll hurt me? *Kill* me?" He laughed. "You can make fire, fantastic. It's a good parlor trick. But you need fire in your heart to be a real threat." He gestured toward Quin's hands. "I don't even have you bound, that's how little you scare me."

He was right. When Quin tried to spark a flame, his hands were blocks of ice. Useless. Weak.

"What do you intend to do with me?"

"I haven't decided. Maybe I'll let you join the revolution, son of Clan Killian." He spun the knife on his palm. "Or maybe I won't."

Quin forced himself to breathe. Callaghan was dead. How could it be otherwise? Furious, he banished the thought from his mind. Cal was smart and resourceful. For all he knew, she had already led the Embers to freedom. In which case it was time for Quin to do his part.

What was his part, exactly?

To die?

He peered down from the parapet. To the south, his kingdom fanned out before him, a moving green-and-blue quilt knit together by the Natha River, the lifeblood of Glas Ddir. He winced at the remnants of Tobin's forest fires, scorched tree stumps like black scars on the earth. It hurt Quin to see his wounded land—though it had hurt worse to see his wounded people. He'd met more Glasddirans over the past few days than he had in the past eighteen years. They had suffered greatly, these good, kind, hardworking women and men he felt proud to know.

To the west, the marshes glittered in the sun. The air was so clear he could see even farther, to the red glint of desert where the swamplands met the sands. He imagined the Twisted Sisters in the glass kingdom. Had they received his letter? He felt ashamed of it now. Would they come to Glas Ddir, expecting a show of force and fire, only to find his burnt head on a spike?

He craned his neck. At his back, looming high overhead, were the northern peaks. Mammoth and immovable, the black cliffs were both above the castle and part of it. Thousands of years ago his ancestors had carved Kaer Killian between the mountain's dark ribs. Even as a child, Quin had resented the peaks for blocking the Opalen Sea. The ocean was so close, tantalizingly within his reach, yet he had never once seen it.

And to the east . . .

He blinked.

There was movement on the eastern road.

A group of people hurried toward Killian Village. He squinted. He hadn't imagined it: they were fleeing the castle, at least several dozen. And two small creatures besides.

He inhaled sharply.

"Yes," Tobin said. "That's her. Leading the precious Embers to freedom."

Hope swelled in Quin's chest. "You let her take them."

"They're a sorry lot of revolutionaries. You said so yourself." Tobin shrugged. "I can find better."

"How?"

Quin wheeled around. He felt braver now, knowing Callaghan and the others were safe.

"Will you ravage more villages? Kill more innocents? Seize other people's power because your own was taken from you?"

Tobin groaned. "Spare me your soliloquy on power."

He gestured toward the retreating Embers with his knife.

"Brialli will lead them to wherever she's been hiding. Domeniq's there, too, yes? If I follow her trail, I don't imagine they'll be difficult to find. Once we've finished here."

Quin looked into Toby's silver eyes. He had spent years dreaming about those eyes. But where he once saw love, he now saw only hate.

And then his gaze lifted to the northern peaks at Tobin's back. Dark and oppressive, forever casting a long shadow. They'd been peering over Quin's shoulder his whole life.

Till the northern peaks crumble.

Promise me, O promise me.

Heat ticked between his palms.

"Do you know what I miss, Toby? Hearing you play. You playing piano was my favorite sound in the world. But now when I try to remember the songs you taught me, all I can think of is that night. I hear you screaming."

"While you vomited," Tobin bit back. "A touching duet."

Quin closed his eyes.

Suddenly his ears were full of sound. It wasn't only his pain and Tobin's that thundered down around him. The whole Kaer roared with suffering. He heard the howls of innocent women as their hands were severed by his father's blade. He heard the sobs

380

of servant girls dispatched to the king's chambers at night. The wails and cries rose in a crescendo, so many he knew they were not from Ronan alone, but from the long lineage of Killians who came before him.

Newer voices mingled with the old. Quin heard the crack of the Hunters' skulls as they fell in the Grand Gallery after Angelyne stopped their hearts. He heard Domeniq shuffling through the corridors, dead-eyed, dragging bodies to the Hall of Hands.

And he heard the sound of the piano in the library, blazing, smoldering, destroyed by his own hand. His own fury. He was a son of Clan Killian. He'd been trapped inside a cycle of rage, fear, and hatred since the day he was born.

Callaghan was right. Quin *was* a soulless tyrant. He carried this legacy in his very blood. He could not rewrite his history.

He opened his eyes.

"You were right about me."

Tobin looked at him askance. "Was I?"

"You said my heart would always surrender to love before hate. Your point stands. I don't hate people. I didn't even hate my father, though he was certainly worth hating. I've seen what hate can do. You're about to kill me, and I don't hate you, either. You're the first person I ever loved. What my father did to you . . ."

He shook his head.

"It was unthinkable. I am so sorry I couldn't save you, Toby. I couldn't even save myself."

He took a breath.

"But you weren't right about everything. You called me a coward. You said I was too weak to make hard decisions for the good of my people. The good of my kingdom. You said I wasn't capable of violence."

Quin held out his hands.

"You were wrong."

The flame leapt from his palms. It arced, casting off red-hot sparks, curling into a spiral of fire that flew upward, picking up speed, until it burrowed into the side of the northern peaks.

"You missed me," Tobin said, incredulous. "From two feet away."

But Quin had not missed.

The rocks fell slowly at first, like crumbling sugar on a cake. Then the crumbles grew larger. The peaks began to tremble, fissures yawning into cracks, the heat and power of the flame cleaving the cliffside. A spray of stones landed on the parapet.

Tobin jumped back. He looked at Quin in disbelief.

"Forgive me, Toby."

He heard a thunderous rupture, like the smack of a waterfall. He saw Mia floating in the Salted Sea, the two of them laughing and swimming, marveling at how they had survived the fall.

Not everything was meant to be survived.

Quin felt the castle shift beneath his feet. The rock walls were caving in, crushed by other rocks, a stone snake eating its own tail.

And as the northern peaks fell, so too did the bloodied Kaer, so too did the reign of Clan Killian, and so too did the last son.

ACT IV

Once upon a time,
a girl came home.

Chapter 43

MODALITIES OF HEALING

MIA RETURNED FROM PRISMA alone.

The pain of leaving Angelyne was excruciating. She felt it in every nerve, every tendon, every bone. As she dragged herself across the white sands of the island, the mist pressed against her ears, a new voice inside the glass terror. A voice that broke her heart.

But Mia didn't push the ache away. She had chosen differently than her sister; her body was still her own. Each step brought her closer to the Bridge—and offered her another chance to breathe. In, out. In, out. She pressed the ruby wren to her chest, let the pain curl into the hollows of her rib cage, hunker down inside her soft tissues. Her body could feel suffering now.

And so, she let it.

The Shadowess was overjoyed to see her. So, too, were Lord Shadowess and all the creatures in the Curatorium, big and small.

When Mia walked into the Creation Studio, Nelladine cried out. She leapt off her stool, clay abandoned, and barreled toward Mia, sweeping her feet off the floor.

"Let me look, just look at you. This isn't my mind playing tricks? You're really here?"

"In the flesh." A truth that still felt miraculous.

"Great sands, Mia." Nell's eyes filled with tears. "No one comes back from the Isle of Forgetting. I thought I'd never see you again."

Amidst the abundant relief on Nell's face, Mia saw another emotion, one she hadn't expected. Guilt.

"The things I said to you . . ." Nell trailed off. "I've thought of nothing else. I had bottled everything up for days, weeks, and it all came bursting out at once. I . . ."

She faltered.

Mia pulled her friend close. Nell was doing it again: putting Mia's feelings above her own. *Everyone's* feelings above her own. She had, after all, been doing it her whole life.

Mia didn't know how to talk about Prisma. She did not yet have the vocabulary to describe her time in that strange and terrible place. But the last thing she wanted was to focus solely on her own pain. Nell's mattered just as much.

"I'm grateful, Nell. Your words helped me find my way back."

They held on to one another, until Nell stepped back. Mia

sensed a kind of severing; she couldn't deny that it stung. But this was probably the most honest interaction they had had in months.

Mia stepped back, too. Her gray eyes locked onto Nelladine's brown ones.

"I'm going back to the river kingdom, Nell. To face Quin—and to do what I can to help innocent Glasddirans. It's time I stopped running."

She took a breath.

"I know I wounded you. I didn't see what you needed, or how much our friendship cost you. But I've spent a good bit of time lately mending wounded things. Even if there's a whole kingdom between us, I'd like to take the time to mend our friendship." She swallowed. "If you'll still consider being my friend."

Nell squeezed Mia's hand.

"After the things we've seen, the things we've *survived*? I think that's a bond worth mending. Even if it takes time." Then she added, "I'm glad you came when you did, I would have just missed you. I'm headed back to Luumia. *Maysha* and I will sail alongside the Snow Queen's party."

"They're still in the House?"

"You've only been gone a few days, Mia."

She was astonished. "I thought I'd been gone for weeks."

"That's island time for you, certainly *that* island. The Snow Queen leaves tonight. Mumma is sending scientists and alchemists—magicians, too—to help the Luumi rebuild. I'll travel with them as far as Valavïk, then make my own way back to White Lagoon."

Mia raised an eyebrow. "You'll get to know my mother, then."

Nelladine laughed her deep, husky laugh. Mia was going to miss that laugh.

"After all the time you've spent with mine?" Nell teased. "Seems only fair."

Now it was Mia's turn to squeeze her friend's hand.

"I can't thank you enough for everything you've given me. I'm glad you're going back to Luumia. You can be brilliantly, wholly *you*. Not what other people need you to be."

A gigantic smile broke over Nell's face.

"Look at you, always the good student! I can't wait to be back, honestly, Luumia feeds my soul. I feel most myself there. It feels like home."

Mia held on to the word, turning it over in her brain.

Home.

In the old language, the word *heim* meant, simply, "dwelling." The deeper connotations—warmth, family, the sense of belonging—came later. Perhaps those things came only with time.

Where was *home* to Mia Rose?

"If you're going back to Glas Ddir," Nell said, "you should join Mumma's caravan of ambassadors. She wasn't going to accompany them, but she's changed her mind, she won't tell me why. We've heard nothing from the river kingdom for days, no news. Other than Quin's letter to you, of course, which he would have sent by courier a month ago. We don't know what has happened in the weeks since, but it can't be good."

Mia wasn't sure what she feared more: a world in which Quin

was dead, or a world in which he was alive—and massacring his own people.

"When does the caravan leave?"

"Tomorrow, first thing."

Mia felt a flicker of hope. She remembered Pilar in the Creation Studio, Quin's letter clutched in her fist. *We have to go back.*

"Is Pilar coming, too?"

"Pilar left three days ago. She went alone."

Mia took very little

"Pack light," the Shadowess told her. "It'll take us a month to cross the desert—and that's if the weather holds. Prepare for a long, bumpy ride."

So Mia stuffed a satchel with clothes, her elixir, the melonfish sketchbook, and the ruby wren. She was pleased at the lightness of her pack. She would conquer the desert like the intrepid explorer she was.

And then she climbed onto her kama.

Pink kamas were indigenous to Pembuk; she'd never seen one in Glas Ddir. They were bigger than horses, with enormous humps on their backs and thick, swooping necks. Her kama had two giant padded toes on each foot, bald knobby knees, and coarse beige hair—except for the tuft of fur on his head, which was a coquettish pink.

Mia had ridden a horse before. Griffin Rose had kept a handsome blond mare in a stable in Ilwysion, and when Mia was little, her father would bring her along, toting a crate of apples and sugar cubes. Sometimes he let her climb into the saddle, then led her on a walk around the pasture, the horse ambling gently with a smooth, even gait.

Riding a pink kama was *not* like that.

The beast moved laterally, jostling her from side to side as it plowed over the red desert. Despite the blankets piled onto his hump, Mia's cheeks were sore and tender. For hours on end, her royal steed kept up a running dialogue with the other kamas, a conversation peppered with bleats and groans, brays and bellows.

"Yours is quite the talker," said the Shadowess, jolting along beside her. Mia took comfort in the fact that Muri and the other ambassadors looked just as uncomfortable as she did. "A bit of a rough ride, isn't it?"

"It does take some getting used to," Mia agreed.

In truth, she was happy. She reveled in the sensation of the scratchy wool abrading her thighs, the constant eyestrain from riding east into the sun, the biting coldness of the desert at night, and the reliably burnt coffee they heated over the campfire each morning. She even found herself savoring the foul odor of the kamas. She could feel, taste, smell everything. Whether it was the elixir, her time in Prisma, or some other mysterious combination of factors, she didn't know. But this time, she hoped the sensations were here to stay.

Mia also felt tremendous guilt over the fact that, in the midst of so much suffering, she took pleasure in these small delights.

"It's all right to feel pleasure," the Shadowess said. "Your happiness can coexist alongside others' suffering. We must hold on to the things that bring us joy, even during difficult times. *Especially* then."

Mia dreamed of Prisma every night. She had vivid nightmares that she'd abandoned her sister; she would hear Angelyne crying out for her, only to wake in a cold sweat. In the most awful dreams, Mia sat beside her sister on the shore, sand eroding beneath them, their bodies rotting away. When she woke, she felt a deep, pervasive sadness.

But she had ample time in the desert—to think, reflect, remember. Mia let her mind wander where it would: to her cottage in Ilwysion, to Kaer Killian, to the House of Shadows. She thought of her parents, Angelyne, Pilar, Quin. Whether the memories arrived as rolling waves or violent sandstorms, she let them come.

She spent long hours with the Shadowess, talking. At night when they made camp, they huddled together by the fire, wrapped in blankets, the stars smeared so thick over the sky they looked like bones.

"The thing I can't let go of," Mia said, "is that Angie gave me the ruby wren. She told me to embrace life, not death. And yet, moments later, she left her own life behind."

"It can be hard to understand why people do things. We don't get to live inside their heads."

"I'm glad I have the wren. There's great healing power inside the fojuen stone; I can feel it. The bird was my mother's, and she was a gifted healer."

Muri smiled warmly.

"From what my husband tells me, so are you. Hold on to those gifts. I expect you'll need them in the river kingdom. The Mahraini mystics say the only way to heal something as large as a kingdom is to heal it in a hundred small ways every day."

"Do you think we'll be able to save Quin?"

Muri didn't know, because no one did. Would they have to take the castle by force? The ambassadors were grateful to have Mia; she knew Kaer Killian better than any of them. She tore out pages from her melonfish notebook and drew intricate maps, sketching alternate methods of entry, such as the secret entrance through the crypt.

"I'm glad to see you kept the melonfish," Muri said. "I've always been so taken with the idea that a creature can illuminate itself from within. Sometimes we need a reminder that we can create our own light."

"That," Mia teased, "is what we call a metaphor."

And when, a week into the journey, one of the pink kamas hurt his foot, shrieking as his cloven toes touched the sand, Mia stepped forward.

"Mind if I take a look?"

She extracted her notebook from her pack and scrutinized a sketch she'd drawn in the Curatorium of a horse's injured hoof. Then she purloined tea leaves from the food stores, a swatch of bloodmoss one of the women was keeping on hand, and a drop of her own elixir. She heated the ingredients over the fire—and applied the paste using the magic in her hands.

By morning the kama had made a complete recovery. He stood

evenly on all four feet, spitting globs of saliva. He brayed, bleated, and—to Mia's ears, anyway—growled his thanks.

From that point forward, whenever any member of the caravan, two-legged or four-, had a hurt or ailment, they came to Mia first.

The days blended into a soothing rhythm. Kamas, campfire, desert, sky. Every talk with the Shadowess buoyed Mia's spirits, and each time she healed a scrape or cut, she felt stronger in her own body, her own mind.

When the caravan crossed the Glasddiran border, the pink kamas struggling to find purchase in the western marshlands, Mia was already dreading the moment they would part ways. But there was something she had to do before she could go to Kaer Killian, and by the time they reached the outskirts of Ilwysion, she could no longer forestall it.

"I'll be in Killian Village," said Muri, hugging her close. "Take good care."

Mia nodded numbly.

She walked all day. She didn't need a map: she knew the way by heart. Her feet found familiar pathways, moss and lichen stitching a soft green carpet on ancient rain-worn stones.

Night had fallen when she made it to the cottage. It was just as she remembered. The sweeping balcony. The gently sloping eaves.

When Mia saw it rising from the bluff, bathed in moonlight, she had an overpowering urge to turn back. She should have stayed with the caravan. Traveled with them to Kaer Killian, even though that, too, filled her with dread, imagining what they might find.

Yet here she was. Standing before her home. Desperately wishing to be anywhere else—and knowing she'd made the right choice. Not in spite of the painful memories. Because of them.

She climbed the old path, touching the birch tree with the knots that looked like eyes, stepping around a colossal white rock. Mia paused for a moment, remembering. As a girl she had argued the rock was a die cast by the four gods in a celestial parlor game. Angelyne said it looked like an elephant. They had never agreed.

Mia scaled the five steps to the porch, skipping the second and fourth, her childhood ritual intact. She swept her hand across glaucous cobwebs draped over two rocking chairs before facing the iron door. She clutched her satchel, drew her shoulder blades down her back—and reached for the rose-shaped knocker.

The staleness struck her first, the damp smell of a house untouched by human feet or hands for many months. The moonlight fell in uneven chunks and wedges, revealing curled brown leaves blown in from some forgotten window.

Mia stood, motionless. Unable to pull her eyes away from the empty kitchen. Always toasty warm and filled with tantalizing aromas, this little room had been the soul of her home.

Now a thick mantle of dust coated the square table. No potato cakes dunked in sweet brown mustard, no twisty pretzels, no garlic goose-meat pies. Mia remembered how, on her fourteenth birthday, her mother had spent all day fretting over a butter cake—only to accidentally send it flying off the cooling rack. The four of them had sat cross-legged, scooping crumbly hunks off the floor, dipping them into a bowl of fresh-whipped cream.

Now, standing in the desolate kitchen, Mia had to remind herself to breathe. She placed one hand on her heart and one hand on her belly, just as the Shadowess had taught her, and felt her diaphragm expand and contract. She sorely missed the blood-bloom charm; she had looked for it everywhere in the House of Shadows. But it was gone.

For a moment she thought she detected the rich, velvety scent of butter. Then it vanished. How could a fragrance—no, the *memory* of a fragrance—bring so much pain?

She heard Muri's gentle voice. *Because the body holds pain, just like the mind.*

Mia took a deep, brave breath and climbed the stairs.

For the first thirteen years of her life, Mia had shared a room with Angelyne. But after her first bleeding, as she teetered on the cusp of womanhood, her parents had decided she deserved her own space. They'd set to work transforming Griffin's study, clearing out his collection of treasures from the four kingdoms— curios, maps, compasses, astrolabes, and countless books on magic.

"Please don't take them," Mia had begged, drunk on the thought of so many precious artifacts from a world beyond her own.

"You can keep the maps," her mother said. "But you have enough books already."

Mia had raved and ranted, refusing to eat for a whole day. What a spoiled brat she'd been. Now, of course, she understood why her mother had forbidden her to read her father's books on magic. They'd been inked with fear and hatred, not to mention lies.

Mia stepped out of the hallway—and into her room.

Everything was exactly as she'd left it the day her father had announced she would marry the prince. Books neatly arranged on their shelves and four walls thatched with maps, anatomical sketches, and, best of all: her life-sized Wound Man, a faceless man with sundry weapons plunged into his body. Beside each wound she had scribbled various modalities of healing.

She looked away sharply. How could an ink outline of an anonymous man first drawn hundreds of years ago remind her so much of Quin?

Mia padded out of the room, closing the door softly behind her. She placed her foot on the top step. She would go downstairs. Even if it was important to remember her past, there was no need to torture herself. She had only come to say goodbye.

But she did not go downstairs. She pivoted, drawn to the room at the end of the hallway. Angelyne's room.

She made it no further than the doorframe. Her gaze snagged on a rack of satin hair ribbons, embellished with feathers in a dozen shades of green. In this room she saw the inchoate dreams of the castle Angie would build on the Isle of Forgetting. The fantasy life she had chosen—by surrendering her own.

The dam broke. Mia staggered backward, consumed by grief.

She fled down the stairs, her feet striking the floor in the exact spot Wynna Rose had stopped her own heart. Impetuous Mia Rose, skipping home through the forest, never suspecting she had just lost her mother. She'd lost her sister, too, though she wouldn't know it for some time.

Mia stumbled over the threshold and into the pale moonlight, leaving the door ajar. She dropped her satchel and sank onto the stoop, eyes blurred with salt water. Hugged her knees to her chest, inhaling, exhaling, even as silent tears rolled down her cheeks.

"I thought I might find you here," said a voice to her right, and Mia glanced up, startled, to find Pilar in a rocking chair.

"I'm glad I found you here," her big sister said, and smiled.

Chapter 44

BLOOM

IT WAS GOOD TO see Mia. Pilar hadn't expected it to feel so good, but it did and she wasn't complaining.

"How did you . . ." Mia touched her wet face. "I'm sorry. I'm a mess."

"Don't dry them on my account. I've been doing more of that myself lately. Got to say: after choking down tears my whole life, crying feels pretty damn nice."

Rose burbled a reply. Something between a laugh and a sob.

Pilar grinned. "So you agree."

She still couldn't believe she'd found the Roses' cottage. All she'd had to go off was the crude map a river guide drew her on an old canvas sack. He was an odd man, dressed in a peculiar costume with long, sagging green sleeves, babbling some nonsense about

Kaer Killian falling off the side of a mountain. After he sailed away, she'd spent half an hour squinting at the map, trying to decipher the mysterious meaning of *OUR* before realizing it was part of *FLOUR*.

It was a flour sack. Typical.

The river guide hadn't known much more than the general area where Griffin Rose *might* live. "The leader of the Circle?" he'd croaked. "I don't reckon you'll find him. I hear he's so far gone he slurps soup from a boot in the castle dungeons." Clearly that rumor had been making the rounds.

Yet here she was. Camped out on the Roses' porch. In no small part because Mia had yammered on and on about the rock that Angelyne insisted looked like an elephant and Mia insisted did not. Angelyne was a murderous delusional liar—but she was right about the rock. Once Pilar saw the elephant, she knew she'd found her way.

What a stroke of luck. Or maybe fate. Pilar wasn't sure she believed in fate, but for the first time in a long time, she wasn't sure she *didn't*.

"When did you get here?" Mia said, freeing a curl glued to her wet cheek.

"This morning." Pilar patted the rocking chair beside her. "Care for a rock?"

"I thought for sure you'd beat us here." Mia stood shakily, then sank into the chair. "Did you take a pink kama through the desert?"

"No. Came by boat. A boat half the size of *Maysha*, with twice as many people."

"That sounds awful."

"Awful doesn't even come close."

The journey had been a monthlong lesson in humility. It had started well enough, when she'd filched a bucket of expensive Black Roses from the Rose Garden. Was she proud of stealing from the House? No. Did she enjoy plucking the heads off Celeste's precious flower children? Oh, fuck yes. She used the roses to barter passage to Dead Man's Strait, where she planned to hop off the ship and head north to Kaer Killian.

Key word being *ship*. Not the bobbing banana peel she'd been prodded onto after surrendering all her roses. The promised three meals a day turned out to be gruel, peanuts, and hardtack so stale one passenger chipped a tooth. Pilar endured a series of dramas, from the annoying—farts upon farts upon farts—to the terrifying, like the night a man got drunk on banana wine, pitched overboard, and never resurfaced.

"You must've missed me terribly," Mia said.

Was Rose joking? Her puffy, tearstained face made it hard to tell. Pilar thought of a few biting gibes she could toss out. She lined them up on the tip of her tongue.

But what she said was, "I did miss you, actually."

Mia sat a little straighter. Listening.

"I couldn't do this part without you, Rose. The epic final battle. That's how every story ends, right? Though to be honest"—she waved a hand around them—"this isn't quite the epic battlefield I was expecting."

"How did you know I'd be here?"

"This is your house. Seemed like a good place to start."

"I meant more, how did you know I wasn't on Prisma?"

Pilar leaned back in her chair. How *had* she known? She wasn't sure she could explain it. But she would try.

"When I left the House," she began, "I was wrecked. Not just because you left. That didn't help, but there were other reasons. I can give you all the gory details if you want. I said goodbye to Stone, swung by the Rose Garden to pick up a few things"—Mia arched a brow, but didn't press—"then wandered Shabeeka until well after dark, plotting what to do next. I was looking for the fastest, cheapest way to get to Glas Ddir. I didn't find the boat as much as it found me."

She scowled, remembering the neat little swindle. The man who sold her the ticket had pointed to an impressive ship docked at the harbor, then goaded her onto a small canoe to ferry her to the larger vessel. Once she and the other passengers were all loaded and the canoe pushed out into the bay . . . the impressive ship sailed off. It had never been theirs to begin with.

"From the dock I was only a stone's throw from the Bridge. The sky was so clear. You know that thick white fog that's always hanging over Prisma?"

Mia gave a hard, sharp nod. There was a story there. Pilar would ask about it later.

"Well, that night, the fog was gone. I could see all the way to the island. Honestly, I was so angry at you for leaving. I'd just left the one place that had started to feel like home—and it nearly destroyed me. And there you were, off lying on a sandy beach, drinking pulped papaya."

"As long as we're being honest," Mia said, "I didn't care for the pulped papaya."

Pilar rolled her eyes. "Hilarious."

"I'm sorry. I don't mean to make light of what you're saying. Go on."

"So I saw the fish trees swaying in the wind. And I had this funny feeling I could hear someone singing. Lots of people, all these voices crammed together. I figured it was probably just the Pearl Moon Festival behind me. But underneath the noise, I felt this sense of . . . quiet."

She cracked her knuckles. Frowned.

"That's not the right word. But it's hard to put into words. It's the way I used to feel when I believed in the Four Great Goddesses. I guess you could call it peace, or a kind of knowledge that comes from something bigger than your own brain. Somehow, I just knew."

"Knew what?"

"That you were going to leave the island."

Rose's rocking chair slowed. "Even though no one's ever come back from Prisma?"

"Even then."

Mia gazed up at the porch ceiling, where the white paint was peeling off in strips.

"Incredible," she murmured. "You knew even before I did."

She lowered her chin, meeting Pilar's eyes.

"Are you still angry I left?"

"Angry. Hurt. All kinds of things."

"You have every right to feel those things." Mia took a breath. "I want you to know I wasn't leaving you. I left because I felt like a failure. I had failed you, Nell, Angie, Quin. I couldn't give any of you what you needed. I hadn't even *seen* what you needed. I went to Prisma because I couldn't bear to live with that failure."

She sighed. Tucked a stray curl behind her ear.

"But I came back from Prisma because I finally understood that failing is the only way to live."

Pilar watched her. Rose did seem different. Calmer. Sadder. And at the same time, lighter. Whatever had happened on the Isle of Forgetting had certainly left its mark.

"Those are pretty words," Pilar said. "But I'm going to need all the gory details."

And Mia began to speak.

Angelyne had an imaginary baby. The white fog was cut-up souls. The Isle of Forgetting swept your memories quietly out to sea, then brought new ones on the tide.

"I don't understand," Pilar said, after Mia had told her everything. They were sprawled out now: Rose with her back pressed against the big iron door, Pilar's feet dangling over the edge of the porch. "I don't see why Angelyne would choose it. Why *you* were going to choose it."

"Haven't you ever wanted to go back and change what happened to you?"

Pilar saw the cottage by the lake. The rafters. Her Dujia sisters. And most recently: Celeste.

"A thousand times. But if erasing my pain meant erasing my *self*?" She shook her head. "Don't get me wrong. I've spent plenty of time hating myself. I'm flawed as all four hells. But at least, at the end of the day, I know who I am."

She thumped her chest. "At least I know I'm *here*."

Mia peered at her intently.

"When you think of yourself, is that the part of your body you think of? Your heart?"

"Doesn't everyone?"

"Fascinating."

Rose rooted around in her satchel, then pulled out the melon-fish notebook she was always lugging around the House. Pilar watched as she scribbled down a note.

"I didn't realize that was noteworthy."

Mia tucked the pen in the crease of her notebook. Her gray eyes had a thirsty spark, the way they always did when she'd made some new discovery.

"When I think of *me* . . . where my true self sits in my body . . ." She touched her forehead. "It's here."

"Huh."

"Huh, indeed. I always assumed a person's essential who-ness—their self distilled to the most vital essence—resided in their intellect. It hadn't occurred to me other people might feel differently."

Pilar chewed it over. Maybe her self didn't always sit in her heart. Maybe it was also in her fists. Her blood. "What would Angie say, do you think? Which body part?"

Mia closed the notebook.

"It doesn't matter now. She no longer has a body. At least not the way I understand it."

Pilar thought Mia might start crying again, but she didn't. She slid the notebook back into her satchel. Then she fumbled around inside, almost by instinct. But her hand came up empty.

"Are you looking for your charm?"

"Oh, the bloodbloom?" Mia looked embarrassed. "It wasn't in my sfeera when I got back."

Pilar couldn't suppress a grin. She knew there was a reason she'd held on to the bloodbloom. She tugged the wooden disc out of her pocket.

Mia brightened, just like Pilar knew she would. She started to reach for it, then hesitated.

"Have you been using it? I don't want to take it from you."

"I don't even know how it works. Besides, you know how I feel about belly breathing."

"You must've held on to it for some reason."

"I kept it because it was yours," Pilar said simply. "I went to your sfeera after you left. I was ready to do whatever it took to convince you to come with me to Glas Ddir. Then I saw your books and that journal and your clothes, and I knew immediately where you'd gone. So I took the charm. It felt like the only piece of you I could hold on to."

"I told you what happened on Prisma," Mia said gently. "Would you tell me what happened at the House?"

And there it was. The wall Pilar had knocked into a million times before. Someone asking to hear her story—and her hands balling into fists. Nails digging into palms. Her body reacting physically, like she'd absorbed a blow to the gut.

"It's . . ." Her throat clenched. "It's hard to talk about."

"You don't have to. I mean that."

Mia placed one hand over her heart and the other in the air.

"I hereby swear: I won't keep trying to fix you, or force you to talk about things you don't want to talk about."

"Thanks for that. The thing is . . . I think I *do*."

Pilar uncurled her fingers. The nail grooves began to fade.

She took a breath.

Pilar told Mia how the Gymnasia smelled like sweat, even in the early morning before anyone sparred. How just being there made her happy.

She described the thrill of teaching Stone, how hungry he was to get better, and the even bigger thrill she'd felt the day Shay pinned her to the floor.

She talked about her fight students, how they wanted to eat with her in the Swallow, tell her stories, make her laugh. When they were hurt or scared or angry, they came to the Gymnasia. Sometimes she'd spar with them. Other times she'd just listen while they poured out their hearts.

She told Mia about the night Stone broke Shay's heart.

She told her about Celeste.

"*What?*" Mia was shocked. "I take back every nice thing I ever said about that woman."

"Blame the Shadowess. She's the one who wanted to get rid of me. Not to mention she appointed a Keeper who abuses her power every time she attacks you with a kiss."

Mia knit her brow. "Something doesn't add up. That's just not who the Shadowess is."

"Maybe you don't know who the Shadowess is."

Rose held up her hands. "I don't want to fight."

"Me neither." Pilar snorted. "For once." She stared at the blood-bloom charm on her palm. "I know I came back to Glas Ddir to stop Quin. And that's still the plan. But I think really, from the moment I got on that sad excuse for a boat . . . I was coming back for you."

The words nested quietly between them. The night was still. Pilar felt still, too. Her body felt the way it always did after a good fight: exhausted but content. Empty and also full. The words had poured out of her, and they were there now, in the space between.

Pilar thought she'd feel exposed. Instead she felt seen. In a good way. Mia had seen and heard her without trying to heal her broken parts.

Maybe that was how it felt to have a sister. To be seen, known, *loved*, exactly the way you were.

"Want to see how it works?" Mia nodded to the bloodbloom tree. "Only if you want."

Pilar realized she'd been rubbing the charm. There was power inside the wood. Inside her hands, too. She could feel it thrumming.

"Do I have to chant?"

"There will be no chanting. I give you my word."

Pilar didn't shrug. Just handed the tree to her sister.

"Let's make it bloom."

Chapter 45

INTO THE HATS

MIA COULDN'T STOP STARING at Pilar's hands. They were so different from hers. Smaller, with shorter fingers and broader thumbs. Far rougher—and infinitely stronger, Mia had no doubt. Weeks on the sea had healed the scabs on Pilar's knuckles, leaving her olive skin a pale, wrinkled pink.

In the Curatorium, Mia had made a tincture that worked wonders on scar tissue. She was dying to offer it. But she refrained. If Pilar wanted to heal her scars, she would heal them herself.

"What I like about the bloodbloom," Mia said, as Pil cupped the charm in her palm, "is that it works in tandem with your own body. We each have great power to heal ourselves, magic or no. But we still need tools, the same way that we need other people."

"And if I don't want to need other people?"

Mia shot her a shrewd look. "I think it might be time you evolve that view."

She waited for Pilar to chuck the charm into the forest and storm off the porch.

To her surprise, Pil didn't move. Her face was open. Curious.

"I suppose all I'm saying," Mia continued, "is that we form communities to survive. Families. Friendships. Whole villages. These people can help us find our way."

She nodded toward Pilar's hands. "Can I ask you to look at your own hands? *Really* look? I'll do it with you. Imagine you're studying for a test and your hands are the primary text."

Pil rolled her eyes dramatically—but complied.

True to her word, Mia began to examine her own hands. Beneath ivory skin dappled with orange freckles, blue veins coursed close to the surface. When she undulated her fingers, the phalanges and metacarpals crested one at a time, each bone exquisitely contoured.

"Other side," she said, and they both flipped their hands palm up.

The human body really was amazing. Mia marveled at the delicate lines etched into her palms: a unique and inimitable map. Each fingertip so distinctive, not even two of her own fingers were alike.

A thought came unbidden: King Ronan's Hall of Hands. Where blood and bone and muscle had once worked together in exquisite harmony, they had been severed, carved into inanimate parts.

What had those hands done in the time before? Had they

turned the pages of a book? Strung an arrow in a bow? Cradled a sick child? Flourished and fluttered to tell a lively story? What kinds of magic had they wrought?

"I understand you like hands an awful lot," Pilar said, interrupting her thoughts. "I get it. You grew up terrified of them. Wearing gloves. All of it. I'm just wondering . . ."

"What this has to do with anything?"

"I'm getting the sense this might be a fetish." Pilar shrugged. "Nothing wrong with that."

Mia burst out laughing. "Your point stands. I'll skip ahead."

She placed her left hand over her belly. Pilar echoed the movement.

To Mia's surprise, she felt nervous. After all those sessions with the Shadowess, this was the first time she had tried to teach someone else. She'd wanted to teach Angelyne, sitting in her imaginary castle: Mia's last desperate attempt to save her little sister. Her big sister, on the other hand, did not need saving. Pilar simply wanted to learn.

Mia's breath was jittery, uneven. She heard a reproachful voice in her head: *Really? Your breath is* still *ragged? Have you learned nothing?*

But as soon as the thought wormed into her mind, she thanked it and bid it farewell. This was simply her breath *right now*. It would be different tomorrow, in an hour, even in one minute. She would breathe smoothly and roughly, roughly and smoothly, for the rest of her life. It didn't mean she was broken. It meant she was human.

"Inhale through your nostrils," Mia said. "Nice, deep breath.

Then let it out your mouth slowly. Feel how your hand actually *rises* when you exhale? That's your diaphragm expanding. You're breathing all the way into your belly, not just your chest."

She winced, waiting for Pilar to say something snide and walk away. She remembered standing in the Creation Studio as Pil had sneered at her for belly breathing. *Rub your little wooden tree. 'Cause that'll solve everything.*

But there was no trenchant commentary. No movement other than Pilar's hand over her belly, rising and falling. Mia felt a tremendous surge of pride.

"Look," she whispered, nodding toward the charm in Pil's right hand.

The little tree had blossomed. Expanding on the inhale, wood creaking, branches reaching toward the starlit sky. On the exhale, wind streamed through the leaves, tiny red flowers opening like jewels.

Pilar stared at the tree growing in her hand. Incredulous.

"It's really me? I'm the one making it do that?"

"You are."

"It feels good. *Really* good."

"You think I'd spend all those hours in the House doing something that felt bad? Give me *some* credit."

"You can be a glutton for punishment," Pil countered, and Mia couldn't disagree.

They breathed together awhile. Left hands on their stomachs. Mia's right hand pressed to her heart, Pilar's cradling the bloodbloom as it creaked and bloomed. Mia felt a profound sense of comfort that they could bring their own breath back into alignment—without manipulating the elements, or siphoning from a history of oppression, or creating any kind of imbalance at all.

The best part was that they didn't need the bloodbloom. It was nice, but it was just a tool. Their hands had the real power.

They could heal themselves.

Mia wasn't sure how much time had passed when she finally let her hands fall. The night had grown colder, but she felt centered and refreshed. The grief that had consumed her as she paced the halls of her childhood home had quieted. She could manage it now.

"Here you go," Pilar said, holding out the bloodbloom.

"Keep it. I want you to have it." She rubbed the heat back into her arms. "We should probably go."

"To Kaer Killian?"

She nodded. "I'm not looking forward to it."

"Me neither."

"I keep seeing Quin under the snow palace. That hateful look in his eyes."

"Me too."

Pilar cleared her throat.

"Listen, I heard something on the way here. It's probably nothing. The river guide was going on and on about how the Kaer fell off the mountainside. But he was pretty old and batty. You should've seen what he was wearing—he had these long, drooping sleeves."

Mia sat up sharply.

"Why didn't you tell me this earlier?"

"I . . . didn't think you cared about sleeves?"

"What color were they?"

"Green and yellow, I think. Though the yellow might've been gold."

Terror seared through Mia's chest. She stood.

"Those are the colors of Clan Killian."

"I mean, is that surprising? We are in the river kingdom."

"You don't understand. Those are the mourning sleeves. They mean a Killian is dead."

Pilar went silent. She, too, brought herself to her feet.

"But *all* the Killians are dead, right? The king, the queen. Karri."

"That was months ago. The sleeves are worn when a death is still fresh."

She saw her own fear reflected in Pilar's eyes.

"Come on. We'll get to the Kaer faster if we ride." Mia leapt off the porch, skipping all five steps at once. "I know where we can find a horse."

They rode through the night, Mia astride her father's blond mare, Pilar on a white stallion they had wheedled out of the sleepy stable boy by promising him a pouch of Killian gold.

"I'm the princess," Mia had proclaimed. Then, with slightly less certainty: "I *was* the princess." And, finally: "I might actually be the queen?"

She had still never managed to confirm the validity of her marriage vows, since the wedding had been so violently interrupted. *Were* she and Quin married? It hardly seemed to matter now.

"I see you're wearing the mourning sleeves," she'd said to the stable boy.

"Don't you know? It's the end of Clan Killian."

Mia's heart contracted. "Isn't King Quin in the Kaer?"

"There is no Kaer," the boy said. "And no king. Not anymore."

After that, she and Pilar said nothing. They rode through the forest side by side, each lost in her own dark thoughts, stopping only to feed and water the horses.

Mia believed she had made peace with Quin's death. After all, she'd lost him months ago, crushed beneath the snow palace. Only when she and Pilar received the letter had she dared imagine seeing him again.

Then why did it hurt so much to know she wouldn't? Was it the knowledge that he *had* been alive, and she hadn't made it back in time? Or was the real fear that he had become the tyrant he'd sworn never to be—and that only in his death, Glas Ddir would finally find its freedom?

No king. Not anymore.

In every village, Mia saw one or two drunken revelers stumbling around the dark, the gold-and-green sleeves draped over their arms.

Every time, she had to look away.

By the time they made it to Killian Village, dawn was breaking. Mia felt weary down to her very bones.

She and Pilar dismounted, tying their horses to the fence beside a snowmelt well.

"You Glasddirans sure do get up early," muttered Pil.

Despite the hour, the town was already abuzz. Mia leaned into the fence, taking a moment to get her bearings. Nearby, a blacksmith hurried out of his forge. In a sudden jolt of recall, Mia remembered standing in the same spot to catch her breath after she and Quin fled the castle.

The man wore the mourning sleeves. Everyone in the village wore them.

But somehow the mood didn't seem quite right for mourning. People ducked into bakeries and out of hat shops, often with a smile on their lips.

"I think that used to be a brothel," Pilar said, pointing. "When I was a scullery maid at the Kaer, I used to go to the village to get food, and there were always ladies standing on the porch in silks and garters."

And indeed, ladies there still were. But these wore neither silks nor garters. They stood behind a long table, handing out baskets of bread—fresh-baked, by the smell of it—cartons of vegetables, and cuts of meat wrapped in crisp brown paper to the people lining up outside.

Mia's jaw dropped. The women had their sacred mourning sleeves rolled up and tucked into the tops of their trousers, leaving their hands unencumbered. What sacrilege was this?

"Pilar!" called a familiar voice. "Mia!"

She turned to see the Shadowess walking toward them. Muri looked tired, dark circles under her eyes, but also happy.

"I'm so glad to see you," Mia said, relieved. Who better than Muri to help her process the loss of Quin?

She felt Pilar bristle at her side. In Mia's joy over seeing the Shadowess, she had forgotten Pil did not share the same cuddly feelings.

"I'm glad to see you, too, Mia," Muri said, though she sounded hesitant. She turned to Pilar. "I'm hoping you and I can speak, Pilar." She paused. "Privately."

It took Mia a moment.

"Oh! Oh. Privately."

She was flustered—and a little jealous. Then deeply embarrassed over feeling jealous.

"If you need me, I'll just be . . ." Mia glanced around, mildly panicked. "In that hat shop."

She turned and fled into the arms of a milliner. Or at the very least, into the hats.

Chapter 46

SOFTER FALLS

PILAR SCOWLED AT MIA's retreating back. She hadn't asked to be alone with the Shadowess, the last person in all four kingdoms she wanted to speak to. *Second* to last. Celeste claimed first prize.

But off Mia went, bolting into a hat shop. Even though she had never once worn a hat.

Pilar fixed her gaze on the Shadowess. Crossed her arms.

"You got what you wanted. I'm out of the House."

The Shadowess's expression was grave.

"There's been some confusion, Pilar."

"Why are you here? You said you were sending your ambassadors to the river kingdom."

The Shadowess removed her glasses. Looked Pilar in the eye, no lenses between them.

"There were things I was only recently made aware of that need to be addressed. In an effort to address them effectively—"

"It's a simple question."

Muri sighed.

"Because of you, Pilar. I came here for you."

She slid her glasses back into place.

"I owe you an apology. Many apologies. And I will give them all to you, happily. Though I would love to sit down first. I'm not quite as young as I used to be, as my knees often remind me. Can I offer you a hot meal and a cup of cocoa?"

Pilar appraised her. She found it hard to believe Muri had crossed a whole desert just to apologize to her. To Mia Rose, maybe. Since when had Pilar d'Aqila mattered to the all-powerful Shadowess?

Pilar stared into Muri's deep brown eyes. She saw kindness. Her mother had had deep brown eyes, too. They were never kind.

"I don't want cocoa," Pilar said. "Thanks anyway."

She savored—she couldn't help it—the crestfallen look on Muri's face.

"That said . . ." She shrugged. "I *will* take a nip of rai rouj."

Pilar did not order rai rouj. It was just past dawn when she and Muri stepped into the inn: too early for spirits. Besides. After the man on the boat from Shabeeka fell overboard from drinking too much banana wine, she had decided to lay off the rai rouj for a while.

When the Shadowess said to get whatever she wanted, Pilar took her at her word. She ordered a cup of coffee and her favorite

Glasddiran breakfast foods—thin potato cakes with honey, salted pork and cheese curds, cornbread dumplings, and sweet buttermilk pudding.

The inn was packed. Every time she saw the mourning sleeves, her stomach tightened. She was having a hard time accepting Quin was dead. The frustrating part was that she thought she'd accepted it months ago. Why was it hitting her so hard now?

Maybe it was less about him and more about her. She'd only come back to Glas Ddir because of Quin's letter. She had sworn to stop him, save him, maybe both. Now she could do neither.

Then what in four hells was she doing here? She had no great love for the river kingdom. She liked the buttermilk pudding—less so the pasty, backstabbing people and their diluted excuse for spirits. This was Mia's home, not hers.

But where else could she go? The volqanoes were actively burying her homeland under burning ash. Even if they weren't, it had been a long time since Fojo Karação felt like home. Pilar was placeless. An island adrift.

"I want to start," Muri began, "by saying how much I appreciate all the time you have spent with Stone. It really does mean the world to him. He has been happier training with you than I've seen him in a long time."

Pilar waited for the *but*. The part where the Shadowess ripped into her for teaching her son something that—how had Celeste put it?—*hinged on physical violence and aggression.*

"You know," said Muri, heaping sugar into her coffee mug, "I used to do a little sparring myself."

Pilar stopped, her fork halfway to her mouth.

"It's true. I may not look like much now, but back when I was a little spryer—and my knees hadn't staged a full-fledged revolt—I loved a good fight. Long before I was the Shadowess, I would stop in at the Gymnasia whenever I came to the House. There's nothing like the satisfaction of working up a good sweat."

Wary, Pilar chewed a mouthful of salted pork, then stabbed another.

"I thought you don't approve of violence."

"Violence?" She shook her head. "When I think of someone being violent, I think of intention. There is an intent to do harm. Violence is by nature destructive. As I see it, sparring is creative."

"Then why did you let your precious Keeper close the Gymnasia?"

The Shadowess's gaze was steady. She set down her spoon.

"I didn't know Celeste had closed the Gymnasia. By the time I did, it was too late."

Pilar dropped her fork, which landed with a clatter.

"What kind of Shadowess are you if you didn't know that?"

Pilar saw the hurt flash across her face. But Muri didn't pull back. She leaned forward.

"Can you tell me what happened, Pilar? All the details you can remember. This is important."

"Why?"

"Because Celeste is not who I thought she was. She's hurt a lot of people. And I will fight any battle, bad knees or no, to make sure she never hurts anyone in the House again."

Pilar remembered *every* detail.

Over the course of her story, she watched Muri's face. The Shadowess swung from shocked to furious to heartbroken, and a hundred shades in between. She interrupted Pilar only to ask for clarification—except for the times she muttered "outrageous" or "unbelievable" under her breath. Twice she swore. Then immediately apologized.

It was the rawest, foulest, least Shadowess-like Pilar had ever seen her.

She loved it.

"I am so sorry, Pilar," Muri said when her story came to an end. By now the Shadowess was on her third mug of coffee. Pilar had switched to hot cocoa. Because why the hells not?

"Celeste's actions are inexcusable. This goes much deeper than I knew. I am, quite frankly, horrified."

"What do you mean, deeper than you knew?"

Muri stared hard into her mug, as if she'd find the answer there.

"The night you left the House, Stone said something that greatly troubled me. He said you told him the Keeper had kissed your cheek and read your mind. To my knowledge, Celeste did not have magic, and never had. We welcome magicians to the House, of course, but we ask that they acknowledge their gifts when they arrive, and then carefully consider the ways in which they use them."

"Sounds like Celeste did neither."

"When she first came to the House, she worked as the gardener.

She had a gift for cultivating plants and flowers—a non-magical gift, she said, though now I wonder. Last year, when my Keeper passed away unexpectedly, Celeste positioned herself as a viable candidate.

"By then she and Shay had spent years in the House. She knew our people and our practices. Because we needed a Keeper and I did not have adequate time to vet other candidates, I said yes—against my better judgment. Even then I had my doubts. I knew her to be somewhat intrusive, the sort of person who always thinks they know best. But she assured me she was working on it. And the House is nothing if not a place for people willing to do the work."

She leaned back. Let out her breath.

"I have launched a full investigation into Celeste's behavior. Others have begun to step forward to share the ways in which she has abused her power as Keeper. She has been actively undermining all my best hopes and intentions for the House. I have worked to foster a community of openness, exploration, and—above all else—support. What you have offered Stone, Shay, and the other young women and men is a community. You've empowered them, making them feel safe and seen. Why would I want to take that away from my child? Why would anyone?"

Pilar grunted. "Ask Celeste."

"Needless to say, Celeste is no longer welcome at the House."

Muri rotated her coffee mug first one way, then the other.

"This has been my greatest challenge as the Shadowess. Especially now, as our world changes around us. I have tried to do

422

everything at once, from the highest goals and missions of the House—our promise to our guests and residents, as well as to other kingdoms who need our help—all the way down to knowing which resident will break out in hives after eating tajin. I clearly should not have spent so much time on the tajin."

It wasn't a great joke, but Pilar smiled. Muri smiled back.

Then she grew serious again.

"People who are hungry for power are always threatened by those who truly have it. You have great power in you, Pilar. Celeste wanted to take that power away. In so doing, she hurt everyone. My son, her own daughter. And you. I am truly sorry."

The words landed in Pilar's ears like a foreign language. Had her own mother apologized to her like this? *Ever?* It was almost uncomfortable.

"Is that really why you came here? You rode a pink kama through the desert to say sorry?"

"Some apologies are worth a trek through the desert." Muri tapped her finger on the lip of her mug. "But that is not the only reason."

Here it comes, Pilar thought. The agenda. The *real* reason the Shadowess had come to Glas Ddir.

"I rode through the desert," she said, "to ask if you would consider coming back."

Pilar blinked. Surely she'd misheard.

"Back to the House?"

"Yes. I never wanted you to leave. That was Celeste's lie. Her attempt to make you feel unwanted."

Starved for attention. Girls who pretend to be victims when they are any-thing but.

Pilar searched Muri's eyes for the coldness she had seen in Morígna's. But she saw only warmth.

"I don't know your history, Pilar, and I don't need to. If you someday choose to share it with me, fine. If you do not, fine. What I want to assure you is that I will work harder to identify the ways in which the House is failing its mission, and where *I* am failing *my* mission. I would like your help in ensuring the House of Shadows remains a haven of safety and support."

The words were coming swiftly. Comforting. Disorienting. Pilar couldn't guzzle them fast enough.

"We are, as it so happens, currently in need of a Keeper." Muri took a breath. "I would be honored if you would consider step-ping into the role."

Pilar was speechless. Not in one million years would she have expected this.

"I would only ask that you come to me the moment you get even the faintest whiff of someone misusing their power. I think you have a gift for discerning the rotten heart of even the most sweet-smelling apple."

"I've had some practice."

"I wish you hadn't had cause to learn. And yet those expe-riences are a part of you. They have sharpened you into a keen blade. If I am to keep the House a safe haven for all, I need a blade like you as my Keeper. Soon my second term will come to a close. Between then and now, I want to do everything I can to put strong structures in place before the next Shadowess or Shadower is appointed."

Pilar pushed her plate aside. Thinking. She was honored by the offer. But something about it didn't sit right.

"I don't think Celeste in the role of Keeper is your problem," she said slowly. "Sure, Celeste is a demon witch. She's the worst Gwyrach who ever Gwyrached. But I think the real problem is the role itself."

The Shadowess looked at her, curious.

"Tell me more."

"The way I see it, two people have power in the House. The Keeper is appointed by the Shadowess, and the Shadowess is appointed by the Manuba Committee. Who are they again? Because I've yet to find someone at the House who's actually met them. But they're supposedly old and wise and important, so they appoint whichever Shadowess or Shadower they think is most qualified. In other words: who looks good on paper, not who the people choose. Don't get me wrong: you're not a bad person. You're good at what you do. But what if the next Shadowess isn't? What if they hurt people, like Celeste? There's no one to hold them accountable. Two people with absolute power really isn't all that much better than one."

The Shadowess held her gaze. Pilar watched Muri turn the words over and over in her mind. With each turn, something else seemed to click into place.

She took off her glasses. Set them down beside her mug. Pilar had started to recognize the gesture. The glasses came off when

Muri was about to say something important.

"Great sands," she said. "You are exactly right."

Pilar almost laughed. Not the appropriate reaction. But she'd won the argument so easily, it wasn't even an argument.

"I would now like to revoke my offer," the Shadowess said. "The offer of Keeper, anyway. I'd like you to come back and help me reconfigure the system, with a focus on accountability of power."

Pilar leaned back.

"What would that look like?"

"I don't know yet. We'll have to figure that out. But we would build a new system, together. And I'd love to hear from the younger members of our community about what they want and need. They already like and trust you, Pilar. How validating for them to share their thoughts and ideas with their favorite fight teacher, then see those thoughts and ideas implemented throughout the House." Muri's face brightened. "We can start by reopening the Gymnasia. Expand it if you like—there is plenty of room. You are welcome to whatever resources you need."

Pilar was having a hard time paying attention. Not because she didn't like Muri's proposal. The opposite. She was imagining a Gymnasia twice the size. Double the sandbags. Thicker floor mats for softer falls. She pictured more students pouring in, her brood growing so large she'd have to hire Shay and Stone to teach some of the new recruits.

She felt a sharp pang.

"If Celeste isn't at the House anymore, does that mean Shay isn't, either?"

"No child should be punished for their parents' crimes. Shay is old enough to make her own decisions. The doors of the House remain open to her."

Pilar grinned. Not just for herself. For Stone. He'd have a chance to apologize to Shay for the things he'd said. Confess his true feelings. For all she knew, he already had.

Muri was smiling, too. She picked her glasses back up.

"There is much work to be done. And much is being asked of us, more than ever before. The four kingdoms need healing. Our world needs healing if we are to survive. So, too, do the young men and women of the House of Shadows. They need a place where they feel safe and strong. They—we—*I*—need you."

Pilar didn't have time to let the words sink in. Behind the Shadowess, Mia stood in the doorway. Her face drained of blood.

She said something. Or maybe just mouthed it. Whatever it was, it wasn't good.

Pilar stood. Locked eyes on the Shadowess.

"Thank you," she said. "I mean it, Muri. Thank you. But I have to go."

She turned and followed Mia out of the inn.

Chapter 47

TOMB

"I CAN'T PUT IT into words," Mia said, leading Pilar through Killian Village. "I just have to show you."

Mia still couldn't believe it herself. Her exhaustion had caught up with her in the hat shop; she'd staggered out into the morning sun, made a few wrong turns, and dead-ended in an alley reeking of excrement and old fish. This was the village she remembered, a warren of huts and hovels she'd only briefly glimpsed when she and Quin escaped.

That night he'd confessed he sometimes went into Killian Village, doing what he could to make amends for his father's policies. Why had she not asked him what he did, or whom he helped? Why had she failed to ask him so many things?

She would do everything differently, if she only had more time.

Heavy with regret, Mia had traced an uneasy path through the village, until a white-haired woman selling flowers hissed, "Where are your mourning sleeves, girl? The king is dead."

The words made the wound bleed anew.

The king is dead.

Quin is dead.

Miserable, she had started wandering toward the eastern road.

That had not been the right decision.

"Where are we going?" Pilar said, as Mia dragged her along. Rose was holding on tight—annoyingly tight—as they stumbled over the uneven cobblestones. Add that to the many failures of Clan Killian: their roads were absolute shit.

"Are you taking me to the eastern road?"

Pilar knew the road well, having tripped down it a hundred times as a scullery maid. The Kaer was so awful she would sometimes hide food stores in dark cupboards so it would appear they had run out, just so she'd have an excuse to leave the castle.

"I'm not taking you to the eastern road," Mia said. Which was, in a sense, true.

They were coming to the edge of the village, where the huts thinned out at the foot of the northern peaks. Thousands of years before, Clan Killian had commanded Glasddiran stonemasons to dig a castle out of the rock, leaving a black scab on the side of the mountain.

The crush of panic was upon her. Mia could no longer avoid it.

"Look," she said, pointing.

Pilar followed Mia's finger. She nearly choked.

There was no eastern road. No mountain.

"No Kaer." She swallowed. So the river guide hadn't lied. "It's just . . . gone."

They stood side by side, awestruck. The entire landscape was transformed. So much so that, if they hadn't been there before, they never would have recognized it. The saw-toothed mountains had been tempered into gentler versions of themselves—their rough edges smoothed, the steep crags filed down to softer slopes. Some hills were blanketed in green grass and varicolored flowers; others were inky black, stippled with charred tree stumps.

"So the rumors weren't rumors," Pilar said. "About the fires."

"Fires can be good," Mia murmured, partly to remind herself. "They're part of a forest's natural life cycle. The fires burn up old dead trees and competing vegetation on the forest floor, leaving more resources for the survivors. Many ancient trees have bark so thick they can survive the flames."

"Never hurts to have thick skin," Pilar quipped.

Mia sucked in her breath. "I think I see the ocean."

Pilar squinted. "Really?"

"Right there." She gestured toward a limpid line on the horizon. "The Opalen Sea."

Rose was right. Pilar could see it now. The rolling hills stopped abruptly at a gash of silver.

She fingered the bloodbloom charm in her pocket. Now she understood why Mia liked it. Just knowing it was there made her feel calmer, even as she swayed a little on her feet.

Why did she feel so unsteady? Pilar hated the Kaer. Hated it as Ronan's scullery maid, hated it even more as one of Angelyne's enkindled. But it didn't feel right that something so big could vanish so completely. Especially if it meant Quin had vanished, too.

"I don't get it," she said. "It looks completely different. Like the mountains were never even here. Since you seem to know a lot about forest fires . . . they can't do *that*, can they? Dissolve a bunch of thousand-year-old rocks and then sprout some nice flowers?" She frowned. "You're not using head magic on me, are you, Rose?"

"Not unless I am inadvertently also using it on myself."

"How could the northern peaks collapse without crushing Killian Village?"

Till the northern peaks crumble.

Promise me, O promise me.

Mia saw Quin's eyes. Scintillating green.

Another wave of grief crashed over her.

She should turn around. Go back. Being here, this close to Kaer Killian—or rather, the ashes of Kaer Killian—was too painful.

"We should go up there," Pilar said.

"Why? It's gone. *He's* gone."

"Maybe he's buried up there. That would make sense, right? That they'd build some kind of shrine? We could . . . I don't know . . . pay our respects."

She could tell Mia didn't want to. Pilar didn't really want to, either. But to stand there, feeling helpless, realizing Quin had been erased without a trace? Surely that was worse.

"Look!" Now it was Pilar's turn to point. "Do you see that?"

Mia trained her eyes on the spot Pilar had indicated. In the middle distance, she saw movement. Blurs of color on a green plateau. And—now that she was looking for it—a narrow white path winding toward them like a strip of gauze.

"There are people up there," said Pilar. "And we're going to find out who."

The people were children. A dozen, maybe two. They wore brightly colored costumes and jewelry, one girl sporting a wig of wild red curls. A blond boy ran around a rough-hewn stage, screeching, then somehow got his foot caught in the blue pendant dangling from his neck and went tumbling into a group of girls. He looked so pleased with himself when he landed at the girls' feet, Mia wondered if he'd planned it.

"Children," called a matronly woman from the edge of the stage. "Children! I ask that you *please* gather yourselves. If we cannot pull ourselves together, there will be no performance tonight."

A hush fell over them.

"Good. Thank you. That's much better. We're going to take it from the top of act two."

Mia exchanged glances with Pilar. What had they stumbled into?

"Oh, hello there," said the woman, noticing them for the first time. "Are you here from the Council? Quin said he'd be sending two members up for a preview."

All the moisture evaporated from Mia's mouth.

432

Quin.

How was she supposed to hold that name in her head? The blistering hope bound up in those four letters? She could not, *would* not dredge him out of the tomb, only to bury him again.

"Wait," Pilar said. "*Quin* told you that?"

"Well, yes." The woman looked slightly irritated. "If you're not from the Council, I'm afraid I am going to have to ask you to leave. You can come to the main performance tonight with the other villagers. Now if you'll excuse—ah, there he is now."

Mia didn't look. She couldn't. If she did, it might not be real.

For years after, she would regret that it was Pilar who turned first. Pilar who saw him. Pilar who spoke his name.

"Quin?" Pil said.

And it was.

Chapter 48

SHATTERED

THE MOMENT WAS INFINITE. In truth it could only have lasted a few seconds. But when the sisters turned toward him—Mia with her wild curls, Pilar with her proud jaw—Quin had the strange sensation that all three of them had been cut loose from time. They were players in a tableau vivant, perfectly preserved under glass: a moment that would stay with him forever.

Quin had known the sisters were in Glas Ddir. He'd spent the better part of last night in negotiations with the Shadowess and her ambassadors, ensuring them that, yes, Kaer Killian had ceased to exist, as had the reign of Clan Killian; no, he was not a tyrant brutalizing his people; and yes, he would welcome both their counsel and assistance, insofar as these aligned with his own plans for reparations.

These reparations had been physically exhausting, mentally draining, emotionally taxing—and by far the most rewarding efforts of his life. He felt sometimes that he had lived more in the last month than he had in the eighteen years before.

And yet, in spite of all that, he still had not anticipated how terrified he would feel, a crate of theatrical props tucked under one arm, as he beheld Mia and Pilar on a sun-dappled hill. The last they'd seen of him, he had been trying to kill them. The last they'd heard from him . . . he had still been trying to kill them He would rue that cursed letter for the rest of his days.

"I . . ." he stammered. "I . . ."

Where to begin? *How* to begin?

"Suffice it to say, I owe you both—"

The apology screeched to an ignominious halt. Pilar was barreling toward him. So swiftly he thought she might tackle him to the ground. She'd be well within her rights.

Quin would not retreat. He was resolved to face her anger head-on, to pay the price for his own actions. He came forward stiltedly, still adjusting to his new gait—and then he saw her eyes and knew she wasn't going to attack him. Quite the opposite. He was so overjoyed, so grateful, that he dropped his crate of props, throwing his arms wide as she plowed into them.

He had forgotten her scent. A touch of sweat and fire. He'd missed it.

"I can't believe it." She pulled back, roughening his curls. "Don't you ever die?"

He knew then that it would be all right. That whatever happened between them—including what already had—things would even themselves out. Not to imply it would be easy. He did not take lightly his turn beneath the snow palace, how he had loomed over Pilar, lifting his sphere of fire. He could spend three lifetimes doing penance and it would still not be enough.

He bowed his head.

"I owe you precisely one million apologies, Pilar, I—"

"Stop. Don't ruin the moment."

He couldn't suppress a smile. She was still Pilar d'Aqila. The love he'd once felt for her was not gone; it had simply grown into a different shape. From the joy on her face, he sensed that, one way or another, the Doomed Duet of Pil and Kill would find a new harmony. Albeit with some discordant notes.

As for Mia . . . he was not so sure.

"Quin," she said. Softly.

She took a careful step toward him.

"You're alive."

Over the last month, Quin had spent countless hours imagining the moment he saw Mia again. Ruminating on what he would say and how he would say it. He had even rehearsed.

Now that the moment had arrived, all his preparations promptly went up in flames.

She felt like home.

Mia was the home he'd longed for, not the dark and fearful home he'd known. He had not expected how desperately he would want to wrap her in his arms and bury his face in her curls. He'd missed her gray eyes and sweet freckles, her fierce independence, her mind working even now to parse the logic of finding him alive. He knew her like he knew his own soul.

Or did he? What if the Mia Rose he'd known was not the Mia Rose who stood before him? They had lived whole lifetimes since they'd last seen each other. He had cheated death and created himself anew. Something told him she had done the same.

And so he willed himself still. Sheer agony, but essential. He would let Mia come to him, if she so chose.

She did not so choose.

Her face remained passive. Inscrutable. Quin's heart plummeted into his ribs. How could he blame her? Last they'd touched, he had burned the flesh off her hands.

"Well, this is quite the performance!" said Prenda, and he gave a start. He had forgotten that the tableau vivant was not, in fact, just the three of them: it included the entire ensemble of orphans, along with Prenda, their mistress of the pretending arts. The children sat and stood in clusters around the stage, all rapt as they watched this real-life drama unfold.

Quin blushed fiercely. Here he was, the props master, facing off with his two former lovers in front of an audience of children.

He cleared his throat.

"Let me just . . ." He stooped and began hurriedly scooping the props back into the crate.

"I'll help." Pilar crouched beside him. "What's all this, anyway?"

"The children are putting on a production," he said, grateful to have something to talk about. "They're performing tonight for Natha Village."

"Natha Village?" Mia echoed. She'd crept a few inches closer.

Unless Quin had imagined it.

"Yes. The Council officially renamed Killian Village after taking a public vote."

He thought he saw a flicker of interest in Mia's eyes, but it faded quickly. If her goal was to keep her face unreadable, she was succeeding. The uncertainty was driving him mad.

"In the old language," she said, "*natha* means 'snake.'"

Pilar snorted. "You named it Snake Village?"

"I like snakes!" piped one of the orphans.

Quin sighed. "I'll bet you do, Victor."

To the sisters he said, "The name was chosen by popular vote. We are the river kingdom, remember, and the Natha is our most prominent river. It was the chief source of trade and commerce under Queen Bronwynis's reign. Our hope is that trade will soon flourish once again."

Quin stood, hefting the repacked crate under his arm.

"Give me one moment."

He moved toward the stage, acutely aware of his leg, and also relieved to have a moment to catch his breath. How had he ever merged Pilar and Mia into the Twisted Sisters? When he looked at Pil, he felt a jolly camaraderie. When he looked at Mia, he went weak at the knees.

The orphans were making noise again, as was their way, their chirps and chatters offering a welcome reprieve from his reunion.

Victor climbed onto Quin's shoulders as he set the props on the stage.

"Children," Prenda said. "*Children.*" She shot Quin a beseeching look. "You are a tremendous help, and an even more tremendous distraction."

"Yes, yes, I know. We're leaving."

He unhooked Victor from around his neck and faced the sisters. Pilar was grinning, clearly amused. Mia was a blank wall.

"Come," he said, walking toward them. "It's been a while since you've both been here, and much has happened. I'll show you everything you've missed."

Quin was proud. He'd never been prouder of anything in his life.

As he led the sisters through Natha Village, he delighted in showing them the various components of reconstruction. "We hand out fresh provisions every morning," he said, pointing to the old brothel. "And over there, see the tavern? We've repurposed the kitchen to provide hot meals to anyone who needs them. Too many Glasddirans have gone hungry for far too long."

He took them to the hospital, the site of his own convalescence, now bustling with other patients in need of care. "We treat anyone," he explained, "whether they have coins or not." Then to the industrial district he had affectionately dubbed Karri Row, a thriving guild of brewers, butchers, blacksmiths, and dairy farmers manufacturing all his sister's favorite things: malts, meats, swords, and stoneberry flambés. "The goal is to offer work to those who seek it. In so doing, we stimulate our own economy— and make our exports more attractive to potential trade partners. Two birds."

He turned to Mia. "Griffin Rose has been a great help to us.

Your father knows the trade routes well, having traveled them so many . . ." Realizing his mistake, he turned to Pilar. "Your father, too, I suppose."

Quin saw a glimmer of interest in both their faces. Perhaps even hope. He imagined they had plenty to discuss with Griffin Rose. Would they choose to forgive their father?

He winced. Would they choose to forgive *Quin*?

"Wait until you see this," he said, eager to change the subject. He led the sisters down to the riverbank, where he showed them a new water-filtration system he'd been experimenting with. When he pumped the lever, bright orange water spurted out.

"A work in progress," he said, sheepish.

"What about the children we saw earlier?" Pilar asked. "Are they one of your good works?"

"I believe you cannot rehabilitate a kingdom without providing entertainment and artistry. I've always been fond of the theater, and as I saw it this was a way to bring the pretending arts back to Glas Ddir. The children have been rehearsing very hard for tonight's performance. You should come."

Pilar grunted. "Will the performance be better than that orange water?"

"I certainly hope so."

Quin considered circumventing the Old Towne, but decided to guide them through. This was the oldest part of the village, a neighborhood many still considered to be dangerous.

"We're trying to stabilize the area," he explained. "Make it safer for all. Illicit enterprise flourished under my father's reign, as you might expect. When a king violates the rights of his people, those violations spread like a virus. It's only a matter of time before they infect others."

As he led the sisters back to the new heart of Natha Village, they fell quiet. Pilar had kept up a lively banter for most of the tour, which only underscored Mia's silence. At each new place, Quin stole covert glances, hoping to see a hint of a smile. But Mia remained stoic.

In the village square, they stopped to rest at the rosewater fountain. Quin's leg ached, as it always did after a long walk. He heard a yip and looked up, expectant.

"Wulf!" Mia cried. "Beo!"

Quin's heart soared at the joy in her voice. His dogs were happy, too. Ears pricked, they trotted toward Mia, skipping over him entirely.

"I suppose I see whom they prefer," Quin said, hoping for an opening.

Mia steadfastly ignored him. She cupped Wulf's chin, scratching him behind the ears, just the way he liked.

"What's that?" Pilar said, pointing to the two-story structure across the street.

"We call it the Bronwynis Chambers. It's where the Council meets. When my aunt was queen, she appointed a council of eight people to help her rule the kingdom."

"Lauriel told me about it," Mia chimed in, to his surprise. "It was Queen Bronwynis who said, 'If we don't invite peasants to sit at our table, how will we learn what they eat?'"

He nodded. "An apocryphal story, perhaps, but I've always liked it. I know she appointed five women and three men. It's recorded in the histories."

Pilar arched a brow. "How many women do *you* have?"

"Four. And four men. A fair divide."

"Plus you the king."

"I sit on the council," he said, "but I am not the king."

How to explain to the sisters the manifold epiphanies he'd had over the last month? About power, duty, politics, love?

He still marveled that a twelve-year-old had taught him the greatest lesson. *That's the thing about power,* Callaghan said. *It corrupts even good people.* Those were the words he'd had in his heart as he hurled his raging flames into the northern peaks. Power was by nature corruptive. The only way to ensure that kings in lofty castles would not abuse their power and exploit the people down below . . . was to ensure there were no kings, and no castles.

His first step had been to renounce the throne. Easy enough, considering there no longer was one. Then, as his body began to heal, he had turned his attention to the Glasddirans. Though he was confined to bed at his physicians' insistence, his brain churned relentlessly. He often lay awake until the wee hours of the morning, concocting some new plan to bring relief to his people.

The most surprising thing was that he was good at it. Wildly good. In addition to his gifts in music and the pretending arts—not to mention his ability to whip up a feast fit for a non-king—he had a natural talent for public works.

Growing up with his sister, he had never imagined he, too, might make a good leader. Karri had excelled at diplomacy and statecraft, which had never been his style. And, as he knew from his short-lived bid for tyranny, he made a gods-awful tyrant. But when it came to the well-being of Glasddirans? Providing care and succor, putting strong checks and balances in place, and dismantling an old system? Creating new practices that would benefit *all* people, not just the rich and powerful? He was a bottomless fount of ideas.

"If you were in the Kaer when it fell," Pilar said, "I don't understand how you survived."

"I don't, either." He had recounted the story a hundred times. "I saw the rocks plummeting down. Felt the Kaer coming apart under my feet. Then everything went black."

He patted his leg.

"When I woke up, this was buried under a boulder, every bone crushed. Femur, tibia, fibula—I'm sure you'd know all the names, Mia, though try as I might I can't hold them in my head. I'm just glad I got to keep it. For a while they weren't sure."

Though he tried to do it with a dose of humor, it was still hard to talk about his leg. He vacillated between anger and acceptance, resignation and gratitude.

So far no one had been cruel. If anything, the people around him had adapted more easily than he had. "So one leg's a little shorter," Callaghan said. "It isn't like you've changed!"

Sometimes when he looked at his reflection, he saw Tobin staring back. At the beginning he had dreamed about him every

443

night; now it was only every two or three. It haunted him how, in that final moment, he had searched Toby's eyes for a flicker of warmth, starved for comfort as the Kaer crushed them from above. Or perhaps what he'd really been seeking was forgiveness.

He hadn't found it. Tobin's eyes had been cold. Hateful.

Quin grieved the loss. He imagined he would for some time. It broke his heart that Tobin had clung to power till the bitter end. In spite of how their story had come to a close, Toby would always be his first love. A love he'd been ashamed to feel—and that his father had extinguished with hate and fear. As long as Quin lived, he would fight to ensure the children of the river kingdom never felt that shame.

Perhaps love was like a rose. Love should always be allowed to grow, between whomever chose to grow it. All that mattered was how well you tended it.

"Why the mourning sleeves?" Mia asked, jolting him back to the village square.

He let out his breath.

"I told people not to wear them. I had renounced both the Killian crown and the royal colors; the sleeves were nugatory. But they insisted." His cheeks reddened. "It became something of a movement. People said it was the perfect symbol for putting the old world order to rest."

"We thought you were dead, Quin," Mia said. "*I* thought you were dead."

She stared at him with such intensity it knocked the air from his lungs.

On the hill he'd felt a kind of transparent wall between them. Even as he stared into her gray eyes, she had hidden from him.

Now the wall shattered. He was defenseless under the ferocity of her gaze.

"Do you two need a moment?" Pilar said.

"No," Mia said curtly. She rose. "You stay. I'm going."

"Going where?" Quin called after her, aware of how pitiful he sounded.

He needn't have worried. She walked away too quickly to hear.

Chapter 49

WIDE AS THE SKY

"I SHOULD GO AFTER her." Quin stared at Mia with such painful longing, Pilar worried for his health. "*Should* I go after her?"

Pilar kicked off her boots. Stretched out on the fountain. Stared up at the sky.

"Give her time. She'll come around."

She had wondered how she'd feel, seeing Quin again. Never had she shared so much of herself with another person. And it had been *her choice*. That was the thing. Instead of having something taken from her, she had chosen to give it.

But the moment she saw him on the hill, holding a box of stick arrows doused in fake blood, it confirmed what she'd known for months. The pleasing shivers were gone. Her body didn't hum with pleasure. More of a nice, steady thump in her ribs: the feeling of seeing an old friend.

Honestly? She was relieved. She had too many plans, too much to do, to throw shivers and hums into the mix.

"Are we going to talk about it?" Quin said.

She groaned. Just when she'd gotten settled.

"Of course you want to talk about it."

"Yes, Pilar, I do. Considering how we parted ways, I'd at very least like to say I'm sorry."

How many apologies was she going to get today?

She sighed. Sat up. Spun round to face him.

"All right, Killian. Have at it."

He winced. "Could you perchance call me Quin? Or really anything but Killian."

"I will call you Quin if you promise to never say *perchance* again."

He grinned. She'd won a small victory.

"I don't even know where to begin," he said, and began anyway.

The apologies came in a strange order. And not always the ones she expected. Quin was sorry for almost killing her. For *wanting* to kill her. That was the big one. Also for knocking her down using her own moves.

"You were trying to teach me to protect myself," he said, "and I used it against you."

He was sorry he had lied a million times while Angelyne was enthralling him. Even sorrier that he'd kept lying when she *wasn't* enthralling him.

He was sorry for other things, too. Undercooking a rabbit on their journey to Luumia. Not complimenting her violin playing enough. His continued inability to correctly pronounce the *i* in P*i*lar. She found these confessions sweet, if somewhat beside the point.

By the time Quin finished apologizing, he looked beat. She got the sense he was relieved to get it all out.

"You do this a lot now, don't you?"

"Is it that obvious?" He shot her a rueful grin. "The Art of Making Amends. I've been getting plenty of practice. You'd think I would have tightened it up a bit by now."

She looked at him. Thoughtful. Did he expect her to forgive him? Did she expect *herself* to forgive him? Under Angelyne's enthrallment, he had broken her trust. She'd felt used. Betrayed.

But magic was tricky. Now, with more distance—and less raw fury—she understood Quin had been used, too. Pilar had blamed the victim for the crime.

As for the snow palace? The moment when some essential part of Quin had broken, and he had decided her life was worth less than his? She didn't know what to do with that. But she knew he was a product of his past—like her, like anyone—and he had known only violence, beginning with his father. She felt real grief over what that violence had cost them both.

"I'm sorry too, Quin."

She touched the bloodbloom in her pocket. Let the air out of her lungs.

"I'm sorry for everything you've had to endure. And I'm sorry

448

I was cruel to you. I blamed you for things that were never your fault. Angelyne hurt us both. I want you to know I admire everything you're doing here to make amends. You should be very proud."

Her apology was simpler than his—and a lot shorter—but it felt right.

They sat in companionable silence. He petted his dogs. She flopped back onto the fountain wall, flung an arm over her eyes. The sun made her sleepy. Who knew apologies were so exhausting?

"Here's a question," she said. "Do you think we ever would have had an honest go?"

"You mean the Doomed Duet of Pil and Kill?"

"The timing wasn't right, obviously."

"*That's* an understatement."

She was about to make a joke when he said, simply, "I've always cared about you, Pil. Beneath all the lies and all the magic, there was always that truth at the core."

Heat rushed to her face.

"I think we each gave each other something we needed," he went on. "You reminded me I might actually deserve to be loved."

"And you made me feel safe again."

He smiled. "These days I think a lot about power. People who've had their power stripped away often seek out others who've been hurt in similar ways. We were both victims, and we clung to each other because there was nothing else to cling on to."

Pilar sat bolt upright.

"We're also survivors, Quin. Don't forget that. We helped each other survive."

She took him in. His fiery green eyes. His taut, lean body, which—she did not mind admitting—had brought her great delight. She thought of every moment they'd spent together. The sensual. The playful. The infuriating.

"Can I ask you something?" she said.

"Of course."

"Did it make you feel strong?"

He looked at her, curious. "Which part?"

"When you did the move I taught you—and knocked me on my ass."

"I don't know if *strong* is the word I'd use. *Powerful*, maybe."

"Do you think if you'd learned to fight when you were younger, you would have felt more powerful?"

He considered it.

"I think so, yes. Perhaps in the end it isn't so different from magic. That night I felt powerful in my body, whether I was using your sparring moves or sending flames from my hands. I had never felt that kind of power inside me. Perhaps my life would have been very different if I had."

Pilar grinned as wide as the sky. She stood. Leaned down. Kissed Quin on the cheek. She was surprised to feel a lump rising in her throat.

"You may not be a Killian," she said, "but you are still a prince to me."

Chapter 50

THE GREATEST LOVE STORIES

Mɪᴀ ᴡᴀsɴ'ᴛ ʜᴀʀᴅ ᴛᴏ find. Pilar went straight to the hospital.

Rose was loitering by the front steps. Staring at the front door. Brow furrowed.

"Or you could go in," Pilar said over her shoulder.

Mia didn't turn. Somehow she'd known Pil was there.

"Why? I'm not sick."

"Only half the people in a hospital are sick. The other half are there to make them better." Pilar plopped herself down on the top step. "You should talk to Quin."

Mia was silent.

Nothing could have prepared her for seeing Quin on the sun-soaked hilltop. She was gripped by shock and joy, hope and terror.

He was alive. She had drunk in his tousled golden curls, his warm green eyes, his tenderness. Even before he'd opened his mouth to bungle an apology, she knew he was not the same person who had penned the letter.

It alarmed her how quickly she forgave him. How easily she let the old tide of feelings sweep her away. She could feel herself tilting toward him, as if pulled by an invisible string. She had taken exactly one step, then stopped. Nell's words pierced her consciousness.

I'm not entirely convinced you know what love is. At least not the kind that's freely given, freely shared.

Mia had grown so much over the past few months. No doubt Quin had, too. But had they grown together or apart? It seemed too much to hope that their separate journeys would now perfectly intertwine. The thought that she would finally choose him—that she was ready to freely give him love—only to have him reject her? She couldn't bear it.

And so, as Quin showed them a revitalized village, she'd kept her face stony and impassive, even though she was deeply moved. At the hospital she'd wanted nothing more than to go inside, yet she had turned away, studiously avoiding eye contact. It wasn't that she was scared of what she might see in Quin's eyes. She was scared she wouldn't see anything at all.

"I have nothing to say to him," Mia lied.

"You have *everything* to say. And you know it."

Mia sighed. That was the thing about Pilar. She could spot bullshit from a mile away—and she never beat around the bush.

Mia sank onto the stoop beside her.

"What did Muri say? I never asked."

Pilar sighed. That was the thing about Mia. She could shift an interrogation so smoothly you were suddenly the one being interrogated.

"You were right. Muri had no idea about Celeste. She asked me to come back to the House, if you can believe it. Told me I could keep sparring. She wants my help rooting out the rotten people no one else can see." Pilar lifted her chin, cocky. "She thinks I have a knack for it."

"Will you go?"

"I don't know." She shrugged. "Maybe."

"Come on, Pil. Don't do that."

"Do what?"

"You so clearly love it there. Your whole face lit up when you told me about your fight students. You love everything about it."

Mia smiled. She liked the idea of Pilar in the House of Shadows. Sweating and sparring; bonding with her brood; holding people to account. The irony was not lost on her. Pilar had stomped around the House, claiming to hate everything, and yet she'd found a home there. A family. Mia had been blissfully in the House's thrall, only to leave it behind.

She felt a twinge of grief. Would she ever see the Curatorium again?

And yet, when she thought of returning to the House—of turning her back on the river kingdom—the grief was far greater.

"I can't go with you," Mia said softly. "I didn't know how

much I missed home until I came back to it."

Pilar held her gaze. "I was thinking," she said. "Pembuk and Glas Ddir aren't *that* far apart. Really the only thing between them is a vast, brutal, endless desert. Now that you're an expert kama rider, a vast, brutal, endless desert is a piece of cake."

Mia laughed. "I think you sorely overestimate my aptitude on a pink kama."

"There's always the water. I know how much you love boats."

Pilar enjoyed teasing her sister. She'd never had a sister she could tease. But she wondered if Mia could hear the fear beneath the jokes. Pilar didn't want to accept that she might never see her sister again. *Couldn't* accept it.

Maybe she wouldn't have to.

When Quin was taking them around the village, Pilar's brain had started popping with ideas. Or maybe it had popped earlier, when she'd seen the children run around the stage, the little boy fling himself onto Quin's back. If she was going to expand the Gymnasia, why not train younger children, too? It would be more tumbling than fighting, but that was fine. It would give them a physical outlet, a way to get comfortable in their bodies without feeling any shame.

The idea made her so dizzy with happiness she actually felt faint.

"I was also thinking," she said aloud, "that I could create different kinds of programs—different sparring styles, sure, but not *only* sparring. A lot of times my brood just wants to talk. What if I started a group where we sat in a room together and talked?

Like the circle, but with actual words."

"No humming?" Mia said wryly.

Pilar grinned. "Never."

"I think that sounds divine."

Pil traced the wooden stoop between them, running her finger down the grain.

"I could offer the same programs to students from all four kingdoms. Teach in different places, or maybe recruit students to come back to the House. I know we can't heal ourselves before we heal the world, or we can't heal the world before we heal ourselves, or whatever it is they say. Obviously you can't spar with a volqano or punch a glacier back into place. But maybe, if I can help my students feel strong and powerful . . . it's something."

"It's more than something, Pilar. It's everything. The whole reason we're in this mess is because people wanted to feel powerful, and they didn't care about the cost. That's why the world is breaking open. My sister . . ." She swallowed. "*Our* sister wanted to feel powerful. She just didn't have the right tools."

Mia had wondered countless times if things would have been different if she—or the Shadowess—or anyone, really—had been able to give Angie the right tools.

But when her mind wandered there, she gently drew it back.

Angelyne had made her choice. It had broken Mia's heart, and yet here she was, with her heart still beating. No matter how well she knew the anatomy of a human heart, she would never be able to understand it. Maybe she didn't need to.

"If you're sailing around the world recruiting," she said, "would you promise to come see me whenever you're in the river kingdom?"

Pilar felt a rush of warmth. So Mia would miss her, too.

"Don't worry. You can't get rid of me so easy." She cocked her head. "Wait, where will you be exactly? Natha Village? Ilwysion?"

"I honestly don't know," Mia answered. Going back to her cottage seemed too sad, too painful.

"I'm not worried," Pilar said. "You always seem to land on your feet."

"Says the queen of feet landing! I hope you know you're well on your way to becoming a legend, Pilar d'Aqila. The girls and boys of the four kingdoms have no idea how lucky they are."

Pil reached out and took her hand.

The only time they'd ever been side by side, hands clasped, was during their Reflections. They had been suspended, almost incorporeal, floating in the dreamlike space between.

Here, in Natha Village, the air smelled of dust and moldy fruit. Two boys unloaded a cart of wares across the street. A little girl coughed violently as her mother shepherded her toward the hospital. A man hocked a wad of spit onto the cobblestones.

"You should really talk to Quin," Pilar said. "I think he wants to apologize. But be prepared, because his apologies are a *lot*."

Mia grew thoughtful. She and Quin had been children when last they'd met. She had thought she knew what love was, the way she'd thought she knew everything. She had applied the same rubric to her feelings for Nell. Those feelings had not entirely dissolved; she could still feel their imprint on her heart.

But loving Nell—or *failing* to—had changed her. She now knew to nurture her beloved's feelings as much as her own. And she knew something else, too: that she could love whom she loved.

For seventeen years she had been constrained by the flawed system she'd inherited. But she had finally shucked off the guilt and constant questioning of her own desire. Now she could come to Quin exactly as she was, because she *knew* who she was.

Something Mia had read in a book long ago drifted through her mind.

"'Perhaps, in the end, the greatest love stories are not about our lovers. They are the stories of how we learned to love ourselves.'"

Pilar let the words wash over her. She'd never been much for love stories. But this one was worth a try.

Mia lifted their clasped hands. Planted a peck on Pil's knuckles before she could object.

"Though, for the record," Mia said, "I do love you."

Pilar pulled her close. Laid her head on Mia's shoulder.

"I love you, too."

Chapter 51

IGNITE

MIA'S HEART WAS SORE. She had already said goodbye to one sister. Must she say goodbye to another?

But as she watched Pilar swagger off down the cobbled road, ready to take on the world, she knew this was a different kind of ache. She would see Pilar again. Unlike Angie, Pilar was not relinquishing her life. If anything, she had finally begun to live it.

Was Mia finally ready to live hers?

She stood, brushing the dust off her trousers. Drew a smooth, steady breath.

The door of the hospital yielded easily as she stepped inside.

It was quieter than the Curatorium. The wide, bright room lined with tidy cots thrummed with the murmur of nurses speaking to their patients and each other. Unlike the long blue robes of the Curateurs, they wore brisk white shirts and unfussy trousers.

A nurse approached her.

"Ill, wounded, infirm?"

"None, in fact."

"Here to visit someone?"

Mia threw back her shoulders. "I came to see if you need assistance."

The nurse looked her up and down.

"You have prior experience?"

"Some, yes."

"You've studied anatomy? Physiology? Wound theory?"

Mia smiled, thinking of Wound Man.

"Extensively."

"How are you with blood?"

"I love blood." That hadn't come out the way she intended. "I only mean I don't get queasy at the sight of it."

The nurse placed a hand on her hip.

"Performed any surgeries yourself? I'd wager not. You look a bit green."

"I once extracted an arrow from a man's back, stanched the flow of blood, and later cured an infection that had gone septic. I saved his life." Mia lifted her chin. "Twice."

The nurse looked suitably impressed.

"There is one thing," Mia said. She braced for the woman's face to cloud with fear and suspicion. "I have magic."

"Healing magic? All the better." The nurse gave a quick nod. "Can you start today?"

After that, things happened fast. Half an hour later Mia, too, was wearing a brisk white shirt and trousers. She was given a whirlwind tour of the facilities—admittance room, patient rows, surgical chambers, restatory—introduced to a few nurses, and set loose.

Mia knew immediately where to go. She headed toward the patient rows, following the sound of the deep, rasping coughs she had heard the moment she stepped inside.

A little girl sat on a clean white cot. Her mother perched in a chair beside her—clearly as frightened as her daughter, but trying to hide it.

"She's been coughing all morning," the woman said. "She can hardly catch her breath."

"It hurts," the girl whimpered. "Like I'm being crushed."

Mia sat beside her. "You're being very brave."

"I'm scared."

"I understand. It's a scary thing, not to be able to breathe. But you are doing beautifully."

She couldn't help but think of Angelyne. The horrible hacking coughs Angie had suffered when her magic first bloomed, the relentless pressure on her chest. Was this girl blooming, or simply sick? Either way, Mia would do everything in her power to lessen the pain.

A new awareness settled comfortably, warming her from the inside. She could no longer heal Angelyne. But, thanks to Angelyne, she could heal this little girl.

She pulled the ruby wren from her trouser pocket.

"This stone has healing magic. As do I." She turned to the

girl's mother. "May I touch her?"

The woman hesitated. "Will it help?"

"I believe so. I've done it before."

Mia thought of Nanu. How Domeniq's grandmother had coughed and wheezed until Mia placed a hand on her chest, summoning the winds of Ilwysion, magic pooling in her fingertips as she smoothed the gaps in Nanu's breath.

She turned back to her patient.

"May I touch you?"

The girl nodded, eyes wide.

"Yes."

Mia cradled the fojuen wren in her left hand, placing it gently on the girl's back. Then she put her right hand over the girl's heart.

In the Curatorium she had learned to temper and refine her gifts. Lord Shadowess had taught her to favor slow, balanced remedies over fast, dazzling cures. "True healing is not a magic trick," he liked to say. "Nor is it about achieving high marks."

And so, as she held the girl's fragile rib cage between her hands, she called on her training, her knowledge, and her magic. She closed her eyes and found what her mind alone could not see: the phlegm clogging the lungs. Quietly, steadily, she drew it downward. She coaxed her patient's humors back into alignment, making sure to rebalance her own as well.

It was not instant. It took time. Though, as Mia was learning, change often did. She held on to the Shadowess's words. The only way to heal something as large as a kingdom was to heal it in a hundred small ways every day.

The girl fell asleep in her mother's arms, exhausted by pain and fear.

Under Mia's hands, her body began to heal.

She lost track of time. After the girl came another patient, then another, a steady trickle of ill, wounded, and infirm. Each one required something different, and Mia rose to the challenge, calling on both her intellect and intuition. She thought critically, acted compassionately—and loved every second. She had never felt so vitally alive.

Only when one of the nurses came bustling toward her, saying something about a visitor, did Mia look out the window and realize the sun had set.

"A visitor?"

The nurse blushed and scurried off.

Mia had a good guess who it was.

She scrubbed her hands in the bath bucket, then wiped them dry. Then scrubbed them again with extra soap. She was stalling. She couldn't stall forever.

Mia marched into the admittance room, hands still wet. After all that, she'd forgotten to dry them.

Quin perched on a stool, a gray blanket rolled beneath his arm. When he saw her, he leapt up too quickly, the stool screeching an inch across the floor.

"Hello," she said. "How did you know where to find me?"

"Pilar might have mentioned it."

"*Might* have."

She felt him searching her face. Trying to assess whether or not it was safe to smile. She wasn't sure herself.

"What is it, then?" she said briskly. "I'm quite busy, as you can see."

"Yes, I . . . I was wondering if . . ." He cleared his throat. "If you would consider accompanying me to tonight's performance."

She raised a brow. "The children's play?"

"That's right. We've got half an hour till curtain. They've been working so hard. As for the play itself . . ." He straightened. "I think you might like it."

He was so earnest, standing there. His charming windblown curls, and boots so black and slick, she knew he had shined them before coming. How could she say no to him?

"Well, then," he said.

"Well indeed."

"I ought to—"

"I should be—"

They both stopped abruptly.

"You go first," he said.

"I was just going to say that if we're going to a performance, I should probably change clothes."

Quin's whole demeanor changed. A smile illuminated his face so brilliantly Mia was certain she, too, would ignite.

"Give me five minutes," she called over her shoulder, walking toward the restatory. Grinning the whole way.

Chapter 52

ENDLESS OPALINE

QUIN LOVED THE HILLS. During the day, whenever he felt overwhelmed by the magnitude of reconstructing Natha Village, he would hike above the hubbub, finding new trails amidst the rubble of his childhood home.

After the Kaer collapsed, the first days were the hardest. As the physicians deliberated over whether Quin would keep his leg, he slipped in and out of consciousness, his head foggy from the medicine they gave him for the pain. He remembered Callaghan had come to see him, as had the du Zols. The twins' banter had lifted his spirits. After Domeniq took them home, Lauriel had stayed by his side.

"Are they still burning?" he'd murmured. Every time he closed his eyes, he saw his fire scorching the northern peaks.

"No, darling. The fire has burned itself down to cinders. The hills are quiet now."

She stood, crossing the room to stoke the hearth.

"Do you know what I have always found peculiar? In your language, you use the word *cinder* interchangeably with *ash*. While they are both something that fire leaves behind, they are not the same. Ashes are merely remnants. Cinders have life in them still."

"But they're dead." Quin fought the tears welling in his eyes. He felt so weak and helpless in his sickbed. "Cinders are useless."

"Insofar as cinders cannot be resurrected into the fire they once were, then yes. They are dead. But cinders have a quiet, untold power inside them."

She came to stand beside him. Gently, so gently, she took his hand.

"They are still burning, darling. But they do not need a brutal flame."

Now, as he walked beside Mia in the brisk evening air, the hills cloaked themselves in quiet. The air was crisp and cool, stars dotting the sky like flecks of buttercream. Sometimes, on very clear nights, he could see all the way to the Opalen Sea.

"Is that really the ocean?" Mia pointed, though as she did, a heavy cloud settled on the horizon. "Let me rephrase. Is that the ocean hiding under that cloud?"

Quin smiled. He shifted the gray blanket beneath his other arm.

"I desperately wanted to see it as a boy. The ocean was so close, yet so maddeningly out of reach. Those pesky northern peaks were always standing in my way."

"Not anymore."

It was strange how little they'd said to each other, in light of how much there was to say. Quin had tried to follow her lead, talking when she wanted to talk, never forcing anything. It was partly why he'd invited her to the play: so they could spend time together without Mia feeling pressured to make conversation.

Now he doubted himself. He was terribly nervous. Should he prepare Mia for what she was about to see? He hoped she would like the performance. His secret desire was that she might even love it. But there was also a distinct possibility that after she saw the play, she would never speak to him again.

They weren't far now. The path wound toward the stage, irradiated by hundreds of torches. They looked to Mia like a trail of fireflies.

Her mind was abuzz. She felt irrationally worried about things that seemed pointless to worry about. Did she still stink of blood and humors from the hospital? Should she have at least *tried* to comb her hair?

The path widened and leveled out, revealing the stage.

The zestful children were nowhere to be seen. The stage itself was swathed in a thick crimson curtain. Beside it someone had erected a large tent—the backstage area, Mia assumed. At least a hundred people sat on the grass, tittering in the restrained way people do before a performance, blankets spread on the ground beneath them.

"Here we are," Quin said, choosing a spot in the back. He didn't want to make the children nervous by sitting too close. He unrolled the gray blanket to stake their claim. "Now if you'll excuse me for a moment."

He hurried backstage, heart pounding.

"Ah!" said Prenda as he ducked into the tent. She looked regal, her hair swept into a bun and skin greases elaborately applied. "It's Quin, children, I told you he'd come backstage to see you. *Quietly*, please! No jumping."

They streamed around him, adorably nervous. He felt the pre-performance tension in the air. It brought to mind a pudding on the stove, simmering with potential. A pudding that might still very well go bad.

"Break a leg, everyone," he said softly.

He felt a tap on his shoulder. Turned to find Callaghan in full costume, sword and all.

"Who's the pretty redhead I see out in the audience? Is it Miiiiiia?" Cal batted her eyes so dramatically Quin laughed. "I want to meet her!"

"If you dazzle us tonight," he teased, "maybe you can meet her after."

"I was *born* to play this role," Cal sniffed.

"I know you were." He appraised her costume. "It's a little more like this," he said, adjusting the longsword so it hung a touch higher from her hip.

He stood back. Nodded his approval.

"Perfect. You're Princess Karri through and through."

This time he didn't try to fight the ache. He missed his sister. He always would. But it was far better to see Callaghan costumed as Karri than to imagine his sister fading quietly away.

"Break a leg, Cal. You're going to be amazing."

"Just don't *you* break a leg," she quipped, as he slipped out of the tent. "You've done enough of that already!"

Mia was exactly where he'd left her. He breathed a sigh of relief. A part of him had been absolutely certain she'd be gone.

"A question," she said as he situated himself, leaving a respectful strip of blanket between them. "What is the play about?"

He was spared from answering. At their backs, the stagehands extinguished the arena torches, veiling them in sudden darkness. A few giddy gasps coursed through the crowd. Then the pretending torches were lit around the stage—and the curtain rose.

Gone was the children's cheerful platform. The stage had been transformed.

The floors were varnished a gleaming black. Dark canvas hung from tall poles to create three opaque walls. In the center, a dangling ring of candles.

Mia shivered. The scene felt ominous, and eerily familiar. A hideous monster loomed in one corner, a mishmash of what appeared to be fused metal tubes.

"The children made that themselves," Quin whispered. "It's supposed to be a pipe organ."

There was a flutter of small feet as the players spilled solemnly onto the stage.

Something strange was happening. Had Mia met these

children before today? She was sure she hadn't. Yet with every new child she felt a flicker of recognition. A girl with lambskin gloves and long ginger hair walked beside a stern-looking boy with a man's beard drawn on his face. A puckish girl strode in with a longsword hanging from her belt. At a bronze table, a boy wearing a green jacket with gold buttons faced a girl in a curly red wig.

A blond-haired boy—the one who had climbed onto Quin's back that morning—sauntered in, promptly tripped on his long robes, and fell facedown onto the stage. The audience went stone silent.

The boy jumped up.

"I'm fine!" he shouted. "I fell!"

The illusion was broken—but the relief was palpable. The audience let out a collective breath. Several people chuckled.

"Oh, Victor," Quin muttered. "A scene stealer till the bitter end."

Victor recovered himself admirably. He was already striding over to the bronze table.

"We have come here today," he crowed, "by royal decree of Ronan, son of Clan Killian . . ."

And suddenly Mia knew why everything seemed familiar. The redheaded girl. The prince.

She was watching her own wedding.

Only, she wasn't. Because she couldn't.

She was on her feet, sprinting out of the arena—and onto the path.

"Mia!" Quin struggled to keep up. "*Mia!* Please."

He cursed his leg. If she kept that pace, he would never catch her. He cursed himself for thinking she would enjoy seeing their story performed onstage. Clearly she had *not* enjoyed it. Of course she hadn't. Who wanted to have their own life paraded before them? He'd done everything wrong.

But as he reached the path, just out of earshot of the performers, he saw that Mia had stopped. She was pacing back and forth. Curls bouncing furiously off her shoulders.

"What was that, Quin? What was that supposed to be?"

"I should have told you beforehand. I just thought—"

"That it would be a nice surprise?"

"I'm sorry, Mia. I am trying so hard to make things right. And I'm failing at every turn."

Mia peered into his eyes. As she'd sat beside him on the grass, watching her effigy totter about onstage, she had wondered if Quin was mocking her. Was this some sort of elaborate ruse? Drag her back through her own failures, her own grief?

But now, standing face to face, she could see he was miserable.

Mia wanted to be angry. At least she knew the weight of anger. Grief was slippery and ever changing. Just when she thought she knew its heft, grief reshaped itself.

"The play isn't satire," Quin said. "I promise you that. Though with Victor slinging himself about the stage, it may well turn into a comedy by the end. I've done my best not to stray from the facts. It's drama, for the most part, though there are silly bits, too. Most of the silly bits are mine. You come out looking quite heroic, actually, whereas I'm a bit of a buffoon."

Quin was flinging words with wild abandon, hoping the right ones would stick.

"You wrote the play?" Mia said.

He scrutinized her expression, pondering which answer would be least upsetting. In the end he went with the truth.

"I've been writing the new histories. *Our* histories. I want to tell the true tale of Clan Killian, including its grisly end."

Behind their backs, the performance was in full swing. Victor was doing a fine job as Tristan, intoning the horrific Glasddiran wedding vows.

Quin shifted his weight, grimacing in pain.

"I could try and heal your leg," Mia said. "If you want."

Mia wasn't sure it was the right thing to say. But she'd been thinking it from the moment they reunited. After spending her whole day healing others, she'd be remiss not to ask.

"Thank you, Mia. But it's all right." Quin's smile was soft. "I spent so many years ashamed of my body. I thought it weak and delicate, not at all befitting a son of Clan Killian. But after the Kaer fell, after my leg was shattered, my body fought so hard. It healed from something that should have killed me. I have chosen to honor that."

Mia understood. Her fingers grazed the frostflower inked onto her wrist.

"Not everything needs to be fixed," she murmured.

He nodded. "We cannot unmake the things that make us who we are."

They were quiet a moment. Gazes fixed on one another. Contemplating their next move in this fragile dance.

Quin broke the silence.

"Do you know where we're standing right now? What was here before?"

To Mia's astonishment, she *did* know.

"The Hall of Hands."

"Yes." He looked impressed. "You sensed it instinctually, didn't you? It's hard to know for sure, of course, since there isn't much left of the Kaer. Our geographers will never be wholly certain."

"*I'm* certain," Mia said. "I can feel it."

Quin gazed toward the ocean. The clouds had thickened, masking all signs of the sea. He drew a breath.

"I don't want to run from my history, Mia. It's a brutal history, written in blood. My father did terrible things, and his father did terrible things before him. The entire Killian line is one long, bloody blade. That's why I destroyed the Kaer. I wanted to bury everything."

He frowned.

"But if we keep it buried, that's no good, either. If we hide the truths from our children, then they will end up making the same mistakes. I want us to learn from them. We learn more from our failures than our triumphs." He brandished a hand toward the stage. "And a good story is a powerful way to learn."

Mia watched Quin's face. When he talked about the children, his students in the pretending arts, a new light burned in his eyes.

She had known him to be many things—frosty, coy, haughty,

kind. She had seen him gripped by fear and consumed by passion. What she saw now was pride.

"Listen." Quin cocked his head. "They're getting to our vows. Soon I'll have an arrow in my back."

Flesh of my flesh, bone of my bone.
I give you my body, my spirit, my home.

Quin and Mia locked eyes. It was strange, listening to their vows in the mouths of two nervous children. But it was also sweet.

Come illness, suffering, e'en death,
Until my final breath I will be yours.

How true those words had been, in ways they never could have known. Each of them had suffered. They had lost sisters they loved dearly. They'd been wounded, enthralled, enkindled—nearly killed. Not *nearly*. Mia had stopped her own heart.

Was it any wonder they had found solace in each other? The weight of so much loss and grief could not be borne in solitude. And so they had grabbed hold of one another, gasping for breath, like the two sole survivors of a shipwreck, certain they could not survive alone.

Till the ice melts on the southern cliffs,
Till the glass cities sink into the western sands.

But it was only once they'd parted ways, Quin pulling himself from the wreckage of the snow queendom, Mia sailing west to Pembuk, that they had finally reckoned with their wounds. They had each made grave mistakes—and faced the consequences.

It had taken far longer than Mia would have liked. But, piece by piece, she and Quin had reassembled who they were. They had, in his words, learned more from their failures than their triumphs. A lesson Mia had only just begun to learn.

Till the eastern isles burn to ash,
Till the northern peaks crumble.

Quin was still the boy she knew. But he was different, too: a man she longed to know better. She held the same union within herself. The girl she'd been, woven into the woman she was. Here, in this new world, she and Quin had come together whole.

Promise me, O promise me.

No. Not whole. A heart was only truly full when it was truly broken.

You will be mine.

From the stage, they heard a squeal, then a thump, then pandemonium erupting.

"You'll be dragging me beneath the castle right about now," Quin said.

"Where I'll be forced to save your life."

His gaze was clear.

"You saved my life many times, Mia, for which I will always be grateful. But I wasn't truly ready to love you until I learned to save my own."

She felt a flutter in her belly. *Love.* He'd said the word so naturally, as if it had always been a part of him. A physiological truth.

Quin loosened his shoulders. He had poured his heart out like a song—and he did not regret it. He was done pretending.

The children had given him a great gift. In their mouths, he'd heard the vows anew. And he had come to understand something.

"I don't know about you," he began, "but I, for one, can attest to the ice melting on the southern cliffs. Seeing as how I was nearly crushed by it."

"And the glass cities are sinking," Mia said. "I saw it with my own eyes."

"What's happening in Fojo is heartbreaking. We've offered sanctuary to as many refugees as we can."

"That's good of you, Quin."

"We should have done it long before the isles began to burn. There's so much work left to do."

"So much work," she agreed. "It all feels a little overwhelming. But perhaps we can take it one day at a time. I'm ready to do the work. And I'd like . . . I *hope* . . . to do it alongside you."

Quin let the air out of his lungs. As if he could exhale centuries of oppression. As if life were as simple as taking a breath.

"And now here we are." Mia gestured around them. "Standing on the crumbled northern peaks."

Quin studied her. Despite everything, the horrors and the heartbreaks and the losses, there was something undefeated in her eyes. He recognized the spark. He hadn't realized how much he had missed it.

Mia twisted a curl around her finger.

"You know, I've never really known if we were married or not."

"A contentious point, to be sure." He tilted his head. "But I think we have our answer. Whatever vows we swore are null and void. You are not promised to anyone, Mia Rose. Your body, your spirit, your home are yours and yours alone."

Mia felt her soul lift its weary head. Her body, her spirit—they *were* her home. Home had been within her all along.

"Your body and spirit are yours, too, Quin. You get to choose with whom you share them. Your life is your own."

He raked a hand through his golden curls.

"Maybe now we get to decide for ourselves."

Mia gasped.

Over his shoulder, the clouds had lifted off the horizon. The ocean unveiled itself in all its moonlit splendor. A glint of endless opaline.

Quin stepped forward. His eyes blazing green.

"May I kiss you, Mia?"

"Yes," she said. "Gods, yes."

And she kissed him, and kissed him, and kissed him, until the sea poured into the stars.

EPILOGUE

Once upon a time,
a girl chose to live.

Acknowledgments

THIS IS A BOOK about healing. It was healing for me to write, in no small part because of the many elixirs I was given.

I owe an endless debt of gratitude to Kyle Boatwright, not just for lending me her speech patterns, late-night brilliance, entire family, and generous heart—but for being my second reader in all four kingdoms. Rise Up, beauty.

Joel Tippie, you Design Dujia: you did it again. Melissa Miller, you helped me build my very first boat, and Katherine Tegen, you made the winds blow. Mabel Hsu and Tanu Srivastava: I couldn't have asked for two better editors to help steer my last ship into the harbor.

Keppie Sullivan, thank you for being my mistress of the sailing arts, and Dave, for being Keppie's first mate. Bridget Morrissey, you are the inspiration behind the Once Upon a Times. Deedee Messana, your emails have lifted my spirits more than you know.

Sue and Katie Howe, my British mum and sis, and Philippa Hayes, my British barrister: you came to my aid when I needed you most. Thank you.

Aysha Mutaywea, you stole my heart in just one week. Sabeeka Al-Shamlan, you share the same grace and courage. I am so grateful for the awe-inspiring work you two are doing. You are the true Mahraini mystics.

Joy Malek, Sara Fraser, Laura Lai, Ashley Rideaux, and all the other therapists and yoga teachers I've been lucky to work with: you are my Curateurs. Thank you for teaching me to heal myself.

To my dazzling, devoted readers: Annabeth Cobb, Fin Daniels, Phoebe Edge, Callaghandra Edison, Cheyenne Faircloth, Marley Martinez, Mia Moore, Victoria Moschou, Callaghan Papavasilopoulos, and Brianna Reed. Do you see yourselves in these pages? Because I do. :)

Finley, I'm so glad you poked your cold nose into this book. Piglet, you get the next one. Chris, you are and will always be my Quin.

And to Anna Prendella: Sorry about that low-key hernia. In the gallimaufry of writing this trilogy, there was only ever one chai robot. This book begins and ends with you.

RESOURCES

NATIONAL SEXUAL ASSAULT HOTLINE
https://www.rainn.org/
1.800.656.HOPE (4673)
Call the 24/7 hotline to be connected with a trained staff member from a sexual assault service provider in your area.

NATIONAL SUICIDE PREVENTION LIFELINE
https://suicidepreventionlifeline.org/
1.800.273.TALK (8255)
The Lifeline provides 24/7, free, and confidential support for people in distress, and prevention and crisis resources for you or your loved ones.

CRISIS TEXT LINE
https://www.crisistextline.org/text-us/
Text CONNECT, HOME, or any message to 741-741
Being "in crisis" doesn't just mean feeling suicidal: it's any painful emotion for which you need support. Crisis Text Line serves anyone, in any type of crisis, providing access to free, 24/7 support and information via text.

Psychology Today

https://www.psychologytoday.com/

A great resource for finding therapists, psychiatrists, support groups, and treatment centers, both outpatient and inpatient.

Rock 'n' Write

https://www.breebarton.com/rocknwrite

This is a fun, empowering workshop I created to merge two things that have been profoundly healing in my own life: dance and writing.

Other activities that have had a positive impact on my mental health: yoga, art therapy, meditation, writing, therapy groups, and talking to good friends. Poke around the internet to see what you can find. Above all, don't hesitate to ask for help. Mia, Quin, and Pilar's journey may have come to an end, but yours is just beginning.